Tony Park was born in 1964 and grew up in the western suburbs of Sydney. He has worked as a newspaper reporter in Australia and England, a government press secretary, a public relations consultant, and a freelance writer. He is also a major in the Australian Army Reserve and served six months in Afghanistan in 2002 as the public affairs officer for the Australian ground forces. He and his wife, Nicola, divide their time between their home in Sydney, and southern Africa, where they own a tent and a Series III Land Rover. He is the author of *Far Horizon*.

Also by Tony Park

Far Horizon

ZAMBEZI

TONY PARK

MACMILLAN
Pan Macmillan Australia

For Nicola

First published 2005 in Macmillan by Pan Macmillan Australia Pty Limited
St Martins Tower, 31 Market Street, Sydney

Reprinted 2005

Copyright © Tony Park 2005

National Library of Australia
Cataloguing-in-Publication Data:

Park, Tony, 1964–.
Zambezi.

ISBN 1 40503678 8.

1. Violent deaths – Africa – Fiction. I. Title.

A823.4

Typeset in 11/15 pt Birka by Post Pre-press Group, Brisbane
Printed and bound in Australia by McPherson's Printing Group
Cartographic art by Laurie Whiddon, Map Illustrations

Papers used by Pan Macmillan Australia Pty Limited are natural, recyclable products made from
wood grown in sustainable forests. The manufacturing processes conform to the
environmental regulations of the country of origin.

Acknowledgments

A number of people kindly helped me with my research for *Zambezi*.

My thanks go to Danny Toplis from the North Fort Artillery Museum in the Sydney suburb of Manly, for access to information about surface-to-air missiles; to Susan Fuchs-Nebel, who helped fill in the gaps in my memories of Zanzibar; to Julia Salnicki for providing information on animal tranquillisers; and to fellow Pan Macmillan author, and pilot, David A Rollins, for his help with the aircraft scenes.

I am also indebted to American author and former Gulf War Apache helicopter pilot Michael T Gregory; and to Ed Delong and Susan Bray Delong, late of the United States, who all read early drafts of the manuscript and straightened out some of my half-arsed Americanisms. Isobel 'Scotty' Wrench was also kind enough to read the manuscript from a Zimbabwean's point of view and made several excellent suggestions.

In Zimbabwe, Dennis, Liz, Don, Vicki, Peta and Andrew have not only all been good friends, but also superb guides to the many wonders of the Zambezi Valley, on many enjoyable occasions.

As is and should be the case, any remaining mistakes in the book are down to me.

My wife Nicola, mother Kathy and mother-in-law Sheila read and re-read drafts of the manuscript and once again all proved they are excellent proofreaders and part-time editors.

At Pan Macmillan, my profound thanks go to Deputy Publishing Director Cate Paterson, editor Sarina Rowell, copy editor Julia Stiles and publicist Jane Novak. Again, you have made my dreams a reality.

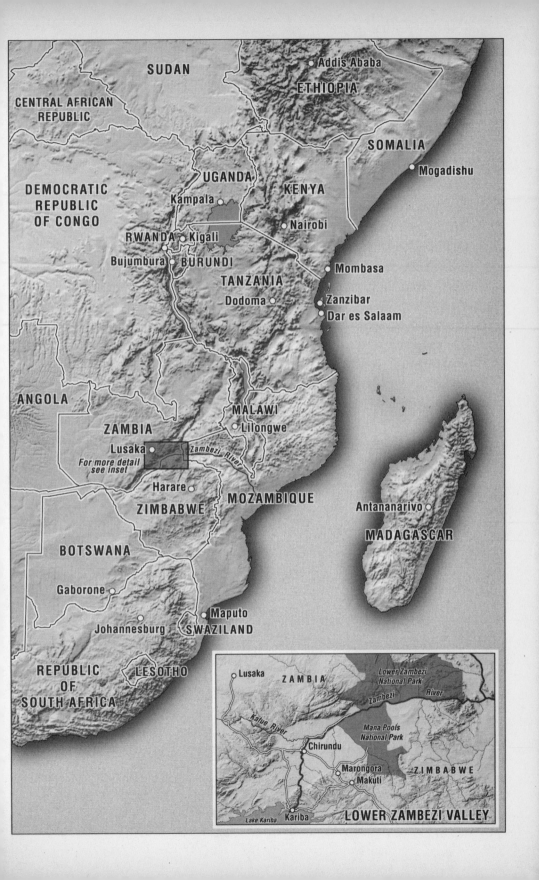

SUDAN

CENTRAL AFRICAN
REPUBLIC

ETHIOPIA
Addis Ababa

SOMALIA

Mogadishu

DEMOCRATIC
REPUBLIC
OF CONGO

UGANDA
Kampala

KENYA

Nairobi

RWANDA Kigali

Bujumbura BURUNDI

TANZANIA

Mombasa

Dodoma

Zanzibar
Dar es Salaam

ANGOLA

MALAWI
Lilongwe

ZAMBIA

Lusaka
For more detail
see inset

Zambezi River

Harare

ZIMBABWE

MOZAMBIQUE

Antananarivo

MADAGASCAR

BOTSWANA

Gaborone

Maputo

Johannesburg SWAZILAND

REPUBLIC
OF
SOUTH AFRICA

LESOTHO

Lusaka ZAMBIA

Lower Zambezi
National Park

Kafue River

Zambezi River

Mana Pools
National Park

Chirundu

Marongora
Makuti

ZIMBABWE

Lake Kariba Kariba

LOWER ZAMBEZI VALLEY

1

Afghanistan

A dead place.

That's how he thought of it. Nothing grew on the plain in front of him. Rock, dirt and dust. Even the target was made of mud, the once straight lines of the compound's walls rounded by the ceaseless blasting of grit and wind. The backdrop was a mountain, jagged and welcoming as a chunk of razor-sharp shrapnel, capped in bitter, lethal snow. The passable areas, the roads and the village pathways; the arable areas, the farms and the populated valleys, were home to seven million landmines.

The land was reflected in its people. Burned by searing summers, hardened in unforgiving winters, brutalised by warfare. Afghanistan didn't have a monopoly on war and killing, it was just a market leader in both.

Master Sergeant Jed Banks blinked and rested his eye from the tiring one-dimensional blur of the view through his night-vision goggles. On the ground, he noticed, in the dust near his elbow, was a half-buried copper cartridge case, green with age. Probably from an AK-47. Maybe a Russian soldier had sat out here under a chilly star-studded night and watched the same medieval mud-brick compound. Maybe an Afghan shepherd had fired at a predator or a thief from a neighbouring village. Perhaps a blood feud had been settled on this spot.

Here they resolved village disputes with assault rifles and mortars, celebrated weddings with a fireworks show of machine-gun tracer rounds, played a game on horseback with a dead animal instead of a ball. Sometimes, depending on who was at war with whom, they used a human instead of an animal.

Jed Banks was here to kill, too. He squinted into the sight of his M4 assault rifle again and scanned the squat tower at the corner of the compound once more. Maybe he would add to the never-ending tally of this country's violent death toll tonight.

'Do you think the US is achieving anything here?' the man beside him whispered as he lowered himself to the dust.

The nasal drawl of the young Australian was a distraction for Jed – and not a welcome one. Nothing good could come of having a reporter along on a mission like this. There was no movement around the compound or on the parapets. The guard in the tower at the north-east corner was still asleep. All was quiet and the snatch team was almost in position.

Jed glanced at the reporter. The man was short and weedy, with a goatee beard and an earring. He had carried a ruck on the walk in from the landing zone and Jed had made sure the stranger also humped the spare radio batteries and a couple of IV drips, just so they would get *some* use out of him. He had stood up to the walk all right, though he still hadn't been carrying near as much as the rest of them.

'Hi, remember me from the briefing? Luke Scarborough,' the reporter whispered.

Jed remembered the man, but ignored him. He scanned the wall again. The reporter worked for some wire service or other. AP, UPI, Reuters, some damn thing. Afghanistan was what was termed an acronym-rich environment. It was hard enough to keep up with the military abbreviations, let alone the media's. He stayed away from the motley crew of journalists at Bagram. He resented having one forced upon the team, but CENTCOM – the US military's Central Command in Tampa, Florida – was red hot on embedding journalists with all units, even Special Forces. Probably seemed like a good idea over drinks in the officers' club. Out here in the dust, it sucked.

'The captain said we'll have to wait a while,' hissed Luke. 'About two hours. How do you pass the time?'

'I sit quiet and do my job.'

'Think about home?'

Jed turned and stared at the man. He didn't get it. He was out on a big adventure, but couldn't see that Jed and the rest of the ODA were totally focused on their mission every second they were out in the field. By contrast it seemed that everything the reporter had been told during the briefing about Operational Detachment Alphas – ODAs, or what used to be known in Vietnam and subsequently on TV as 'A Teams' – had gone in one ear and out the other.

'Nothing to think about,' he said, hoping this would shut the reporter up.

'No one back home? No parents, no wife, no girlfriend? A boyfriend?'

'Can't you see I have a loaded weapon?'

Luke grinned.

Jed wiped his forehead with the back of his hand, mopping away the sweat with his black Nomex fireproof gloves. It was hot at this time of year in Afghanistan. A country of extremes, the reporters called it, and they were right about that. At the end of winter, when he'd started his tour, he'd been operating in the mountains and it had been bitterly cold, with snow on the peaks. Now, in August, it was sometimes over fifty degrees Celsius during the day and damn near as hot even at night.

'A daughter.' Immediately Jed regretted giving this away . He couldn't help it, though. She was on his mind too much these days.

'How old?'

'None of your fucking business.'

The radio hissed in his earpiece. He held up a hand to silence the reporter.

'Hawk, this is Snake, go.'

The reporter pulled out his notebook.

Jed listened intently for a few seconds, held the headset's microphone close to his lips and whispered: 'Roger that. Six, this is Snake. They're in position. Show time is in two-zero mikes, over.'

Jed took another sight picture on the sleeping guard.

'How old's your daughter?'

'I was hoping you had left.'

'Give me what I want and I'll get out of your hair.'

Fat chance, Jed thought. 'She's twenty.'

'College?'

'Was. She's in Africa. Zimbabwe. Researching lions.'

'Cool,' Scarborough exclaimed.

'Keep the fucking noise down.'

'Sorry. But, hey, that's interesting. That's my usual beat – Africa. I normally work out of Johannesburg; I've just been up here for a few weeks covering for someone else. I'm going back next week.'

'Don't even think about asking for her phone number.'

'She got a degree?'

'Science. University of Massachusetts. She's studying for her masters in wildlife conservation and working as a researcher while she writes her thesis.'

'What does she think of you being over here?'

'I don't know. Proud, I guess. Not as proud as I am of her. She's the only good thing in my life.'

'Do you worry about her, being out in the wild in Africa? Zimbabwe can be pretty hairy.'

'Thanks for the tip. But yeah, I do worry about her. She tells me it's fine, though, so don't spoil my illusions, OK, asshole?'

'Sure. You're the one with the gun.'

Luke chuckled to himself. He had got the soldier talking. That was ninety per cent of the job done. He had cracked the tough guy wide open and got his story.

4

He made some notes. The moon was full, so he could see enough to write. *M/SGT Jed. The captain is the senior man, but Jed runs the team. 6'2", broad shoulders; long, fair hair past his collar, bushy beard – the Special Forces types grow them as it gains them more respect with Afghan tribal elders. Crow's feet at the corners of his eyes – sun-bronzed, weathered face. Veteran of Grenada, Somalia, Desert Storm, Kosovo. The last patrol of his tour. Daughter, aged 20.*

'What's her name?'

'Miranda.'

Miranda. Zimbabwe. Researches lions. The one person this soldier cares about. A little corny, Luke thought, but he'd finesse it a bit. Tough guy with a heart of gold always worked. He wondered what the daughter looked like. A blonde, if she took after her dad. Couldn't be too many blonde, female American lion researchers in Zimbabwe.

Jed couldn't stop himself from thinking about Miranda. He really did worry about her. He was due out of this godforsaken dustbowl of a country in four short days. He had a ticket booked to Harare, Zimbabwe. He was going to spend four weeks of his leave with his baby girl and he couldn't wait.

'Where's Miranda's mom?' the reporter asked.

'Boston.'

'And your unit is based in Fayetteville, North Carolina, is that right?' He wrote it all down.

'Yep. Work it out yet, genius? We split when Miranda was about three years old.'

'How did it feel not being around when she was growing up?'

'They teach you how to piss people off in journalism school, or does it just come natural?'

'They teach us to ask loaded questions,' Luke laughed. 'Sorry. It must have been tough, being away from your kid. How come you're so tight with her now?'

'She found me. Looked me up a couple of years ago. She made the effort and I guess that's why I love her so much. I always sent presents, called in on Patti maybe once or twice a year. There was no bad blood between us – not after the first couple years, anyway. Miranda reached out for me at a bad time – I hadn't seen either of them for a while, and, well, she really helped.'

'Why did you lose contact?'

'None of your business.'

'But things are good now?'

'Couldn't be better.'

'Got a picture?'

'Remember the weapon.'

'Hey, I didn't mean it that way.'

'We don't take anything personal out with us in the field. Nothing that identifies our families or loved ones, nothing they can use against us if we're captured. You were told that during the brief. I don't want to know what you're carrying.'

'I'm a reporter. No one's going to harm me.'

It was Jed's turn to laugh now. 'You're in civilian clothes – they'll think you're OGA, so they'll torture you and kill you first. Give the rest of us time to escape.' OGA – Other Government Agencies – was a euphemism for the CIA in Afghanistan.

'Really?'

Jed shrugged. He'd had enough of the interview. A green shadow flickered in the night sight.

'Six, this is Snake, over. We've got movement in the tower, I say again, we have movement in the tower.'

Jed's voice was calm and matter-of-fact, as if he were asking for more chow in the D-FAC, the dining facility at Bagram, Luke thought. Luke hunkered down lower in the dust when he saw the *muj* in the tower stretch and yawn. He was picking up the Special Forces language quickly; a *muj* – short for *mujahideen* or holy warrior – was the common term for any Afghan adult male.

A goat bleated somewhere in the shadows at the base of the compound wall. The turbaned guard placed his hands on the earthen wall and looked over the edge. He straightened, scratched his beard and picked up his AK-47.

'Six, this is Snake. Subject is moving. He has his weapon. Climbing down from the tower. I think he's going to get that stray goat.'

'What does that mean?' Luke asked too quickly, giving away his rising panic.

'Quiet, buddy. Stay low and be cool.' Jed reached over with his left hand – his right didn't leave the pistol grip of his M4 – and patted Luke on the shoulder. He smiled and the Australian tried to force a grin back at him. Poor kid was shit-scared.

The captain's voice came over the radio, asking for a situation report. Jed ignored him. He was more concerned about the snatch team, four men lying in the cover of some boulders not twenty metres from the compound.

'Hawk, this is Snake,' Jed whispered into the microphone. 'Can you see the subject?'

The only reply was a single click that brought a burst of static. The signal meant yes, but also told Jed that the subject was probably close enough for the team not to risk speaking, even in a whisper.

The goat bleated again. Jed saw the Afghan, if that's what he was, emerge from the shadow of the wall. He held his AK-47 by the barrel and whacked the animal on its rump.

'Stay cool, Hawk,' Jed whispered.

The goat did a one-eighty and scarpered towards the boulders. The guard laughed and turned to follow it. Instinctively he turned his rifle back the right way so the barrel was pointing forward again. He walked to the boulders.

Jed pressed the switch on the black box fixed to the stock of his M4, activating his laser night-aiming device. He closed one eye and looked through the night-vision monocle strapped to his face. The bright dot of the laser beam rested in the middle of the subject's back.

The man stopped suddenly. He brought his AK-47 up into his shoulder with the practised speed of an old warrior. Jed pulled the trigger and felt the recoil in his shoulder. The silencer muffled the noise of the round exploding from the barrel.

The Afghan pitched forwards and his rifle clattered against the boulders. A split second later the noise of a gunshot destroyed the night's peace.

'Jesus Christ,' the reporter said.

Jed spoke into the mike again. 'Subject is down. Hawk, what is your status? Repeat, what is your status? Who fired that shot?'

'What's happening, Snake, what's happening?' the captain hissed in Jed's earpiece.

Jed was concerned now. It was going to shit. One of the guys in the snatch team, Murphy probably, who didn't have a silenced weapon, had panicked when he saw the Afghan raise his rifle and fired a shot as well.

'We're fucked, Snake. We're pulling out,' said Kirby, the leader of the snatch team.

Jed knew there was no alternative. 'Roger that. All call signs, abort. I say again, abort. Move to emergency LZ. Fall back through my position.' Jed moved the mike away from his mouth and turned to Luke, whose face was a ghostly white. 'Keep it together, man. As soon as the captain gets here, you go with him. I've got to wait here for the other guys. OK?'

Luke nodded dumbly.

Jed pressed his night-vision monocle against the aperture of his rifle scope again and saw the four men from the snatch team running back up the hill away from the compound towards him. The picture was lime-green and grainy, clear, but devoid of depth. Another movement caught his eye. First one, then two men appeared in the watchtower. They were struggling with a tarpaulin.

The captain and McCubbin, the team's radio operator, appeared from Jed's right, panting as they knelt next to him.

'What happened, Banks?' the officer demanded.

Jed ignored the stupid question. 'Get Boss Man on the radio, Mac. It looks like they've got a Dooshka in the tower.' Boss Man was the

United States Air Force Airborne Early Warning and Control aircraft, orbiting unseen somewhere above them.

'What?'

The radioman was thinking faster than the captain. He spoke rapidly into the handset of the radio he carried in his Alice pack. 'Boss Man, Boss Man, Boss Man, this is Cougar one-five. Request immediate CAS, over.'

Jed saw the reporter had stopped taking notes and was balling his fists to try to stop his hands shaking. 'It's OK, Luke,' he said softly. 'We're calling up some CAS – Close Air Support. They've got a Russian DSHK heavy machine-gun down in the tower, a Dooshka we call it. Just be ready to move if I tell you.' The Australian nodded. Jed licked his lips to stave off the dryness in his mouth. The weapon was probably older than himself, but it was built to last and the 12.7-millimetre rounds in its belt would tear a man in half.

Jed continued to watch the tower. 'Get the Harriers on station, Mac. We need them close, but we don't want to blow the whole place up if we don't have to. There are women and children in the compound.'

The long barrel of the Dooshka swung up in profile momentarily as the two Afghans readied it.

Jed placed the point of the laser on the man on the left, whose torso was visible above the mud-brick wall. He squeezed the trigger again and the man careened backwards. The other man, however, was out of sight, presumably behind the weapon. 'I'd get down if I was you, Captain.'

The machine-gun opened up with a din like a giant striking an anvil five hundred and fifty times a minute. The heavy bullets split the air a couple of metres above the heads of the small group of Americans. Every now and then a green phosphorescent tracer round arced into the sky. The captain landed in the dirt beside Banks, sending up a cloud of dust.

'Put some fire down, sir,' Jed said to the captain. To the best of his knowledge it was the officer's first time under fire. He was Special Forces, but a staff officer from CJSOTF – Coalition Joint Special Operations

Task Force – headquarters. He'd been assigned to accompany the reporter and supposedly make sure neither Jed nor any of the other ODA team members said the wrong thing – like how much they resented having a newsman and a rear-echelon dude from HQ along for the ride.

The captain screamed at his radio operator. 'Mac, call in the CAS. Wipe that fucking compound off the face of the earth. Now!'

McCubbin hesitated.

'Don't look at Banks, goddamn it! I just gave you an order.'

Jed ignored the screaming captain. The man behind the machine-gun had raised his head a little, desperately trying to see his target. The gunfire stopped. Jed placed the dot of the laser on the man's head and pulled the trigger. The silenced rifle coughed. The pale-green face disappeared.

'Sir,' Jed said, 'here comes the snatch team. Mac, call up the CH 47. It's time for us to get out of here.'

'On its way, Jed.'

'Good man. Sir, we've silenced the gun for the time being. If you lead the men back to the emergency LZ I'll tidy up here.'

The captain realised he had been overruled, but Banks had given him an out. 'Right, you men, let's go. Now! You too, Luke.'

Jed reached for his pack and unstrapped a sixty-six-millimetre light anti-tank weapon, a disposable one-shot rocket-launcher that was pretty well useless against modern tanks, but still handy for busting open buildings and bunkers. He slung his M4 and extended the telescopic case of the rocket-launcher. The weapon was not overly accurate and he needed to get closer to the compound. There was enough explosive in the rocket to wreck the machine-gun if he could score a direct hit.

'You need a hand, Jed?' McCubbin asked. The captain and the snatch team were disappearing over the brow of the barren hill.

'No thanks, Mac. Won't be but a minute,' he said. 'Don't dick around now.'

Jed half ran and half slid down the face of the dry slope. He cut right and started to climb again, then moved forwards once more until he was within a hundred paces of the compound's tower.

Someone shouted. Jed could see a big man with a white beard climbing the inner steps to the compound wall. He couldn't be sure from this distance, but he looked like one of the four men they had been sent to capture or kill. Intelligence said they were Al Qaeda, Arabs who had crossed over from Pakistan with a couple of shoulder-launched surface-to-air missiles which they planned to use against Coalition aircraft.

Jed pulled the safety pin from the rocket-launcher and flipped up the crude sights. He squinted through the aperture. He could see the Dooshka and one of the bodies of the two men he had killed. The white-bearded man came into view as he swung the machine-gun around. Jed realised he was silhouetted on the slope, casting a telltale shadow on the ground from the moon's illumination.

The first rounds from the machine-gun brought up geysers of dirt in front of him. He pressed down on the launcher's firing mechanism and the rocket screamed from its tube. A cloud of dust erupted behind Jed from the back blast. He dropped to his knees and watched the projectile find its mark. The explosion lit up the compound, and the timber roof of the guard tower disappeared in a thousand splinters.

Jed tossed away the used launcher and ran back up the hill.

He paused on the other side of the crest and punched in the pre-set waypoint for the emergency helicopter extraction zone on his wrist-watch GPS. He started jogging again, following the illuminated arrow on the display. He ran for three minutes, until the GPS told him he was only two hundred metres away. Gunfire once again ripped apart the night. AK-47s, two probably. An M4 was returning fire. Dead ahead. Shit.

Jed heard the clatter of approaching rotors. There would be an AH64 Apache attack helicopter escorting the big Chinook. He cautiously crested another rise and instantly saw the cause of the problem. There was a Toyota Land Cruiser parked in the middle of the track. Two men were out of the vehicle, lying on their bellies and firing at the fleeing Americans.

Jed brought his M4 into his shoulder, lased the first man with his night-aiming device and fired. The man writhed on the ground, wounded but not dead. The Chinook was coming in fast, unaware of the gunfight below. Why hadn't McCubbin warned them? The answer was plain a couple of seconds later. Murphy and Kirby came into view from behind a boulder, dragging the radioman between them. Mac's feet dug twin furrows in the powdery dirt.

Just as Jed took a sight picture on the second man the Chinook started its descent. The downwash of the giant twin rotors stirred up a dust storm that obscured the terrorist from view. Jed unsnapped a small pouch on the front of his combat vest and pulled out a grenade. He'd never pulled a grenade pin with his teeth, but he had his rifle in his other hand and there was nothing else for it. He was glad none of the others could see him as he extracted the pin – he'd never live it down. He spat the pin out and lobbed the deadly orb in the direction he had last seen the enemy rifleman.

The sight and sound of the explosion were all but lost in the cacophony of noise and dust generated by the huge transport helicopter. The snatch team were dragging Mac and his heavy pack onto the rear ramp of the Chinook. The captain was already aboard by the look of it. The fat rear wheels of the machine were barely touching the ground.

Jed saw Luke scramble aboard, two crewmen in bulbous helmets and tan flight suits reaching for him. Jed sprinted for the helicopter and saw one of the crewmen waving to him. Luke was standing on the ramp now, waving as well, urging him on.

From his left, above the din of the screaming engines and the *thwop* of the blades, Jed heard the unmistakable pop of AK-47 fire. The bullets found their mark, stitching a line of holes in the helicopter's metal skin. One of the crewmen held his helmet mike close to his mouth and the machine started to rise. Jed dived for the ramp and managed to get his torso on board as the chopper lifted off, his legs kicking in the air as he tried to find purchase.

The gunman fired again. The door gunner positioned at the Chinook's front hatch returned fire with his M60. Luke was down on one knee, grabbing at Jed's combat vest, trying to pull him aboard. The helicopter rocked to the right and suddenly Luke slipped. Jed watched in horror as the young man fell past him, his arms windmilling. He dropped three metres to the ground and landed on his back. Jed looked up at the crewman, but the man just shook his head and screamed something the Green Beret could not hear.

'Fuck it,' Jed said, and let go of the ramp. He fell, maybe five metres now as the chopper was still rising. It was a heavy fall, but he rolled over, unhurt. He had dropped his rifle and couldn't see where it had fallen. He crawled to Luke, who was still lying on his back, and drew a nine-millimetre automatic pistol from inside his combat vest as he moved.

'Luke! Talk to me!'

The reporter coughed and tried to sit up, but the fall had winded him.

'Steady, son. Anything broken?' Jed yelled over the engine noise.

The Chinook was still rising, the door gunner firing blind into the night. Jed hoped the fool didn't cap them by mistake. The AK man had stopped firing.

'Don't think so . . .' Luke spluttered.

Jed helped the young man to his feet, then reached into a pouch of his vest and pulled out a battery-powered strobe light. He flicked it on. The flashing infra-red beacon was invisible to the naked eye but would be easily picked out by the pilots and crewmen through their night-vision goggles.

There was a noise like a buzz saw fifty metres off to his left. Jed heard the sound of lead tearing into metal. The Apache had let rip on the Land Cruiser with its thirty-millimetre chain gun in a long swooping pass. The gas tank caught and the vehicle erupted in an incandescent orange fireball that lit the surrounding hills.

Jed looked up and saw the Chinook swinging around again. There was no sign or sound of the enemy rifleman. He waved the strobe above his head. The Chinook came back around and Jed shielded his eyes from the stinging dust it stirred up. His other arm was wrapped around Luke, supporting him.

The Chinook blocked out the night sky and the moon with its dust and its fat-bellied green bulk as it descended once more. As the edge of the lowered ramp neared the ground, Jed pushed Luke into waiting arms.

One of the crewman who dragged Luke aboard was wide-mouthed for a split second. In the next instant he was thrown backwards into the bowels of the chopper. Jed turned and saw the enemy rifleman not twenty metres away. The man stepped from behind his rock and swung the barrel of the AK towards him.

Even though it was dark and the air was thick with dust, Jed saw the man's face clearly and was struck by his piercing eyes. Jed was quicker than the gunman. He raised his arm instinctively and fired two shots. A double tap. Both rounds hit the man in the chest and he pitched backwards.

Jed felt hands on his shoulders, dragging him back. He didn't resist. He landed on his backside on the helicopter's cargo ramp, feet still dangling in space as the Chinook rose like a big, noisy elevator.

It was over. He shook his head. More action in the last ten minutes of his last patrol than in the rest of his six-month tour of duty. In a few days he would be finished with Afghanistan and reunited with his daughter. He closed his eyes and tried to think of Miranda, and not of the wide-eyed look on the face of the man he had just killed.

Zambia

Hassan bin Zayid put down his chilled Mosi Lager and reached for the remote. He turned up the volume on the television set in the lodge's bar. He was alone in the cool, dark retreat. The staff had returned to their compound for lunch and he had no guests at the moment. It was CNN, something about Afghanistan.

The announcer said: 'Five known Al Qaeda terrorists were killed yesterday in a raid on their hide-out in eastern Afghanistan, near the border with Pakistan. US military sources said the men, all natives of unspecified Arabic countries outside Afghanistan, were in the process of shipping anti-aircraft missiles deeper into the country for use against Coalition aircraft. Two American servicemen were injured in the shoot-out but are said to be recovering. CNN's Mike Porter has more, from Bagram, Afghanistan . . .'

The report continued with file vision of the rugged mountains and desolate plains of the war-ravaged country, then the reporter threw back to the studio announcer, who said: 'Thanks, Mike. We're going to go now to the Pentagon, where senior US Army officer General Donald Calvert, who until recently commanded the Coalition forces in Afghanistan, is holding a live press conference.'

The vision cut to a shot of a man with a bristly grey crewcut and the lined face of one who has spent years outdoors. Silver parachutist's wings and myriad colourful medal ribbons stood out in stark contrast to the dull green of his uniform tunic. On his right shoulder was the yellow embroidered shield of the First Cavalry Division with its black bar and horse's head. On his left, the blue dragon's head of the 18th Airborne Corps. He stood at a podium, a map of Afghanistan on the plasma-screen television behind and to one side of him.

A reporter off-camera asked: 'General Calvert, a few months ago you were the commander of Coalition forces in Afghanistan. When you left you were, quote, "confident we had disrupted Al Qaeda's ability to mount major offensive operations inside Afghanistan". What's gone wrong since you left and do you stand by your earlier comments?'

The general smiled, leaned a little closer to the microphone in front of him and said: 'Stu, what we've seen in the last few days is proof positive that we are making headway against terrorism. Acting on accurate, timely intelligence, our Special Forces soldiers were able to intercept this band of killers and their deadly hardware and prevent a missile attack from taking place. Call me old-fashioned, but I'd rate that a pretty good success.'

Another reporter said: 'Rachel Wise from the *Post*, General. On another matter, now that your retirement from the military has been announced there's been a flurry of speculation about what you will be doing next.'

Again the easy smile. 'Well, Rachel, right now I'm still an officer in the US Army. My future's my business, for now, but the first thing I'm going to do when I finish up here is go on a safari holiday. Now, if there are no more questions about Afghanistan . . .?'

Hassan hoped Miranda's father hadn't been involved in the attack, or been one of those injured. The raid had occurred near Pakistan. Iqbal was in Karachi, studying at an Islamic university. He was nowhere near the border, thank God.

Hassan pushed aside his half-drunk beer and strode across the polished stone floor of the bar to his private office. Next to his computer a portable satellite phone sat in its desk charger. He picked it up and started to scroll through the saved names, glancing at the silver-framed photo beside the charger. Taken ten years earlier, on the day of his graduation from Cambridge University, it showed him in academic robes, smiling broadly, his darkly handsome father in a western business suit. Iqbal, his twin brother, stood on the other side of their father, wearing a *kansu*, the traditional loose-fitting white robe of the Zanzibari–Omani man. A year after the photo was taken, Hassan senior had succumbed to lung cancer.

Hassan found the number and pressed the dial button. The feeling of unease, a mixture of guilt and dread, started to spread through him once more. He changed his mind and pushed the cancel button before the phone on the other end started to ring. It was nothing, he told himself again.

He put on Ray-Ban sunglasses and a New York Yankees baseball cap as protection against the glare and heat of the African sun and walked along the riverside track to the enclosures.

'Hello, Maggie,' he said fondly.

The cheetah, the eldest of his breeding females, responded to his voice, got up and walked to the gate. Hassan opened it; Maggie made no move to escape. Instead she rubbed her flank against his leg like an overgrown household cat. 'How are your babies today, beautiful?'

16

He walked to the shade of the apple-ring acacia inside the enclosure, drawn by a series of high-pitched squeaks.

The cat's latest litter of five strong, healthy cubs turned their tiny faces to him. The little balls of fluff knew his scent as well as their mother's. He picked one up and stroked it. Another clawed at the fabric of his tan trousers, while a third tried to trip him up by attacking the laces of his kudu-leather boots.

One day these cheetahs would take their rightful place in the Zambezi Valley, patrolling the riverine forests and floodplains of the great river. He had helped save Maggie, and a few other heirs to the natural paradise that bordered his own private game reserve, from extinction.

Hassan bin Zayid also thought himself an heir to the valley. His family had made their fortune in this part of Africa hundreds of years earlier. His people, on his father's side, were Omanis. Great traders and seafarers, they had left the Arabian Gulf and followed the east coast of Africa in search of exotic animals, spices and the most valuable cargo of all – slaves.

Hassan certainly did not think of Juma or his other staff as slaves, just as loyal paid servants, but his ancestors had not been as benevolent. They had forged deeper and deeper into the forests and savannas of central and southern Africa, spreading Islam as they went and returning to their bases at Zanzibar and Bagamoyo with dhows crammed with live cargo.

He thought of the news item he had just seen. The war against terror, as the Americans called it, had touched many more countries than Afghanistan and Iraq. His ancestral homeland of Oman had lined up with the Americans, the oil-rich state providing land for US bases. The place of his birth, Zanzibar, had seen a drop in tourist numbers because world events and his family's fortunes had suffered as a result.

Hassan found himself missing Zanzibar less and less and spending more time at his game reserve in Zambia with every trip. He loved the island where he had been born, with its azure waters, white sands and heady aroma of cloves and other spices. But the paradise he had known as a child was changing, and not for the better. Each year hotels encroached a little more on the beaches. Even now, with tourist numbers down it seemed to him there were still more European faces than Arabs or Africans on the streets of Stone Town, and that dance music and hip-hop were drowning out the gentle melodies of his own people.

Of course, he didn't mind the presence of tourists when it came to the monetary aspect – they had made him and his family extremely wealthy over the years. Since the demise of the trade in slaves, ivory and, more recently, rhino horn, the bin Zayid family had made their living from the development and running of hotels on Zanzibar and the Tanzanian mainland. Hassan liked to think of himself as a progressive man. He didn't hate westerners and, although he had been raised a Muslim, he did not follow all the rules of his father's religion. Neither had his father, for that matter. Hassan had inherited from him a weakness for malt whisky and a fondness for women with golden hair.

He thought for the hundredth time that day of Miranda, just across the Zambezi from him. He would send the boat for her tonight, to her camp on the Zimbabwean side of the river. They would dine and share a bottle or two of fine wine from his cellar. There were so many things he wanted to discuss with her, but they could wait until after they had made love. He had fallen under her spell so quickly and completely that it still amazed him. He, the millionaire bachelor, with a string of sexual conquests to rival a Hollywood leading man, had found himself ensnared by her beauty, her wit and their shared love of Africa's precious wildlife. There were still, however, so many things he needed to clear up with her.

'Boss, excuse me.' It was Juma, returned from lunch. He strode down the pathway, carrying the satellite phone. The African was not given to smiling, but his face looked more solemn than ever.

'There was a telephone call for you. The caller wouldn't wait, but I have a message.'

'What is it?' Hassan asked as he gently laid the cheetah cub back amongst its siblings.

'I am sorry, boss, with all my heart, but there has been a death.'

*

South Africa

Panthera Leo. The African lion. This one was a beauty. She guessed his weight at close to a hundred and ninety kilograms – nearly four hundred and twenty pounds where she came from. A big boy.

Professor Christine Wallis flipped open a cheap photo album and leafed through the pages until she found Nelson. To a casual observer the pages and pages of digital photo prints would have all looked the same. All big, tawny lions. Nelson was a little easier to distinguish from the rest because, like his namesake, British admiral Horatio Nelson, he was a one-eyed warrior.

His disability had not affected his ability to fornicate and fight – the king of beast's two top, and pretty much only, duties in life. Chris put down the album and made some notes in her journal, recording Nelson's condition – good – and activity – nil.

The lion yawned, baring yellowed fangs the length and girth of a man's finger. He curled his long pink tongue. It was roughened, like a domestic cat's, and made for flaying the skin off a dead animal. Chris was three metres away from Nelson, but the predator paid her no mind. The shape of the four-wheel drive she was sitting in was as familiar to him as the striped zebra, or the fearsome bulk of an elephant. Nelson lowered his head, rolled onto his back, wriggled a little to dislodge an annoying tick, then sat up.

Chris took up her camera, focused tight on Nelson's sleepy face and snapped off three frames in succession, getting a better, closer shot of his scarred face. He blinked lazily at the whirr of the camera's motor wind. He'd heard that sound his whole life. He was all power, Chris thought. The top of the food chain, irresistible to the six females in his pride, respected by his dozen children and feared by his enemies. He was the reason why she was living in South Africa's Kruger National Park instead of her other home town in Virginia, USA.

Nelson sniffed the air, reassured himself all was well in his kingdom and, content in the knowledge that his wives were either caring for his children or hunting for his supper, laid his big maned head down and fell asleep.

Lions. Chris shook her head. For all their majesty, the big cats were also some of the most boring animals in Africa to watch and study – most of the time. Nelson was doing what every lion did for about eighteen hours a day – nothing. But it was those rarely glimpsed moments of the hunt and the kill, where the members of the pride came together instinctively as one to bring down their prey in a tawny blur of dust and blood, that made her rise before dawn six days a week and drive out into the bush. Taking her lead from the lion, Chris laid her head back and closed her eyes.

Her home for the past eighteen months had been a caravan parked under a marula tree in the camping ground of Pretoriuskop rest camp in the south-west of the Kruger National Park. An American university had provided funding for research into the feeding habits of lions and other large predators in the southern part of South Africa's premier park. A particular focus was the prevalence of humans as prey for large predators. The reserve's eastern boundary was also the border with Mozambique, and illegal immigrants from that country had for decades been risking the natural hazards of the bush in their quest to find their fortunes in comparatively prosperous South Africa. Even though Mozambique's prolonged and bloody civil war had long since ended, the flow of illegals had continued unabated. Many of Kruger's lions, beloved and photographed by tourists from around the world, had feasted on the flesh of luckless refugees. Chris wanted to find out how many lions were man-eaters, and whether there were individuals or prides that now specialised in hunting humans. She had interviewed rangers who had come across human remains on the veldt and, with the help of the local police, with whom she maintained an excellent relationship, she had also been able to speak to detained illegal immigrants about their brushes with wildlife. So far she had not actually seen the remains of a human killed by a lion. That was just fine by her.

The noise of a vehicle engine woke her from her doze. A game-viewer – an open-top Land Rover with a canvas awning roof and tiered bench seats crammed with tourists – pulled up in front of her truck. Chris waved when she recognised the driver.

The tourists were open-mouthed with awe at the sight of the lion. However, their silent fascination soon gave way to chattering in at least three languages. Cameras flashed and a child shrieked as Nelson rose on his front legs and yawned. He looked at the game-viewer, considered moving, but couldn't be bothered. He fell asleep again.

Chris knew most of the safari guides and rangers in her part of the park, including the 'jeep jockey' driving this vehicle, a South African guy named Jan. He was young, blond and attractive. Not her type, but he looked good in his short khaki shorts. Jan was sitting up on the backrest of his seat, facing his passengers and explaining some facts about lion behaviour to them.

'We're safe as long as we stay in the vehicle, but if you got out and tried to pat the big kitty it would be the last decision you ever made in your life,' Jan said. There were a few nervous laughs from the crowd.

Jan started his vehicle and edged it around Chris's until he was parked beside her window. 'Morning, Professor,' he said, smiling.

'Had much luck, Jan?' Sometimes the jeep jockeys were a pain in the ass, getting too close to animals in order to present a better photo opportunity for the tourists, and scaring off the game in the process. Jan, she recalled, was studying zoology and seemed to have a genuine respect for wildlife.

'Only need a leopard and we'll have nailed the big five this morning.'

'Head via the Klipspringer kopjes on your way back to camp. That big male was out on a rock sunning himself this morning.'

'Thanks, Professor. I'll buy you a beer with my tips if we catch up with him. Hey, how's Miranda doing up in Zim? You heard from her lately?'

'She's fine. Working hard and much better able to concentrate on her studies now that she's away from you guys.' Chris attracted her fair share of attention from the men in the national park, but Miranda, blonde, blue-eyed, gorgeous and thirteen years her junior, sent the South African young bloods into a frenzy of competition for her affections whenever she passed through Kruger.

Jan laughed. 'She wasn't interested in any of us last time she was here. Oh, by the way, I nearly forgot. The gate guard said there's a message for you at reception.'

Chris checked her mobile phone. She was out of range, even though much of the park was now covered by the cellular phone network. 'Thanks, Jan. I'd better be getting back, then. Good luck with your spotting.'

She followed the game-viewer back onto the main tarred road running through the park, then overtook Jan and drove as fast as she dared back towards Pretoriuskop camp. When she was close to the camp and its tower, her mobile phone beeped. Chris pulled over, ignoring the bull elephant snapping branches from a tree a scant fifty metres from her. She dialled the number to retrieve her message.

It was the embassy. A female secretary started to dictate the number for her to call, but she cut the woman off, ended the call and started to dial again. She knew the number by heart. Bad news, Chris thought. The embassy only ever called when something terrible had happened.

Afghanistan

Jed's spirits were high as he walked down Disney Parade, the main thoroughfare through Bagram Air Base. The road was named not after the cartoon creator, but a US Army soldier who had been killed in a welding accident in the early days of the American occupation of the old Russian base.

The jet engines of a C-17 transport aircraft screamed at full pitch and the fat-bellied bird roared down the runway. Jed smiled. He had just visited the APOD, the aerial point of debarkation, and confirmed his seat on a flight out of Afghanistan that night.

The dust by the side of the road was ankle-deep and as fine as talcum powder. It broke over his boots like the foamy edge of an ocean tide. The wind picked up and he shielded his eyes from the flying grit. He could no longer see the foothills of the Hindu Kush mountains, couldn't even see two hundred metres down Disney. A convoy of Hummers rumbled down the road, stirring up even more dust. The paratroopers manning the .50 calibre machine-guns and Mark 19 automatic grenade-launchers mounted in the turrets of each vehicle had their faces wrapped in Arab *shamags*, their eyes protected by goggles. He would not miss Afghanistan.

From the runway to his left, on the other side of the old Russian aircraft hangars, he heard the whine of helicopter turbine engines winding up to full power. Another patrol, another search for an enemy who was both hard to find and hard to identify. He thought of the men he had killed on his last mission, a few days earlier. He pressed his fingers to his eyes to wipe out some particles of dirt, and to squeeze out the image of the face of the man he had shot at close range.

He had killed before. He had called in airstrikes on Iraqi Republican Guard positions and armoured columns during the first Gulf War. He had seen the burned and shattered bodies of some of his victims, become hardened to the grotesque face of death, but he had never been close enough to one of his victims to look into his eyes. He had no doubt about himself as a soldier, the righteousness of his cause, or the fact that the man would have shot him without blinking if he had been quicker on the draw.

The rangers who had swept the compound the day after the mission had found two Hongying 5 surface-to-air missiles, Chinese knock-offs of the portable shoulder-launched Soviet SAM 7, or Strela. Although based on nineteen sixties technology, the lightweight missiles were still a serious threat to modern aircraft. There was no doubt the team had hit the right target at the right time and probably saved Coalition lives. But still the face of the man haunted him. He supposed it was only normal.

Two Black Hawks and an Apache rose above the dust stirred up by their rotor wash and headed south. Khost, he guessed. Afghanistan might have dropped off the front pages of the world's newspapers, but Americans were still fighting and dying there. He wondered how long the war would go on. He believed the operations in this blighted country had made a real dent in Al Qaeda's ability to conduct terrorist operations around the world, but their enemy was like the mythical Hydra, growing a new head as soon as one was lopped off. The war, such as it was, had spread to Asia and Africa, where terrorists had tried to down an Israeli airliner in Kenya with weapons identical to the ones discovered after his last mission.

He thought about Africa. It was ironic that at a time when much of the rest of the world was preparing itself for possible terrorist attacks, Miranda was probably safer in strife-torn Zimbabwe than anywhere else.

'Jed!' a man's voice called from behind him.

Jed turned. 'Morning, sir. Hell of a day for a walk,' he said to his commanding officer, a full colonel who had served in the Army since Vietnam. Jed had enormous respect for the old man. A veteran of too many firefights to count, with more combat experience than any of them, he was also a devoted family man who cared for his soldiers like they were his sons. He almost always had the makings of a smile on his face, no matter how bad the situation.

'Just got a signal from the States, Jed,' the colonel said. 'Thought I'd better come find you in person.'

Jed looked into the other man's eyes. There was no smile.

'It's not good, Jed. There's been an accident . . .'

2

J ed drained the last of the Scotch from the plastic tumbler and let the single ice cube slide into his mouth as the fasten-seatbelt sign chimed and lit up. He turned and stared out of the window of the United Airlines 737-300 and chomped on the ice as the plane descended through the clouds.

He needed a clear head for his meeting with Patti – she had sounded incoherent on the phone – but at the same time he had needed a couple of Scotches to calm his own nerves for the flight. A combat veteran and paratrooper with more than two hundred jumps on his log card he might have been, but he was still scared of flying. Also, there was the constant pain, a feeling deep in his core, every time he thought of Miranda.

She couldn't be dead, he told himself over and over again. There was no body, according to Patti, who desperately wanted to believe Miranda was hiding, or maybe alive but lost in the African bush.

'I don't know how to tell you this,' the CO had said to him on the dusty roadside at Bagram, 'but it seems Miranda has been killed by a lion in Africa.'

For a moment he had thought the colonel was joking. Everyone in the unit knew his daughter was researching carnivores in Africa. The guys in Special Forces were hard men and, Lord knew, some of them had twisted senses of humour, but one thing a guy would never do was joke about another man's kids.

It was no joke, but it was absurd. Miranda had lived in the African bush for six months and she had repeatedly told Jed in her emails that she knew how to take care of herself. Also, he remembered her reassuring him in one message that when she camped out in the field there was always an armed ranger or safari guide in the party. What had happened to the guard? For the man's own sake, Jed hoped he was dead. If not, he would be by the time Jed finished with him.

Boston looked cold and bleak through the gaps in the cloud cover. He had never liked coming here, although the thought of meeting Miranda had always made the trip worth it. Nightmarish scenes played over and over in his head as he prepared to face Patti. The thought of his baby being torn apart by a wild beast was too much to bear. He screwed his eyes tight for a couple of seconds to rid himself of the recurring image. He was tired, fall-down tired, but there would be time to sleep on the next flight, later that evening.

He pulled his green suit bag from the overhead locker. He had about an hour with Patti. He doubted he could take more than that.

She was waiting for him when he emerged from the air bridge. They stared at each other for a few seconds. She was wearing jeans and high-heeled boots, a white T-shirt and a cropped black leather jacket. Her golden hair was piled carelessly high, stray wisps framing her face. She was a little fuller in the face, but still as beautiful as the day they had met. He saw Miranda in her eyes and mouth. It was all he could do to fight back the tears.

Patti Vernon had transferred to his school in his senior year. They had started dating a week after she arrived. She lost her virginity to him on prom night. It seemed as though they would live happily ever ᵃᶠ ᵗᵉʳ il he made a spur of the moment decision to join the Army going to college. They had planned to marry as soon as d he wanted to start earning money. She had reluctantly become a soldier's bride, on the promise that he would eventually go to college with the money he made from his first enlistment.

Their teenage passion lasted for the first year of marriage. Patti was on the pill and took it religiously, except for the weekend between Jed's basic training and advanced infantry training. They went away to a country hotel and she forgot her oral contraceptive packet. They risked it. Patti fell pregnant.

Jed loved his baby girl, but he was being seduced away from his over-tired wife, who seemed to blame him for the fact that she had to drop out of college and could barely afford to make ends meet. Domestic duties left Jed cold, particularly when compared with the excitement of airborne school at Fort Benning, Georgia, and ranger training in the Florida swamps.

Grenada, in 1983, was the first time America had seriously flexed its military muscles since Vietnam. The brief conflict also marked the beginning of the end of Jed and Patti's marriage. The Army had shaken off the shame of defeat in south-east Asia and Jed Banks had discovered that he was born to be a warrior.

Patti's lower lip started to tremble and Jed walked to her. He folded her in his arms as she started to cry.

'Oh, Patti,' was all he could say.

'Jed, it can't be true.' She leaned back and wiped her face with the back of her hand.

'I know, Patti. I can't believe it myself.'

'She's all right, Jed, I know it. She might be hurt, but she's not dead.'

Jed wanted so much to believe Patti was right.

'Let's find somewhere to sit down. Are you alone?'

'Rob's outside. It'll take an age for him to park the car. How long have you got?'

'Less than an hour, and I've got to check in for my connection to Johannesburg. Let's get a coffee.'

He ushered her across to a cafe, his hand on her elbow. He sat her at a table and she blew her nose on a tissue.

'OK, tell me about this email you got,' Jed said when he returned from the counter with two black coffees.

She sniffed again, then rummaged in her big leather handbag. 'It's from a professor. Wallis is her name, Christine.' Patti pulled a crumpled print-out from the bag and smoothed it out on the laminated tabletop. 'Miranda met her during her final year at college – said the professor ran a postgraduate program for zoology majors in the Kruger National Park in South Africa. Professor Wallis was the one who put Miranda onto this research project in Zimbabwe.'

Jed nodded. He remembered Miranda's description of the program, if not the names of the people involved. Zimbabwe had been short of foreign aid for years, because of its political and security situation, and it seemed the few foreign wildlife researchers left in the troubled nation were welcoming with open arms any contributions or volunteers. Miranda had mentioned that she was being funded by a US-based wildlife conservation group, as an offshoot of the program being run by Christine Wallis in South Africa. He couldn't remember the name of the organisation. 'So what did the professor have to say?'

'Well, the media were reporting Miranda's . . .' Patti's lip began to tremble again.

'It's OK, Sugar,' he said, a little surprised at how easily the old nickname came back. 'I saw the reports.' He had printed them off at Bagram. 'They said it appeared she had been sleeping with her tent flap open and that a lion had entered.'

Patti nodded, took a deep breath and held up the paper. 'Professor Wallis says, "*These reports surprised me greatly as Miranda is always so sensible when she spends time in the field. She always made a point of making sure her tent was completely secure, and was well aware of a recent case in which a young man was taken by a lion because he slept with his tent open on a particularly hot evening.*" '

Jed nodded. He wondered why anyone would sleep in a tent when there were lions around. 'I don't know, Patti. People get lazy when they get out into the field.' That was true. He'd had a buddy who had been bitten by a snake at ranger school because he had left his sleeping bag unrolled during the day, allowing the reptile to slither inside.

'This goddamned professor sent her there, Jed, and now she feels

28

guilty. That's what I know. But she *does* say that the press reports don't tally with what she knew of Miranda.'

Jed took the offered print-out and scanned it. 'Says she's going to go to Zimbabwe to talk to the authorities herself.'

'Find her, Jed. Talk to her. Find out if Miranda could still be alive. I know she's not dead, and the police and park rangers say they haven't found her body.'

Jed nodded. There were explanations for that, but he didn't want to voice them in front of Patti. She was conveniently ignoring the media reports that human remains had been found at the scene of the attack. Now wasn't the time to remind her. 'I'll do what I can, Patti. There will be arrangements to make with the embassy in any case.'

'Thank you, Jed.' Patti looked as though she would cry again.

'You look great,' Jed said, trying to get her to relax.

She looked down at the table and felt her cheeks start to colour. She glanced up at him. God, she thought, he looked even better now than he did when he was nineteen. Patti hated the way she felt right now. So distraught over Miranda, so devoted to her second husband, but still captivated by that sandy hair and those blue eyes. It was the way he fixed her with them like she was a butterfly pinned to a board, helpless around him. She'd had the courage to move on with her life when Miranda was still young, and given Miranda and her other children a great life with Rob Lewis, but there were times, like now, when she wondered if she shouldn't have stuck it out a couple more years.

'Here's Rob,' Jed said. 'I should be going.'

'Stay a while.' Patti wiped her eyes again and waved to a handsome man in chinos and loafers and a blue button-down shirt. A gangly ten-year-old boy loped along behind him and the man carried a three-year-old girl, Louise, in his arms.

'Hi, Jed,' Rob Lewis said. 'I'm so sorry about Miranda. It's good you can go over there at such short notice.'

'I had a ticket booked.' Jed didn't dislike Lewis. He was a nice enough guy, for a lawyer. He supposed he envied the normality of the

29

relationship he and Patti had – the very domesticity he had turned his back on nearly two decades before.

Patti stepped between the two men and took Louise in her arms. 'Jed, find her, please.'

Jed picked his green beret up off the coffee-stained table and put it on. He shook hands with Lewis and turned to face Patti.

'Be strong. You know I may find nothing.'

She nodded, tears welling in her eyes again. 'God, Jed, I just want to know for sure, even if it's . . . '

Jed knew enough about death and grieving to understand that the recovery of a body gave closure, allowed relatives to grieve, services to be said and life to go on. He hated to think he was going to Africa in search of the mortal remains of the one good thing he had given to this world.

'I'll bring her back with me, Patti. I promise. I've got to go check in. They'll be calling my flight soon.'

He kissed Patti on the cheek, smiled down at her son, who had been too shy to talk to the uniformed stranger, and shook Rob's hand again.

'Travel safe,' the lawyer said.

Jed reflected that he had never travelled anywhere safe in his life.

In truth, he still had forty minutes until his flight boarded, but he wanted some time alone, to think. He didn't want to be reminded of the family life he had forsaken.

He walked the length of the terminal and stopped at a bar. He ordered a beer and took it to an internet work station on the other side of the lounge. He popped some change into the slot and sipped his beer while the browser loaded. His life was governed by planning and routine and he was about to travel halfway around the world with the benefit of neither. All he knew of Zimbabwe and South Africa was what he had seen on the Discovery Channel or read in tattered copies of *National Geographic* while waiting for dental appointments.

In the browser's search field he typed in *Mana Pools National*

Park – the place where Miranda had been doing her research. He clicked on a site that boasted maps. The park, he learned, was in the far north of Zimbabwe, in the Zambezi River Valley, below Lake Kariba and the dam of the same name. Mana Pools was a World Heritage-listed area, valued for its scenic beauty and abundant wildlife. *Mana* was a local word for four, referring to the number of large pools of water which were cut off from the river after the dam was constructed. Jed was surprised to learn from his web surfing that tourists were allowed to walk freely without an escort around the park – something that other national parks did not allow. Miranda had told him that she was accompanied by an armed guard when she did her research. He wondered now if she had lied to help convince him she was safe.

The four websites he investigated were all run by private safari companies and offered 'exclusive', which he took to mean expensive, guided tours into the Zambezi River Valley and Mana Pools National Park.

He took out his hardcover Army notebook and a pen and started writing. He didn't know how long he would be in northern Zimbabwe. As a military man, he did his best to make a logical judgment of the situation and what he was setting out to achieve. His mission was to find out what had happened to his daughter and discover some concrete evidence of her fate. From the scant information available to him, it seemed there was little reason to be optimistic.

Under the heading *Police* he made a note to contact the local station. From his brief internet surfing he deduced the cops who investigated Miranda's death would most likely be based at either Kariba or Chirundu, the two towns nearest the national park. Kariba was further away from Mana Pools, but appeared to be the larger centre.

Miranda was his next entry. He needed to find out her movements in and around the park, to talk to other people she would have come into contact with. *Rangers? Colleagues? Prof Wallis – visiting Zimbabwe?*

Scene. He wanted to see where Miranda had been camping and to conduct his own investigation there. He had done tracking courses in the jungles of Central America, but he knew there was never a substitute for local knowledge and skills. *Hire local guide/tracker.*

31

Logistics. He needed to be flexible and self-sufficient. He would have no choice in Mana Pools, as there appeared to be no shops or restaurants in the park. He needed a vehicle, tent, camping gear, food, water. Some of the basics were in his Alice pack – the common name for the capacious US Army-issue LC-1 rucksack – which was with his checked-in luggage. He had a sleeping bag, fatigues, mess tins, water bottles, combat boots and other odds and ends that would come in handy. He wished he could take a weapon with him, but from what he had read he would have to surrender any firearms on entering the national park, or risk being shot on sight by an anti-poaching patrol.

His mobile phone chirped and he fished it from his uniform coat pocket. He made a mental note to call his service provider before he got on the plane to check whether the device would work in Africa.

'Banks,' he said.

'Jed, glad I caught you. It's Tom Cookson. How are you keeping, buddy? I'm so sorry to hear about Miranda.'

Jed was surprised. Tom Cookson was a retired lieutenant colonel, an ex-Green Beret officer who had been invalided out of the military due to injury. Jed recalled he had taken up a civilian analyst's position of some sort with the defence department and was working in the Pentagon. 'How did you find out, sir?'

Cookson hesitated. 'It's been in all the papers. Where are you, Jed?'

The last time Jed had seen Cookson was inside Iraq. Tom, then a captain, had been in charge of Jed's patrol, until he had trodden on an anti-personnel mine. The last Jed had seen of him was when he slid him into the medevac Black Hawk.

'Her name hasn't been released – at Patti's request,' Jed said, immediately curious.

'Aw, hell, Jed, I'll level with you. I saw a report from State. Her name was in the regular sitrep out of the Africa desk. I'm so sorry. She was such a bright kid.'

'You're talking like she's dead, sir.'

'Cut the "sir" crap, Jed. The report was pretty conclusive.'

'Yeah. Well, thanks for the call. I'll be sure and let you know if I find anything different.' Jed was irrationally angry at the man. He knew Miranda probably was dead but, like Patti, part of him refused to accept what he had been told.

'Hold on, Jed. What do you mean, "if you find anything different"? You're not going to Africa, are you?'

'What if I was? Is this you or the Pentagon asking?'

'Jed, I owe you one. I would have died if you'd followed my orders and left me in the minefield, but you crawled through and dragged me out.'

'No big deal.'

'Bullshit. You should have got the Congressional Medal of Honour for that stunt. God knows, I recommended you for it. But, Jed, I believe the best thing you can do for Miranda is to stay at home and comfort Patti. State will get news to you if they hear anything more about her.'

'What is this bullshit, Tom? What are you trying to tell me? Are you warning me off? Since when does the Government of the United States of America investigate lion attacks?'

'Jesus, Jed. I'm just trying to help an old friend. Sit tight on this one . . . that's my advice to you.'

'Yeah, Tom?' Well, *screw* your advice, sir, he wanted to add, but held his tongue. 'It's my daughter who's missing and I'm not waiting around while some pimple-faced Ivy League prick from the Timbuk-fucking-tu embassy conducts some sorry-assed excuse of an investigation.'

'Jed . . .' Cookson's voice dropped to a whisper. 'Look, I can't talk any more, but just be careful, OK?'

The call dropped out and Jed walked back to the bar. He ordered another beer, downed half of it and forced himself to be calm. What did Tom mean 'just be careful'? He supposed Cookson was warning him about the general security situation, but, hell, Jed had just spent six months in a country where people had actively been trying to kill him. How dangerous could Africa be?

He reopened his notebook and wrote *Cookson – check.*

Jed upended his beer glass, steeling himself as he felt the first twinges of nerves that always preceded flying. He picked up his suit bag and walked into the men's room. In a cramped cubicle he changed out of his Class A uniform into comfortable travel clothes – a short-sleeved navy Ralph Lauren shirt, lightweight tan trousers and hiking boots. It would be hot where he was heading, and it was definitely not a place where he could wear a US Army dress uniform. He needed a shower and a bed to sleep in. He would get neither for more than twenty hours. He folded his uniform and gleaming patent leather jump boots into his bag and zipped it shut.

He left the cubicle and checked his reflection in the mirror. He'd shaved off his beard prior to leaving Afghanistan and his chin stood out white compared to his cheeks. He didn't feel as though he was getting older – he was still in excellent physical shape – but his face showed all its forty years and then some. He closed his eyes and saw Miranda again. He couldn't lose her.

Jed walked through the brightly lit airport terminal, past eager holiday travellers and grey-faced men and women in business suits. He had nothing in common with any of them.

It was probably his imagination, he supposed, but the immigration officer seemed to be taking a long time to inspect his passport. 'Is there a problem?' he asked.

The officer looked up at him but said nothing as he continued typing on his hidden console. Jed checked his watch. The final boarding call had been made five minutes earlier.

At last the officer looked up and said, 'How long are you intending on staying in Africa, sir?'

Jed felt like telling the man it was none of his damned business. 'I don't know. A couple of weeks, maybe more.'

'I need to know countries and duration, sir.'

This had never happened to Jed before, although most of his international travel was courtesy of the USAF's Military Airlift Command and the places he tended to visit didn't require passports or customs declarations.

'South Africa for one night. Zimbabwe for, say, two weeks. It depends.'

'It depends on what, sir?'

Jed was close to the brink. 'It depends on how goddamned long I want to spend in the country. Look, buddy, my flight is boarding.'

'It's not my fault, sir, if you haven't left enough time to clear immigration.'

Jed wished he had his nine-millimetre with him.

The man tapped away on the keyboard again, then looked up and smiled insincerely as he handed back Jed's passport. 'Have a nice flight, sir.'

Jed nodded and walked past the desk. When he turned and looked over his shoulder the immigration official was ignoring the next person in the queue and talking into a telephone.

'Would you like a drink from the bar, sir?' the flight attendant asked as the aircraft levelled out.

'Scotch on the rocks, and a beer, please,' Jed said.

He'd slept for three hours on the flight from Boston to Amsterdam, Holland, where he'd picked up his connection to Johannesburg, on KLM Royal Dutch Airlines. He covered a yawn with his hand. It would be three flights over three continents before he made Zimbabwe.

The immaculately groomed young Dutchman gave a large smile as he handed over the drinks and opened the can of beer. 'My pleasure, sir. Just holler when you need another.'

'I think he likes you,' the woman seated next to Jed whispered as the flight attendant moved past them to the next row.

Jed smiled. 'Not my type.'

'Mine either, he's too young for me. I'm Eveline, by the way.'

'Jed.' The woman was well off, judging by the gold earrings and necklace. In her late fifties, or early sixties. Still attractive, and a real looker in her day, Jed imagined. He didn't really want to get into conversation, but felt it would be rude to cut her off straightaway. 'You're South African?'

'I live there, but I was born in Rhodesia – Zimbabwe to you. Just

35

been visiting some friends in the States. We Zimbos are scattered all over the world these days.'

'I'm heading for Zimbabwe.'

'Do you hunt, or are you going on a photographic safari?'

'Neither. Family business to attend to.'

'It's just that most of the Americans I've met who have the gumption to travel to our part of the world seem to be hunters.'

'I thought that was pretty much out of vogue these days.'

Eveline shook her head. 'No, no, Jed. Hunting's alive and well in southern Africa. In Zim, it's one of the few activities that still brings in hard currency. The local people get a cut of the proceeds as well. You'll find we're not as politically correct as other parts of the globe, although we're very conscious of conserving our wildlife. If we can make some money out of it on the side, well, all the better.'

Jed nodded. 'What about the Zambezi Valley, around Mana Pools National Park. Do you know the area?'

'Know it? I practically grew up there. You hear a lot of people talk about God's own country, but let me tell you, Mana Pools is *it*. Garden of Eden. One of the last truly wild places left on this earth. Are you going there?'

'Yes. For a few days. You say it's a wild place. Is it dangerous?'

'Many people are a danger to themselves in the African bush, Jed. If you don't know what you're doing you become a risk to yourself and the wildlife.'

'Are many people killed by wild animals?'

'Probably more than you read about.'

'What species?'

'Not counting the mosquito, hippos top the list, you may be surprised to learn. Yes, they look like big friendly creatures, but they'll chomp you in half as soon as look at you. They're incredibly territorial. If you stray into their part of the river you can be in real trouble. Tourists on canoe safaris on the Zambezi are forever bumping into submerged hippos and getting tipped out of their boats when the animal, quite rightly, shows its annoyance. Crocs also nab quite a few people in the valley – a lot more than you ever hear about.'

Jed tried to sound casual. 'What about lions? Do they take many humans?'

Eveline took a sip of her gin and tonic. 'Well, Jed, your lion, he's a different prospect. In fact, I should say she, as the females do most of the hunting. Had a couple sniffing around my tent at Mana years back. They'll leave you alone if you stay quiet and don't bother them.'

'Are there really man-eaters – lions that develop a taste for humans?'

'I don't know enough about the scientific side of it, but there are certainly plenty of reports, even these days, of lions feeding on humans. They regularly take Mozambicans trying to cross the border into South Africa illegally.'

'Really?' Jed said, showing his surprise and disliking his ignorance of the continent where his daughter had chosen to live. 'And elsewhere?'

'Careless or reckless safari guides, tourists who don't have the sense to zip up their tents at night . . . most of them had it coming.'

Jed had heard enough, but Eveline went on. 'What's the family business you have to attend to, if you don't mind me asking?'

'It appears my daughter may have been taken by a lion.'

Eveline fumbled with her plastic glass, spilling half the contents into her lap. Jed had had enough of talking anyway, and he needed some sleep.

The flight attendant woke him an hour before landing. 'You've been out for *hours*.'

Jed rubbed his eyes.

Eveline leaned over. 'I'm so sorry about my comments last night. Please forgive me. I'm sure your daughter hadn't done anything foolish.'

Jed shrugged. 'It was rude of me not to warn you what I'm going to Africa for, and I'm sorry for that. But I'm looking for honest information – for facts – not sympathy. My daughter's missing, but I don't know for sure yet that she's dead.'

'Well, I'm sorry anyway. There's a man you should talk to, if you need a guide or a tracker. He worked for me for a few years before I left

Zimbabwe. I wrote down his address while you were asleep. Here, please take it. He lives in Kariba – at least, he did the last time I heard of him. He'll look after you if you tell him Eve sent you.'

After landing, Jed shook hands with Eveline and before they parted, she asked, 'Was your daughter a smart girl?'

'She was studying for a masters in zoology, researching carnivores, and she was no stranger to the African bush.'

'Don't give up on her, then. Africa's a place where someone can easily get lost – whether they want to or not. Call the man whose number I gave you. If anyone can find someone, it's him.'

'Thanks.'

'You're a soldier, aren't you?'

'Is it that obvious?' He didn't recall his occupation coming up in their brief conversation.

'I lived through fifteen years of war in my country. I've known a soldier or two,' she smiled, her cheeks colouring a little. 'Be careful up there in the valley. It can be a dangerous place if you don't know what you're doing – and you can't take a weapon with you.'

'So I've heard, and thank you, I'll watch out.'

'Good luck.'

Jed was surprised how modern Johannesburg International Airport was. He could have been anywhere in the First World. And as the hotel shuttle bus drove through an industrial area flanked by a multi-lane freeway Jed found himself thinking he could have been in any airport suburb in any major town in the western world.

The Holiday Inn Garden Court was a sprawling affair in a mock hacienda style, complete with terracotta roof and stucco façade. The analogy was marred, somewhat, by the presence of an Irish Bar, but to some extent reinforced by a Wild West theme steakhouse. Of Africa, there was still no sign. The porters were black Africans, though the receptionist was white. She was blonde, blue-eyed, and efficient. Jed found her Afrikaans accent oddly appealing.

'How long will you be staying with us, Mr Banks?'

'Just overnight. I'll need a wake-up call for seven tomorrow morning.'

'Certainly, sir. Oh, by the way, Mister Banks, did your friend catch up with you?'

Jed was confused. 'What friend?'

'There was a woman here about two hours ago, asking after you. When I told her you hadn't arrived she said she would try to meet you at the airport.'

He had no idea what she was talking about. 'I think there must be some misunderstanding. I don't know anybody here and I'm not expecting to meet anyone.'

'She seemed certain. She also asked if you were checked in under your rank. Is it Sergeant Major?'

'Master Sergeant. But no, I still don't know who it could have been.'

'Don't worry, sir. If I see the lady again I'll be sure and call your room.'

In his room at the end of a corridor on the second floor Jed tried to think who the mysterious woman could have been. He had meant to ask the receptionist for a description, but his brain was addled from jetlag and booze. The only explanation he could come up with was that the woman was from the American embassy.

He opened the curtains of his room and saw there was a small balcony. Beyond the railing, at the same level as the floor, was the roof of one wing of the first storey. His was a smoking room and Jed lit a cigarette. He opened the door and stepped outside. The night air was refreshingly crisp – he'd expected it to be hotter.

Despite his fatigue, he was restless. He thought a couple more beers might help him sleep, and he wanted to stretch his legs.

The bar was noisy and smoky. Imitation Irish bric-a-brac, horse brasses and signs to towns such as Dublin and Killarney cluttered the walls. People were talking over the top of each other and a jukebox pounded out rock classics.

Jed made his way to the bar and ordered a beer. 'Whatever's most popular,' he replied when the barmaid asked him what brand. She wore a black crop-top stretched tight across her ample breasts, and had hennaed hair and green eyes. Jed guessed she was in her late twenties.

'You staying long?'

'Just a night. From what I've read I'm better off in here than out painting the town.'

'The crime?'

He nodded. 'Is Johannesburg as bad as everyone says?'

'Sure, it's bad in parts, but other parts are fine. Mind you, a friend of mine was carjacked the other day. Two bullet holes through the windscreen.'

'Sounds like she was lucky they didn't hit her.'

The barmaid laughed. 'Ach, no, man. It was *she* who fired the shots! From her automatic. The carjackers took off, but now she has to buy a new windscreen! I don't go out at night without a weapon.'

She opened a bottle of Castle Lager and slid it across the polished wooden bar.

'Put it on my bill, please,' he said after he'd drunk his beer and ordered another. He was beat. He held a hand over his mouth to cover a yawn. 'If it's OK with the house rules, I'll take this one up to my room.'

'Of course, sir, no problem.' The woman punched the amount into the cash register and printed out a docket for Jed to sign.

Jed signed and passed the paper across the bar. The barmaid picked it up and paused for an instant. Jed noted the look of surprise in her eyes as she read the docket.

'Hey,' she said, 'I nearly forgot. It's two for one tonight. A special promotion, but your free beer has to be a draft, so you'll have to stay here and drink it. We don't allow guests to take drinks in glasses out of the bar.' Before Jed could protest, she reached into the fridge and pulled out a chilled glass and started filling it from a spigot. She sat the beer down in front of him.

'Funny, you didn't mention that when I ordered the first beer,' Jed said.

The woman looked away for a split second, then back at him. 'I forgot. I'll get you another, if you like.'

'No thanks, don't bother. Someone was looking for me earlier, at reception. Did anyone ask after me in here?'

The woman turned away from him and picked up a cloth. She

started to move away, busying herself by wiping down the bar. 'No, not that I know of.'

'Not too many Americans around tonight. Probably not too many by the name of Banks. I saw the look on your face when you read my name on that docket. What gives?'

'Sorry, man. I've got other customers to serve.' She turned away from him, but he could see there was no one waiting for a drink.

He followed her to the other end of the bar, watching unnoticed as she grabbed her handbag from under it and, lifting a hinged panel, stepped through into the main area.

Jed touched her arm and she jumped. 'Hey, don't do that. You scared me. You forgot your beer.' She pointed to the other end of the bar, where he had left his glass and bottle.

'I'm not thirsty any more. What's going on?'

'Like I told you, it's happy hour.'

'Bullshit.'

'Look, I'm supposed to be going on my break now. Why don't you give me the extra beer if you don't want it.'

'Right. Sit down. I need to talk to you.'

When he returned to the table, the woman was rummaging in her handbag. She pulled out a packet of cigarettes and a lighter. 'Smoke?'

'Thanks. Now tell me, why the special treatment?'

'OK, there is no happy hour. You're new here in South Africa, you seem like a nice guy and I thought, hey, I'll be welcoming to the tourist and give him a free beer. No law against that, is there?'

'Yeah. In my country stealing from your employer is a crime.'

She looked past him, towards the door, and Jed glanced over his shoulder. 'Looking for someone?'

'No.' She lit her cigarette and slid the lighter across the table to him.

Suddenly Jed stood up and pushed back his chair. He cursed his jet-lagged brain for not seeing what was obvious – the woman had been deliberately trying to get him to stay in the bar. She was keeping him from his gear, in his room.

Jed forced his way past a group of young men and women who were entering the bar and hurried back out into the lobby. He saw from the lighted sign above the elevator that it was at the third floor. He turned left and ran up the staircase, taking the steps two at a time.

As he approached the door to his room he slowed his pace, forcing himself to breathe slowly and deeply. The door was still locked. That meant nothing. It would be relatively easy for a professional thief to get hold of a hotel's skeleton key card or manipulate the lock in some other way. He pulled out his own card and slowly inserted it. He leaned against the door and, when the little light above the lock flashed from red to green, barged into the room.

One of the bedside lights was on and there was enough illumination to see the intruder clearly.

He was tall, slim and dressed in black, with a black ski mask and gloves. He was bending over the low luggage table where Jed had left his suit bag. His Alice pack was on the floor and appeared to be undisturbed.

Jed ran at the man but he was already moving. The balcony door was wide open and Jed, remembering he had neglected to lock it after his cigarette, cursed himself.

The man was through the external door before Jed could lay a hand on him and he vaulted the wrought-iron balcony railing easily. Jed snatched up a heavy table lamp, sparks flying from the power socket as the cord came free.

He drew back his arm and threw the metal lamp as hard as he could at the fleeing figure. His aim was good. The base of the lamp hit the man on the back of his head, causing him to stagger. The trailing electricity cord fell between his legs, and he missed a step as the lamp bounced on the flat roof of the first floor.

Jed was over the railing and onto the roof without breaking his stride. He dived at the man and brought him down. The man twisted onto his back, but Jed was faster. He grabbed the thief's skivvy top with his left hand and punched him in the jaw with his right. The man's head snapped back and hit the rough surface of the roof. But he was quick to recover and brought his knee up into Jed's groin. Jed gasped in

42

pain and leaned away, giving the man room to land a punch of his own. The intruder reached up and clasped Jed to him, and the two of them rolled over.

Jed, underneath his attacker now, rammed two fingers towards the man's eyes, forcing him to twist his head aside to avoid the attack. Jed reached around and punched the man in the kidney, then raised his knees and thrust the man off him.

They both scrambled to their feet, circling each other. The intruder looked to the edge of the roof. He reached into the back pocket of his jeans and drew out a knife. The silver blade flicked free at the touch of a button. Jed skipped out of reach and snatched up the fallen desk lamp by its cord. He started to swing it. The heavy ornament quickly gained momentum as he swung faster and faster. He hoped the cord would hold. The man started to back away out of range of the spinning weight. Jed brought his arm above his head now and charged at the man.

The cord connected with the man's raised arm and the lamp swung around and glanced off his head, causing him to lose his footing. Jed closed in on him and kicked the man in the groin, causing him to double over and fall to his knees. He stomped on his hand, forcing him to drop the knife. Jed picked it up. He kicked the prone figure in the side again. They were on the edge of the roof now. The man tried to roll away, but stopped when he reached the precipice.

Jed stood over him. 'Who are you, and what were you doing in my room?'

The intruder said nothing. From below them there was the squeal of rubber as a car pulled up. The man craned his head and looked over the edge of the roof.

'Up here,' he yelled.

Jed grabbed him by both feet and started pushing him over the edge of the roof. The man's arms flailed in the air. 'Tell me who you are, asshole, or I'll fucking send you over to meet your friend right now.'

The intruder stayed silent and stopped struggling. Jed knelt down, putting his weight on the man's shins, and reached over towards his face. The man tried to grab Jed's arms but he was too quick. He grabbed at the ski mask and yanked it off. The man had cropped red hair and a pale complexion.

'Last chance. Who are . . .?'

Jed ducked instinctively as he heard the sound of gunfire. Two bullets split the air above his head. He grabbed the man's skivvy and rolled backwards and to one side. The man had tried to rob him, but he didn't really wish to push him off the roof and leave him dead or crippled – he had more questions to ask him.

The gun fired again and Jed rolled further away from the edge, letting go of the intruder. The man saw his chance. He stood up and kicked viciously at Jed's kidneys. Jed arched his back and rolled on his side, watching in agony as the man lowered himself over the edge. The tyres protested as the car took off. Jed crawled to the roof's edge and saw the vehicle racing through the half-empty car park. It was a sedan, white. Maybe a Mercedes. It was already too far away for him to read the licence plate. Peering over the lip of the roof he could see the man had shimmied down a drainpipe.

A small crowd of people had spilled from the restaurant and bar inside the hotel to see what all the noise was about. A couple of young males, one white and one black, had pistols drawn. He had heard that many people carried guns in South Africa for personal protection because of the high crime rate. He stepped back from the edge of the roof – he didn't want to provide target practice for a civilian with an itchy trigger finger.

Jed brushed himself off and started back towards his hotel room. He felt his body, assessing his injuries. He could tell he would be badly bruised, but none of his ribs were cracked. He touched the inside of his lip with his tongue and tasted blood.

In his room, things looked as he had left them, apart from the missing lamp. His suit bag was zipped shut and his Alice pack still buckled closed. He must have arrived just after the man had entered his room, and before he'd had time to steal anything. He picked up the telephone and dialled reception. 'Send your security man up here now and call the police. There's been a break-in.'

'The police are already on their way, Mister Banks. There have been gunshots outside.'

'Tell me about it.'

'Excuse me?'

'Forget it. Put me through to the bar, please.'

The receptionist connected him and a deep-voiced man answered.

Jed wiped more blood from his lip with the back of his hand. 'I'd like to speak to the woman serving behind the bar.'

'She's left. Family emergency. Who's calling, please?'

'I think I left something in the bar,' he lied. 'When is her next shift?'

'She's a casual. Only comes in here now and again. Can I help you? What did you lose?'

Jed hung up. He'd leave the girl to the police. He unzipped his suit bag and reached inside for his toiletries bag, but couldn't see it. He had been carrying his airline tickets, passport and all his money in his pocket. There was really nothing else of great value in either his bag or pack. He rummaged through his clothes and, finally, located his wash bag and took it into the bathroom. He stripped and turned on the shower. The water stung a cut on his face, but the hot jets soothed the ache in his side. As he turned off the water there was a knock at the door.

He pulled on a white bathrobe and tied it around his waist. 'Who is it?'

'Police, sir.'

Jed opened the door. 'Come in, please. Excuse my appearance,' he said to the two officers. Both wore dark-blue fatigue trousers, shirts of a lighter hue and military-style boots. They removed their peaked baseball caps as they entered the room.

'Good evening, sir,' said the taller of the two, who looked more Indian than African. 'I am Sergeant Vincent Sakoor and this is Corporal Tshabalala. We hear you've been robbed.'

Jed ran a hand through his wet hair. 'My room was broken into, but I don't think anything is missing.'

'You disturbed the man in the act?' Sergeant Sakoor asked.

'I did. He put up a fight, but he got away.' Jed told his story, describing the suspicious behaviour of the barmaid, the scuffle and the man's escape in the getaway car.

'Ah, these people are professionals, I think. You say the man was white?'

'Yes. I was surprised by . . .'

'You are surprised we have white criminals? You think only black or coloured people commit crimes in this country?'

'No, Officer. I was about to say I was surprised by the apparent level of organisation behind a simple break and enter.'

'As I said, it looks like the work of professionals. If it is whites, it's probably drug-related. Addiction to hard drugs knows no racial boundaries, Mr Banks.'

Jed nodded, but the intruder was no strung-out heroin addict. He was clean-cut and, now that he thought about it, had a military look about him.

'Can you give me a description of the car?' Sergeant Sakoor asked.

'White sedan. Mercedes, I think.'

The two policemen looked at each other and Tshabalala consulted his notebook. 'There's a Mercedes on fire a couple of blocks from here. The licence plates match one that was stolen earlier this evening.'

'Carjacked?'

'No,' Sakoor said. 'Hot wired from outside a restaurant in Sandton. An area inhabited mainly by wealthy *whites*. A European man trying to break into a Mercedes would probably be assisted by a passer-by, someone who thought it was the owner who had locked himself out. A black man caught in the act of car theft would probably be shot by vigilantes.'

Sakoor sat down at the table and gestured for Jed to take the other chair. He took down a statement in longhand.

When they had finished, Jed said, 'I take it you're not overly optimistic about catching these guys.'

'Consider yourself lucky, Mr Banks. And keep your balcony door locked next time.'

That night, when Jed finally fell into a fitful sleep, he dreamed he was chasing the black-clad man out of the room again. When they got to the edge of the roof, the criminal's body hanging in space, Jed again ripped off the ski mask. This time the face that stared back at him was Miranda's, her blonde hair cascading free in the breeze. He recoiled in shock and lost his grip on her. She fell, arms windmilling, her mouth opening as if she was trying to tell him something. But he could not hear her.

3

Jed woke in a cold sweat. The glowing red numerals on the bedside clock told him it was a little after four in the morning. He was sore from the fight and his head throbbed from the combination of too much alcohol and not enough sleep. To top it all he was jetlagged and couldn't get back to sleep. He rose, showered, then smoked a cigarette while he shaved around the reappearing stubble.

He wiped his face and replaced the razor and shaving cream in his wash bag. As he zipped the bag closed, a shiver ran down his spine.

The wash bag.

When he had reached into his suit bag last night it had taken him a few moments to find his toiletries. He was a disciplined soldier, a creature of habit, and, like it or not, a slave to order, precision and routine. He always placed his wash bag in last, on the top right of his bag. It had not been in its usual spot after the intruder had left.

Jed unpacked his suit bag and then turned it upside down. He sorted through his underclothes, his shirts and spare pair of trousers. He upended each of his combat boots and his running shoes, but nothing fell out. He checked the zippered pockets of the bag and then ran his hands over the lining, feeling for any irregularities. He took his camera out of its case and examined it. He hadn't loaded it with film and it was still empty. As he shifted one of his running shoes the camera case dropped from the bed onto the carpeted floor. It landed with an audible thud.

Jed was surprised by the noise. He picked up the empty case; it was heavier than usual. He took a closer look inside and found a removable divider in the bottom of the pouch, fastened to the interior with strips of Velcro. He took out the padded piece of material and turned the case upside down. A black pistol magazine filled with snub-nosed bullets slid into his hand. He examined the mag and thumbed the rounds onto the unmade bed. There were thirteen of them. The magazine was made of metal and bore no markings, but he recognised it instantly as belonging to a Browning nine-millimetre pistol.

'Bastard,' he said.

He scooped up the rounds and reloaded the magazine. He searched his gear again and then emptied his Alice pack on the floor. He checked and rechecked every piece of kit and every item of clothing. Then he re-examined both the pack and the travel bag to make sure there was nothing else in there that didn't belong to him.

The magazine was small enough to be easily concealed but there was no way it would not be discovered by an airport metal detector. It was in his carry-on bag, as well. The intruder had not planted a pistol, just the ammunition.

Jed had been set up. He would have been stopped by airport security on his way to check in for his flight to Zimbabwe, and probably taken away for questioning. The security men would have discovered from the identification card he carried that he was US Army. The fact that there was no pistol in his possession would eventually be discovered, after they had searched both his bags and his person. He could imagine the process taking a long time, maybe hours. Would he have been charged with a criminal offence? Possibly: he didn't know. Would he have missed his flight? Definitely.

And who was the intruder? If not a thief, who did he work for? Jed had been clearly visible over the roofline when the man's accomplice had opened fire. He had been shot at with a pistol – not an accurate weapon over any great distance, but even so the rounds had sailed harmlessly high over his head. Had the man pulling the trigger simply been trying to scare him off?

Jed had carried his passport and tickets with him down to the bar. Still, the intruder had somehow known that he would be catching another flight the next day. Then there was the mysterious woman who had been asking about him. It was all too weird for words.

Inside the crowded airport terminal Jed took the lift to the departures floor, and joined a queue of people waiting to put their bags onto the conveyor belt of a large X-ray scanning machine. The machine was big enough to take suitcases, and the departing passengers were being told to place all their luggage, not just their carry-on bags, onto the wide rubber belt for inspection.

As Jed approached the machine, a European man in jeans and a spray jacket walked over and stood beside the seated security officer. It was close to a hundred degrees outside and warm and sticky inside the terminal, despite the airconditioning. Jed guessed the man wore a jacket to conceal a shoulder holster. He peered intently at the screen as Jed dropped his suit bag and then his pack onto the conveyor. As he walked through the metal detector, the beeping alarm sounded.

The man in the civilian clothes looked up and stared at Jed as a second uniformed security officer, an African woman, ran a metal-detecting wand over his body. The wand made a buzzing noise as it passed over Jed's pants pocket. The woman asked him to empty his pockets. Jed noticed out of the corner of his eye that the conveyor belt had stopped. The man was alternating his gaze between the machine's monitor and Jed.

Jed reached into his pocket and pulled out his mobile phone. The female security guard made him walk through the detector again and, when the alarm did not go off, she handed him back his phone. The conveyor belt started once more and Jed's bags emerged. As he picked up his pack, the man in civilian clothes whispered something to the male security guard, who called a third colleague.

'Please empty the contents of your bag on that table, sir,' the standing security guard said.

'Why?' Jed asked.

'We need to check something, sir. Now, if you don't mind . . .'

'What if I do mind? What are you looking for?'

'We're not sure until we inspect your bags, sir.'

'Both bags?'

The security guard looked over at the man in civilian clothes, who nodded.

Jed emptied his pack and then his bag, keeping his eyes locked on the European man the whole time. The man held his gaze, but did not come closer or take part in the thorough examination of the bags' contents.

Amongst his civilian clothes were a few items of military-issue gear he thought would come in handy in Africa. He had a web belt with a couple of water bottles in their carriers, an ammo pouch, his green mosquito net, and a pair of tan battle dress utility trousers and matching bush hat. His pack had originally been drab olive-green, but he had lightened the colouring with liberal splashes of sand-coloured paint for his time in Afghanistan.

'You are in the military?' the security guard asked.

'No, I'm in real estate.'

The guard looked confused. He held up the fatigue pants. 'Why do you have these then?'

'Because it would be embarrassing walking around in my boxer shorts.'

'And this hat?'

'Prevents skin cancer.'

The security guard gave up. He turned to the man in civilian clothes and shrugged.

Jed repacked his bags, without any help from the guard. As he shouldered his pack he said, 'Whatever you're looking for, I don't have it.'

The man took a mobile phone out of his jacket pocket, punched in a number and started speaking, his free hand covering his mouth. Jed picked up the suit bag and left.

He found a coffee shop on the departure side and ordered himself a cup of black coffee. He pulled out his wallet. In it was a picture of Miranda, taken during her summer vacation the year before. She was wearing a cropped green T-shirt and khaki walking shorts, her blonde hair tied back in a ponytail. She was smiling wide, hands on her hips. She had grown into a beautiful young woman and he had missed so much of her life.

The picture had been taken at a campsite on the Appalachian Trail. They had spent a week together, just the two of them, hiking a demanding stretch of the route through steep valleys and dense woods.

'On nights like this I can see why you joined the Army,' she had said the night after the picture was taken.

'How do you mean?'

'You must spend so many nights out under the stars, away from it all. The peace, the freedom, it must be such a blast.'

'Sometimes more of a blast than you might think. It's not all camping out, you know.'

'Hey, I know it's dangerous, but tell me you don't love being out in the field, away from the rat race.'

'I'd be lying if I said I didn't,' Jed admitted. 'Though it sounds like you'll get your fair share of nights under the stars in Africa.'

'Yeah, that's part of the attraction. Also, I want to make a difference.'

'You will – hell, you'll end up saving some endangered tiger or something.'

Miranda had laughed.

'There aren't any tigers in Africa?'

'Stop kidding.' Then her tone was serious again. 'I want to make a difference. Like you do.'

'I don't know that I make a difference. I'm just a small part of a big machine.'

52

'Don't give me that simple soldier crap, Dad. I thought about military service myself, you know, after nine-eleven.'

His heart skipped a couple of beats. 'You haven't done anything stupid, have you?'

'Relax. I thought about the reserve, but I think I'm better off channelling my energies into other areas.'

'Like your studies, right?'

'Sure. But serving your country is not something to downplay, Dad. You know how proud I am of you, don't you?'

Miranda had gone to Africa to study man-eaters. Her mentor, this damned Professor Wallis, had sent her into the Zambezi Valley – to look for animals that ate people. How could Jed have let this happen? How could this goddamned academic have consigned his daughter to an early death?

Most other fathers in America would hire a lawyer and sue the ass off Professor Wallis. If the professor had been a man, Jed would have killed him. At least, that was how he felt now. In fact, his plan was to track her down as soon as he had finished his business in Zimbabwe – although exactly what that business would be he still did not know. He needed to talk to the police and the National Parks staff, Miranda's fellow researchers, and the people from the US State Department who had so far been handling the matter of his daughter's disappearance.

After all that was done, Jed wanted to look Wallis in the eye and ask her to account for her actions. Jed knew Miranda was a wilful young woman, passionately committed to wildlife conservation, but he wanted to make sure she had been fully aware of the risks she would face.

Part of him knew that she would have gone into her assignment with her eyes wide open. She was a smart girl, a straight-A student, yet had a practical side to her and was at home in the outdoors. He had seen her change a tyre on his SUV – just to prove to him that she could – replace the oil and fuel filters on her own car; start a fire in the wilderness; hike all day; and climb a vertical cliff face unaided.

What he feared, though, was that she had taken unnecessary risks.

She had backpacked around Australia and New Zealand in the year after she graduated from college and he knew she had used the trip to feed a growing hunger for adventure sports. High-speed downhill mountain biking, whitewater rafting, bungee jumping, heli-skiing, sky-diving, hang-gliding and para-sailing, she had tried them all. Patti had blamed him for Miranda's wild streak. He took risks for a living, but, if he was honest with himself, he had the same passion for danger and addiction to risk as his headstrong daughter.

Miranda had chosen to go to a politically unstable continent to study dangerous animals. In Mana Pools National Park, Miranda had boasted in one of her emails, she slept in a tent in the middle of the bush without a fence of any kind to keep wild animals at bay. How had it happened? he wondered. Had she been careless, and simply left the door of her tent open? Had she left the tent to answer the call of nature? Had the lion, or lions, been brazen enough to rip through the flimsy nylon walls? He chided himself. He was already accepting the official version of events – that Miranda had been taken by one of the animals she was so intent on saving. He wanted so much to believe that she was still alive. He forced the morbid thoughts of her death from his mind.

4

He was the heir to one of the last remaining natural paradises on earth.

He lived in harmony with the animals around him, but there was no disputing that he was the boss, and that the environment in which he lived, as beautiful as it was, was there solely for his pleasure and sustenance. It was, if not in name or on paper, his kingdom, and he was, if not by decree or charter, the king.

Mashumba was a warrior. An old man, as was plain to see, but still a fighter and, when opportunity arose, a lover of note. He had sired more offspring than he cared to remember and had been in more fights than there were butterfly-shaped leaves on a mopani tree in the height of summer.

He rested by the river now, for the sun was high above the valley and the sands that flanked the shimmering blue ribbon were so bright with reflected light it hurt the eye to look at them. And so, with a yawn, he shifted his position to get back into the shade and, as was his norm at this time of day, drifted off into sleep.

In his dreams he saw the herd of zebra grazing on the grass of the floodplain, the stallion raising his head and sniffing the breeze. He saw the fleet-footed impala leaping through the bush, the docile waterbuck grazing in the marshes. He saw the cantankerous old bull buffalo, the most dangerous prey a hunter could face. He remembered glorious feasts he had presided over, and saw again his offspring and wives and his dear departed brothers.

His family was gone now. It belonged to others. He and his brother had been kicked out of their own extended clan, replaced by younger, fitter contenders for their fickle wives' affections. Such was the way of his tribe.

His world was changing, little by little every year, but he had learned long ago to cope with change. He had learned to live with the white man and his strange ways, and to make little adjustments in his day-to-day life so that he could exist side by side with him. There was room in his valley for everyone, even the whites and their noisy machines. As long as they respected him, he would allow them to visit his home.

Of his brother there was no sign. He had seen him in the night, but lost sight of him before dawn. He too was probably sleeping away the hottest part of the day. They would see each other for a drink in the evening, if not before.

A fish eagle landed in the tree above him. Its mournful, whining call woke him. He opened one eye and looked at the bird. It was the definitive sound of the valley, but it never ceased to annoy him when he was trying to take a midday nap, or hunt. If he could have reached the bird, he would have killed it.

Mashumba yawned again and thought about dinner. The thing he missed most about his ex-wives, even more than the coupling, was the way they fed him and his brother. How sweet it was at the end of a hard day or a long night to find a feast waiting for him. It was the natural order of things. He and his brother took care of them – in every sense of the word – and, likewise, they were fed. That was what he missed most.

He stood, for the sun had caught up with him yet again, scratched himself and then pissed on the opposite side of the tree to where he intended to sleep for the rest of the afternoon. He was very particular about some things. As he was settling down for the remainder of his nap a flicker of movement caught his eye. It was down on the river-bank, on the sand.

The people in the village knew about old Mashumba and his brother. They told stories about the two old men of the bush and how they now lived as bachelors. The children of the village knew to stay clear of them, not to wander too far down the river, past the bend, into the area that was their home.

Occasionally he would roam down the road, close to the village, but the women and the children stayed inside, or close to their green-painted houses inside the compound, when Mashumba was about, because since his wives had left him he had become a danger to them. The first occasion Mashumba had been tempted by a young woman from the village had taught him a lot. She had been walking to her work in the National Parks compound and he had seen her, across the floodplain, near the firewood stacks. She had screamed and Mashumba, realising he had been spotted, had run off into the bushes. Some of the men from the village had come looking for him, but he had hidden up in some reeds and watched and waited until night had fallen and the rattling, smoke-belching Land Rovers had gone. He had returned to his part of the valley, where he still reigned supreme, but he had remembered the sight of the woman. How easy it would have been to have her; how defenceless she had been.

The second one had been different. He had stalked her, carefully, through the bush, and watched her movements for a full day. The next day he had waited for her, lying in the shadows of a big Natal mahogany tree. She had almost walked right up to him. She had been fair-skinned, not like the village women, but colour meant nothing to him. A white woman was as good as a black one as far as he was concerned. He felt no guilt about it at all, for the hunt and the capture came naturally. It was a necessity, since his wives had left him. It had been satisfying enough but, in a strange way, also mildly disappointing. It had been so easy to overpower her; there had been no great skill needed to catch the woman, no thrill of the hunt, no intense physical exertion.

The men had come looking for him again, as he knew they would, but he had melted further into the bush, and then cut back down to the river. He had continued to lie low, away from the roads, for many more days and, eventually, they had stopped looking for him.

And here was another one, down by the river. He felt the old desires coming back.

Precious Mpofu carried a fishing rod over her shoulder and a plastic bag full of tigerfish in her hand. The prize catch of the Zambezi River, so named because of the yellow and black stripes down his shiny flank, was as good to eat as he was hard to catch. Precious and her family would eat well that night. Two tigers, maybe six kilos all up, and a couple of chessa as well.

It would have been safer to walk back along the riverbank, she had strayed too far as it was, but the afternoon sun was setting fast and the dirt road provided a quicker, more direct route back to the village. Precious decided the sooner she got the fish on the fire, the happier her ranger husband and two hungry children would be.

Precious had finished her morning's work cleaning the big two-storey lodge she looked after. She had swept the floors, emptied the garbage bins into the incinerator and made the beds. The warden had said a new guest was arriving that day – a woman, by herself. The woman was from America, like the young one, Miranda, who had been killed by the lion. Precious liked Americans because they tipped in US dollars, although she had never received a cent from Miranda – one of the other maids washed and ironed her clothes and washed up her dirty dishes. Precious and the other maids were jealous of their colleague, whose name was Violet. Precious was sad that Miranda was gone – she was a nice person, even if she didn't share the work around. However, Precious was not sad that Violet had gone. No one knew where she was, but everyone presumed she had hitchhiked out of the park to Kariba to change the US dollars Miranda had given her. With her benefactor dead, maybe Violet had decided to take her money and have a holiday.

Precious had decided she would do what she could to earn some foreign currency from the new American. She had cut some wildflowers from down near the river and put them in an empty half-litre gin bottle that one of the South African fishermen had left on the dining table. When she replaced the tablecloth she had set the flowers in the middle. She was glad the men had gone. They were loud, drunken and uncouth, and they had left the lodge in a disgusting mess. She had collected two bin bags full of empty beer cans and one of the men had let a cigarette burn down on the armrest of a lounge chair. She had reported the burn mark to the head ranger, but she doubted anything would come of it. Precious knew how desperate the park was for guests, so the authorities would do nothing to penalise the fishermen, even if they were pigs. They hadn't tipped her either.

After making the beds with fresh linen she had polished the concrete floors with Cobra wax until they gleamed. The lodge was old and had seen better days, but no one could say it was not clean. Her work finished, she had grabbed her fishing rod and one of the discarded plastic supermarket bags the South Africans had left behind in the rubbish, and set off to do her fishing. One nice thing the Boers had done – the only nice thing in nine days of drinking and singing and fishing – was to leave their worm box behind.

Precious had employed the worms to catch some small bream and, using the still-squirming fish as live bait, she had caught her tigers. Yes, she thought, the walk upstream had been worth it. The current in that particular spot was running well and the speed of the water had made the dying fish seem that little bit more alive. She had fooled the wily tiger and turned the tables on the hunter. She sang to herself as she walked up off the sand. The grass was cool on the bare soles of her feet after the sun-soaked riverbank.

Mashumba licked his lips in anticipation. He lowered himself into the grass as the woman walked up the sandy bank towards him. He would take her by complete surprise, just as he had taken the pale-skinned

59

one. He felt a slight breeze coming down the valley, from behind him, and the wind ruffled his long hair.

The woman stopped and looked around. She raised her nose slightly in the air and sniffed.

Mashumba grunted. It would be a close-run thing.

Precious knew that odour and she was instantly terrified. She smelled his scent in the bushes, but did not run. Slowly she turned her head, scanning the dry yellow grass from left to right, looking for him. She looked down on the ground and cursed her stupidity. His foot-prints were there for her to see, if she had taken the time to look down instead of daydreaming. Her heart beat faster and sweat beaded her broad ebony forehead. I must not move, she told herself, although her legs wanted to break into flight. She wondered if she could make it to the river before he caught her. Stupid girl, she chided herself silently. The river was full of crocodiles and hippos. Death awaited her at every turn.

Mashumba saw his prey was alert now. The time for stealth had passed. He stood, raising himself to his impressive full height. The breeze caught his hair again. He took a step forwards, then another. Still the woman did not move. Mashumba was annoyed and he yelled at her, wanting to scare her. It was the way it should be – she must fear him and run from him. Without the chase it was not right.

Precious stared into his cold, emotionless eyes and doubted she would ever see her little boy and girl again. She was so scared she began to sob. Her knees started to shake from the fear and the urge to run, but everything she knew, taught and inherited, told her to stand her ground against the fearsome bully.

Mashumba shook his head and yelled at her. He told her to run, in fear, from him, to leave his place. But she defied him. So be it. He started walking towards her, but still she held her ground.

Precious kept her eyes on him, hardly daring to breathe as he stopped, no more than twenty metres from her. Sometimes the men, when faced with a bully, would make a noise or scream at him and often as not the troublemaker would back down and run away. But the men had rifles to back them up. She had only her fishing rod and her tigerfish.

He yelled at her again and her whole body seemed to vibrate from the noise. The tears rolled over her full cheeks, carving rivulets in the dust that had settled on her during the minutes that she had stood motionless.

The bully started towards her again and she was more scared than she had ever been in her whole life. She wondered again if it was worth risking the river, hoping that the crocodiles were asleep and the hippos not close to shore.

'You will run! I am the one in charge here! You will run and I will chase you. That is the way of things, the way it should be.' The white one had run. He had caught her and he had played with her and he had killed her. His life had changed, but at least the white one had done as he had expected.

Precious raised the plastic bag above her head and started to swing it. Round and round went the heavy fish. Her arm moved like a windmill, faster and faster. She could see the confusion in his evil glassy eyes and this gave her courage.

She shouted at him. 'Go away! Go away! You will not have me today, you bastard! Go away and leave me!'

Mashumba stopped in his tracks and blinked at the strange sight. He was not scared – just confused.

The woman let go of the bag and it sailed towards him. He dodged to one side to avoid the missile. The bag thudded into the ground next to him and skidded along the dirt, giving him a fright. He spun around and retreated a few paces. He sniffed it. It was quite pleasant, but it could be investigated later. He turned his head and looked back at the woman.

Precious had summoned the last of her courage to throw the bag. Her heart had leaped at the sight of the foul bully running from the flying fish. She did not wait around to see if the heavy missile hit his big scarred forehead. She dropped her fishing rod, turned and ran. Precious didn't feel the sharp rocks and prickles, nor the heat of the sand as she reached the riverbank. She nearly stumbled, but regained her balance in a heartbeat. Her dress rode up her thighs as she ran, exposing slim, muscled flanks. Her arms pumped like an athlete's and she felt the breeze from the river on her face. The shimmering water was so close and she could see no dark humps of the hippos' backs, no furrow in the bank where a crocodile had dragged its lethal tail.

She would make it. Once in the water she would be safe, because everyone knew he could not swim. Everyone knew the hated one feared the water. Twenty metres, ten . . . She could do it. For her son and her daughter, she would do it. Precious risked a glance back over her shoulder.

She screamed, louder than she had ever screamed in her life. '*SHUMBA! SHUMBA!*'

Not that it would do her any good. Not that anyone would hear, but if there was, maybe, a fisherman, or a tourist, or a ranger within earshot they might come and save her. She cursed herself for running – she knew she should have stood her ground.

At last, she was running from him. It was as it should be. Mashumba lowered his head and charged.

Christine Wallis was no stranger to the Zambezi Valley – the broad, shimmering river; the stagnant, reflective pools surrounded by wildlife; the quaint old-fashioned lodges; the scenic campground; the man-made dirt roads and the timeless game trails. She knew them all, the same way other people know the route from their home to their office or the stops on a subway.

Chris had devoted half her working life to the preservation of wildlife, but she could shoot almost as well as a professional hunter. The rifle was as familiar a tool to her as the pen or word processor. She didn't think twice about picking up the ranger's AK-47 assault rifle when she heard the woman scream. She pulled back on the cocking handle with her right hand, chambering a round, flicked the selector to semi-automatic, and raised the scarred wooden butt to her shoulder.

The running woman suddenly burst into view and Chris followed her flight through the open sights. Chris shifted the aiming mark a little to the left, looking for the real target. This was not how it should be, damn it. Killing an animal went against the grain, against everything Chris stood for and had worked towards. But the woman's life was clearly in danger.

Lloyd, the uniformed park ranger, burst from the bushes, hastily pulling up his green trousers. 'What are you doing, Professor?' he asked in alarm. 'Put down the rifle, please!'

'*Shumba.*'

'I heard the scream too,' Lloyd said, fumbling with his fly buttons. 'Where?'

'God, I don't want to do this,' Chris said. She aimed just in front of the lion's big head, leading him a little.

'I see him! Shoot, Professor. Shoot now! It's her only chance. He is nearly on her.'

Chris pulled the trigger.

Precious screamed as she felt him grab her. In the same instant she heard the shot. She fell, face first into the sand, his huge weight on her.

Mashumba had her, just as he knew he would. But as he grabbed her he felt something slam into his right flank, knocking him sideways. He took the woman with him as he landed and rolled in the sand. He yelled in pain and the valley heard his bellow.

She wriggled and writhed in his grip and he thrashed in the sand to make the pain go away, but he did not want to lose her. It was all wrong. It had never ended like this before. He shook his big head, but still the pain was there.

Precious beat at him with her fists and screamed again when she saw her blood on the sand. She had never known such pain and he would not let go of her. He had her legs pinned, but she was able to twist her body to one side to stay away from the big shaggy head and the long yellow teeth.

*

Chris jumped down onto the sandy riverbank and ran towards the struggling woman and her attacker.

'Finish the job, or give me the rifle – now, Professor!' Lloyd barked. He liked the American woman, remembered her from her previous stays in the park, but by snatching up his rifle and firing it she had broken too many rules to count. The only way either of them would get out of this without a fine or worse was if Precious Mpofu escaped with her life.

Chris walked closer, stopped, took a deep breath, and aimed carefully. She did not want to hit the woman by mistake. Chris pulled the trigger and the copper-jacketed lead projectile smashed a path through the lion's brain.

Mashumba lost sight of his valley forever.

Chris shrugged off her daypack and unzipped it. She pulled out the bulky first-aid kit and found a plastic bottle of iodine. As she squirted the antiseptic into the crying woman's wounds, tears welled in her own eyes. She had come to Africa to save, not to kill, and she would have given anything not to have destroyed the beautiful creature lying beside her.

'You had to do it, Professor,' Lloyd said, reading her thoughts.

Chris nodded. 'It's OK, you're going to be fine,' she said to the woman as she bandaged her leg.

'I have radioed for the Land-i Rover, Professor. Help will be here soon.'

'We'll have to take her to Kariba.'

'What about the lion? We have to –'

'I know what we have to do,' Chris snapped. She was sorry as soon as she saw the look on Lloyd's face. He was a good man. She softened her tone. 'Lloyd, I know what we have to do, but that doesn't make it any easier for me.'

'If he is the one, then you do not need to feel sorry for him, Professor,' the ranger said as he helped her bandage Precious's wounds. 'If he killed Miss Miranda then it is against the natural order of things. We cannot have a man-eater on the loose in the park.'

God, but I need a drink, Chris thought. She hadn't known what she would do if they did finally find the lion they thought responsible for Miranda's death, but it looked like the decision had been made for her. It was only a theory that the old male was the killer, but the tragic irony was that the only way to prove his innocence was to kill him and cut him open. The rangers and their families in the staff village had no doubt he was the one, and they wanted him dead because of his increasingly dangerous forays around their homes. Chris had wanted to capture him alive – to dart him – and to take a blood sample and compare his DNA with evidence from the scene of Miranda's disappearance. It would take time and there were no guarantees that it would work, but she would have gone to any lengths to save the life of this magnificent beast.

Chris brushed a bang of coppery hair from her eyes and looked over her shoulder. A green National Parks Land Rover was swaying down a rutted game path towards them. Now that the adrenaline rush was subsiding, Chris thought again of Miranda. She dreaded what grisly remains might be found in the belly of the big battle-scarred cat at her feet, but she had to find out, one way or another, what had happened to her, no matter how gruesome the truth. She had known as soon as she had received the message in the Kruger National Park that the news from the US embassy in Johannesburg would be bad. The voice on the end of the line had told her that Miranda was missing, presumed killed by a lion. Chris had packed her bags the same day and travelled to Mana Pools in two hard days of driving. The police were being obstinate, not letting her have access to Miranda's personal effects and research equipment, which actually belonged to Chris, as she was not a family member. Such were the vagaries of African bureaucracy. They also said, as had the embassy, that Miranda's father was on his way to Zimbabwe.

Two African rangers climbed out of the Land Rover's cab and, together with Chris and Lloyd, lifted Precious into the rear of the truck.

'Give me a hand, fellas, we've got to take him with us too,' Chris said, pointing to the magnificent bloodied beast on the sand.

*

65

Mashumba's brother crouched in the long golden grass and watched the Land Rover depart.

He had always been the smarter of the two, if not the larger. Between them they had ruled the pride for many years until a triumvirate of younger, stronger males had ousted them and set them on their uncertain path.

Mashumba's brother had initiated the hunt against the white woman, but instinctively he knew this type of prey was trouble. Humans, he had learned, were easy to catch, and reasonably good to eat, but he had grown cautious following the first one. He remembered how the noisy machines had come in the wake of that easy meal, how he and Mashumba had had to walk for days to escape the two-legged hunters. He sniffed the air and padded across the dirt to where the bag of fish lay. He ripped the plastic with his claws, scoffed the tasty morsels inside and licked his lips. Not as good as half of a two-legged creature, but enough. He was the smart one. He was still alive. He would hunt again.

5

Harare International Airport was a gleaming white elephant. The new terminal was all chrome and glass and white walls, but the place was empty. There was only one aircraft parked on the tarmac: the one Jed had arrived on. The other air bridges were all empty. A dozen customs men leaned against a wall watching the forty-odd passengers pass through immigration and collect their bags from the carousel. Jed did the math and thought it pretty likely he would be stopped and searched.

'Over here, please,' a customs man said as Jed approached.

He laid his suit bag and pack on the burnished aluminium tabletop and said nothing as the man and a female colleague emptied his possessions.

'These look like military trousers,' the man said.

'Really?'

'Are you a soldier?'

'Yes, I'm a soldier. I may be doing some hunting. That's why I brought those old trousers.'

The man looked dubious. 'You must not give or sell these trousers to any Zimbabwean. Do you agree to this?'

'I'd look a little silly walking around the bush in my underpants.'

'This is a serious matter.'

'I understand. I promise not to give away my pants.'

'Where are you staying?'

'Waldorf Astoria. Penthouse suite.'

The man nodded. 'Is that in Harare?'

'It's on the cheap side of town.'

'Be careful then,' the man said with a smile.

An overweight European man with thinning grey hair combed over a sunburned pate was holding a sign with *Mr Banks* written on it.

'That's me,' Jed said.

'Lawrence Howie.' The man grabbed Jed's hand in a sweaty greeting. 'Welcome to Zimbabwe. Business or pleasure?'

The man looked to Jed like a talker. 'Neither.'

Howie frowned when Jed said nothing more. 'Very well. This way.' He led the way out of the terminal.

Jed squinted in the glare of the morning sun. The fat man took him along a row of parked cars, finally stopping next to a dark-green Land Rover Defender.

'Don't come much tougher than this,' Howie said. 'Are you going hunting?'

'Kind of.'

'Well, this vehicle will get you anywhere in the country.'

'Where's the rooftop tent?' The vehicle, according to the travel agent who had made the booking, was equipped with all the camping gear he would need for a protracted stay in the bush, including a fold-out rooftop tent.

'South Africa,' Howie said.

'Long way for me to go to sleep.'

'I ordered four of them three months ago. Thought they'd be here yesterday. Sorry.'

'Let me guess . . . still in the mail?'

'Nothing works in this bloody country any more. I've thrown in a canvas dome tent – no extra cost. There's a fridge in the back – it works off the car battery – and a crate of cutlery and crockery, a gas cooker, foam mattress, shovel, table and fold-out chairs. I've topped up the tank with diesel and you've got four full jerrycans. Fully equipped.'

Jed considered arguing about the tent, but he just wanted to get on the road. He studied the dashboard and Howie threw in a few hints about where everything was. 'Is there a map?' Jed asked.

Howie pulled a map of Zimbabwe and a Harare street directory from the glove compartment and explained to him how to get out of the city and onto the main road heading north.

'Follow the signs to Kariba. The road splits at Makuti – Kariba's to the left and Mana Pools is straight on, but you won't get to the park before nightfall. You have to register at a place called Marongora and they won't let you in after dark, so you may as well plan on spending tonight on the lake.'

'Lake Kariba?'

'Yes. Try the Lake View Inn. It's not a bad place to stay. And be careful.'

'Why does everyone keep saying that to me?'

Jed had seen Land Rovers in Afghanistan. The Australians and British had a few like this one, the commercial version. The Defender was big and square – as aerodynamic as a house brick on wheels. The roof-rack would do nothing to increase his speed. However, the truck had power steering, and a turbo-diesel engine with a five-speed gearbox, so it moved OK. Jed was used to driving the American Army's low, squat Hummvees. He found it a pleasant change to be riding high, and there was plenty of legroom in the cab, though it felt strange driving on the other side of the road.

At a stoplight an emaciated man in dark trousers and an off-white business shirt tried to sell him a newspaper with an inflammatory anti-government headline. A car waiting beside him played African music at full volume and he found he quite liked the drums and the beat. Harare, like its airport terminal, had some of the trappings of prosperity, but Jed couldn't help but feel the place was like a fake Wild

West town in a Hollywood back lot – just propped-up façades instead of real buildings and businesses. Here and there he saw a European walking along the sidewalk or driving, though for the most part they tended to be elderly. He'd read enough about Zimbabwe to know that most of the white people who could were leaving the country to start over somewhere else.

An African woman in ragged clothes carrying a tiny baby rapped on his window as he stopped at another red light on a choked main street. He tried to ignore her. At the next intersection was another newspaper seller. This time he saw the headline. WOMAN HAS NARROW ESCAPE FROM MAN-EATER. He saw the word *lion* in the first paragraph and wound down his window, fishing in a pocket. All he could find was an American five dollar bill. He handed it to the young man.

'I'm sorry, sir, I don't have change for this.'

'Keep it,' Jed said as he grabbed the paper and accelerated. The man was wide-eyed.

Jed tried to read as he drove. The attack had happened in Mana Pools National Park, the day before. He wondered whether it could have been the same lion that had supposedly killed Miranda.

He finally escaped the blue-smoke fog of the choked city centre and took a turn towards Kariba. Outside of town he recognised a large roundabout from the directions Howie had given him and saw, to his left, a sprawling suburban shopping mall. A uniformed security guard handed him a plastic laminated card as he passed under the centre's boom gate. He pulled into the first available car space, some distance away from the two-storey white stucco complex.

Jed unfolded the newspaper and read.

A National Parks employee narrowly escaped death yesterday when she was attacked by a lion at Mana Pools National Park. A National Parks spokesman said Precious Mpofu was walking home to the staff village when the lion pounced on her and mauled her leg. Mrs Mpofu's life was saved by the quick actions of ranger Lloyd Nkomo and a visiting academic, Professor Christine Wallis. The lion was shot and killed and

Mrs Mpofu was transported to hospital in Kariba. Her condition is listed as stable. National Parks have initiated an investigation into the shooting of the lion and will attempt to establish if the animal was also responsible for the killing of a young American scientific researcher last week.

Jed felt the hair rise on the back of his neck at the reference to his daughter in the cheap newsprint. He had nearly convinced himself that Miranda could somehow still be alive, and seeing the newspaper refer to her death so bluntly was a rude shock. And there was the reference to Professor Wallis. That also surprised him as he had assumed the scientist who had despatched his daughter to this godforsaken country was still in South Africa. At least there was now a good chance of them meeting face to face.

Jed wondered how the Zimbabwean National Parks authorities would 'establish if the animal was responsible' for the death of his daughter. It was too gruesome to contemplate, even for a man who had seen death in many violent forms.

There were more white faces inside the shopping centre and the Africans looked well dressed and affluent. He checked a map of the mall and found a camping store. The shop was an outdoorsman's dream come true and smelled of canvas and gun oil.

'Can I help you, sir?' the bearded giant behind the counter asked.

'I need a hunting knife, and some web gear or a vest. What's the policy on gun ownership in this country?'

'Ah, you're American. It's not like in the States, sir. Our Government takes a dim view of people like . . . well, white people, to put it bluntly, owning too many weapons. Where are you headed?'

'Mana Pools.'

'To the National Park? You can't take a weapon in there. They'll shoot you on sight, chum. Only the rangers can carry firearms in the park.'

The man's accent sounded to Jed like a cross between the guttural English of an Afrikaner and an Englishman.

'Fine, then just give me the knife.'

The man showed Jed a range of edged weapons in a glass cabinet.

Jed selected a hunting knife with a wickedly sharp eight-inch blade. He didn't know exactly what he would be trying to hunt with it, but it made him feel better to have a weapon of some sort. He went to the clothing section of the shop and picked out a green canvas hunter's vest. The pockets on the front were big enough to hold a couple of magazines for an assault rifle – if he'd had one. He threw the vest on the counter and asked for a map of the Zambezi Valley.

It was after one in the afternoon when Jed surrendered his parking pass and headed out of the mall and back onto the main road north. The driving was easy, once he got used to being on the left-hand side of the road. It was pretty countryside, but most of the farming land looked idle. Here and there were stretches of wheat, waving in the gentle afternoon breeze, but more often than not he saw only weedy half-tilled fields. He'd read about the redistribution of land away from white farmers to Africans, but it didn't look to him as though anyone was doing too well out of that process.

The succession of farming towns he rolled through looked tired and dusty. People thronged the streets but there seemed to be a general lack of purpose to their ambling. Too many idle youths, most of them males, stared at the shiny Land Rover with envious eyes.

He swerved and swore when a shiny new black Mercedes barely made it back into the oncoming lane after overtaking a donkey cart driven by two young boys in cast-off shirts and ragged shorts. The boys waved at him as he passed. Here were the extremes of Africa – the businessman or government functionary in his limousine, the children on the cart, visible in his rear-view mirror, pulling up beside a roadside trash bin to supplement their meagre diet. He shook his head. It had been the same in Afghanistan. Warlords – or regional leaders, as they preferred to be called these days – growing fat on the proceeds of opium and marijuana while ordinary people starved and struggled to rebuild their war-torn lives.

He stopped in a town called Chinhoyi to refuel his vehicle and himself. He bought two chicken pies and a Coke in an old-fashioned glass bottle while he waited for the driveway attendant to top up the tank. The pies were cold and the soft drink warm, but he didn't care. He wasn't in Zimbabwe to sample its culinary delights. He wanted to make Kariba by nightfall, but when he checked his watch and his map, he reckoned that would be a long shot.

'What's the road like down to Kariba?' he asked the attendant.

'Ah, sir, that is a very winding road,' the young man said as he peeled off Jed's change in grimy one-hundred-dollar notes. 'Very many animals. Be careful if you are driving at night.'

'Animals?'

'Yes, sir. Elephant, buffalo, zebra, leopard, maybe even lion.'

'I didn't know Kariba was inside a national park.'

'No sir, it is not. It is a wildlife area, though. Kariba has much wildlife, but it has no fences, no rules. It is a wild place, sir.'

The shadows were lengthening as Jed pushed on northwards, past some well-tended orchards and more straggly-looking fields of carelessly planted corn. It was not how he had pictured Africa. He had imagined either wide-open savanna grasslands or equatorial jungle, not a poor man's version of the Midwest. The people seemed friendly enough, although every now and then he would pass a young male who stared sullenly at him.

He reached the turn-off to Kariba as the tip of the red sun disappeared behind the hills to his left. He switched his headlights to full beam as he took the winding road down off the escarpment into the Zambezi Valley. The sign had said it was seventy-three kilometres to Kariba. There were no lights at all on either side of the road, just rolling tree-covered hills and valleys. He wound down the window and switched off the airconditioning, hoping the night air would help keep him awake. As he descended he felt the humidity and temperature rise, despite the fact that it was now dark.

Suddenly Jed saw a movement in the corner of his eye, off to the left side of the road, and he stood on the brakes. A tiny antelope leaped into the beam of his headlights, paused in the glare for a second and then skittered away to the other side of the road. He put the truck into first carried on, a little slower, his eyes roaming left and right in search of other game.

For half an hour he saw nothing unusual and he started to speed up again. The moon was beginning to rise, and every now and then he would catch a glimpse of the wide man-made lake in the distance. It took him a couple of seconds to realise something was not right.

It was the road. The white line running down the centre had suddenly disappeared, as though the paint had run out when the road workers were marking it. Then the line became visible again. Jed blinked and then braked hard as the massive black shape reared up in front of him.

'Fuck!'

It was an elephant. It had stopped in the middle of the road and its great bulk had blocked out the centre line. Jed turned the wheel to avoid slamming into the huge beast. He skidded to a halt on the dirt verge. He rammed the gearstick into reverse as the elephant raised its trunk and stuck out its great sail-like ears.

The animal trumpeted, so loud that it seemed the Land Rover was vibrating with the noise. Jed stood on the accelerator and the vehicle zigzagged backwards as he overcorrected left and right with the steering wheel. The beast was coming towards him, still blowing shrill angry notes and shaking its massive head.

Jed had been looking over his shoulder to make sure there was nothing behind him. He looked forward again and saw the elephant had stopped. It looked to the left and then to the right and then straight at him. As he watched, stupefied, a baby elephant emerged from the bush to the left. It barely reached the underbelly of the big one. It paused for a second, looking in his direction, its wriggly trunk flopping wildly as it tried to sniff the air. The adult, which he guessed was the mother, nudged the youngster with her trunk and the pair of them carried on across the road.

He stayed parked for a full five minutes and counted fourteen of the gigantic creatures cross the road in front of him. It was an awe-inspiring experience and he realised, with sadness, that he wished he had

74

someone there to share it with. Most of all, he wished Miranda was with him. This was the sort of thing he had hoped to experience with her on his planned visit. He edged the vehicle forwards and watched the last of the massive baggy-skinned rumps disappearing into the gloomy undergrowth. His heart was heavy as he changed gear and drove on.

The winking lights of Kariba were a welcome sight and he stopped for directions to the Lake View Inn at a gas station on the edge of a steep drop that overlooked the lake. Even at night he could get a feeling for the immensity of the man-made inland sea. Out on the water he saw bright pinpricks of light, which he assumed were fishing boats. Jed was exhausted after his long journey. All he wanted was a beer, a steak and a bed.

The hotel had a nineteen-sixties feel about it – flagstone floors, and a mix of heavy dark timber framing and asbestos sheet walls. The rooms were arranged in long flat-roofed buildings set above each other in tiers on the side of the steep slope overlooking the lake. The place seemed to Jed like a twenty-five dollar a night Midwestern roadside motel with a million-dollar view.

In the lobby he was greeted by a smiling African woman. 'How much for a room, please?' he asked.

'Where are you from, sir?'

'The United States.'

The rate she quoted was about ten times what he had expected. 'What?' he exclaimed.

'There is a different rate for foreigners, sir, and you must pay in foreign currency, not Zimbabwe dollars.' She shrugged and gave him a sympathetic smile, as though she didn't necessarily agree with the policy.

He peeled off the green notes. He was in no position to argue and in no mood to go searching for a cheaper alternative.

After a porter had shown him to his room, Jed made his way to a terrace overlooking the lake. A few guests, most of them African, were sitting down to dinner at candlelit tables. Jed took an empty table at the edge of the terrace, next to the wrought-iron railing. A waiter sped to his side. The place was only about a third full. Business was bad, so the service was good.

'Beer, please.'

'Zambezi Lager, sir?'

'Whatever, so long as it's cold.'

When the waiter returned with his beer, Jed ordered a fillet steak and a second drink. The night was humid and the green beer bottle was slippery with condensation. The glass that came with it was frosted, straight from the freezer. He'd really had no idea of what Africa was going to be like, and things like chilled glasses and elephant roadblocks came as pleasant surprises. The ice-cold amber fluid was a balm and he reached in his shirt pocket for cigarettes and lit one as he drank.

'Excuse me, have you got a light?'

He turned around at the sound of the woman's voice and was momentarily taken aback. Everything about her was a surprise. Her red hair, her American accent, her smile.

'Sure.' She leaned closer as he flicked the Zippo and he smelled her perfume. 'It's surprising finding another American here.'

'I know what you mean. We're thin on the ground in these parts – it's not exactly a tourist Mecca any more,' she said, exhaling. She made no move to leave. 'So, are you a tourist?'

'No. It's complicated. I'm looking for someone.'

'Well, I hope you find her, or him. Sorry to intrude.'

'No, not at all,' he said quickly. It had been a long day and he ached from the drive, but, as tired as he was, he found himself wanting to keep the conversation going. 'Are you here alone?'

She laughed and said, 'That's one step removed from "Do you come here often?" Yes, I'm alone. You?'

'Travelling solo. Divorced, a long time ago.'

'Oh, I see. Sorry.'

'Don't be. We made a great kid, so it wasn't all bad. Look, would you like to join me for a drink?'

'Sure. I wouldn't mind catching up on some news from home.'

'If it's home-town gossip you want,' he said, 'you might find me lack-ing. I spend more time away from the States than in 'em.'

'What do you do?' She leaned back in her chair and crossed her legs.

'Government work.'

'Sounds mysterious, or boring, depending on the type of work.'

He studied her. He guessed her to be in her mid-thirties. Attractive. Very attractive. She wore a sleeveless shirt with the top three buttons undone. Her breasts strained pleasingly against the fabric. Her arms were toned and slender. Her green eyes glittered. He thought her ances-try might be Irish.

'I could work for the IRS for all you know,' he said.

'You look like you pound more than a keyboard.'

He smiled and wondered if she was flirting with him. 'I get paid a pittance to sleep in the dirt, get shot at and eat crap food.'

'Army or marines?'

'Please. I might not be a genius, but I'm not a retard.'

'Army it is then.'

'But that's enough about me, except for my name. Jed. What brings you to Zimbabwe?'

'Jed?'

'That's right. And you're supposed to tell me yours at this point.'

'Not Jed Banks?'

'The very same. How did you know that?'

'My God, I'm so sorry I didn't ask sooner. I'm Chris . . . Christine Wallis. I don't know if Miranda . . .'

Jed was surprised. He drained his beer to buy himself some time.

'Miranda's mom told me about your email,' he said eventually.

'I see. Mr Banks . . . Jed, please understand how sorry I am . . . I can understand how you must feel.'

'Do you have kids?'

'No.'

'Then you haven't got a fucking clue how I feel.'

She looked down at her lap. 'You have every right to be angry. I know what you must think of me.'

He said nothing.

'I wouldn't have sent her here if I didn't think it was safe. Please understand how bad I feel about this.'

'How you feel isn't exactly at the top of my list of concerns, Professor.'

She looked up now, and he saw something flash in her green eyes. 'Don't you think I'm hurting too? She's a smart girl and if anyone can handle themselves in the African bush she can! Don't come in here and tell me I've done something terrible. Miranda was a grown woman who made her own choices.'

It was Jed's turn to be taken aback. 'You spoke about her in the present tense. Do you think she's still alive?'

Chris sipped her Scotch. 'I don't know, and that's the truth. There was a lion shot yesterday that had attacked a local woman.'

'You think it might be the same one that supposedly attacked Miranda?'

'I took it to the police. They've got it in the local morgue and they're going to get a vet to open it up tomorrow.'

'Jesus.' Jed shook his head.

'I want Miranda to be alive just as much as you do, but if she wasn't taken by a lion it's hard to know where she went or what happened to her. There are some remains too. Not much.'

'Would madam care to order something from the menu?' The waiter had slipped in behind Chris without either of them noticing.

'I don't know,' Chris said, looking at Jed.

Jed was in two minds. As much as he seethed at the woman's decision to send his daughter to such a dangerous place, she was his only source of information. Plus, she was disarmingly attractive.

'Be my guest,' he said with a wave.

Chris glanced at the menu. 'The bream. And a glass of Mukuyu Colombard, please.'

'Is it any good? The wine, that is,' Jed said.

'Cheap, locally made, but drinkable.'

'Sounds like my kind of beverage. Make it a bottle, please,' he said to the waiter. 'When did you last see her?'

Chris hesitated, glancing out at the lake. 'Let me see, she was with me in Kruger for about a month, so she would have arrived here in Zimbabwe three months ago.'

'When did you get here?'

'Yesterday. I drove here as soon as I could mothball my research operation in Kruger. I visited Miranda's campsite briefly this morning, but didn't hang around once we picked up some lion spoor.'

'The one the ranger shot?'

'Actually, I shot it,' she corrected him.

He looked at her with grudging respect, but he would be damned if he'd praise her. 'I thought you were into protecting big cats.'

'A woman's life was at risk. I won't put animals before people, although I know a few zoologists and conservationists who wouldn't agree with me.'

'I've met a few people I wouldn't put ahead of a snake.'

'I know what you mean.'

She laughed and he felt angry with himself that he had relaxed around her. He wanted to stay mad for a little while longer. Besides, it was impossible to forget why he was here – why both of them were here.

'So, what happens tomorrow? With the lion?' he asked.

'I know the local vet here. The police will get him to do the . . . the autopsy.'

'What time and where?'

The waiter arrived with the wine. Chris tasted it and nodded. 'I don't think that's a good idea, if you're planning on being there. I can have the police let you know –'

'I don't care about what you say, I've got more right to be there than you and I *will* be there. I want to view the remains that were found at the scene as well.' He took a sip of wine, then asked, more gently, 'What will you do after the lion's been examined?'

'That depends on the result, I guess. I need to collect some equipment I loaned to Miranda, as well as some reports she was working on for me, but the authorities won't let me near her stuff. It'd really help me if you gave the police permission to release Miranda's things to me. I'll make sure you get all her personal effects.'

'That won't be necessary.'

Chris looked confused.

Jed refilled her glass, then his own. 'You won't need to pass anything on to me, because I'll be with you.'

'Look, Jed, I've spent a lot of time in this part of the world. I know some of the police here, I know the vet, I know the National Parks people. I can get a lot done by myself, using my personal connections, and –'

'And if you try to keep me out of this you'll regret it.'

'You can't order me around. I'm not one of your soldiers, you know.'

'I know that. But you can't get your stuff back without me. Also, I wonder how long your funding would last if the press learned how you sent an inexperienced college girl out on her own, ill prepared, unprotected and alone in a dangerous country.'

'Are you threatening me?'

'Yes.'

'Well, it won't wash. You don't even know what you're talking about. You don't have all the facts.'

'Fill me in,' he said, leaning back in his chair. 'What facts am I missing?'

'How I run my research projects is none of your business. Suffice to say that they meet the most rigorous safety and academic standards applicable for this sort of work.'

'Then you won't mind the press asking you a few questions. I'm surprised they haven't already.'

Chris looked him straight in the eye and said, 'I don't think we need reporters sniffing around here. You don't want any more publicity about Miranda's disappearance, do you? Won't that just add to the burden your ex-wife must be carrying?'

Bullshit, he thought to himself. She was hiding something and that only made him all the more determined to follow her every move. The waiter arrived with their meals and he let the conversation drop while the man slowly but attentively served them.

She looked out over the lake and he studied her profile in the candlelight. Pretty, for sure, but there was a steely strength within Professor Christine Wallis evidenced by the set of her jaw and her unwavering gaze when she had locked eyes with him. Her body was lean and toned, as though she worked out. He remembered Miranda complaining that it was almost impossible to exercise in the African bush. One could hardly go off jogging or power-walking amidst wild animals, and there were certainly no gyms. It would have taken a strong will and a good deal of self-discipline for Chris Wallis to stay in shape, and she obviously did.

He left the argument about him accompanying her – anyhow, she would have no choice once he confronted the police in the morning – and changed the subject. 'How far away was the lion when you shot it?'

She swallowed a mouthful of fish, took a sip of wine and wiped her lips. 'Oh, about two hundred metres.'

'Moving?'

'It didn't exactly pose for me. It was charging the woman and had just started to leap on her when I fired.'

'What weapon did you use?'

'An AK-47. It belonged to the ranger who was supposed to be protecting me. But he was taking a dump.'

He didn't detect any bravado in her simple account. The AK was a reliable, sturdy weapon, but to hit a moving target at anything over a hundred metres required a good measure of skill or luck. In her telling, though, it was as if taking the shot was simply part of her everyday work, something she had no qualms or excitement about.

'Quite a shot. Where did you learn to fire a rifle?'

'The eighty-deuce.'

'Eighty-Second Airborne Division?' He couldn't mask the surprise in his voice. 'You didn't tell me you were a soldier.'

'We haven't done a lot of talking about me.'

'Touché. When did you serve?'

'Eighty-nine to ninety-four. I stayed in long enough to pay for my college tuition.'

'What was your MOS?' Every soldier had a military occupational specialty, a primary job he or she was trained for.

'I was a clerk, in C1 – personnel. My drill instructor at basic training told me I would have been a sniper if I'd been a man.' A touch of pride there, he noted, and resentment too.

'Why didn't you try for officer candidate school? You must have had the grades.'

'I never planned on making a career out of the Army. It was a means to an end. I figured I'd do my time and get out. I had my sights set on other things. Besides, they wouldn't let me be a sniper.'

He smiled. He sensed that in other circumstances they might hit it off. However, she was holding something back from him and for some reason didn't want him nosing about. He guessed that his bluff about going to the press was a very real concern in her mind. Conservationists lived on public donations and corporate sponsorship and couldn't afford a whiff of controversy.

'How did it feel when you killed the lion?' he asked.

She answered without a pause. 'I didn't want to do it – hated it, in fact – but after it was done I didn't feel a thing. There was no joy, if that's what you mean. Men and women are both capable of killing, but they do it for different reasons. It's the same as in nature. A female lion will kill to provide for her pride or to protect them. A male lion, on the other hand, will kill to meet his own ends, to demonstrate his dominance. Did you know that when a male takes over a pride, as well as killing or vanquishing the old male, he also kills all the cubs his predecessor has sired?'

'I've heard that stepchildren are a pain.'

'Not very funny.'

'Best I could do at short notice.'

'Have you ever hunted?'

'No.' He took a drink.

'Why not?'

'I never saw the need to kill an animal. I've never had to hunt for food, never been threatened by an animal in the wild.'

82

Chris looked at him with those penetrating green eyes again. 'But you've been in combat?'

'Yes.'

'And?'

'And what?'

'Have you ever killed a man?'

'Most people are too polite to raise that question.'

'How did it feel?'

'I'm sure I saw on Discovery Channel that male lions also kill to protect their prides.'

'What's your point?'

'I like to think that what I do is about protecting people – innocent people. It's how I manage to sleep at night.' In fact, there were some nights when he didn't sleep at all, but he wasn't going to tell that to Christine Smart-Ass Wallis.

'That's a good answer, although you didn't really answer my question.'

'Where are you going after you've been to the police tomorrow?' he asked.

'Look, Jed,' her tone was softer now, 'I know you've come all this way to find Miranda, but you have to prepare yourself for the worst. The National Parks rangers have scoured the campsite where Miranda was staying for clues and tracked the lions as far as possible. There's really nothing more any of us can do. I'm sorry, but I think we've both got to face the facts.'

She was right, of course – he did need to prepare himself for the worst. But she was also right in the first part of her comment – he had come a long way to find his daughter – and he would be damned if he would leave without some concrete evidence of her death.

'You can't stop me talking to the police and you can't stop me visiting the National Park.'

'I'm not going to try. It's just that I don't think you'll be able to find out any more about what happened to Miranda by blundering around on your own. Despite what you may think, I do wonder if I was some-how responsible for her disappearance. As her supervisor I promise you that I will pass on any information I get from the police or other sources about her whereabouts. I know you want to help, but it will be better for all of us if you sit tight for a couple of days and wait and see what turns up.'

'I didn't come here to sit tight. I came here to find my daughter and bring her home.'

'So did I.'

'Well then, don't get in my way.' He wiped his mouth with his napkin and tossed it on the empty plate.

She took a deep breath. 'I don't want to argue with you, Jed. I want the same thing you do – to find Miranda alive. But we both have to start preparing ourselves for the fact that might not happen.'

'Don't try to shield me, Professor Wallis. I'm no stranger to death. I also know the best way to deal with grief is to confront it, head-on. I want to be there when they open that goddamned beast. If my daughter is dead I want to see it with my own eyes.'

Chris shrugged. 'In the end, these are matters for the police to decide. You're a blood relative and you have certain rights. I'm a scientist and Miranda's employer. I have certain rights too. As I said, we're all working towards the same goal.'

Jed looked into those green eyes that had sparkled with warmth a few minutes before. Now they seemed as cold and hard as cut emerald. As she stood and excused herself from the table, he wondered if the two of them were, in fact, working towards the same goal. He doubted it.

6

Jed woke late.

He had finished off two more beers after Christine Wallis had left him, nursing his anger and resentment at the fiery-haired female. It had been nearly midnight by the time he had made it back to his room.

Heavy curtains kept the place in darkness but Jed saw from his watch that it was after nine in the morning. He had been operating on minimal sleep since Afghanistan, so it wasn't surprising. However, he was annoyed with himself – he had wanted an early start. The morning sun blinded him as he pulled back the drapes. He fetched his sunglasses from the pocket of his trousers and stepped out onto the little balcony, clad only in his green boxer shorts. The lake stretched to the horizon, glittering silver in the harsh glare, like a pool of spilt mercury. It was hard on his eyes and his head hurt. He had been alcohol-free for months in Afghanistan and it would take a while to rebuild his tolerance level.

'Any messages for me?' he asked the woman at reception after a breakfast of toast, coffee and tomato juice.

'No, sir.'

'One of your other guests, Professor Wallis, is she still in the hotel?'

'Oh no, sir, she left about five o'clock this morning.'

That was odd. He didn't imagine veterinarians anywhere in the world started work before dawn.

The security guard in the car park saluted him as he opened the door of the Land Rover. It was sweltering already and the steering wheel was hot to the touch. Jed rechecked the map of Kariba and set off.

The countryside was spectacular. Below him were myriad little inlets. Fingers of water divided brown hills studded with acacias and trees with copper-coloured butterfly-shaped leaves. The land was criss-crossed with clearly visible paths, which he presumed were made by animals of some sort, as there were no signs of houses away from the water's edge. Bays that had been wooded valleys before the man-made flood now sheltered houseboats and sailboats. The skeletal white tops of dead trees protruded above the surface of the lake, their boughs blanched with droppings from the many different types of waterbirds that roosted in them.

The Zimbabwe Republic Police camp was perched on the top of a high hill with a panoramic view across the lake. Jed parked the truck and walked into the two-storey concrete building. It looked as though it had been built to withstand a direct hit from a rocket-propelled grenade, which probably wasn't far from the truth as the country had been at war for most of the nineteen sixties and seventies. A bored-looking policewoman in a blue-grey uniform was seated reading a magazine and picking her nose. Jed cleared his throat. She didn't look up.

'Excuse me,' he said.

She got to her feet ponderously. It was stifling hot and the woman moved slowly to the long wooden charge counter. 'Yes, sir, can I help you?'

'I'm looking for someone I can talk to about the disappearance of my daughter, Miranda Banks. An American citizen. She was research-ing carnivores in Mana Pools National Park.'

'What is the name again? Hanks?'

'Banks.' Jed spelled it out. He wondered how many Americans disappeared in presumed lion attacks.

The female constable opened a large book on the counter and ran her finger down the margin. She looked puzzled.

'The initial report we had was that she had been taken by a lion,' Jed said, trying not to let his frustration show.

'No, I do not think so.'

'Can I see your superior?'

It was the woman's turn to look annoyed. 'You can see me. First name Miranda?'

'Yes.'

'We have a report about an American woman disappearing, but her name was Miranda Lewis.'

Jed was embarrassed. 'Yes, of course. That's her mother's name.'

'So she is not your daughter?'

'She sometimes called herself Banks-Lewis.'

'Not according to her passport she didn't.'

Jed was surprised. He wondered at what age his daughter had gotten her new passport. Had Patti organised it for her when she was a child and left his name off it in spite?

'She's my daughter.'

'And you have proof of that, sir?'

Damn. He had no proof at all that Miranda Lewis – or even Miranda Banks, come to that – was his daughter. He had not realised it would be necessary. 'The US embassy in Harare knows of my relationship to my daughter. They advised my wife of her disappearance.'

'Perhaps you can call and get them to send us a letter.'

'Can I use your phone, please?'

'Ah, I am sorry, the phone is not working today.'

'Jesus Christ.'

The constable frowned at the blasphemy.

'Who is your superior?'

'Why do you want to know? The member in charge will only tell you the same thing.'

Jed was ready to hit someone.

Voices echoed from down the corridor, behind the charge desk. He heard a woman's laugh.

'Mr Banks. How are you today?' Chris Wallis asked as she came into view.

Jed thought that she didn't seem surprised to see him. She was escorted by a tall African police officer in a grey-blue shirt and khaki trousers. He was a distinguished-looking fellow with a grey moustache and silver crowns on his epaulettes.

'I'm fine,' Jed said. In fact, he was seething, but he didn't want to betray his emotions to her.

'This is Superintendent Ncube. He is the member in charge here – that's like the station captain back home.'

'I get the picture. Will you tell him that Miranda Banks-Lewis is my daughter?'

'Professor Wallis told me you would be visiting us today, Mr Banks,' the superintendent said. 'Please accept my apologies that I have not yet had the opportunity to brief all of my officers on your impending arrival.'

'No problems,' Jed said. 'Has the lion been examined yet?'

'We are on our way to the morgue now, Mr Banks. I would invite you to accompany us but I fear the experience could be quite . . . traumatic.'

'I'm a soldier, Superintendent. I won't see anything I haven't seen before in combat.'

'Mr Banks . . . Jed, I think –' Christine began.

'Professor Wallis, with all due respect I don't give a flying you-know-what for your thoughts. Superintendent, I am Miranda's father and I demand to be present at this examination.'

'Mr Banks, I understand your concerns. Normally I would not let any family member view such a procedure, but you have come a long way to learn of your daughter's fate. Professor Wallis means no disrespect, I am sure. You are welcome to accompany us.' Superintendent Ncube led the way out of the police station, donning his peaked cap once he was in the open air. He saluted two male constables who were entering the building and thrust an ebony swagger stick under one arm.

'In times such as these, when fuel is short, it is silly to take three vehicles. Won't you both please join me?' Ncube offered.

Jed and Chris exchanged glances. Jed wasn't thrilled with the idea of sharing a ride with the obstructive scientist and it was clear she felt the same way.

'It will be our pleasure, won't it, Mr Banks?' she said sweetly.

Chris climbed into the front seat of the superintendent's white Land Rover and Jed took the rear bench. They sat in strained silence as Ncube drove recklessly down the hill and into a ramshackle township.

It was the superintendent who started the conversation again. 'This is Mahombekombe township. It was built as a temporary village for workers during the construction of the dam around forty years ago. As you can see, it seems no one told the inhabitants it was only temporary.'

The place was a crowded mini metropolis of corrugated tin and asbestos fibreboard. It reminded Jed of shantytowns he had seen in the Philippines and Central America, but without the litter. The people here were poor, but proud enough to keep their meagre homes and neighbourhood tidy. He wondered what their lives must be like.

'Most of the people here make their living from the lake and the tourist industry – fishing, maintaining the holiday houseboats, working in the hotels. Times are tough, though, because of the lack of foreign visitors.'

'Is that elephant dung on the road?' Jed asked.

'Yes, it is,' Ncube said. 'As Professor Wallis knows, there is still a healthy wildlife population around Kariba.'

'Poaching has been bad here in recent years, but Kariba remains one of the few places in Africa where you can see humans and the big five – well, minus the rhino – living side by side,' Chris said.

'I nearly collected an elephant on the drive in, but I didn't expect to find evidence of them this close to people's houses,' Jed said.

'You'll see people and elephants walking along the same roads around here. The locals know how to deal with dangerous game, but that doesn't mean there aren't fatalities on both sides,' Chris explained.

Superintendent Ncube chimed in again. 'Just last week a local man was killed by an elephant. He ran into it with his vehicle, driving too fast at the time, but the elephant was only injured, not killed. The animal crushed the car and, as the man fled, he charged him.'

'Was he gored by the tusks?' Jed asked.

'That's a common misconception,' Chris said.

'Indeed,' Ncube continued. 'The elephant knocked the man to the ground with his trunk and then knelt on him with one of his front legs, crushing him to death.'

'Despite the occasional accident, though,' Chris added, 'Kariba is proof that if people take care they can live in close proximity to dangerous game.'

'What about lions?' Jed asked.

'There's actually a fairly large pride living close to the outskirts of town at the moment. But there've been no reported cases of attacks on humans locally. I'd be interested in studying that particular group sometime.'

'Is that where you were this morning?'

Chris nodded.

'Five a.m. is probably a good time to go looking for big cats, I guess,' Jed said.

Ncube looked at his watch. 'Do you mind if I turn on the radio to listen to the news?'

Jed shook his head.

Ncube leaned over and turned up the volume.

A female announcer said: 'And repeating our top story of the hour, a bomb has exploded on a tour bus in Dar es Salaam, Tanzania. Police say at least fourteen tourists, all of them Americans, are believed dead, with up to twenty more injured in what they claim is a terrorist attack. No one has claimed responsibility for the act.'

'Jesus Christ,' Jed said.

Ncube grimaced. 'This is not the first time terrorists have struck in East Africa. Remember the failed missile attack on the Israeli airline in Kenya and the bombing of your embassy? Fortunately, in southern Africa we have yet to be targeted by religious extremists or terrorists.'

Jed looked at Chris. She was staring fixedly out of the window. She said nothing and her face looked pale.

'Here we are,' Ncube said, pulling up in front of a whitewashed building. 'This clinic doubles as our overflow morgue. We thought it best to bring the lion here as there will be no other families of victims here today.'

'Please go ahead without me,' Chris said. 'I'll join you in a couple of minutes.' She pulled a mobile phone from the pocket of her tan safari trousers and walked away.

Jed raised an eyebrow but said nothing. Instead he followed Ncube inside. They were greeted by a nurse, who spoke to the superintendent in their shared language. 'The doctor is waiting for us,' Ncube translated. 'Please take a seat, Mr Banks.'

Jed sat in a moulded plastic chair, which creaked under his weight. The clinic smelled strongly of disinfectant. The walls were whitewashed, but stained here and there with flecks of brown. The linoleum tiles under his boots were scrubbed but pitted. Dirt had collected in the tiny holes, giving the flooring the appearance of being covered in fly specks. He reminded himself to try not to get sick in Africa.

'Would you like tea or coffee while you wait?' the nurse asked.

'Coffee, no milk or sugar, please,' Jed said.

The policeman ordered tea. The nurse returned a few minutes later, a tall, thin grey-haired man in tow.

'How are you?' Ncube said as he extended his hand in greeting. 'Mr Banks, this is Doctor Leslie Reynolds.'

Jed shook hands with the man, surprised to find a European vet working in such austere surroundings. Reynolds wore a frayed white lab coat over grey trousers that stopped at his ankles. Jed wondered if they were second-hand. He also wondered how much a vet working for the Zimbabwean public health system made in a year.

'Please, sit down, Mr Banks,' Doctor Reynolds said as he took a cup of tea from the nurse and pulled up a chair.

'Apologies, everybody,' Chris Wallis said as she came in through the door.

'Christine, how nice to see you again, though I'm sorry it's in such difficult circumstances,' Reynolds said with a forced smile.

Chris shook hands with the vet then turned to the other two men. 'Sorry about that, but I have a friend who drives a tour bus in Tanzania and I was worried he may have been hurt in the bomb blast. He's fine, thank goodness.'

'I'm glad to hear it,' Doctor Reynolds said. 'Terrible business. Now, Mr Banks, first let me say how sorry I am for the distress your daughter's disappearance must be causing you and your family. I'm afraid my findings won't give you the closure you need, but you should –'

'Have you already opened the lion up?' Jed's voice rose in annoyance.

'Mr Banks, I can assure you that the business of dissecting an animal such as a lion is not something anyone would wish to sit through. The carcass was starting to decompose, so I had to act quickly. The job was done last night.'

Jed noticed the older man's hand shook as he raised the chipped china mug to his thin lips. He had a ruddy face and a bulbous nose that marked him as a drinker.

'What did you find?'

'Some fragments of clothing, Mr Banks.' Reynolds paused and no one spoke.

Jed found himself suddenly short of air. He took a deep breath and a shot of coffee. The liquid burned his tongue and the roof of his mouth. 'Please go on.'

'There is no doubt this lion feasted on a human being, Mr Banks. I can show you the material fragments. The fabric appears to be green, lightweight. Possibly a shirt, or a woman's blouse. Bush clothing. Very common around here, of course. The animal's digestive system would have processed and passed any skin and flesh by now, assuming the consumption happened around the time your daughter disappeared. However, the fabric would have taken longer to pass.'

Jed swallowed hard. 'Tell me about the remains that were found at the scene. I want to see them.'

'There isn't much to see, Mr Banks. A hand and part of the attached forearm, and part of a skull.'

'Show me.'

The doctor looked at Superintendent Ncube, who nodded. 'Come this way, please. Will you be joining us, Christine?'

She looked at Jed.

'You can if you want,' he said.

They followed Reynolds down a corridor with an even stronger smell of disinfectant. The vet opened a heavy sealed door and they stepped into a coolroom. Jed's rubber-soled boots squeaked on the white tiled floor. There were a dozen drawers with enamelled metal doors set into the wall. Reynolds checked the cardboard tag slotted into a holder on one of them, opened it, and slid out a long tray. The plastic bag took up a pitifully small portion of the space normally occupied by a body. He untied the rubber band holding the bag closed and rolled down the sides. 'I'm afraid this is it.'

Jed felt as though he were outside his body, watching from a distance. He'd seen body parts before, thought he was numbed to the sight. He was wrong. He barely heard his own words as he spoke. 'Any rings, a wristwatch, or anything else at the scene?'

'No. Did your daughter wear a ring?'

'Nothing special that I can recall.' He didn't touch the hand. Couldn't run his fingers over the cold skin, didn't want to feel the smoothness of the cleaned-out skull pan. There would be no closure in this macabre trove.

'There's been some decomposition, as you can see, but you notice the skin is white, and it certainly looks like a woman's hand,' the doctor said.

'Were there any other European women in the area?' Jed asked.

Ncube, who was standing away from the group, spoke up. 'We questioned everyone in the lodges and the camp ground. No visitors have been reported missing.'

'But how can we tell for sure if it's . . . if the remains are Miranda's? What about DNA testing?' Jed asked.

'This is Zimbabwe, Mr Banks, not the United States, and a far-flung corner of Zimbabwe at that, but I did anticipate your question. I've spoken to a former colleague who is now a professor at the university in Harare. He can perform a DNA test but, of course, we require some sort of sample from your daughter.'

At first the idea sounded ridiculous, as his daughter was missing presumed dead, but then Jed recalled something he'd seen on a TV cop show. 'Like hair, you mean?'

'Precisely.'

'Where are Miranda's personal effects?' Jed asked.

'They were collected by the National Parks people once our investigators had finished at your daughter's campsite. I made sure all her belongings were stored under lock and key in the park armoury,' Ncube said.

'I was planning on collecting them for you,' Chris said.

Jed recalled that the professor wanted to get her hands on some work Miranda had been doing for her. The woman's businesslike interest in Miranda's belongings grated on him.

'I'll be collecting my daughter's stuff myself,' he said to Chris. To Reynolds, he added, 'I've seen enough, thank you, Doctor. And I'll find a hairbrush or pillowcase or sleeping bag or something you can use as a sample for the testing.'

'That's good, Mr Banks, but I think you should prepare yourself for a positive match. There have been no other reports of Europeans, male or female, being attacked by lions in Mana Pools recently and, again, all I can tell you is that in my best estimation the remains probably came from a white woman.'

'I understand, Doctor.' Despite the evidence, Jed wanted so much to believe in the impossible. But in his heart of hearts he was beginning to realise that he had lost his daughter.

7

Jed sat on the concrete stoep of the police station smoking a cigarette and reading a report of how his daughter had died.

He was in the shade, but he figured the mercury had topped a hundred. Sweat rolled down his forehead into his eyes, forcing him to blink every now and then. A passer-by, although there weren't any at this hottest time of the African day, might have thought he was crying. He wasn't, but the lump in his throat got bigger as he read on. The police station's photocopier was broken and Superintendent Ncube would not let him take his only copy of the investigation report away, so Jed was forced to read it on the premises.

The victim's tent was found to be open and there was evidence a single lion had entered, in the form of muddy paw prints on the nylon floor. The camping stretcher inside the tent was on its side.

Jed reread the section of the report and made a note on the sheet of A4 paper he had liberated from the broken photocopier – much to the chagrin of the cranky policewoman at the charge desk.

The victim's mosquito net was outside the tent. It is believed the net became entangled with the victim and/or the lion as it removed her.

He closed his eyes tight and tried to imagine the horror of being seized by a massive cat and dragged along the ground. Huge jaws clamping down on her slender body, piercing her smooth skin. Blood flowing from her.

He scanned the page again. No mention of blood in the tent. He imagined he would see it for himself when he recovered Miranda's effects.

Outside the tent a number of different footprints were observed. These were believed to belong to the victim, several National Parks officers who were first on the scene, and another female person – possibly a National Parks maid who occasionally visited the victim's campsite.

Jed lit a second cigarette from the first, something he hadn't done for many years, and continued to read.

A large bloodstain was found in the grass eleven metres from the tent. Drag marks and lion paw prints continued from this point to a location forty-three metres further away, towards the Zambezi River, at the foot of a large tree. Another bloodstain was found here. It is believed that this was where the victim's body was consumed.

Consumed. Jesus Christ, Jed thought. It was the twenty-first century and his daughter had been raised in suburban USA. People didn't get *consumed* by wild animals any more. Even warfare was more understandable, to him at least, than being preyed on by an animal. He wished it had been him and not Professor Wallis who had shot the man-eater. He wanted to hunt down this beast as it had hunted his baby girl.

Hyena tracks were also discovered at this site, leading off in several directions. It is believed that these animals disposed of the victim's bones after the lion had finished feeding.

Jed felt sick to his stomach.

'Are you OK?'

He looked up. Chris Wallis stared down at him. He couldn't think what to say.

'I'm sorry I had to leave so quickly before, but I had some urgent errands to run in town. I'm glad you haven't left yet. I thought it'd be better if we travelled together.'

He didn't care about her errands or her plans. The woman seemed to alternate between wanting him out of the country and trying to spend every waking minute with him. 'Whatever,' he said, then stubbed out the cigarette and coughed. At least talking to her would take his mind off the vision of Miranda's bones being ground up by a pack of scavenging hyenas.

Chris saw the pain in his eyes and said, 'Jed, I know this must be heartbreaking for you. Take your time. I'll wait while you go to town, get organised.'

'Thanks. Actually, I need to look for someone.'

'Oh? Maybe I can help. I know Kariba pretty well. Who is he – or she?'

'A guide. A tracker. He was recommended to me. I want to do some looking around while I'm at Mana Pools.'

'There's a National Parks ranger I've been working with. He knows the area better than anyone and I'm already paying for his services as a guide. You can tag along with us if you like. It'll save you money.'

'I've been in Afghanistan for six months with nothing to spend my money on so I've got cash to spare. Anyway, I wouldn't want to tie you up or distract you.'

'No bother.'

'Look, I'm not trying to be rude, but I like to do things my way, OK?' Jed stood and collected the pages of the investigation report, which he had spread around him on the stoep.

'Do you still hope she's alive, that the investigators got it wrong and she's lost in the bush somewhere?' Chris shook her head.

'I don't know what I'm hoping for. I won't know until I start. I don't expect she's lost and, from what I know of this place, if she did get lost she probably wouldn't have survived. Until we know for sure that it was Miranda's remains the doctor found, you can't blame me for wanting to at least check out the place where she disappeared.'

Chris nodded and bit thoughtfully on her lower lip. 'But please, let me help you into the park. The bureaucracy can drive you crazy, and at least I can take you and your tracker straight to the spot where Miranda's camp was. Might save you some time.'

Jed realised it would be hard, if not impossible, to shake the professor now, so, somewhat reluctantly, he nodded his head.

The soundtrack to Mahombekombe township was African music played at full bore from a car stereo, a lively mix of plinking percussion backed by a solid beat. People chattered around Jed. An urchin in ragged clothes tugged at his trousers and asked him for a ballpoint pen as he walked from the supermarket. A minibus taxi piled high with luggage and cardboard boxes buzzed past him, leaving a fog of blue smoke. On the unpaved roadside women sold lace tablecloths, printed fabrics and basket ware.

'That looks like a bachelor's shopping trolley,' Chris said with a smile as he returned to his Land Rover.

'Thanks,' Jed said to the young African who had wheeled the trolley out for him. The man unloaded Jed's supplies – four dozen bottles of Zambezi Lager, a few packets of steak, a bag of potatoes, cornflakes, milk, three loaves of bread, a few packets of crackers, peanut butter and a bag of assorted condiments.

'I see you have all of the food groups covered.'

'Except for red wine. They were out. So I bought Scotch instead. Not bad for two bucks a bottle.'

'Don't be too pleased with yourself, you haven't tried it yet.'

It was afternoon, and still oppressively hot and muggy down near the lake shore. A little boy pushed a carved wooden Land Rover along the ground and looked up enviously at Jed's and Chris's vehicles.

'Hello, Mister,' said the boy.

'Hello yourself.'

'Jason,' the boy's mother called from her stall. She nursed a baby in the crook of one arm and carried a white doily in her free hand. 'Come here, boy. A present for your lady friend, boss?' she added, catching Jed's eye and waving the intricate piece of lacework.

Jed was surprised by the greeting. Black people didn't call white people 'boss' where he came from. 'She's not my friend,' he said.

'Oh.'

'Thanks,' said Chris.

'I mean that in the nicest possible way.'

'I bet.'

Jed turned back to the stall keeper. 'I was wondering if you could give me directions. I'm looking for someone.' He produced the piece of paper from his pocket on which Eveline had written the name of her former employee.

The woman took the paper from him, read it, then threw back her head and laughed long and hard.

'Ah, sah! What do you want this man for? Does he owe you money?' She laughed again.

Jed smiled politely. 'No, he was recommended to me as a safari guide.'

'The only thing Moses Nyati will guide you to is a hangover, sah!' she cackled. 'This man is no good. He is a bad man. Ask any woman in Kariba.'

'Sounds like quite a guy,' Chris said from behind him.

'Sounds like my kind of guy,' Jed muttered. He asked the woman how to find Nyati and she gave him directions to a shebeen in another township, called Nyamhunga.

'I take it a shebeen is a bar,' Jed said to Chris after he had thanked the African woman for her help.

'You got it. And if you don't mind some advice, be careful if you're going to track him down in one of those places. We're not exactly talking cocktails at the Ritz.'

'I've been in some pretty basic joints in my time.'

'In South Africa they put battery acid in the local beer to give it a kick.'

'Well, maybe not that basic. I'll stick to the bottled stuff.'

'Good idea. Want me to lead?' Chris asked as she opened the door to her Land Rover.

Jed shrugged, resigned to the fact that she seemed intent on chaperoning him around Zimbabwe.

He climbed into his Land Rover and started the engine. He swigged from a bottle of warm water as he followed Chris Wallis's vehicle out of Mahombekombe and back onto the main road that led up away from the lake. She seemed to know Kariba well and he wondered how much time she had spent in the town.

He knew very little of her background, her experience, her qualifications or her relationship with his daughter. In short, Chris was a mystery, except for being stubborn, and with a fiery temper he'd already been on the receiving end of. She hadn't wanted him to go to the vet or to the national park to collect Miranda's things but, when it became clear he would anyway, she seemed determined to be by his side at all times. He wondered again what she was trying to hide.

They reached a plateau, leaving the lake behind them. The bush stretched off to the horizon on either side, a tan and dull-green expanse of wilderness. He wished Miranda, and not her guarded mentor, was there to show him around. With Miranda, this would have been an exciting, fun-filled journey of discovery. Without her, it was like a mission in any other Third World country he had ever visited. Chris drove fast, too fast for his liking, but he kept pace with her on the narrow, winding black-top. He wondered what would happen if they hit an elephant or some other large animal at speed. It seemed every kilometre or so there were ribbons of burned rubber where some speedster had had a near miss.

There was a beeping from the daypack on the passenger seat next to him. Steering with one hand, he reached over and fished out his mobile phone. He looked at the screen and saw he had a message. It was from Patti, asking him to call. He would, but not right now. On impulse, he decided to make a different call, to the States. He knew the number by heart.

'Fort Bragg, how may I help you?' the reassuringly southern female voice said.

'Can you put me through to the C1 shop, headquarters 82nd Airborne Division, please?'

'Anyone in particular, sir?'

'Major Hank Klein.'

'One moment, sir, connecting you now.'

A man with a gravelly voice answered. 'Major Klein.'

'Fritz, you Kraut bastard, how they hanging?'

'Jed? Is that you, Banks, you pussy?'

'The very same.'

They had been privates together in the 75th Ranger Battalion many years before, but a partial parachute malfunction and the resulting hard landing had left Klein with a couple of compressed vertebrae and no chance of staying at the fighting end of the Army. Reluctant to leave, he had transferred to a desk job, in C1 – personnel – and eventually earned a commission. His latest promotion had come with a new posting to the 82nd Airborne Division in North Carolina.

'OK, out with it, Banks, what do you want?' Klein asked after Jed had enquired about his family. 'You were never one for social calls.'

'I'm overseas, Hank. Can't say where.' Of course he could, but Jed didn't want to go into the details of Miranda's disappearance all over again. 'I need some background on a player working in my AO. She's ex-eighty-deuce so I thought you might be able to pull up some info from her jacket.'

'She? You dog.'

'It's not what you think.'

'Wouldn't blame you if it was. You know it's highly illegal to delve into someone's personnel file without authorisation?'

'And you know I wouldn't ask if it wasn't important.'

'You owe me, Banks. Big time. Name?'

'Wallis, Christine. Served in your pogue area – C1 – with the Div from eighty-nine to ninety-four.'

'OK. Might take a while, buddy. It's Miller time over here right now.'

'At least you're not making up some bullshit excuse. Enjoy your beer, but see if you can get back to me first thing tomorrow, pal. I may not be in phone range for long.'

'You got it. Stay safe, bro.'

'All the way, *sir*,' said Jed, giving the catchcry that enlisted men used when saluting an officer in the 82nd Airborne.

'Airborne,' said Klein, giving the customary reply, 'you wise-ass sonofabitch.'

Ahead of him, Chris Wallis was taking a right turn off the main road into a township of prefabricated houses. The dwellings here were modest by world standards, but a world away from the tin shanties of Mahombekombe. This, according to the road sign, was Nyamhunga.

Jed soon saw that the appearance of comparative prosperity was just that. He drove past barefoot children and women so thin their knee and elbow joints were thicker than the rest of their limbs. He wondered whether it was AIDS or malnutrition – or possibly both – which seemed to afflict so many of the people who thronged the busy but crumbling sidewalks of the township. He drove past half-stacked market stalls selling bruised fruit and wilting vegetables, roadside tailors, a metal-work shop and a car repair garage where mechanics worked on the pavement, in the sun. He guessed from the stares of the inhabitants that not too many Europeans visited Nyamhunga.

Chris took a left up a side street and Jed instinctively scanned left and right and his rear-view mirror, looking for signs of trouble. He'd been on close personal protection duty before – bodyguarding, in civilian parlance – but everything here looked quiet. Chris parked in front of a Corolla sedan with a smashed-in driver's window. A small boy stopped kicking a beer can and stared at him as he got out of his vehicle. Jed waved and the boy smiled and waved back.

'This is the place,' Chris said as she closed the door of her truck.

Jed looked at the stark, bunker-like concrete building. The bar had no name, but a price list painted on the wall advertised *Scuds* and *Bombers* at four-figure prices. 'Scuds?' Jed said to Chris.

'Slang for the big plastic containers of local beer. A bomber is a seven-fifty-mil bottle of lager.'

'Sounds like the lunchtime crowd is already in full swing.' Muted peals of laughter could be heard over the blare of music.

'Be careful in there, Jed,' Chris said, placing a hand on his arm.

He was surprised by her touch, and her concern. 'I take it you won't be accompanying me?'

'Thanks, but I think I'll sit this round out. Most of the ladies in these places tend to be there on business.'

'I'll bring you back a scud. You gonna be OK out here alone?'

'I'll be fine. You watch your back.'

'Call in an air strike if I'm not out in twenty minutes.'

'I'm serious. Don't spend all day in there.'

Jed walked through the rusted security gates. The front yard was littered with beer cans and brown plastic containers about the size of large coffee jars – disarmed scuds, he presumed.

Inside it took a few moments for his eyes to adjust to the gloom. The floor was bare concrete. The place smelled strongly of cigarettes and yeasty beer, and faintly of vomit, or urine, or maybe both. So far, nothing he hadn't encountered in a thousand other bars around the world. The place was about half full, with people mostly sitting on bare wooden benches along the walls. He felt a couple of dozen pairs of eyes on him as he strode to the bar. In the far corner of the room a man sat on the floor with his back against the wall. He was asleep, or unconscious. An upturned scud lay next to him on its side. A pool of dark beer was slowly drying around him.

'Beer, please,' he said to the middle-aged barmaid. She wore a low-cut white blouse which her ample breasts fought hard to escape.

'What type?'

'I'll have what he had.' Jed motioned to the comatose patron on the floor.

'*Chibuku?*' she asked, wide-eyed.

'What?'

'African beer. Most of . . . most visitors don't really like it. We serve it warm.'

'Something cold will be just fine.'

The barmaid reached into an old-fashioned top-loading chest fridge and pulled out a bottle of Castle Lager. She deftly took the top off.

'Planning on staying with us long?' she asked, looking past him with a wary eye at the crowd of mostly male drinkers.

Jed noticed the boisterous conversation had dropped to murmurs and whispers. 'Long as it takes.'

'For what?'

'To finish this beer, and maybe another, and to find someone.'

'You're American.'

'Does it show?'

She chuckled. 'Are you a hunter?'

He thought about the question for a second. 'Yes. A friend of mine recommended a guide. Moses Nyati.'

The woman shrieked. She covered her mouth with her hand and doubled over as her whole body shook with laughter.

Suddenly she straightened and stopped. Jed looked over his shoulder and saw two men had entered the bar. He knew from a first glance that they were bad news. He judged them to be in their early twenties. Knock-off designer T-shirts and black jeans, gold chains and dressy, but heavy, boots. Both big, one with a scar running down his right cheek. Both had shaved heads.

The nearer of the two took off his black wraparound sunglasses and scanned the room. He nodded towards the sleeping man and his partner said, 'That's him.'

'Go now, quickly,' the barmaid whispered to him. 'You're not the only one after Moses.'

'That's him? The dead guy?'

The woman nodded. 'He's not dead. Not yet, anyway.'

Jed walked across the room to where the man was slumped. He dropped to one knee, feeling the eyes of the two thugs drilling into his back. He grabbed the man by the shoulder and shook him.

'Moses? Moses Nyati?'

The man didn't respond, so he shook harder. 'Hey! Wake up. Moses?'

Slowly, painfully, Moses Nyati opened one bloodshot eye, and then the other. He burped, long and loud, and Jed recoiled involuntarily.

'What? Who are you?'

'I'm looking for a tracker. I was told you were the best.' Jed wondered what he was getting himself into. The man's head lolled to one side and he burped again. He was either completely wasted or sleeping off the mother of all hangovers.

Moses shook his head and winced at the resulting pain.

'I think it might be better if we talked outside.' Jed offered his hand. He looked over his shoulder and saw the two heavies were approaching.

'We have business with this man,' one of the men said to Jed.

'So do I, friend.'

'I suggest you leave this place now,' the second man said.

'We're going,' Jed said, hauling Moses to his feet. He was surprised by the man's weight, not to mention his height, as he swayed unsteadily. Moses was easily six-five and had a heavyweight's build, though he looked anything but ready for a fight right at this moment.

'Not "we". Just you. Leave now, man.' The man switched to an African language and spoke rapidly to Moses.

'Maybe you should leave, boss,' Moses croaked.

'What's the problem?'

'Money.'

'How much?'

'Too much.'

The first man brushed past Jed and drove his fist into Moses's stomach. Too groggy even to try to evade the blow, the big man doubled over and fell back against the wall.

'It's time to pay up, Moses,' his assailant said as he stepped forwards and drew back his fist for a second strike.

Jed grabbed the man's arm and he turned around, fast. But not fast enough. Jed warded off the man's redirected punch and landed a sharp left hook on his jaw. The man's bald head snapped back and he reeled, fighting for his balance. Jed knew the man's partner would be behind him, so he stepped back and drove his right elbow rearwards, hard and fast, catching the second guy in the gut. He snapped his forearm straight back up and smacked the back of his fist into the man's nose. Jed spun on one foot and jabbed two more blows into the man's solar plexus.

The first man was recovering and now closed on Jed. Any time, Moses, Jed said to himself. Feel free to join in.

Jed bunched both fists and rocked from one foot to the other, waiting for the man to make his move. 'Maybe you should leave, friend,' he said.

'This is my country, *friend*.' The man reached into the pocket of his jacket and Jed heard a snap as the spring-loaded blade popped out of the flick-knife.

Jed sidestepped the first lunge and then stepped back, leading his attacker across the room. The bar's other patrons had gravitated to the walls, but none of them was going to miss out on – or join in – this fight. The man lunged again and Jed jumped back, landing on both feet like a cat. The pool table was behind him and he reached around for the cue he had seen before.

'Shit!' he said as he ran his hand along the felt tabletop.

'Lose something, white boy?' a scar-faced man called from the far wall as he brandished the cue. A few of the other patrons laughed.

The attacker slashed the blade in a wide arc, aiming for Jed's stomach, but he was too slow. Jed jumped again, landing on the table on his butt, and then rolled into a backwards somersault down the length of the green felt. He swung himself off the other end and reached into one of the pockets.

His assailant bolted towards him, but Jed was already moving. He kept the table between them and they circled it, like kids playing tag.

'Get up,' the first man called to his comrade, who was groggily rising to his feet. 'Come help me finish off this stupid tourist.'

The second man drew a weapon himself, a wicked-looking cutthroat razor. He gathered his senses and courage and charged straight for Jed. The first man came around the table from the opposite direction, planning on trapping him.

Jed drew back his arm and threw the pool ball as hard as he could. It hit the first man between the eyes with a crack and he crumpled. Jed turned but was too late – the second man's arm was a blur as he slashed. He felt the sting on his forearm as he instinctively raised it to ward off the blow. Jed reeled backwards and lost his footing in a puddle of beer. He dropped to one knee, his arm still up. Hot blood dripped from his elbow onto the slick concrete. The man kicked him in the stomach and he doubled forwards onto both knees.

'Your mother won't recognise your face after I've finished with you,' the man said, drawing his arm back for another cut.

Jed turned over to one side, beer and blood soaking his shirt. The razor flashed within inches of his face. The man swung back in the opposite direction. Jed rolled towards the edge of the dance floor, sending other patrons scattering. He was against the wall now. No escape. He wished he had a gun. He grabbed an empty beer bottle by the neck and smashed it on the floor.

The man laughed and lashed out with his booted foot, shattering the bottle easily. Jed threw the splintered remains at the man's face, but he dodged to one side and the glass sailed harmlessly across the bar.

'You're finished, my friend, well and truly.' The man raised his hand and the razor sparkled evilly as it caught the golden light from the low-amp bulb in the ceiling.

There was the sound of wood snapping and the man dropped to his knees in front of Jed. The broken end of the pool cue landed at Jed's feet and he looked up to see Moses Nyati, towering, hungover and smiling, holding the splintered other half in his hands. He held out a huge hand and Jed grasped it for a moment, then yelled, 'Behind you!'

Moses turned. The first man, blood streaming from the gash between his eyes where the pool ball had hit him, was drawing a silver-coloured revolver from his pocket. 'I was hoping it wouldn't come to this, Moses. But this is how it ends.' He cocked the pistol and started to raise it.

'Wrong, asshole.'

Jed looked around Moses's bulk and saw Chris Wallis ram the muzzle of a Glock automatic pistol into the gunman's temple. The man started to turn.

'Drop it, motherfucker. Now!'

Jed was as impressed with her profanity as he was with her timing –

not to mention the accessory she carried. The thug kept the pistol in his hand and tried again to turn to get a look at the woman.

Chris shoved the pistol so hard into the man's temple that his head rocked across to his opposite shoulder. 'I SAID DROP THE FUCKING GUN!' Finally, the man got the message. The revolver clattered to the ground and Jed scooped it up.

'Time to go, boys,' Chris said to Jed and Moses.

'Yes, madam,' Moses said, then laughed.

'Consider this man's debt cancelled and the police will hear nothing of this,' Jed said to the two men as he, Moses and Chris backed out of the gloomy bar, pistols raised and ready.

'Get in the truck, quick,' Chris said once they were outside.

'Wait a minute.' Jed opened the door of his vehicle and reached into his daypack for his Leatherman. He strode across to the black BMW that hadn't been there when they first arrived. 'This their car?'

'Yes, but hurry,' Chris said. 'Here they come.'

Jed unfolded the sharp knife blade. He stabbed the two front tyres of the Beamer while Chris kept the wounded gangsters at bay with her levelled Glock. The nose of the car sagged as the air rushed out.

'OK. Moses, climb in,' Jed said.

'Let me drive, boss. You're cut bad.'

Jed looked at his arm for the first time and saw the guide was right. He reached in his pocket, also aware of the pain for the first time, and tossed Moses the keys.

'I'll lead,' said Chris. 'Let's go!'

Once they were out of Nyamhunga, Chris pulled over at a picnic site on the main road into Kariba and jogged back to Jed's Land Rover.

'Here, take this, it'll slow the blood flow until we get back to the hotel.'

Jed knew what was in the small green packet without reading the writing on the wrapper. It was a US Army field dressing.

'Want some help, boss?' Moses asked as Chris got back in her vehicle.

'I can handle it. Just keep up with her . . . and don't call me boss.'

'Right, sah.'

Jed ripped the dressing open with his teeth, placed the sterile pad on the cut and wrapped the bandage attached to it around and around his arm. He was sore, but his heart still thudded with adrenaline from the fight.

They followed Chris back up to the Lake View Inn.

'Come to my room, Jed, I'll fix you up there,' she said, pulling a bulging green rucksack from the back of her Land Rover. Jed recognised the pack as a combat medic's kit, again US Army issue.

'Moses, why don't you wait for us on the terrace? Have a cup of coffee, or a beer or something.'

'Sure, just one thing . . .'

Jed fished in his pocket with his good hand and pulled out some Zimbabwe dollars.

'I'll pay you back. By the way, can you tell me what this is all about?'

'I'll take the money out of your first day's pay. The rest of the story can wait.'

Moses thanked him again and headed for the terrace.

'Excuse the mess,' Chris said as she opened the door to her hotel room. 'Once I left the military I promised myself I would never submit to neatness again.'

'Did someone drop a grenade in here?' Jed found it hard to believe one person could strew so much junk around in such a short time.

'Get that field dressing off and run some water over the wound. Use the bathroom,' Chris said as she unzipped the first-aid kit on the unmade double bed.

Jed turned on the bathroom light and saw more clothes tossed around. He couldn't help but notice she had washed out her underwear and left it hanging on the shower rail. There were two thongs, one black, one red, and a black sports bra. He thought she might look pretty good in them.

He unwrapped the bloody bandage and peeled the dressing off the wound. The cut stung as he ran cold water over it, and fresh blood started to well up.

'Here, let me help.'

Chris was behind and, given the confines of the small bathroom, she had to reach around him to place a clean gauze pad over the weeping wound.

'Turn around,' she said. 'There's blood on your shirt. Let's get it off.'

He stood in front of her, holding the gauze in place as she unbuttoned his khaki shirt. He could smell her hair as she bent forwards to get the last couple of buttons. The scent of her shampoo and the sight of her underwear strung around the bathroom brought on an involuntary reaction. He hoped she wouldn't notice.

She looked up and smiled as she pulled the shirt off him.

'Where did you get that?' She ran the tip of her finger around a white puckered circle the size of a dime, just below his right collarbone.

'Somalia. Lucky shot.'

'Lucky for who?'

'My buddy, who the bad guy was aiming for. For the bad guy, because he managed to hit at least one of us, and for me, because it missed the lung by an inch or so.'

She let her finger linger for a second. 'Exit wound?'

He turned and pointed to a lump at the very top of his back, just below the ridgeline of his shoulder.

'You *were* lucky. Through and through, too close for the bullet to start tumbling.'

She touched him again and he shivered. He was facing the mirror and he caught her eyes in the reflection when he looked up. He turned around again, noticing that her nipples were straining against the fabric of her shirt.

She turned and headed back out into the bedroom. 'Come and let me see to that wound. Sit down on the bed.'

She brushed a strand of hair away from her forehead and knelt on the carpet in front of him. 'Hold your arm out for me.' She squirted iodine around the wound and Jed winced.

'Be still, big brave soldier boy. It won't sting for long.'

'I've had worse.'

'I'm just going to put some of these butterfly plasters on it. That should keep it closed.' When she finished she wrapped the wound in a bandage. 'That should do it. We need to keep it clean where we're going.'

'That's quite a first-aid kit you have there, and you seem to know what to do with it,' he said, flexing his fingers.

'I did the combat survival course when I was with the 82nd and bought this kit from an Army and Navy store back home a couple of years ago. In the places where I work you need more than a packet of Band-Aids and some Tylenol.'

'What else is in there?'

'The usual. Saline, sharps kit, sutures, field dressings, splints, pain-killers. But for now I prescribe a cold beer. I could certainly use one and you probably don't want to keep your friend waiting.'

'You're right,' he said, although he wouldn't have minded sitting and talking to her in private for a while longer. 'Thanks, Christine.'

'Chris is better. And don't mention it – it wasn't exactly major surgery.'

'No, I mean thanks for before as well. Those guys had us on the ropes. You were pretty cool, looked like you knew what you were doing. Are you always armed over here?'

'Whenever I go on long journeys outside the national parks. Four-footed predators I can deal with – it's the two-legged variety you can't always predict.'

She picked up her keys. 'Come on, let's go see your friend.'

An hour ago Jed would have resented the fact that she was inviting herself along to see Moses – he would have felt she was intruding on him, shadowing him. Now, after the scuffle with the thugs, it was as though they had broken through a barrier. She had got him out of a tight spot and he was man enough to cut her some slack as a payback.

Jed carried his blood-stained shirt back to his room and Chris waited outside as he put on a fresh one. When he emerged, they walked together to the bar.

Moses sat at a table by the wrought-iron railing. A lithe young waitress was standing close beside him, laughing at something he had just said. He stood when he saw Jed and Chris approaching.

'What would you like to drink, boss? Madam?'

Jed smiled. 'Beer, please.' He noticed Moses was drinking Coke, and appreciated that the man hadn't used his first advance to get hammered.

'Same for me,' Chris said. 'And Moses, it's Chris. Call me madam again and I'll shoot you where you'll feel it most.'

He laughed. 'I do believe you would, Chris.'

They all sat down and Moses looked expectantly at Jed.

'OK. Can you tell me now where we're going? Is this trip for business or pleasure?'

'Business, I'm afraid,' Jed said.

'I'm a man looking for business. But it's been very slow. Even the hunters are going elsewhere these days.'

Jed leaned over. 'I don't want to be rude, Moses, but first up, what were those men after you for?'

'Money. Nothing illegal. I fell behind on payments on my Land Cruiser. I took out a loan from one of them to cover my original repayments. Stupid, I know, but I had a hunting contract lined up, just needed to cover things for a few weeks until the client arrived. He was a German. He never showed.'

'How much do you owe them?'

'Two million dollars.'

'For a Toyota?' Jed asked, eyes wide.

'Zimbabwe dollars. It's about two hundred of your American dollars.'

'And they were coming after you with a gun and a razor for a couple hundred bucks?'

'That's a lot of money here. They would have repossessed my truck, except I've hidden it.'

'How much do you charge as a guide?'

'Fifty a day.'

112

'Zimbabwean dollars?'

Moses laughed. 'No, American.'

'I don't know if what I'm offering will stretch to four days, but if you want the job, it's yours,' Jed said.

'Sure, what is it?'

Jed explained about Miranda's disappearance and his desire to repatriate her, one way or another.

'I read about her in the newspaper. It's hard to lose a child, I know.'

'I'm sorry for your loss,' Chris said. 'You're married?'

Moses nodded. 'I have a wife and one son. We had a daughter. She was two years old when she died. In another country, a trip to a hospital might have saved her. I had the money – they ask you to pay in advance in Zimbabwe – but the hospital didn't have the drugs. I had to cross the border into Zambia, using a temporary travel document, and get a bus to Lusaka. By the time I got home, my daughter was dead. My wife and I . . . it got hard for us after the girl died. Being out of work hasn't made it easier.'

'I want to know for sure what happened to my daughter,' Jed said to Moses.

'I can't offer you false hope. If your daughter wasn't killed by a lion and she hasn't shown up by now, she probably died from some other cause. I don't think we're going to find her lost in the bush.'

Jed took a sip of his beer and stared out over the shimmering lake. 'I know, Moses. To tell you the truth, I don't know what I hope to find, or even what I'm looking for. If nothing else, by spending some time in the African bush at least I'll get a feeling of what was so important to her these last few months.'

'The African bush I can certainly show you.'

'Excuse me, please, I want to watch this,' Chris said suddenly.

She hurried between the tables and stood in front of the bar, staring up at a television mounted on a shelf above the spirit bottles.

Jed turned and strained to hear what was being said. He saw pictures of westerners carrying bags filing onto buses outside an office building. The caption on the bottom of the screen said *US embassy*

113

staff evacuated from Tanzania.

'What's going on?' Moses asked.

'Another bomb threat, I guess.' After six months in Afghanistan Jed had ceased to be surprised by the reach of global terrorism.

'The sooner we get to the bush, the better,' Moses said, raising his Coke bottle.

'Amen to that, Moses.' Jed clinked his bottle with the guide's, but his enthusiasm for their coming safari was hollow. He was, after all, looking for proof that his only child was dead.

8

Hassan bin Zayid wiped his sweaty palm on his Tommy Hilfiger T-shirt then returned it to the grip on the throttle of the outboard motor.

The inflatable Zodiac tender bore the name *Faith* in white on its sleek, grey rubber flank, the lettering the same as that on his forty-foot motor cruiser. Underneath the name was the port of registration, *Zanzibar*. While Hassan spent most of his time these days at his private game reserve in Zambia, he would always consider the aromatic island off the coast of mainland Tanzania his real home.

It was to Zanzibar that he had retreated to deal with the shock of the news that had come by telephone a few days earlier. As he had sat in the cool, dark interior of the lodge's bar, nursing three fingers of Scotch on ice, he had realised that the one person left in the world whom he truly loved was dead.

He had summoned Juma, the lodge's manager in his absence and his personal valet while Hassan was in residence. Juma was a devout Muslim, so Hassan did not insult him by offering him alcohol. Instead, he poured the tall African a glass of orange juice as he walked into the bar.

'Sit, old friend,' Hassan said.

Juma nodded and seated himself on a bar stool. 'I am sorry for your loss. I feel your pain.'

'Thank you, Juma. Things have changed for me with this news. I must leave the lodge.'

Juma nodded again. 'You will go to Zanzibar?'

'Yes. And I may not return.'

Juma's eyes widened. His whole adult life had been in the service of Hassan bin Zayid and Hassan's father. His mother had been Hassan's mother's maid. He and the handsome, pale-skinned heir to the family fortune had played together as children. Hassan's schooling abroad had separated them, but the bond between them could never be severed, not even when they had inevitably settled into a master–servant relationship. 'Am I to stay here?'

'For the time being. There are things we need to discuss, you and I. You have served my family, served me all your life.'

'Yes. Willingly.' Juma suddenly feared that his employment was about to be terminated, along with his association with the sad-eyed man opposite him.

Hassan forced a smile, but only a brief one. 'Don't worry, old friend. I'm not giving you the sack. In fact, I need you now more than ever. I need to know if you will help me through this difficult time.'

'You know I would die for you.'

There was an awkward silence. Neither man was given to emotional outbursts – not in front of another man, at least – and the declaration took them both a little by surprise. Hassan felt tears welling up behind his eyes, but blinked them back. 'Thank you, Juma, but I hope it won't come to that.'

Their conversation ended with a set of orders. Once Juma had left, Hassan dialled the number of a travel agency in Dar es Salaam. The owner answered the phone. They exchanged the briefest of pleasantries.

'You are coping . . . with the news?' the man asked.

'I am. I'm planning a trip, away from here for a while. I'm leaving late tonight or early tomorrow. I'd like to catch up with you.' He paced around the stone floor of the bar as he spoke into the portable phone.

116

'That could be difficult. I'm going to be very busy in the next few days.'

Hassan panicked. Having made his decision, and enlisted Juma's support, he could not afford to be brushed off. 'Remember you asked me something a year ago, when you came to stay at my lodge?'

There was a pause on the other end of the line. 'This is not a good time to talk, Hassan.'

'That's why I want to see you in person. But you do remember the conversation? The *business* proposition you put to me last year?'

'Of course.'

'I want in.'

'It's not as easy as that. I'm not even sure you would fit into our organisation.'

Hassan's worry turned to annoyance. 'You were keen enough when you wanted my money.'

'You're not the only rich man in Africa.'

'How about money plus local knowledge and contacts? You know the resources at my disposal.' Hassan was aware the man was just being cautious. It paid to be in his line of business. He guessed he knew that Hassan's change of mind had been brought on by the sudden death of the person closest to him.

'OK, Hassan. We can meet. At the hotel. The one you wanted to buy a few years ago.'

'I'll come by boat. At the beach bar, on Tuesday, midday.'

'I will be there.'

He replaced the portable phone in its cradle and sat down heavily on the bar stool. As he poured another Scotch the shaking in his hand caused the neck of the bottle to tinkle on the rim of the heavy cut-glass tumbler.

He stared again at the photo of himself with his father and twin brother, Iqbal.

The brothers dressed differently, they wore their hair differently, they dated completely different types of women. Who was his girl at the time the photo was taken? Felicity, that was it. The blonde from conservative middle England who'd been a classmate at university. She'd

117

said she loved his hair. She'd sought him out – not surprising as he gave his father's Zanzibar address to almost any pretty girl he met. Iqbal had spoken of a Pakistani girl, from a reputable family, who was returning to her home country. In so many other ways the brothers were growing apart, but neither of them could turn a blind eye to a pretty woman.

Their eyes, however, marked them as twins. So similar, as blue as the Indian Ocean, his mother had always said. Yet even here, in this blurred snapshot, one could see different souls behind each pair of indigo portals. Hassan's sparkled with carefree abandon – he'd either just had sex or was about to, he couldn't quite remember which. Iqbal's were cooler. Distant. Barely tolerating the forced bonhomie of the reunion, eager to get back to something else, something more . . . meaningful. His woman? No, she was already in Pakistan by then, and he would follow a few days after the brief holiday on the island. Was it a woman who had lured his brother so irrevocably away from his own world?

No, he didn't think so. It might have been easier for Hassan to understand his brother, and his fate, if he had been led to it by his prick. But it was something with an even stronger influence, something which Hassan had never had, that separated them so completely.

Faith.

Sometimes, when he sat on the verandah and watched a breathtaking sunset – he remembered one particularly vivid crimson and gold cloud show he and Miranda had witnessed before making love – he was tempted to believe there was a God. But his God, at least the God of his father and his brother, would not tolerate his union with the American woman, an unbeliever. His father had married outside his religion, although Hassan's mother had apparently promised to convert. She never did, though, and her husband never forgave her, and not only for her failure to relinquish Christianity. Neither the Christian nor Muslim god had blessed the union of the elder Hassan bin Zayid, tour guide and coffee-shop owner of Stone Town, Zanzibar, and Margaret Wilks, British Overseas Airways Corporation air hostess, of Buckinghamshire, England.

'The only good thing that ever came of it was you two boys,' their father had told Hassan and Iqbal on many occasions. Usually after he had partaken of the better part of a bottle of expensive Scotch. The funny thing was, Hassan remembered his mother saying almost exactly the same thing when he last saw her. He had few recollections of her from his childhood. Margaret had left Zanzibar for good shortly after the twins' third birthday. All Hassan remembered was a golden-haired woman singing to him and, significantly, crying. The only version Hassan had of the marriage was his father's.

'She left you boys. Abandoned you when you were tiny. What mother would leave her children?'

One night when the boys were eleven they snuck out of their bedroom window and dropped as silently as they could onto the tin roof of the next-door dwelling. It was a favourite game, scrabbling across the interconnected rooftops, peering through skylights and neighbourhood windows, daring each other to leap the gaps between houses. On this night they were returning to bed, after seeing old Mrs Jamal getting undressed – an experience neither of them wanted to repeat – when they overheard their father's baritone voice. The smell of his Marlboro cigarette smoke wafted up from where he sat on the stone steps leading to the reception area of the small hotel he owned. Another man sat in a plastic chair beside the steps. Hassan didn't recognise the stranger's voice, but that didn't matter. Thinking his sons were tucked in bed asleep, his father was telling the story of his failed marriage.

'She was a beauty, that much was true.'

'And good, eh? I hear the English girls *love* it,' the stranger interjected.

Iqbal looked at Hassan with puzzlement in his eyes. He thought his mother was *bad*. Hassan shrugged, just as confused.

The elder bin Zayid gave a little grunt. 'Yes. At first, I suppose. As in any marriage. Except we weren't married.'

'Ah . . . and she got pregnant.'

'It happens, Bilal.'

'But a foreigner . . . why didn't she have an abortion? Surely you offered.'

'I did. But she would not hear of it. I didn't mind marrying her.'

'But your father?'

'God rest his soul, he refused to speak to me.'

'What's an abortion?' Hassan whispered.

Iqbal pantomimed a hand holding a knife, then plunged it into his belly. 'Women kill their own children when they do not want them.'

'No!'

'Yes. Mohamed's sister, the older one. She has a woman's magazine, from England. There is an article in there about it.' Iqbal explained, revelling in his worldliness.

'I'm glad our mother didn't do that!' Hassan said.

'Shush! Listen.'

Their father stubbed out his cigarette. 'Everyone thought I was mad, of course, not just my father. I was shunned but, to tell you the truth, I didn't mind at first. I had a sexy, worldly wife and I wanted the children.'

'So what was the problem?'

'She said she wanted to come live here, to quit her job, to which I said, "Of course, this is the way it should be."'

'What was wrong with that?'

'Even me saying that. She said she was making decisions because they were what *she* wanted, and that if she wanted to return to work when the boys were older, then she would.'

'A woman working while her children are at home? Preposterous.' Bilal shook his head emphatically.

'That's what I told her. I also suggested that she might like to dress a little more conservatively once we were married. That did not go down well either.'

'Why do they insist on dressing like whores, these western women?'

Hassan senior smiled. 'Of course, I didn't mind when we were dating, but she was pregnant with my sons, and we were married, so I naturally thought she would start acting like a proper, modest wife. But me telling her to do things only made her do the opposite.'

'In Pakistan, we know how to treat women.' Bilal held up a fist.

Hassan senior nodded. 'I never hit her. Maybe I should have.'

'Let's go,' Hassan whispered to his brother. He had a feeling he didn't want to hear any more of this conversation. He had recently found a photograph – old, faded, dog-eared – in the drawer of his father's desk. The study was out of bounds, but his ballpoint pen had run out of ink and he needed another in order to finish his homework. His father had been downstairs in reception, welcoming a couple of foreign tourists. Amidst the clutter of the drawer was the picture. It was of a slender, fair-haired woman in a uniform. She was standing outside the terminal at Zanzibar airport, the name visible in the background. She had one hand on her hip and a handbag hanging on her shoulder. Hassan had replaced the photo, wondering if it was his mother.

'No, this is just getting interesting,' Iqbal insisted.

'So things got worse?' Bilal asked.

'They were good for a while. She settled down while she was pregnant, but there were problems after the birth.'

'Medical problems?'

'No, it was her head. She was depressed. We had a nanny, of course, an African woman whose husband had drowned while fishing. She had a baby boy of her own, little Juma. Ended up raising my two in the end. But the boys' mother . . . it was as if she didn't want them. It was strange, because she had been against abortion.'

'Women are strange creatures.'

He shrugged. 'Anyway, she got used to the boys, but after a few months she started all that nonsense again about going back to work. I mean, jet-setting around the world, here today, gone tomorrow . . . how can a woman raise kids like that, Bilal?'

'Impossible.'

'Of course, I forbade it. She threatened to divorce me.'

'On what grounds – that you cared about her and wanted her to be a good mother?' Bilal's incredulity was clear from the tone of his voice.

'She said it was like being in prison. Like I was treating her as my slave.'

'This is no prison. More like a palace.' Bilal looked up at the four-storey whitewashed hotel, sandwiched between a souvenir shop and

121

the small cafe Hassan had owned when he met the twins' mother. The boys hastily ducked their heads back away from the rain gutter as the stranger looked up.

'It got worse. I went to the mainland for a few days, on business. I came home a day early and there was a man in my house. An Englishman.'

'A married woman entertaining another man in the family home? Were they . . . ?'

'They were clothed, if that's what you mean. Having coffee at ten in the morning, on *my* balcony, in *my* home. She didn't try to hide him. Said he was a *friend*. That's what made it worse, Bilal, that she had no shame about having a strange man in the house.'

'So, had she been sleeping with him as well?'

'Yes. The truth came out eventually. She said I did not pay enough attention to her, treated her more like a slave than a wife. What a joke. At least from a slave I would have had sex.'

Bilal shook his head and made a clucking noise with his tongue.

'She said the man had just come to offer her a job. He was from the airline. I told her that there was no way she was going back to work. I said her *job* was raising her beautiful young sons. She told me she didn't feel like the children were hers any more, that the nanny was doing a better job than she ever could. In that, Bilal, she was right.'

Hassan thought about what his father had said. It was true: the only motherly figure he had ever known was Aisha, his nanny and Juma's mother.

'It is late, and I should let you get back to your business, Bilal,' Hassan senior said wearily.

'Tell me how it ended.'

He shrugged and stubbed out his cigarette on the hotel steps. 'Simple. She left. No note, for me or the boys. One day we woke up and she was gone. Back to England, I presumed, and the bloody village of Oving in Buckinghamshire where she came from.'

*

122

He sought her out, against his father and brother's strongest wishes, when he started university. All he had to go on was the name of the tiny village, Oving, where her family was from.

Outside the train cold rain pelted the windows of the British Rail service from Marylebone. Inside it was stiflingly hot. The countryside was still alien to him. More a universe than a world away from the cluttered bustle of Stone Town or the palm-fringed white beaches of the coast.

The town of Aylesbury was the end of the line. An overweight lady with a turned-down mouth directed him to the bus terminal. It was the middle of a work day and the bus was empty, save for an elderly couple who ignored him. He was beginning to think the English a cold race. Perhaps some of the bitterness his father felt towards his estranged wife was not totally without merit after all.

Aylesbury's suburbs of crammed council houses soon gave way to verdant pastures and tiny villages of whitewashed cottages with thatched roofs. A ruddy-faced woman in a green waterproof jacket and wellington boots walked a pair of beagles in the drizzle, her breath a white mist. Hassan wondered how his mother could have forsaken Zanzibar's weather, let alone her twin toddler sons.

In Oving, Hassan walked along the grassed verge of a narrow two-lane road and came to the high brick walls of a country manor house. He stopped and stood on tiptoe. Over the wall he could make out man-icured lawns and hedges, and a gravel path fringed with lichen-covered statues. The great home seemed to have a frontage as big as the House of Wonders, the sultan's palace in Stone Town. There was money here. His father was wealthy – he had to be to send two sons out of Tanzania to study: three hotels now, two on Zanzibar and another in Dar on the mainland – but this was a different class of wealth.

'Quite a pile, isn't it?'

Hassan turned and saw a thin-faced man with curly grey hair. He guessed him to be in his early fifties. He wore faded grey overalls and carried a pair of garden shears.

'You look too smartly dressed to be a thief casing the place, but I've not seen you around the village before.' The accent was soft, with a slightly rolling lilt.

'I'm looking for someone, a distant relative,' Hassan replied.

'That so? I'm Ernie. I do most of the gardens around here. Lived in the village all me life.'

'Do you know the Wilks?'

'Mrs Wilks passed away just last year. But you'd know that if you were related, surely?' the gardener said, raising an eyebrow.

Hassan saw the suspicion in the man's eyes. 'I'm from abroad. Tracing the family tree, so I'm not close. Mrs Wilks, you said? That must be . . .' he stopped himself from saying 'my grandmother' as he didn't want news of his arrival all over the village, in case it embarrassed his mother, 'Margaret's mother?'

'Yes, yes. That's right. She's living in the big house, next to her mum's old place.'

'Could you give me some directions to her house, please?'

Ernie looked him up and down, unashamedly assessing him. 'I'm heading that way right now. Doing the hedges at the house two up from Margaret's. I'll take you there.'

Hassan had to stretch his legs to keep up with the older man as he turned down a narrow lane that led to the heart of the tiny village. At the end of the street he saw a quaint pub, called the Black Boy, and an old stone church. Ernie stopped outside a thatched cottage with a bed of red roses out the front.

'This is it,' he said.

Hassan opened the wooden gate. He looked back and saw Ernie waiting. Probably wanted to make sure everything was OK, Hassan thought. He was suddenly very much *not* OK. His heart thudded. His mouth was dry. He wiped his hands on his jeans. There was a heavy brass knocker on the wooden door. He knocked and a few moments later the door opened.

It was her. He had sneaked a peek at the photograph in his father's desk drawer whenever he could, until he had been caught. His father had said nothing, simply taken the picture from him and torn it into tiny pieces. She was still beautiful, though there was something not quite right about her. Her hair was blonde, her eyes the same blue as his, but they were shadowed and recessed too far into their sockets. Her face was too thin. She wore a baggy red jumper over jeans that encased slender legs. In her high-heeled boots she was only an inch or two shorter than his six feet. She put a hand to her mouth.

'Morning, Margaret,' Ernie called from the gate. 'This fellow says he's family. I showed him the way here.'

She blinked. 'Um, yes. Thanks, Ernie. Good of you to help. I've been expecting him for some time.'

Ernie looked puzzled, but nodded and forced a smile. 'I'll be on my way, then. Just doing Joanne's hedges.'

She waved, to show him she was all right.

'I'm . . .' Hassan began.

'I know who you are.'

It hadn't been anger in her voice, or surprise, or resentment. Certainly not love. More a tone of resignation, as though she had, indeed, been expecting him and now he had finally come.

'You'd best come in, Hassan.'

He wiped his muddy feet on the doormat and had to duck a little to get through the door. It was warm inside. The furniture was modern, in contrast with the seventeenth-century exterior. The ceiling was not much higher than the doorframe and, though he could stand up straight, he felt very confined. 'How did you know it was me, and not . . .'

'Iqbal? You were the same when you were tiny. You were always hanging off my skirt, and Iqbal was always running after his father. I knew that it would be you if either of you ever came looking for me. Sit down, I've just boiled the kettle. Tea?'

He was suddenly very angry. There was so much to talk about, so much for her to explain, and she wanted to make *tea*. He had expected an outpouring of emotion. 'Coffee, if that's OK.'

He took a seat on the white leather sofa and looked around the small living room.

'Are you living in England or just visiting?' she asked from the kitchen.

His eyes were drawn to a beechwood wall unit. Above the television was a family portrait. His mother, but not his family. A man with red hair in a uniform of some kind, two girls, in their early teens by the look of it. Pretty, with Margaret's eyes. His eyes. 'Studying. I'm doing a degree in economics at Cambridge.'

She returned with two cups and took a seat in an armchair opposite him. 'Good for you. I'm pleased you turned out smart. Pleased Hassan is making enough money to send you abroad to study. And Ikkie?'

Hassan smiled. He knew how much his twin would hate that baby-ish nickname. 'Arts, with a philosophy major, at Cape Town. He wasn't interested in coming to England.'

She noticed him looking at the photo again. 'I remarried. Soon after . . . soon after I returned home.'

'The man in the photo, your husband. He is a pilot?'

'Yes,' she said guardedly, trying to guess how much he knew, how much he had been told.

'You left my father, us, for him.' He blurted it out.

She moved from the armchair to the sofa, sat down next to him, put a hand on his. Her touch was cold, her fingers bony. He looked into her eyes. No tears, only that same resignation he had seen earlier.

'I'm not proud of what happened. Not pleased with myself, but not really ashamed either. What he wouldn't have told you, Hassan, was that I *tried*. I tried damn hard to make a go of it. I was young, in trouble. I suppose you know you and your brother were conceived before we married?'

He nodded.

'I loved Zanzibar. I think I loved your father, for a time. But that island paradise quickly became a prison for me. He wouldn't let me work, wouldn't let me travel, hardly let me out on the street, wanted me to become something I couldn't.'

'He is a good man,' Hassan mumbled.

'God, I know that. And I'm a *good* woman. Ask anyone in the village!' She forced a smile, but he was unmoved. 'The point is, Hassan, that I couldn't live like that. When it was over, when I knew I had to leave, I wanted to take the two of you with me.'

'You did?' Surprise and disbelief permeated the two words.

'Of course. Don't you think I loved you? Your father called in the lawyers, made all kinds of threats.'

'He said, once, that you did not want us once we were born, that you rejected us.'

'He would, wouldn't he? Postnatal depression, Hassan. Look it up in any medical book. I had it. Boy oh boy, did I have it. Hardly surprising given that I was thousands of miles from home, imprisoned by a domineering husband and stuck in a stone house in one hundred and five degree heat!'

He shrugged.

'I got over it, Hassan, and learned to love you both, but I still couldn't change my world, my circumstances, for the better. Also, by then that bloody Aisha was virtually caring for you and Iqbal twenty-four hours a day. She hated me, and I her from the start. I'm surprised your father didn't marry her.'

Hassan was taken off guard by her comment. Although when he thought about it, the idea of his father having some sort of romantic involvement with his nanny didn't seem so strange. She was still an attractive woman, full-breasted with a sensual mouth and dark, inviting eyes.

'I don't suppose he told you I tried to come back, to visit you both?'

'No.'

'Well, I did. Two years after I left. I was back at work with the airline. Three separate times I tried. He wouldn't let me past the door of the cafe. On my last visit I tracked down the school you were both attending. I stood at the fence, picked you two out immediately. I wanted to come inside, to hold you, to tell you I loved you.'

'But you didn't.'

'God, the teachers would have had a fit. A strange, blubbering white woman barging in to molest two little boys.'

He didn't smile at her levity, just wondered what else had kept her at the fence. He finished his coffee. Suddenly he wanted out of this poky little cottage. He understood her reasons for leaving, even guessed that his father's cloying love might be misconstrued as dominance, but he doubted he could ever really forgive her. 'I'm sorry for taking so much of your time.'

'You're leaving already?'

No hug, no invitation to stay, to meet his stepsisters. Not that he expected or wanted either. 'There's another bus soon. Forgive me for saying so, but you look a little tired, like you need a rest.'

She shrugged as they stood. 'Need more than a rest. Radiotherapy takes it out of you.'

'You're ill?'

'Breast cancer, Hassan. The doctors aren't hopeful . . . But please, if you want to visit again . . .'

'I hope your treatment goes well. And thank you, but I doubt I'll be back.'

'Don't leave angry.'

They were at the door now. It was a day of shocks and now he simply felt numb. The news the mother he'd never known was dying was just one more revelation. He found it hard to arrange his thoughts. He needed fresh air. 'I'm not angry.'

'I can't do the tearful reunion, Hassan. I'm sorry, but I can't. I've got a new family now and I'm faced with the problem of how to say good-bye to them.'

The door was open now and she wrapped her bony arms around herself to ward off the chill and, he thought, to avoid any public display of emotion. She smiled. 'Bet you have to fight the girls off?'

He shrugged, embarrassed by the question. How could he tell her his first sexual experience had been with a blonde English girl, a back-packer staying at his father's Stone Town hotel? His subsequent conquests had all been western girls as well, Dutch, German, Swiss and two more Britons. What would she make of that? 'Better run if I'm going to catch the bus.'

'Stay well, Hassan. If you do want to come again, do me a favour and call first. Will you tell your brother you saw me?'

He thought for a moment. 'No. I don't think so.'

'Probably best. It'll be enough for me, as things draw to a close, to know that you realised that I did try.'

'I understand. Goodbye then.' No contact. No kiss, no hug, not even a handshake. All so damnably British.

He never saw her again, didn't know whether she had fought off the cancer or died in pain. It wasn't hatred he felt, or bitterness. Just resignation. He had *tried*, as she had. About as hard as she had, he reckoned.

His university days were enjoyable. He spent his free time like any other student did, partying, drinking and doing his best to have sex with as many members of the opposite gender as he could. In the last endeavour his good looks and exotic background gave him an edge over most of his fellow students. He preferred blondes with blue eyes, and there was no shortage of them in the university and the bars of Cambridgeshire.

The girls he'd met invariably asked him how often he'd gone on safari and what he knew of Africa's big game. The first few times he'd been embarrassed to admit he knew little of the continent of his birth beyond Zanzibar's white sand shores. He'd seen his first rhinoceros at a wildlife park in Bedfordshire, of all places. He'd started reading up on African wildlife in his spare time. What began as another way to impress girls turned into an interest, and, after a couple of visits to Tanzania's Serengeti National Park during college vacations, something of a passion.

Having fulfilled his father's wish for him to take a business qualification, he returned to Zanzibar after graduation and threw himself into more study, this time a subject of his own choosing – zoology. By day he worked for his father in the Stone Town hotel. After a year he took over the family's shabbiest hotel, in Dar es Salaam, and turned it from a run-down dive frequented by sailors, truck drivers and whores into a trendy, vibrant backpackers' lodge. The hotel's rooftop bar with its eclectic mix of carved African curios, Persian rugs and western music drew overland tour groups and independent travellers from other hotels in the port city. Most travellers through the region stopped over in Dar on their way across to Zanzibar. Sometimes a pretty girl – or two – usually fair-haired, would stay over a few extra nights, at no extra cost. The cash he generated from the fleapit-turned-hotspot helped him finance his first solo commercial purchase, the luxury bush lodge on the Zambezi River, in the wilds of Zambia.

He had come far, successful in business in his own right, and independently wealthy since his father's death. He had spent the last few years indulging his two great passions – beautiful women and African wildlife.

But Miranda Banks-Lewis had offered him the one thing that was missing in his life. True love. Such a confusing, alien emotion, it had surprised him like the sudden rearing of a cobra in the grass. She had everything he might ever look for in a mate – beauty, intelligence and a passion for wildlife conservation. He had made his decision, had decided to commit himself to her totally, to curb his hedonistic tendencies.

Hassan sighed and squinted, even though he was wearing sunglasses, at the bright whiteness of the sandy beach in front of the low-rise luxury resort just north of Dar es Salaam.

The nose of the Zodiac fell, like his spirits, as he cut the power to the outboard motor. He had chanced everything on the beautiful American researcher, had risked his emotions just as he had when he confronted his mother. And, as in England, he had gambled and lost. The man he had come to meet slid off his stool under the beach bar's awning and walked down the sand to greet him.

9

Jed woke up with a hangover. He was drinking too much, but he didn't care – he was looking for evidence his daughter was dead. He showered, then smoked a cigarette while he dressed. Outside the lake shimmered pale-gold in the dawn's light.

Christine had suggested they make an early start. She had grown silent after watching the news report and had never really rejoined their conversation as he and Moses swapped stories and male bullshit. She had left them straight after dinner, while he and Moses stayed behind for more drinks – beer for Jed and coffee for Moses. He liked the big Zimbabwean and felt at ease in his company.

Moses, Jed had learned, had been kicked out of the family home the night before he and Chris found him and had slept in the bar. It wasn't the first time it had happened. From what the tracker told him, the drop-off in tourism and hunting had left the family increasingly short of money. Moses's wife had a job as a sales assistant in a clothing shop. The pay was lousy, but her husband hadn't made a cent in two months. Jed sensed the big man's shame at his lack of employment. While he disapproved of the fact that Moses had been able to find enough cash to get dead drunk, he was pretty sure he believed the African when he said his latest binge was not a regular occurrence.

'I do lots of things my wife accuses me of, Jed,' Moses had told him as he finished his black coffee. 'I am not a saint, but I don't drink when I'm working for a client and I wouldn't let my child starve. If I do a good job for you, I can go home with money in my pocket and my head held high. It has been a long time since that happened.'

Jed had offered to pay for a hotel room for him for the night, but Moses had taken a cab back to Nyamhunga to ready his gear for the trip. Jed arranged to pick him up at the turn-off from the main road to the township the next morning.

Jed packed his gear and checked out of the hotel. There was no sign of Chris in the car park, so he smoked another cigarette while he waited, savouring the mild morning air, which would soon give way to another hot, sticky day.

'Sorry I'm late, I was making a call home,' she said, hurrying up the stone steps from reception.

'Let me give you a hand with those.' He reached for the aluminium case she was carrying.

'It's OK,' she said, holding the bag away from him. 'You could give me a hand with the pack, though.'

'Sure. What's in there anyway?' He nodded to the silver-coloured case.

'Photographic gear. It's expensive.'

He nodded, tossed her backpack into the rear of her Land Rover and stood aside while she loaded the case.

It was a beautiful morning. As they climbed up out of the valley Chris slowed her Land Rover and Jed geared down to keep the interval between them. He wasn't sure why she had dropped her speed to a crawl, nor why she turned on her right-hand indicator, even though there was no side road. He looked again at the trees to his right. Emerging from the forest was a zebra. He was surprised to see the exotic animal so close to a built-up area. In his mind, animals were found on the savanna or in dense jungles, not on the side of a black-top highway within view of a busy town.

The zebra stopped at the edge of the tree line and sniffed the air. Jed could see now it was a stallion. He was fascinated by the way its stripes continued unbroken from its body up into its bristling mane. The animal turned and stared at Chris's Land Rover for a few seconds, then continued walking. Four more zebra, including a tiny foal on spindly legs in the middle of the procession, emerged from the trees and crossed the road in front of them. A zebra crossing, Jed thought to himself, smiling at his own stupid joke.

God, he wished Miranda was with him.

Moses was waiting for them at the Nyamhunga turn-off, sitting by the side of the road on a green canvas rucksack.

'Climb in.' Jed reached across to open the passenger door and Moses tossed his pack onto the back seat.

They drove on in companionable silence for a while.

'Lion,' Moses said.

'What?'

'Lion,' he repeated, matter-of-factly.

'Where?'

'Up ahead. Slow down now. See her?'

Jed's heart was racing as he scanned the road ahead and the bush on either side. 'I still can't see it.'

'Flash your lights – Christine hasn't seen it yet either.'

Chris caught the winking lights in her rear-view mirror and slowed down.

'Look, to the left, at about ten o'clock. A lioness. Here she comes now.'

Jed strained, holding a hand up to shield his eyes from the morning sun's glare. 'I see her!'

'She is alone. She has young cubs denned somewhere. See how full her teats are. She is waiting for the cubs to grow stronger before she takes them back to the pride. She's returning from a night hunt.'

'How can you tell?'

'See the dried blood around her mouth.'

The lioness was big. Long-limbed, spare, all muscle – now that he looked closer Jed could see how her belly bulged with the night's kill. As she crossed the road she paused for a couple of seconds and bared long yellowed fangs, panting slightly as she stared at Jed's vehicle.

Jed felt a chill down his back at the sight of her. He wasn't scared so much as awed by the raw power the animal exuded. He took in the rippling neck muscles, the huge padded paws, the pitiless amber eyes. Here was power, pure and simple: nature's ultimate killer. He could barely imagine the primal terror her victims felt as those powerful jaws entrapped them.

The lioness padded across the tarmac road and disappeared into the long golden grass on the far side.

Jed's pulse was racing. 'Incredible.'

'You're lucky. I haven't seen lions on this road very often.'

'Tell me, what would she have done if I'd got out of the car?'

'One of two things. Most likely, she would have run away. She's used to seeing cars, but the silhouette of a man means danger for most animals. On the other hand, if her cubs are close by, and she considered you a threat to them, she would have charged and killed you.'

The road snaked upwards, the gradient getting steeper and the hair-pin bends tighter as they made for the ridgeline that carried the main road from Harare. The rolling tree-covered hills that stretched away in front of them were beautiful, studded with flat-topped acacia trees. The road followed the ridge for a while and, as they drove through a high pass, Jed again caught a glimpse of the wide valley below, then they dropped down and started their descent into the Zambezi Valley. Jed saw a cluster of buildings ahead and to their left.

'This is Marongora,' Moses said, 'where we have to sign in and get permits to enter the national park.'

The two vehicles crunched up a curving gravel driveway and stopped under a shady tree, outside a single-storey building painted a dull olive-green. An assortment of large whitewashed animal skulls was dotted around the pathway leading to the National Parks building. It was cool inside the office and Jed scanned a large-scale map of the Zambezi Valley pinned to the wall as Moses and Christine went through the formalities of arranging permits. Both of them greeted the ranger behind the desk like an old friend.

'We have to pay for the vehicle entry here,' Moses explained to Jed. 'You pay for your own entry once we get to the main office inside the national park. As a foreigner, you have to pay more money, and in US dollars.'

'Nothing like being made to feel welcome. What about you?' he asked Chris.

'I've got a permit already, it's still valid. You have to sign the register as well.' She pointed to a book on the polished wooden counter.

The ranger handed him a pen. He filled out his name and address and scanned the page. Apparently there were few visitors to the park these days, as the entries on the single page in front of him covered a three-month period. He noted the countries of origin of the visitors – a few British, a couple of Germans, some Danes and a smattering of New Zealanders and Australians. He saw Chris's entry in the book, but apart from her there was only one other American visitor to the park.

Miranda Banks-Lewis. He stared at his daughter's large, bold handwriting and ran his forefinger along the dried ink.

'Come on, Jed, we've still got a couple of hours' drive to reach the lodges,' Chris said.

'Just a minute.' He checked the date. Miranda had entered the park three weeks ago to the day. He was confused – he thought she had been in Mana Pools for three months. He looked up at the ranger. 'How often does someone need to purchase a permit?'

'It depends, sir, on the length of their booking.'

'If someone was staying in the park on a research project for six months, could they get a permit for that long?'

'Yes. As long as they had their campsite or accommodation booking for the same period.'

'What about if they wanted to go out and do some shopping, to stock up on supplies?'

'A person could leave for a day or two, but as long as they keep

135

paying for their accommodation they would not need a new entry permit each time.'

'Do you keep records of when people leave the park?'

'Jed, we're burning daylight,' Chris interrupted, pointedly looking at her wristwatch.

He turned to her. 'Go on ahead without us, if you like.'

'I'll wait.'

He turned to the ranger. 'What happens when someone leaves for good?'

'The gate officer collects your permit and it is brought here and filed.'

'This lady, Miranda Banks-Lewis,' he pointed to the registry entry, 'bought a permit to enter the park three weeks ago. As far as I know, she would have been living in the park for about three months prior to this date. This seems to indicate that she left Mana Pools, maybe for some time, and then had to buy a permit to re-enter.'

The man's eyes widened. 'Miranda! Oh, this lady, I don't know if you have heard about her, but –'

'She's my daughter. It's OK, I know. It's why I'm here.'

'Oh, sir, I am so very sorry. She was a wonderful, wonderful person. I used to see her every couple of weeks when she went shopping in Kariba. I would sometimes give her money and she would collect food from the supermarket for my wife and drop it off here. One time she took my wife and baby son to the hospital when the little one was sick. My wife cried and cried when we heard the news.'

Jed was touched by the man's emotion, but he needed answers. 'So why did Miranda have to buy a permit three weeks ago if she was living here?'

'She was gone for quite a while, about two weeks, when she went to South Africa.'

'South Africa? Did she say what for?'

'It was for her research, I think, sir. She had to go to a meeting with someone, I think she said it was her boss, and to collect some more drugs for the sedation of the lions. These things are hard to get in Zimbabwe.'

'Her boss?' He turned to Chris Wallis, but she was no longer in the room.

'That's what she said, sir.'

'And how was she when she got back?'

The ranger looked puzzled.

'Was she happy, sad, angry . . . ?'

The man was silent for a moment. 'She was . . . I don't know, sir . . .'

'She was what?' Jed tried to hide his impatience.

'Well, sir, I don't wish to speak ill of Miranda but . . . she seemed not as friendly as usual . . . more businesslike. Yes, that's it, more businesslike than usual. I remember she didn't have time to stop and talk. Often I would make her a cup of tea, but this last time she said, "Phinias, please just give me my permit, I'm in a hurry."'

Jed knew his daughter had a way of winning people over. He'd seen her on camping trips strike up conversations with strangers and end up with their email addresses and phone numbers.

'Did she say when she would be coming back through here, to see you again?'

'No sir, but I was a bit surprised not to see her a week ago. She had said to me many times before that as much as she loved the bush she needed to get out to Kariba every two weeks to keep her sanity.'

That fitted, Jed thought. It had surprised him that a girl who loved other people's company would commit herself to a monastic life in the middle of nowhere. 'So she didn't show up for her regular shopping trip?'

'Not unless she didn't bother stopping here on the way out or back into the park. But that would have been very strange indeed. She should have gone on her trip a week ago.'

Jed checked the date on the register. 'So you should have seen her two or three days before her disappearance was reported?'

'Yes, that would be right, sir.'

'One more question, if you don't mind.'

'Of course not. No one here was more upset about what happened to Miss Miranda than I was.'

'Did she have any close friends or acquaintances in the park or the local area? I'd like to talk to anyone who knew her well.'

'You'll find down in the park that she was a friend to everyone. She would often give lifts to the maids and rangers' wives.'

'Any male friends?'

'I only saw her with a man once.'

'An African man?'

'No, sir, a white man.'

'When?'

'I remember now that it was the day she left for South Africa. He came here, to the office, but did not want to enter the national park. He had a Zambian-registered vehicle, which made me curious about him. He said he owned a lodge on the other side of the river. He had crossed the border to attend a meeting with our conservation people at the Kariba office, but he came here to meet someone first. He was waiting for your daughter.'

Jed noticed the ranger was shifting his weight from one foot to the other and looking out the window, as if the questioning was suddenly making him uncomfortable. 'Sorry, I've kept you long enough, but just a couple more questions, please.'

'Yes, sir?'

'Have you seen the man again since then, and can you describe him?'

'No, not since then. He was tall, with dark hair, and brown skin . . . tanned, you know? Not young, not old.'

Jed decided to take a gamble. He smiled and leaned in close as if he was about to share a confidence. 'My daughter told me she had met a special man. She didn't mention his name, but she said he was bit older than her. It sounded to me like she might have been in love with this man. Do you think this guy could have been the one?'

The ranger smiled. 'Well, since she mentioned it, I don't suppose there is any harm in telling you that she kissed him when she said goodbye. I went outside to have a cigarette and saw them in the car park. So sad, sir, that Miranda had found someone, and then . . .'

'Yes, it is sad,' Jed said.

He thanked the ranger for his help, then stormed outside to find out why Christine Wallis had lied to him.

'Where is she?' he demanded of Moses.

'She left a few minutes ago. She said she would check in for us at park headquarters, save us some time at the other end.' Moses was leaning casually against the front fender of the Land Rover.

'Fuck.' Jed was fuming. 'Well, we won't get any more answers here. Let's go.'

They left Marongora and, a little further down the main road, took the turn-off to Mana Pools National Park and the Zambezi River. At a checkpoint they showed their permit and were waved on.

'It's about another eighty kilometres to the park headquarters,' Moses said.

Jed nodded and tried to relax his grip on the steering wheel as the Land Rover juddered along the heavily corrugated dirt road. He was furious with Chris, for not mentioning she had met with Miranda so soon before her disappearance, and for deliberately avoiding him once she realised he was onto her. Thinking it through, though, he was glad she had taken flight. He would have time to compose himself. If he started demanding answers from her she would probably clam up.

As they crossed a low concrete bridge over a wide, dry river Jed noticed three holes that appeared to have been dug in the middle of the sandy bed. 'What are those?'

'They were made by elephants,' Moses said.

'Were they looking for water?'

'Yes. They smell it. They'll dig with their tusks and their feet in order to find the sweetest water. It's long, hard work, but they know that the end result is worth it.'

Jed nodded. That was how he felt at the moment.

'We will find out what happened to your daughter, Jed. I think the professor is as concerned as you are, and misses your daughter as you do.'

Jed had said nothing to Moses of the professional relationship between Chris and Miranda. 'What makes you say that?'

'She said she wanted to go ahead and sort out our bookings . . .'

'So you said.'

'But there was something else.'

'What?'

'I saw it in her eyes. She had been crying.'

They caught up with Chris at another National Parks checkpoint at a T-intersection on the far side of a dry riverbed.

'This is the Nyakasikana Gate,' Moses said. 'They will check our papers again here. I'll take them inside for you.' He left the Land Rover and walked across to a small green building bristling with radio antennae.

Chris was at the boom gate, talking to a uniformed African ranger. Jed lit a cigarette, biding his time while she finished her conversation. Sitting in the shade cast by the green building were five men wearing camouflage fatigues. Their black faces were streaked with sweat and grey dust. One of them waved to him and he waved back. They had the hard, spare look of men at home in the bush. Scattered around them were the accoutrements of battle – bulging rucksacks, web gear, a radio and an odd mix of western and eastern bloc weapons – Russian AK-47s and the long-barrelled FN Self-Loading Rifles favoured by the British Army until the early nineties.

As Chris walked over, Jed nodded towards the men in the shade and she said, 'They're field rangers. Anti-poaching patrol. They go out for a week or two at a time. They're good, experts at tracking and living in the bush, but underequipped. If they see an armed civilian inside the park they'll shoot on sight.'

'Why did you leave before?' Jed asked.

'I told Moses, I wanted to sort things out here and –'

'Bullshit.' He dropped his cigarette on the ground and stamped it out. 'If you wanted to help you could have told me you saw Miranda only a few weeks ago.'

'How would that have helped?' She met his accusatory stare defiantly, hands on hips.

He took a breath and forced himself to regain his composure. 'I'm trying to find out what happened to her. It would help me to know what she had been up to before her disappearance, what her frame of mind was. Was she happy? Was she sad? Was she alone? Did she have someone in her life?'

She let the questions, especially the last one, hang in the air. 'Here comes Moses. We can talk about this later.'

Jed swore under his breath, got back in the Land Rover and slammed the door.

'What's wrong?' Moses asked.

'Forget it. Get in and let's get going.'

Jed hung back from Chris's vehicle to avoid the wake of choking dust. He drank warm store-bought water from a plastic bottle and wished he had a cold beer. However, he held off, knowing that he needed his wits about him when he went to look at Miranda's gear. The police superintendent had told him that her effects had been stored in a locked room in the Mana Pools National Park staff village. Because of the amount of equipment she had with her, the police had been unable to cart all of it away. Rather than splitting the possessions and risk losing some of them, they had left the lot in the care of the park's warden.

The dirt road deteriorated, alternating between deeper corrugations and soft red sand. Jed adapted easily to the poor surface, which was like a highway compared to some of the roads he'd driven in Afghanistan. Parts of that mountainous country were unnavigable by vehicle and some Special Forces patrols even got around on horseback. He'd quickly learned that when driving at maximum speed, one actually sailed across the corrugated ridges in a bad road. When he hit a patch of sand he slowed down and followed the ruts made by Chris's truck. Dense vegetation soon gave way to wide-open grassy plains.

'We are in the floodplains now, except it doesn't flood here any more, not since they built the dam at Kariba,' Moses said, trying to engage

Jed in conversation. 'Before the dam all the pools would be joined when the river flowed and the animals would move inland. Now the animals are here year-round. That's what makes this place so special. See the waterbuck?' He pointed off to the right.

Jed looked across and, after a couple of seconds, picked out five of the shaggy grey antelope.

'See the white rings on their behinds?'

'Nice target.'

Moses laughed. 'No, take a look at the shape. It's where the Hyena played a joke on the waterbuck by painting the toilet seat white.'

'How many times have you told that one?'

'Oh, about a thousand, I think. Do you know how to tell the difference between a male zebra and a female zebra?'

'No, but I suspect you're going to tell me whether I want to hear it or not.'

'A male zebra is black with white stripes, while the female is white with black stripes.'

'You're a riot, Moses. Any more riveting animal tales?'

'I told a lady from Kansas once that the difference between male elephant dung and the female's is that hers tastes sweet and his tastes sour. She didn't believe me, so . . .'

'Don't tell me you let her have a taste test.'

'She said the dung must belong to a male because it tasted disgusting.'

Jed laughed. 'Did you ever come clean to her?'

'She went back to camp that night and told my boss she had tasted male elephant dung. I had to go find a new boss when we got back to Kariba.'

Jed laughed again. 'You're kidding me.'

'It's true, I swear, man.'

'Was it worth losing your job over?'

'Sure.'

'Remind me never to believe anything you say.'

'See, you're already smarter than most of the tourists I deal with.'

Jed smiled, pleased he had Moses along for the ride. He was certain the amiable tracker would help him in his quest – all he needed to work out now was what he was looking for.

10

She found that if she dived deep and kept swimming she eventually passed through the warm water into a deliciously cool layer. She levelled out and swam as far as she could in what she had nicknamed the fast chill zone. It refreshed her body and her mind. The ascent back to the surface was just as nice, but in reverse, warming her skin as she kicked for the light.

The whine of a marine engine made her look around as soon as her head broke the still surface of the Indian Ocean.

It was the Zodiac inflatable, its big outboard screaming at full pitch. She smiled. She had been looking forward to his return. She raised an arm and waved. She felt guilty about what she had done in his absence, but at the same time she was relieved. He had been gone for half the day, a business trip to the mainland, giving her plenty of time to search the luxury cruiser. The vessel was like something out of *Miami Vice*. Long, sleek, powerful – the ultimate rich boy's toy. If she didn't know better she would have said he was compensating for some anatomical deficiency.

After he had launched the boat and was out of sight, she had padded on bare feet along the thickly carpeted companionway from the saloon to the master bedroom at the bow, where they had made love and slept together these past two nights. They had been sharing a bed for a month, alternating between her place and his. She had been sure enough of him to have sex, but today had been her first chance to investigate his things, to delve into his private life, without him being present. Perhaps it was some niggling doubt in the back of her mind that made her conduct the search.

The master cabin smelled of his aftershave. His fragrance was subtle, not overpowering like the cheap stuff. She searched the cupboards and found a couple of expensive linen suits, tailored shirts, chinos, shorts, boxers, socks, running shoes and loafers. Nothing incriminating in the pockets. Nothing hidden beneath the underwear. She pulled out each drawer and checked underneath to see if anything was taped there. Again, nothing. There was a small amount of cash in a water-proof wallet in the drawer of the bedside table, and a box of condoms. She smiled and replaced them exactly as she had found them. In the second drawer was a binder with loose-leaf clear plastic inserts holding various documents. These were for the boat – registration papers, insurance, receipts for maintenance and provisions. There was a magazine face-down at the bottom of the drawer, a cigarette ad on the back cover. She picked it up. It was a glossy pornographic magazine. She sat on the bed and leafed through it. It was much more explicit than she would have imagined. Attractive models, males and females, females and females, in elegant settings doing some very inelegant things. She felt her cheeks redden, but kept turning the pages. The pictures did nothing for her, but she skimmed a couple of outrageously pornographic letters. She swallowed hard. She felt the wetness well between her legs and, not a little embarrassed by her involuntary arousal, quickly closed the magazine and replaced it, cover down, and shut the drawer.

No safe, no bundles of cash, no drugs, no fake passports, no weapons, nothing. Of course, there were lots of places to hide contraband on a boat which she could never hope to find, but the things she did find were helping her make up her mind. In the galley she found a gourmet French cookbook. She already knew he loved to cook. In his brushed aluminium briefcase she found a thank-you letter from the children of a Catholic orphanage in Zambia he had donated five thousand American dollars to. The bookshelf in the galley held a few mass-market paperbacks, but also some modern classics and non-fiction books about a range of subjects from world trade and business administration to the Gulf War. There was a copy of the latest biography of the President of the United States.

She powered up his laptop and was relieved to see he did not use a password. Nothing to hide, she told herself. She found files relating to his hotels and the lodge. She found letters to universities in Zambia and Tanzania offering to establish scholarships for underprivileged students in his father's name. She did a search and found the internet browser cache file. By opening that she could get an idea about what sites he surfed, through files that had been automatically downloaded. She clicked randomly on jpeg picture files and found images that related to online electrical goods stores, an international wildlife conservation charity and a British bank.

The evidence had confirmed what she already knew of him – that he was a philanthropic, progressive, successful heterosexual business-man with a passion for wildlife conservation, who was also wealthy, well read, well dressed and well educated. She'd shut down the computer, sunbathed on deck for a while then gone for a swim.

He cut the Zodiac's motor and coasted up to where she trod water. He reached over the edge, offering his hand, and hoisted her effort-lessly up over the side of the boat.

She kissed him.

'Nice and salty,' he said, 'like a mermaid.'

She smiled at him. In addition to being an all-round nice guy, he also happened to be muscled, deeply tanned, extremely good-looking and sexy as hell.

'Sorry I've been gone so long.' He handed her a towel from the back of the Zodiac. 'I've brought you some presents from the mainland.'

Even his teeth were too good to be true, she thought. 'Show me,' she said, drying her legs.

He opened the plastic cooler box between his feet and pulled a single, long-stemmed red rose from the top of the ice layer.

'Thank you, Hassan. It's lovely.' She smelled the flower and held it against her cheek; it was cool and satiny. She saw he was staring at her, saw the lust in his eyes, and it made her feel sexy, like she was in control. She noticed a long wooden crate on the floor of the boat. 'What's that?'

'Car parts. But I think you'll be more interested in this.' He rummaged deeper into the ice in the cold box. 'Moët et Chandon. Non-vintage, I'm afraid, but this is Africa, after all. I also picked us up a lobster from the market at Mombasa. It's at the bottom of the cold box, but I won't get it out.'

'Please don't,' she laughed.

'Don't worry, I'll cook it. You only have to sip champagne and relax. Remember, this is your holiday, you deserve a break.'

'How can I argue with that?'

'You can't,' he said, and restarted the motor.

After lunch they sat under a white canopy at the aft of the main deck. They had finished the champagne. Hassan drank from a dewy bottle of Safari Lager. She sipped chilled chardonnay from a voluminous glass.

The sun and the wine had left her warm and tingly inside and she knew it would only take another long penetrating stare from his clear blue eyes to turn the warmth to a molten flow. She drained her glass and put it down on the deck. He put down his beer on the table and moved to the upholstered bench she was sitting on. The rose he had given her was on the table. He took up the flower, sniffed its aroma then moved the petals to her lips.

She swallowed hard, not moving at all. The textured surface of the petal brushed her mouth. She looked into his eyes as he trailed the flower down over her chin, along the line of her neck, to her collarbone and over the curve of her breast above her white bikini top. He leaned closer to her, and she parted her lips, quickly moistening them with her tongue.

He tossed the rose onto the deck and their lips met. She hungered for him, as he did for her. Their hands explored each other's bodies as they kissed. The muscles in his shoulders and back were like cables, and the thick hair on his chest was rough and springy. He was older than any other man she had been with, not that there had been a lot, but he was a better lover than any of them. She felt small and fragile in his strong embrace. He moved his mouth from her lips to kiss her neck and she arched her back and ran her hands through his wavy black hair.

She closed her eyes and felt his touch trail lower, down over her chest. He cupped a breast in one hand and moved his mouth to the nipple, sucking it through the thin fabric of her bikini. She gave a low moan of pleasure. He reached around her with his free hand and deftly unhooked the top. She felt it fall away from her and her nipples come fully erect to the touch of his tongue, his teeth and his fingers. She moved her hands down, lifting his shirt and scratching his back. He moved from the bench and knelt on the bleached deck. He placed a hand on each of her knees and moved her legs apart. She did not resist, instead sliding her butt down the upholstered seat. He kissed her belly and moved his mouth lower until his lips caressed her through the fabric of her panties, as he had done with her top. He traced the outline of her sex with fingertips and lips. She lifted her bottom off the seat, wantonly thrusting her mound against his mouth, eyes closed, giving over to her desires. Her bikini pants felt wet and clingy from her own dampness. Her fingers were entwined in his hair, urging him, directing him.

He hooked his fingers in the waistband of her briefs and slowly lowered them. She closed her legs to let him remove them and felt gloriously exposed and open to the sun and the hint of breeze off the ocean. She shuddered as his tongue and lips met her naked, dewy flesh. He grabbed the cheeks of her bottom in his big hands and lifted her as he buried his tongue deep inside her. Involuntarily she tried to close her legs, but his broad shoulders forced them apart, kept her open to him. She hooked her legs over his back and slid further down, moving one of her hands to her nipples, alternately tugging and rolling them in her fingers.

Her breath quickened as he trapped her swollen clitoris between his tongue and top teeth, sucking and teasing the swollen little nub. He moved a hand from under her and eased a finger inside her as he licked. Withdrawing his wet finger he slid it slowly down between her legs, to the cleft of her buttocks, trailing her hot, sweet lubricant with his movement. She ground herself into his mouth and lifted her hips higher.

She gasped when she felt him probing her anus with the tip of his finger, but didn't want to do anything to make him stop. He ceased before it became uncomfortable and, when he slid another finger into her vagina, she accepted the new sensation as a thrilling addition to the pleasure that was engulfing her.

'Oh, yes,' she breathed. She felt the waves of pleasure start deep within her. Just as she was about to climax he stopped. He withdrew his fingers and lifted his face.

She opened her eyes and stared down at him.

'On your knees,' he said as he stood.

He stared down at her, unsmiling. 'Touch yourself.'

She blinked in surprise.

'Now!'

She flinched at the barked command, then realised it must be part of some new game. She could do that, she told herself. To date he had been a considerate, gentle lover, something of a change from the boys she had dated in college. This was a new turn, ordering her around, dominating her. She realised she didn't mind being told what to do. She looked up into his eyes, thought she saw a softening of his hard stare, then nodded. She closed her eyes and leaned back on her haunches, moving her right hand between her legs and lifting her left to her breast.

She felt the pleasurable sensations return in response to her own touch. She threw her head back and let out a little moan, and found she was enjoying putting on a show for him. When she opened her eyes he was standing over her, his shorts partly pulled down, his thick, engorged penis in his right hand.

'Take it,' he ordered.

She looked at him wide-eyed for an instant. Again the scowl on his face. She knew he was really a pussy cat at heart, which made this little game all the more fun. She reached out with her left hand, encircling him, stroking, massaging him. She slid off the bench to her knees. Still touching herself with her other hand, she moved her lips to the swollen head of his penis. She looked up at him, locking eyes. She took him in her mouth, stroking him with her hand as she closed around him.

He looked down at her. He was fiercely aroused, and surprised how compliantly she had given herself to his commands. He wondered how far he could take her. He'd never been into bondage or discipline. He was only doing it now to demean her, to see how far she would go to please him, to trap him. He had loved her. He had been ready to commit himself to her for life, to have her bear his children. Now he looked down at her sucking him and saw her for what she was.

A whore.

He wrapped a hand in her blonde hair and pulled her face from his penis, then dragged her to the deck.

'Ow! Not so hard!' she yelped.

He knelt between her knees and raised his finger to her lips to silence her.

She grimaced then smiled. 'I'm new to this, lover, but I kind of like it. Just not *too* rough.' She licked his finger then raised her eyebrows, inviting him to continue.

She thinks it's a game, he thought to himself. 'Keep quiet. I'm going to give you what you want, now, what you've been paid for.'

'Mmm. Oh, *yes*.'

He pinned her wrists to the deck with his hands as he lowered himself to her, teasing her dripping opening with the engorged head. 'You want it, don't you, bitch?'

She'd had a boyfriend who talked dirty to her during sex and she'd found she didn't mind it when she was in the right mood. It was so out of character for Hassan, though, that part of her wanted to flash a red light to this little charade and get back the sensitive, loving guy she'd fallen for. But another part, deep inside her, was inflamed even more by his crudity. 'Mmm, yes, give me your cock,' she whispered.

'I'm going to hurt you now, you whore.'

11

Jed's mind was still racing with questions as they pulled up, at last, outside the Mana Pools National Park headquarters building. It was single storey, L-shaped, with the two arms linked by a shady verandah. The building was painted the same uniform olive-green as the permit office at Marongora and the structures at the two check-points they had passed through on their way in.

Christine was waiting in the shade of a spreading Natal mahogany tree, sitting in her Land Rover with the door open. She climbed out and walked over to Jed and Moses.

'You going to stay mad at me forever?' she asked, trying a smile.

Jed had fumed all the way for the rest of the drive into the park, barely distracted by Moses's running commentary on the wildlife and vegetation. Chris had held back important information from him and he wanted to know why.

'Look, I'm sorry, again, that I didn't tell you I'd seen Miranda a few weeks ago,' Chris said.

Jed ignored her apology. 'Do you know who the man was who saw her off on her last trip to visit you?'

'What do you mean?'

'The ranger up at that other place . . .'

'Marongora.'

'Right. He mentioned he saw her with a guy when she left for South Africa. He apparently kissed her goodbye. Did she say anything about this guy when she saw you?'

Chris narrowed her eyes as she thought about the question. 'There was a guy she had some dealings with up here. They spent time together – he's into conservation in a big way, breeds cheetahs. But I wasn't aware of any, um, personal connection between them.'

'You can tell me everything later. Right now I want to take a look at her stuff,' Jed said.

'Me too,' said Chris. 'Don't forget that a lot of her equipment belongs to me. The local authorities haven't let me near it yet.'

They walked into the headquarters building. Thankfully, the polished concrete floors and thick walls kept out a good deal of the midday heat. Jed noticed a poster decorated with photos of lions. According to the text, visitors to the park could accompany the resident ecologist when he went tracking lions.

'Was Miranda working with this guy?' Jed asked Chris.

'Not really, he's a National Parks employee. His work is separate, but Miranda's research was complementary to his and all of her findings would be shared with him. I checked yesterday and he's been on leave, in Harare, for the last three weeks.'

Chris greeted the ranger behind the desk with a handshake.

'It's good to see you back, Professor,' the man said, smiling.

'This is Mr Banks, Harold. I think it would be best if he stayed in my lodge for a few nights.'

'No problem, Professor. Mr Banks, if you will just pay the park entry fee, please.'

'I'd like a lodge of my own, if you don't mind,' Jed said to both of them.

'Ah, but I'm sorry sir, all the lodges are booked,' the ranger said.

'But I thought few people visited the national park these days. Are you telling me all your accommodation is full?'

'It's all booked,' Chris explained, 'which is not to say that it's actually full. Tour companies and local people block book accommodation here months in advance, but the companies rarely get enough customers to proceed with the bookings and the local people are often kept at home by things such as fuel shortages.'

'So if someone isn't coming, why can't he give me a lodge?' Jed was trying to keep his annoyance in check.

Chris explained. 'The people who have booked the accommodation have until five-thirty on each day of their booking to show up. It's only then, if the guests haven't arrived, that the rangers here can release the lodging to people without a booking.'

'Fine, I'll wait until five-thirty.'

'Then you have to be out by ten tomorrow morning and come back at five-thirty in the afternoon to see if the lodge is free again, Mr Banks,' the ranger added.

'This is ridiculous.'

The ranger smiled patiently.

'This is Africa,' Chris said.

'What about camping? Can I get a campsite?'

'You're not exactly set up for it, Jed,' Chris said.

'Camping is no problem, sir,' the ranger said, beaming again.

'Great, I'll take a campsite.'

'Except for one problem, sir.'

'What's that?'

'No water, sir.'

'What?'

'I'm afraid the pipe to the ablution block sprang a leak and the elephants dug it up and –'

'Jesus Christ.'

'There's always a room in my lodge, Jed,' Chris said.

Jed shook his head. 'OK, a bed for Moses as well?'

'Of course.'

Jed filled in the visitors' register and paid his park entry fee.

'You've been informed that I'm here to collect my missing daughter's possessions?' he asked the ranger.

'Ah, of course, Mr Banks. The police have contacted us.'

'How soon can I see my daughter's stuff?'

'Right now, if you wish, Mr Banks.'

Chris had been to the Mana Pools staff village on a number of occasions, even though ordinary park visitors were prohibited from driving the dirt road behind the headquarters she was on. She had struck up a good rapport with the National Parks staff here, but their goodwill had not been sufficient for them to allow her access to Miranda's equipment until the police had authorised it. That was the perennially annoying thing about African bureaucracy: it knew only two extremes – laxity bordering on corruption or a pathological adherence to orders. She was eager to see the state of the equipment she had loaned Miranda for her project. She was also concerned that some of it might be missing. All of it was expensive, sensitive and, in the wrong hands, dangerous.

Chris was also concerned about Jed Banks. She had hoped to be in and out of Mana Pools with as little fuss as possible, but the Special Forces soldier's arrival had put the brakes on her plan. She needed, as a matter of urgency, to get into Miranda's laptop and check her emails for any sign she'd been up to something Chris didn't know about. In the back of her mind was the disturbing revelation of a possible romantic attachment between Miranda and a man.

Her own concerns aside, she also felt sorry for Jed Banks. No, it was more than sorry, she told herself as she drove into the dusty staff encampment. She shared Jed's pain. Miranda was more than just a research colleague or protégée to her. Chris had seen herself in Miranda. Her idealism, her devotion, her need to do good and right in a world with precious little reserves of either. She had worried about sending Miranda on her assignment to Zimbabwe, but it was nothing she would not have done herself. At the time, the risks had seemed acceptable. Chris had never had a child, but she could imagine, and see in Jed's eyes, the unbearable pain of losing your only offspring.

Chris also couldn't help but see Miranda's striking looks mirrored

155

in her father's fair hair and blue eyes. Although twenty-odd years of outdoor military life had crinkled the tanned skin around his mouth and eyes, there was no denying he was a handsome man. There were flecks of white in his sprouting gingery beard, but his T-shirt hugged biceps and pectorals that would cost a city executive thousands of dollars and buckets of sweat in a gym. Jed Banks had got to look that way by getting up and going to work each day, sometimes not knowing if he would live to see the next dawn. She didn't think she could ever really fall for an office worker. The guy from the embassy had been nice, but his hands were too soft, his tummy too flabby and his discomfort tolerance too low for her liking. The ranger in Kruger was cute, and energetic, but arrogant as hell and too young for her.

At another time, in another place, if she had struck up a conversation with Jed Banks, if he had made a pass at her, she . . . well, she might have dropped her guard. But here and now she had to concentrate on finding out once and for all what had happened to Miranda. Chris was worried, very worried, that the girl was gone for good. However, like Jed, she needed proof.

The circumstances and timing of Miranda's disappearance were more of a concern to Chris than she was prepared to admit to Jed. To Jed the time, place and manner of his daughter's disappearance seemed random. To Chris they were suspicious, but she wasn't about to let Jed in on her darkest fears.

The first thing Jed noticed about the staff living quarters, simple rendered brick buildings with corrugated asbestos roofs, was that they were painted grey instead of the usual olive drab. Nothing like a little variety, he supposed. The accommodation wasn't bad, considering what Jed had seen so far of the way ordinary Africans lived, but neither could it be described as modern or even comfortable.

An elderly bald-headed ranger in a pressed khaki uniform with sergeant's stripes on the sleeve walked out of the deep shade of a mature tree.

The ranger greeted him and explained what the group was doing in the staff compound.

'Welcome,' the older man said solemnly. 'I will show you where the storeroom is.' He led them away from the housing complex to a grey building isolated from the others by a rusting wire fence.

The headquarters ranger tried three keys in the padlock before he finally said, 'Ah, this is the one.'

The hinges protested as the door swung open. The ranger reached in and pulled an old-fashioned light cord, illuminating a single naked bulb.

'Your daughter's things are all at the far end of the building, Mr Banks.'

It was hot and musty inside and Jed felt his shirt stick to his back immediately. Looking around he saw broken furniture, presumably from the park's lodges, and mould-spotted cardboard boxes over-flowing with carelessly archived paperwork. There was a crate of long-empty beer bottles in one corner and, of passing interest to Jed, some metal ammunition tins and some more boxes containing green army web gear, including packs, belts and pouches. A wooden gun rack ran along a section of one wall, a chain passing through the trigger guards of five AK-47s and three FN Self-Loading Rifles.

The ranger, who was leaning half in through the doorway, said, 'The anti-poaching patrols store some of their equipment here, but they have not disturbed your daughter's possessions. I am always here when they secure their weapons.'

Miranda's possessions were stacked neatly at the far end of the room. Loose floorboards creaked under Jed's feet as he approached the pile of belongings. He did a quick inventory. Most obvious were six aluminium trunks, the kind professional photographers used to ship expensive gear and, he realised, the kind the Army used to house breakable stuff, such as computers and radios and some weapons systems.

Next to the boxes was a purple backpack, which he remembered Miranda carrying on their camping trip. A lump came to his throat and he fought to retain his composure. There was a camping fridge, the kind that ran on gas, electricity or a car battery; two liquid petroleum gas bottles; a shovel; a folded camp bed; a rolled foam mattress covered in green canvas; two green plastic boxes with lids; and a bulging black plastic garbage bag tied in a knot. There were also two green canvas bags that, from their shape, he guessed contained Miranda's folded tent and its accompanying poles.

He ran his hand over one of the metal cases. His fingers left a bright trail in the thin coating of dust. She'd been missing for nearly a week now. Was the trail impossibly cold? Before moving anything he noticed that the layer of dirt was uniform across everything. Nothing had been opened or moved since all the gear was deposited in the storeroom. Jed kneeled and stared at Miranda's backpack for a moment. He was almost reluctant to open it. What good would it do anyway? He heard the floorboards creak behind him and turned. Chris stood, her hands folded across her front.

'It's OK,' he said. 'Come take what you want. I only want her personal things.'

Chris moved forwards and counted the boxes. She stood beside Jed and checked the fastenings on each box.

'They're all locked,' she said.

'Funny, so is the backpack.' Jed fingered the tiny brass padlock. The lock was the cheap kind sold in airport shops, hardly a deterrent to any determined thief.

'It was good of your staff to pack everything so neatly and lock all the baggage,' Chris said to the ranger, who stood inside the building, still holding his bunch of keys.

'No, Professor. Everything you see here is exactly as we found it, except for the tent, of course, which we packed after the police had finished their investigation. All of the boxes and the pack were locked and there were no signs of keys anywhere. The plastic bin bag has a few loose pieces that were in the tent.'

Jed reached for the bag and undid the knot. He opened it and peered inside. 'Not much. A black tin kettle, a gas burner and some barbeque utensils. A gas-powered camp light and a torch.' Next he lifted the lids on the green plastic boxes. 'Plates, pots and pans, cutlery.'

Jed opened the pouch on his belt and pulled out his Leatherman. He unfolded the pliers and used them to grip the padlock on Miranda's pack. The lock sprang open with one good twist and he unzipped the bag. Inside were neatly folded clothes, most of which seemed to be heavyweight items – woollens, jeans and a parka. He lifted a sweater and raised it to his face. It smelled musty. A quick sniff of a couple of other items of clothing yielded the same thing. 'This bag hasn't been opened for a long time.'

'She wouldn't have had much use for those clothes up here in the valley. They were probably her spare things,' Chris said.

Jed rubbed the prickly hairs on his chin. 'Presumably she used a laptop computer to record her research findings. I'd like to have a look at it, if you don't mind, in case she kept some personal stuff on the hard drive.'

'What? Oh, sorry, I was thinking about something else. The computer, ah, sure, no problem.'

'Same with notebooks, letters, that sort of thing,' Jed was watching Chris's face.

'Um, yeah. No problem.' She looked back at the stack of locked boxes. 'I'll go through all this stuff later and do a double-check.'

'Right,' he said.

'Right.'

Moses walked in, breaking the awkward silence that had descended. 'I've brought some Cokes from the car fridge, Jed.'

Jed felt somehow comforted by the big man's presence. 'That's great, Moses. Can you give us a hand to move all this stuff?'

'Got to earn my money some way.'

Jed took a swig of the cold soft drink then asked the ranger, 'Can you take me to my daughter's campsite?'

'Ah, of course, but it is getting late now, sir. The guides are all finished for today, but maybe tomorrow.'

Moses spoke rapidly to the ranger in Shona, then said to Jed, 'I know this place well, where your daughter camped. I can take you there, no

159

problem. But this man is right, it is getting late. I think we should wait until tomorrow morning.'

'Today's been tiring,' Chris said. 'I'm for calling it a day once we get this stuff stored in the lodge.'

'OK,' Jed agreed. However, his mind was anything but tired. It was racing.

Chris had rented a two-storey lodge on the banks of the Zambezi River.

'I'm gonna take a shower,' she told Jed. 'Make yourself at home.'

Chris took a refreshingly cool shower downstairs, looking out at the bush through slits in the brick wall, which also allowed the last vestiges of the afternoon breeze to brush her wet skin. She had no concerns about anyone seeing her, as the lodge attendant had retired to the staff compound and the nearest building was a couple of hundred metres away, out of sight and earshot. Moses had politely declined her invitation to stay, for this first night at least, saying he had friends in the staff village he planned on visiting. Chris smiled to herself at his poor attempt to hide his embarrassment. The tracker's inability to meet her eye told her that at least one of those friends was a woman. Good luck to him, she thought as she rinsed the soap from her body and struggled to shut off the rusting taps.

She towelled off and wrapped herself in a colourful African-print sarong. The shower was in the lodge's open car port, and she walked back inside through the kitchen. The cooking area looked a little sad, with its cheap cupboards, scratched benchtops and antiquated gas cooker, but it did the job. The paneless windows were covered in chicken wire and mosquito gauze to keep out primates and insects. She stopped by the big gas-powered deep-freeze in the dining area and grabbed two green bottles of Zambezi Lager.

She padded barefoot across the stone-floored lounge room, past low armchairs made of heavy dark wood. The zebra-print cushions on the chairs matched the curtains. The park's lodges were simple and functional, not as tastefully decorated as their privately owned counterparts in safari camps, but they provided Zimbabweans and tourists with affordable accommodation and a measure of comfort in one of the wildest places on earth. Upstairs there were beds for eight people, with most of them arranged on a wide verandah under mosquito nets suspended from wooden frames.

She entered one of the two upstairs bedrooms and changed into a diaphanous long-sleeved blouse, khaki trousers and boots and socks. It was still warm even though the sun was behind the Zambian hills across the river, but she covered her body to protect herself from malaria-bearing mosquitos. She unfurled the mosquito net hanging over her bed, tucked its edges securely under the mattress and then sprayed the net with insecticide. Outside, she lit citronella oil candles at intervals along the verandah. As an afterthought, she returned to her room and opened her toiletry kit. It was a green canvas zip-up affair, designed for a man. She found the old, nearly empty bottle of perfume and sprayed a little on her wrists, then wiped the residue behind her ears. Before leaving her room she checked herself in the mirror and decided there was nothing more she could do about her wet hair, which was tied back in a simple ponytail.

She knocked on Jed's bedroom door.

'Come in.' He was sitting on the bed, the contents of Miranda's backpack spread around him on the floor.

'Brought you a sundowner.' She held up the two beer bottles. 'Although I'm afraid you've just missed the sunset.'

'Thanks,' he said, accepting a bottle. He gestured to the still-folded winter clothes around him. 'This is all I have left of her. It's her stuff, but there's nothing of her here, if you know what I mean. No pictures, no trinkets, no letters, no personal stuff. What have you found?'

'Nothing yet. I'll inventory the boxes tomorrow, but they only contain the monitoring gear – radio-tracking collars, transmitters and receivers, that sort of stuff.'

Chris extended her free hand. 'Come with me.' Jed looked up at her, surprised, then reached out and let her gently lead him up off the bed and outside onto the verandah. The Zambezi shone like a river of red-gold lava in the last light of the departed sun. Exotic birds farewelled the day. The sting of the tropical sun was gone, but Jed was still hot.

He let his hand slip from Chris's and stood, leaning on the verandah railing, staring blankly and sipping his beer. The dew from the bottle was wet on his fingers and soothed his brow when he went to wipe the sweat away. 'What does it all mean, Chris? It's like she vanished.'

'She has vanished, Jed. There is absolutely no doubt about it. Miranda has gone from both of our lives.'

He turned to look at her. 'But where are her day clothes, her personal things, her goddamned toothbrush? It looks more like she packed for a trip away and left without telling anyone.'

Chris finished her beer and stood next to him at the railing, closer. She looked straight ahead and said softly, 'Jed, there are a thousand explanations for not finding all of her personal stuff, and you know it. The Africans who work here are good people, but this country is crippled by inflation and poverty. If anything was to go missing from Miranda's tent it would be things the park workers thought no one would miss – her day clothes lying across a chair, her food supplies, her toiletries, even her toothbrush. It doesn't surprise me a bit. People here wouldn't steal expensive electronic gear or break the lock on a backpack, because that would lead to an investigation.'

As she turned to look at him she could see the doubt in his face and the softening of his anger, along with the pain that lurked just beneath the surface. He rubbed his eyes and looked back out at the darkened bush.

'You'll still check her laptop for me, won't you, for anything personal?'

She laid a hand on his arm. The muscle was hard as rock, but warm. 'Of course, Jed. I'll do it in the morning. The lodge attendant lit a fire in the barbeque before she left. It should be about right for cooking now. Let's get some steaks on and open some wine.'

They walked down the creaking wooden stairs to the kitchen and Jed took two bottles of beer from the gas fridge to keep him going during his barbeque duty. Chris started fixing a salad and said, 'I'll come and join you soon. Take that with you,' she added, pointing to a long black flashlight that reminded Jed of a nightstick. The cooking fire embers glowed a warm red in the darkness beyond the pale pool of light cast by an outside bulb.

'Should I take a gun with me too?'

'You may laugh. I'd take a knife if I were you, though.'

'For the lions?'

'For the steak.'

Chris heard and smelled the sizzling steaks as she stepped from the lodge carrying a bowl of green salad and a bottle of wine. She watched Jed staring intently at the hot coals beneath the meat. She wondered if checking through Miranda's things had taken some of the fire out of him. He hadn't asked her about her last meeting with his daughter, but there was still a look of puzzlement on his face as he placed the steaks on a platter and carried them to a large outdoor table whose top was a single slab of stone.

As he uncorked the wine, he said, 'So you don't think there's anything unusual about all of her bags and equipment being packed away?'

'That's how I'd keep my stuff, particularly the valuables. If you leave stuff unattended and unlocked, you've really only got yourself to blame if something disappears. She might have been packed up in preparation for a day walk in the bush.'

'You say you'd keep your gear secured, but don't forget I've seen your hotel room. Forgive the observation, but you'd hardly be classed as anally retentive by a shrink.'

Chris faked a look of indignation. 'You're saying I'm a slob! Anyway, it's one thing to be messy, but I always leave my valuables locked away.'

'But don't you see, that's my point. Even if Miranda did lock away her expensive monitoring or photographic gear or whatever all that shit is, where was the rest of her stuff? The odds and ends that all of us leave lying around?'

'I'd get Moses to ask around the staff village if I were you. Some of her bits and pieces could have found their way there.'

'Don't you think it's at all unusual there was no trace found of the clothes she was wearing? No shoes, nothing?'

Chris finished the last of her steak. 'Not really. What the lions don't eat, the hyenas and the vultures pretty well clean up. It's not unusual to find a victim's clothes inside a man-eater – they don't stop at anything when they're in a feeding frenzy.'

'Would it have done much damage to her tent, if that's where it took her?'

'Hard to say, really. We do know that lions don't, as a rule, break into tents to get their victims, even though it would be easy enough for them to do so. The best defence for campers is to stay inside with the zipper shut and the lion will walk past, thinking the tent's just another anthill or mound.'

'Surely they have a good sense of smell?'

'Oh, they do, but they don't hunt by smell. Their olfactory senses are primarily for detecting other members of the pride and intruders in their territory, or for sniffing out carrion. Lions are great scavengers. They hunt by sight and sound. You've watched a domestic cat hunting birds or mice?'

'Sure.'

'It's the same thing. The cat notices movement and that's what gets it going. They see in black and white, so movement is crucial to allow them to detect something. Once they see that little twitch, or the prey making a dash for it, they charge and pounce – just like a little kitty cat back home.'

'That's why the guide books tell you not to run?'

'Exactly. If you stay rock still, the lion will, theoretically at least, lose interest in you or lose sight of you. However, if I'm ever out with you in the bush and we come across an angry lion, I'm going to run.'

'Don't tell me you can outrun a lion?'

'No, but I don't have to be able to outrun the lion – I only need to be able to outrun you.'

He laughed. 'I'll have to remember that one.'

'Don't try it on anyone over here. It's an old joke, I'm afraid.'

'Funny how we're laughing about it like this. It's the same as in the Army – using black humour to get through the worst of it.'

'I'm sorry, Jed, I didn't mean to . . .'

'No, really, Chris, I mean it. It does help in an odd kind of way. I'm clinging to the hope that Miranda is still alive, somehow, somewhere, and that maybe this has all been a terrible misunderstanding, that she'll pop up at her mother's place in a week's time, broken-hearted over a guy or something. But in the event that doesn't happen, I want you to know that coming here . . . meeting you . . . well, it's sort of helping me to come to terms with it, to prepare myself for the worst.'

'Thanks, Jed.' She reached forwards, across the table and touched his arm again. She really did feel for him. 'Let me get us both another beer.'

Inside the lodge she stood in the kitchen, leaned against the sink and gripped the cool stainless-steel edge with all her might. Oh, God, she said to herself, I don't know if I can keep this up for much longer. Then she started to cry.

12

The beer was an anaesthetic; the warm Indian Ocean a soothing bath; the English girl's kisses a soft, moist balm on his bruised skin. Luke Scarborough was in paradise, Zanzibar-style.

He opened his eyes and stared up through the mosquito net at the lazily rotating fan and painted white ceiling of the bungalow. She lay on her back beside him, all pink and warm and smelling of last night's sex. She wasn't overly attractive, but she was relaxed and experimental in bed and had a wicked sense of humour. He didn't want to leave her. He reckoned he could easily spend a fortnight drinking, dancing and practising new positions, but he had work to do. He climbed out from under the grubby white gauze and padded across the linoleum floor, fine grains of sand sticking to the soles of his feet. He shifted her brightly coloured sarong, called a Zambian in this part of Africa, and her lime-green bikini from the chair and found his own clothes. He pulled on still-damp board shorts and a T-shirt that smelled of sweat, cigarette smoke and spilled beer.

He was technically on the island for business, but after a night at the budget beach bungalows at Nungwi, at the northern tip of Zanzibar, the visit had quickly slid into pleasure. He had arrived at Dar es Salaam on a flight from Dubai the previous morning. The swaying green palm trees, white sandy beaches, azure waters and industrious bustle of the Tanzanian port city were a world away from the barren mountains and deserts of Afghanistan. He'd taken the first ferry out of Dar – a catamaran constructed in his native Australia, of all places – and feasted on fresh cashews and Coca-Cola on the hundred-minute trip across to Zanzibar Island. A young African tout had attached himself to Luke as soon as he stepped off the ferry, offering him in a single breath a hotel room, hashish and a spice tour.

'No thanks,' Luke had tried politely. It had been hot and sticky and Stone Town, the island's historic Arab trading capital, loomed ahead of him, a daunting maze of narrow alleys and decaying once-grandiose buildings.

'Please, you let me take you to a hotel and I get some bread, man.' The tout was still pestering him.

Luke smiled at the out-of-date hippy slang. 'I'm not looking for a hotel and I don't need your help, thanks,' he said, more firmly this time.

'Stupid fucking tourist,' the African said.

Luke stopped and turned. 'Now you're insulting me? That's no way to make money, my friend.'

'I'm not your friend. You people, you start wars and invade other countries. Go back to where you came from, you stupid tourist.'

Luke looked around. The boy was lean and hard and his dark face bore more than one scar. Other people had stopped to watch the exchange, including two Arab women dressed from head to foot in black *kangas*. Luke shook his head and walked on. He lost the tout by walking into a shop on the waterfront advertising scuba diving. Although rattled by the man's quick aggression, Luke now had a lead-in for his story.

At the dive shop he booked a seat on the next minibus shuttle to Nungwi. The drive took him through swampland and crowded villages, and past dense groves of palms. The vibrant greenery assaulted his eyes after the lifeless browns of Afghanistan, but the conservative dress of the island's African and Arab inhabitants and the village mosques reminded him he was still in the world of Islam, even on the east coast of equatorial Africa. It was not until he climbed out of the minibus at Nungwi and stretched his cramped muscles that he realised just how beautiful the beach and water were. He peeled off twenty-five grimy dollars for a bungalow and dumped his backpack inside the door without bothering to inspect the room.

Luke had been born in Sydney and grown up in the northern beaches suburb of Avalon. The ocean had been part of his life since before he could walk and he headed for the water with the same ingrained need as a hatchling sea turtle. He peeled off his T-shirt and kicked off his sandals on sand as fine and white as icing sugar. The water was blue and inviting and he lost himself in it, diving and corkscrewing like a dolphin as he shook the last imaginary grains of dust of the windswept Shomali Plain from his locks.

Two English girls, lobster-red from their first day of sun, giggled at his abandon as they silently appraised his lithe body and unruly curly hair. They chatted to him when he eventually returned to land, and arranged to meet for drinks at the resort bar later in the evening.

The bar was perched on a wide deck of bleached, rough-hewn timber shaded with a steep-pitched thatch roof. The music was a mixture of rap and Bob Marley. Luke didn't mind either but, as he knew from his time in the Jo'burg bureau of International News, Africans tended to have only one setting on their stereo volume controls – max. He dragged his chair out to the balcony away from the booming speakers, the water visible under his feet through gaps between the planks. As the sun dived for the horizon the English girls joined him, along with a mixed bag of South African divers, Italian honeymooners and German backpackers.

They'd chatted, as travellers do, about prices and hotels and ferry timetables, trying to outdo each other with how little they'd paid and how much they'd seen. Luke stayed silent for most of it, his mind still in the foothills of the Hindu Kush though the delicious smells wafting from the bar's kitchen reminded him he was a world away from war-ravaged Afghanistan. There he'd eaten courtesy of the US Army – reconstituted eggs, powdered potatoes and chunked steak. The cooked meals were prepared four thousand kilometres away at a base in Germany, frozen and then flown by C-17 to Bagram, where they were reheated and slopped onto polystyrene plates. The meals did not travel well. For lunch he'd eaten Army MREs, which officially stood for 'Meal, Ready to Eat'. The brown plastic packets of brown plastic food were referred to by the troops as Meal, Rarely Edible or Meal, Rejected by Ethiopians.

That night Luke gorged on grilled Zanzibar rock lobster and fried fresh calamari, washed down by ice-cold Safari and Kilimanjaro lager. After dinner, as a DJ pumped up the volume in a bid to get people dancing, the talk turned to politics.

'Fucking Americans. They want to rule the goddamned world. They think they can bomb civilians and invade any country they want to,' one of the South African divers, tanned and muscled with his blond hair plaited in incongruous dreadlocks, said.

'*Ja*,' a German guy agreed. 'They are all, how you say, Rambos. All they do is kill, kill, kill. It makes me sick.'

'One saved my life,' Luke said, only half aware he'd spoken. The Safaris had dulled his senses and he was losing himself in the alcohol's ministrations and the bright white smile of one of the English girls.

'What do you mean?' she asked.

He told her about Jed Banks and the helicopter being fired on, and the Arab he'd seen gunned down in front of him. He said it in a quiet, matter-of-fact voice that belied the terror and the nightmares, and the rest of them sat in stunned silence.

Afterwards, he'd been embarrassed, and had walked down the stairs from the wooden deck onto the sand at the first opportunity. The girl in the lime-green bikini had followed him to the beach and, later, to his bungalow.

Now, the next morning, Luke walked back out onto the bar's terrace. He lit a cigarette and thought about what he must do. A fisherman in an outrigger canoe, his chiselled black body impervious to the sun's rays, paddled effortlessly past the resort on his way to work. Luke, too, had work to do, and it scared as much as excited him. Here, on this island paradise, Afghanistan was still very much on his mind. Rather than running away from the horror he'd experienced, he would be chasing it, holding onto the beast's tail and shaking it for all it was worth.

He walked back to the bungalow to see if the English girl was awake yet. She stirred and opened her eyes at the squeaking of the door. She smiled. When she spoke, her voice was hoarse from the cigarettes and vodka. Sexy as hell. 'Leaving already?'

'I'm afraid so. It was great. Thanks. I mean . . .' She did not look angry or disappointed, he thought.

'What time's the minibus?' she croaked.

'Ten.'

She checked her Swatch. 'It's only eight-thirty. That gives us an hour and twenty-five minutes.'

He smiled. 'An hour and twenty-five?'

'You'll have to comb your hair and dress, won't you?'

She lifted the mosquito net and threw back the sheet. Luke climbed in.

Beneath him, Stone Town snoozed the afternoon away, but Luke was hard at work, his mobile phone clamped to his ear.

'Zanzibar, not *Zimbabwe*. I'm in Zanzibar, Stone Town.' The signal was weak and he was almost shouting. He was on the top floor of a small, cheap hotel behind the *Beit el Ajaib*, the House of Wonders – a former sultan's palace so named because it was the first building on the island to have electricity and an elevator. Through the gap between the palace and the whitewashed mosque next door he glimpsed a silvery slice of the Indian Ocean, as still as a pond.

It was four in the afternoon and most other people on the island were taking a nap. Luke cupped his free hand over the mouthpiece so as not to wake the entire building.

'How long are you going to be there and how much is it going to cost?' Bernie, the International Press chief of staff in London, asked down the line.

'Bloody hell, Bernie, I'm onto a ball-tearer of a story and all you care about is the bloody bucks. Give me a break. I nearly fucking *died* in Afghanistan – you should be giving me this trip as a holiday!'

Bernie laughed. 'Spare me your Aussie wit and tell me again what you're doing there. I've got the afternoon news conference soon, so make it good.'

'It's a follow-up to my last story, the one out of Afghanistan about the Al Qaeda guy that was killed on the patrol I was on.'

'Yeah, right. Not exactly Osama bin Laden, was he?'

'No, but he was from here – Zanzibar, remember? Iqbal bin Zayid. Plus, there was that bomb in Dar es Salaam yesterday.'

'Yeah, we've got that. Judy in Dar filed last night. Also, they've evacuated the US embassy today, following a bomb threat.'

'Shit, I didn't know that.'

'Check the website, the story's up now. Do you think you can get some more colour for us? Find out if terrified backpackers are leaving Zanzibar in droves, crippling the local tourism industry, that sort of crap.'

Luke paused to sip on his bottle of Safari. 'Sure, I'll get you something, but I want to chase down the dead terrorist's family, find out more about him and if there are more like him at home.'

'All right, but keep your eye on the ball, Luke. Look, this isn't getting personal, is it? The guy did try to kill you after all.'

'No, it's not bloody personal.'

'Right. But seriously, take a few days on the beach when you finish there before you go back to Jo'burg. You've probably earned it.'

Luke snorted. 'OK, and I'm going back via Zimbabwe.'

'Zimbabwe? What is it about you and all these bloody "Z" countries?'

'There's someone I want to catch up with. The bloke who saved my life in Afghanistan. You know, the father of the girl who was killed by a lion. I heard from his ex-wife that he's over there, though God knows what he expects to find. Thought I'd see where the investigation into her death is at, what the fallout is.'

'That was a hell of a good story, Luke. US Special Forces soldier kills a wanted terrorist, saves a dumb journo's life and then finds out his only child has been killed by a wild animal. Talk about the mother of all human fucking interest stories!' Bernie laughed.

Luke shook his head. Everyone in the game knew journalists became desensitised to tragedy. Like most of his colleagues, he coped with the day-to-day exposure to death and sorrow with a mix of black humour and alcohol, but Bernie was talking about someone he knew personally – someone who had indeed saved his life.

'Yeah, right,' Luke said. 'Anyway, this line's crap. I'll be in touch soon, Bernie. I'll file a couple hundred words on the post-bomb tourism situation tonight. See ya.'

'Cheers then. Find yourself a Swedish backpacker and a beer, you'll be OK.'

'Who needs Swedish girls when there are pommies around?' Luke replied, smiling at the memory of the morning's hot, sweaty sex.

'You colonial cad. Don't tell me you've been deflowering some innocent English rose?'

'Rosy all right, but not too innocent,' he said.

Luke finished his beer as he looked across the roofs of Stone Town. The ocean beyond the city's crumbling edifices reflected the changing colours of the fading sun. A mix of medieval dhows and state-of-the-art luxury cruisers sat motionless at anchor in the breathless afternoon. He wanted another beer, but he knew he should stay clear-headed for this evening's business.

He closed his eyes. In an instant he was back there. They happened a lot, the flashbacks. At the oddest times, and most nights in his nightmares, he could see himself there, hear the bullets, see the wounded helicopter crewman, feel himself falling from the Chinook. My God, he thought. I was going to die. They would have left me if Jed Banks hadn't jumped to the ground, rescued me and killed the man he now knew as Iqbal bin Zayid.

Luke placed a hand on his left side. His cracked ribs still hurt whenever he took a deep breath. The doctor said it would be weeks before they healed completely. The scab on his shoulder where he had cut himself had fallen off during his time on the beach. The skin was pink and puckered, a reminder that all of this had taken place less than two weeks ago. Despite the protests of the US Army medics Luke had filed the story of the firefight as soon as he returned to base. His fellow reporters had toasted him with cans of British beer, smuggled past the puritanical American military police, as he'd sat at his laptop, blood oozing from his shoulder, hair matted, face dirty and his side afire with pain. Afterwards, he had stumbled up Disney Parade, checked into the American field hospital and passed out.

The next day the camp was abuzz with news of the raid on the compound and the battalion-sized sweep that followed it. The sky was browned-out with dust from wave after wave of Chinooks and Apaches. Luke didn't even try to get on a flight – he spent the next four days in hospital. As soon as he was discharged he set off to find Jed Banks and thank him. Freshly bandaged, he reported to the front gate of the Coalition Joint Special Operations Task Force compound and asked for the master sergeant. The ranger on guard duty spoke into his radio and asked Luke to wait. That wasn't unusual, as reporters were not allowed into the compound. He hoped Jed would take the time to meet with him. In the end, it was the task force chaplain who came to the gate and explained to Luke that Jed had left because of a family emergency.

The following day International Press's regular Afghanistan correspondent returned from her two weeks' leave in Turkey, annoyed to hear that Luke had encountered the first serious action in months and that IP had scooped the world with the story of the firefight. Luke gratefully said his goodbyes and hitched a ride out on a USAF C-17 transport to Qatar where, the next day, he caught a connecting civilian flight to Dubai and made an onward booking for Johannesburg.

Luke had planned a week's leave at Durban on the South African east coast to recuperate from his time in Afghanistan. However, while in Dubai airport he had seen a newspaper report about a young female American wildlife researcher who had been killed by a lion in Zimbabwe, in the Zambezi Valley. He had spilled his coffee on the table of the cafe in his haste to find his mobile phone in his daypack. The story said the woman's name had not yet been released. How many American women were researching wildlife in the Zambezi Valley? It had to be Miranda. That was the personal tragedy that had taken Jed Banks out of Afghanistan. It was all coming together.

Luke recalled that Miranda had lived with her mother before going to Africa. He dug out the grubby, sweat- and dust-stained notebook he had used in Afghanistan and flicked through the pages. Patti was Miranda's mother's name – probably short for Patricia. Luke got out his laptop and connected to the internet using the infra-red connection on his mobile phone and international roaming software that gave him a dial-in number in Dubai. Within a few minutes he was checking telephone listings in Boston. He found dozens of entries. The phone bill would be horrendous, but the company would pay. On the twenty-second call a woman answered the phone and Luke said, 'Good morning, ma'am, my name is Luke Scarborough, I'm a friend of your ex-husband, Jed, and I was just calling to express my deepest condolences about what happened to Miranda . . .'

The first twenty-one Lewises who picked up the phone had thought him a madman or a prankster. This woman was silent for a moment, then said, 'Um, thank you. How do you know my ex-husband, and how did you find out about Miranda? Her name wasn't going to be made public until tomorrow.'

'I was with your husband in Afghanistan, Mrs Lewis. Jed saved my life over there. He was telling me about Miranda's work in Africa the night he rescued me. He loved her very much. I'm on my way to Zimbabwe now, and –'

Miranda's mother cut him short. 'Are you going to see Jed over there? Will you meet up with him?'

Yes! Luke mouthed silently.

The call proved a gold mine of information. Before Patti went on too much longer Luke identified himself as a reporter, fearing as he did so that she would hang up the phone. In his experience, people who had just lost a family member under tragic circumstances responded in one of two ways. Some would tell a reporter to go away, in language as

174

strong as they could muster, while others, the majority in his experience, would want to talk at length about their loved one's life, from cradle to grave. To be honest, Luke preferred the former reaction, so that he could go back to his bosses and say he had tried to get a comment or a picture of the deceased, but the family would not co-operate. The alternative was heart-wrenching, and sometimes exceedingly boring, as teary relatives poured their hearts out.

Patti Lewis was still in shock, neither unfriendly nor effusive. She answered Luke's questions about Miranda's life and her work and gave him enough colourful quotes for a good story. She was resigned to talking to him, on the basis that the State Department would release Miranda's name the next day, and she partially bought his line that there would be fewer callers from the media once his story was on the wire. On top of all that he now knew that Jed was heading to Zimbabwe, to investigate the circumstances of Miranda's disappearance. He *had* to get down there and see him. It would make a sensational colour piece. And, the story aside, he wanted to thank Jed and maybe talk through a few things.

He telephoned the IP central newsroom in London and briefed Bernie on his conversation with Patti Lewis. It was Bernie who gave him the news that the US had released the name of the Zanzibari Al Qaeda terrorist who had been killed in Afghanistan during the firefight Luke had been involved in. The man was a middle-ranking commander who had fought in Chechnya, where he was believed to have been responsible for the downing of a Russian army helicopter which had resulted in the deaths of nearly sixty soldiers.

The many threads of the story had coalesced magically in Luke's mind. As he'd typed he had smiled to himself as the string of heroic and tragic events filled the page – the brave US Army hero who kills the wanted terrorist, only to find his beloved daughter has been killed in a freak accident. Patti Lewis's quotes had rounded it out nicely.

Below him now, somewhere in the winding alleys of Stone Town, was the missing piece of the story.

Luke walked downstairs to his room and took a cold shower. There was no hot water, even if he'd wanted it. The room was cheap but functional, about a quarter of a star above fleapit status, but his daily expense allowance didn't allow for much better. He dried off with a threadbare towel that smelled as though it had been washed with hand soap, and put on a navy long-sleeved cotton shirt and a pair of light-weight khaki trousers and sandals for his foray into the labyrinthine alleys of Stone Town. He was looking for leads about the life of an Islamic fundamentalist and was culturally aware enough to know that shorts and a singlet top would not endear him to the man's family or friends. He shouldered his camera bag, which contained a professional Canon digital body with a twenty-eight- to fifty-millimetre lens attached, and a three hundred for long-range shots. He also checked he had his notebook and two pens, and that there was still life in the batteries of his mini cassette recorder.

As he walked out of the hotel, shopkeepers were opening their doors and shutters in the narrow winding lanes of Stone Town as the old quarter came alive again in the comparative cool of evening. A young boy on a bicycle rang his bell and chicaned his way around a couple of blonde German backpacker girls. Luke, for one, wasn't culturally offended by their cut-off denim shorts and he turned to give the pair a second glance, nearly walking into an Arab merchant in a long white cotton robe carrying a silver antique tea service.

'Excuse me,' Luke said to the man.

'Not at all. Would you care to look inside?' The man gestured to an antiques shop.

'Why not?' Luke said. He had to start asking questions somewhere. His eyes wandered over shelves crammed with brass and silver knick-knacks. Some, he supposed, were antiques, though he expected most were modern replicas. 'How's business?'

The Arab shrugged his shoulders. 'A little bit quiet now. Iraq, SARS, bombs . . .'

Luke inspected a brass telescope, raising it to his eye and looking out into the street, unable to focus on anything.

'Are you looking for anything in particular, my friend?' the shop-keeper asked.

'Actually, I'm looking for a telephone book.'

'A telephone book? An antique?'

Luke smiled. 'No, actually, I'm looking for a person, by the name of bin Zayid.'

'Interesting. A name that has appeared in the newspaper recently.'

'Iqbal bin Zayid.' Luke set down the telescope.

'Do not believe everything you hear from the Americans, young man. What are you, a journalist?'

'Yes.'

'I have no problem with journalists – they are only as good as the information they are given. People who say Iqbal bin Zayid was a terrorist do not know him or his family. His father, Hassan, God bless him, was a good man. He was married to an English woman. A non-believer! How could a boy who was the son of a western woman, a Christian woman, be a terrorist?'

'You knew the family?'

'A little. They own some hotels here and on the mainland, and Hassan the elder would sometimes buy antiques from me to decorate the reception rooms and so forth.'

'Hassan the elder?'

'He is dead now, may God keep him, but his son helps keep me in business.'

'Can you tell me where I can find the family?' The old man looked wary, Luke thought, perhaps wondering if he had given away too much already.

'As I said, Hassan is dead, and his wife ran off with another man, back to England, many years ago, when the boys were both small. I heard she died. Iqbal is gone, killed by the Americans, and young Hassan is rarely here. He travels a lot to the mainland, looking after the family's business.'

'I only want to talk to someone to get the other side of the story. If Iqbal was innocent, then the world deserves to hear that.' It was one of the oldest lines in the reporter's book of half-truths. Iqbal the Innocent had tried to kill him with an AK-47.

177

The antique dealer scratched his chin. In his other hand he fingered a set of ivory worry beads. 'Very well. I will give you the business address of the bin Zayid offices. Hassan may not be there, but you will be able to leave a message for him, I am sure.'

'Thanks. How much for the telescope?'

The directions the Arab shopkeeper gave led him deeper into Stone Town. As he wound his way through the maze of lanes, the sights, sounds and smells of the ancient precinct assaulted his senses. Every breath he drew of cloves and other aromatic spices was countered by the odour of rotting garbage or an overflowing sewer. For each ornately carved and studded door, there was another devoured by damp and termites. Each giggled *'jambo'*, Swahili for hello, from a shyly smiling child was matched by a cold stare or sneer from a surly youth.

'Osama bin Laden,' a young African man in an LA Lakers basketball shirt murmured as Luke walked past a shop selling gaudily painted Zambians and women's clothing. Luke didn't know whether the man had mentioned the name as part of a conversation with the youth standing beside him, or if it was some form of veiled threat directed at him. Either way, he did not stop to quiz the boy. He felt eyes boring into his back as he strode on down the lane.

Modern politics, religion and prejudices aside, there was no denying the appeal of the claustrophobic old town. In some quieter stretches of alleyway, where he passed men in flowing robes and black-veiled women, the only reminders he was in the twenty-first century were the signs directing him to yet another internet cafe.

Luke found the offices of Zayid Enterprises in a three-storey renovated stone building at the eastern end of town, not far from the Africa House, a rowdy pub inhabited most hours of the day by young backpackers.

A brass plaque beside an ornate wooden door decorated with pointed brass studs confirmed he had found his quarry. Luke knew from his guidebook that the door of a Zanzibari building said a lot about the occupants. This portal was dark and formidable, steeped in history, and almost impregnable. It was flanked by an intercom system

178

with a built-in camera. When he pressed the buzzer, someone inside released an electronic lock. For all its old-world charm, the building was protected by the most modern of security systems. Luke wondered if the surviving bin Zayid had anything to hide.

He pushed open the door and walked up a short flight of stone stairs. At the top he found himself in a tastefully decorated reception area. In contrast with the exterior, the building's interior was ultra-modern, lots of chrome and glass, whitewashed walls and cubist prints. An attractive young African woman in a short-sleeved white blouse said good afternoon to him from behind a large white desk.

'Hello, I was wondering if I could speak with Mr Hassan bin Zayid, please?'

'Do you have an appointment, sir?' the woman asked, checking a large desk diary.

'No, my name's Luke Scarborough. I'm a journalist from the International Press news agency. I've been told your company runs a few hotels in the region and I'd like to speak to Mr bin Zayid about visitor trends in East Africa.' His story was close enough to the truth to allow him to sound convincing.

'I'm sorry, sir, but Mr bin Zayid is not here.'

'Do you expect him back today?' He watched her face carefully and noticed her eyes flick towards an antique brass clock on the wall.

'I can't say, sir. Mr bin Zayid sees no one without an appointment. If I can take your name and number I will call you back if he can fit you into his schedule.'

Luke looked around the office. On the walls were half-a-dozen large glossy colour photographs in polished brass frames. The same man was in each shot. He was youngish, maybe thirty, with dark wavy hair, immaculately dressed and with a face that was not quite European and not quite Arabic. The pictures showed the man in a variety of situations, mostly standing side by side with people who looked to be of some importance. He was with an Arab sheikh in flowing robes; an elderly African man in a suit, perhaps a politician; cutting the ribbon at the opening of a new building, presumably one of the family's hotels. The odd photo out showed the man standing at the stern of a luxury cabin cruiser. The name of the vessel was clearly visible on the back, written in English – *Faith*. There was Arabic script underneath, probably the same word.

'Thanks,' Luke said to the receptionist. He took out a business card and pen from his pocket and underlined his mobile phone number. 'I've also written the name of the hotel where I'm staying on the back of this card. I'll be there for a couple more nights. Mr bin Zayid can contact me at any hour of the day or leave a message at my hotel. I really am very keen to talk to him.'

'Of course, sir. I will be sure to pass on the message.'

'And may I please have your telephone number in case I need to check back with you later?'

'Certainly, sir.' She recited the office telephone number and Luke wrote it in his notebook.

As he turned to leave he took a closer look at the picture of the coffee-skinned man and the sheikh. Piercing blue eyes stared back at him from the broad handsome face. The last time he had seen those eyes was the second before Jed Banks shot the life from them. This man was not only the brother of Iqbal bin Zayid; he was his identical twin.

Luke waggled the fingers of both his hands as he walked out onto the narrow street, a gesture that came to him involuntarily when he knew he was on the verge of a sensational story. This was one of those yarns that would write itself, if only he could make contact with Hassan bin Zayid.

He decided to take a walk down to the harbour, to see if he could find out where bin Zayid moored his boat. There was an off-chance the man might even be lounging aboard the luxury vessel. The odds were slim, but he was at that early stage of an investigation when he would pursue any lead at all. Luck played a part in investigative journalism, but luck wouldn't find you if you sat in a bar or office all day.

As he strode along the foreshore that skirted the Ras Shangani district he pondered the bin Zayid lineage, mentally composing a few background paragraphs for the article he would write. He'd brushed up on the island's history from a guidebook on the ferry trip from the mainland. Arabs from Oman had rounded the Horn of Africa and ventured down the continent's east coast as early as the eighth century, beginning a trade in spices, cloves, hides, rhino horn, ivory and humans that would last for centuries. How long ago, he wondered, had the bin Zayid family arrived? What events in Zanzibar's rich history had shaped the family's political and religious views? The British had progressively ended the slave trade from the early nineteenth century, but Zanzibar continued to thrive, with cloves replacing men, women and children as the island's main commodity.

Luke presumed from their appearance that Hassan and Iqbal bin Zayid came from Omani stock, as these original merchants rarely intermarried with the local African population. Not so the Shirazis, the other dominant Arabic influence in East Africa, who had migrated from Persia in the tenth century. The Shirazis mixed with local Africans and created the coastal people known as Swahili, whose language and culture spread inland along the routes of the infamous slave caravans. The antique dealer had spoken of Hassan and Iqbal's father marrying a western woman, a nonbeliever, and that was something else Luke wanted to look into. Even if Iqbal had been a lone zealot in the family, the bin Zayid family tree would make an interesting background for his feature.

Luke slowed down as he neared the sprawling Old Fort, built by the Omanis in 1700 to withstand attacks by the Portuguese. By the nineteenth century Zanzibar had become a British protectorate, with a constitutional monarchy in the form of an Arab sultan. The sultan's descendants had stayed in power until a coup by Africans in 1964, following several years of increasing discontent by the local majority, and the deaths of dozens of Arabs. The new, independent Zanzibar did not stay so for long, and soon merged with the independent mainland nation of Tanzania.

That was the trouble with Zanzibar, Luke mused. So much history it was hard to encapsulate in a news story and relate it to the modern world. Did the bin Zayid brothers feel some resentment at the waning of Arab influence in East Africa? Were they offended by the growing numbers of western tourists in their homeland, who seemed, even in Luke's opinion, to get younger, wear less, drink more and use more drugs with every passing year? There had been terrorist-sponsored backlashes against westerners in other Islamic tourist destinations. Was Iqbal bin Zayid's transformation from the heir to a prosperous tourist business to Islamic holy warrior a by-product of the industry his family had helped to create? Great angle, Luke thought, if only he could get someone to say it.

A dhow glided through the Zanzibar channel off to his left, its two African crewmen singing as they pulled on the lines of the lateen sail in order to catch the dying gasps of the day's breeze. Ahead, Luke could see the mooring it was headed for, a small floating dock overcrowded with dhows and tourist boats. Half-a-dozen teenage touts raced towards him from the dock.

'Dhow, mister? You want go to Dar tomorrow? Pemba? Mombasa maybe?'

'You want somewhere to stay, mister?'

'Marijuana, my friend. You want dope?'

Luke smiled and said no to all, but walked along the waterfront inspecting the various vessels moored off a wedge of yellow sand.

'Hey, you kids, scram now!' a voice called from a long wooden boat with a big outboard on the back. A European man about Luke's age jumped onto the sand in front of him. The man wore loud board shorts and a ragged tank top. His bare skin was tanned the colour of walnuts and his shaggy blond hair was stiff with salt. 'Don't worry about the kids, hey, they don't mean you any harm. Just ignore them and they'll leave you alone, eventually.'

'Thanks, I've learned that the hard way. You're a fair way from home?' Luke picked the man's accent as South African.

'From Durban. But not so far as you. Aussie?'

'Yeah, just here for a few days. I work out of Johannesburg.'

The man laughed. 'Hey, you can rest easy here, man. Don't need to carry a gun, like back in Jo'burg. Do you dive?'

'Who's touting for business now?'

The South African laughed again. 'Sorry, you got me. But watch out who you go out with. There are some scaly operators up here, man.'

'I'll bet.'

'Still can't beat this place, though.' He looked out towards the huge orange ball falling rapidly towards the distant mainland. 'Hey, check that cruiser. That's the kind of tub I want one day. That's *Destiny*. Owned by one of my countrymen. A gun-runner, no less.'

'You been working here long?'

'Couple of years. Beats working behind a desk back home.'

'You got that right. Do you recognise all the regular big boats by sight?'

'Most.'

'Do you know a boat called *Faith*?'

'Sure, that's Hassan bin Zayid's. Owns a couple of hotels here and a *lekker* backpacker joint on the mainland. Also tied up in a game farm somewhere. I run dive tours as a package from his hotels here. Hell of a nice guy. You looking for him?'

'Yeah. I'm a journalist. A contact told me he'd be a good person to talk to. I'm doing a story on how the terrorist stuff around the world is affecting the tourist business here.'

'He'd be a good guy to talk to about that stuff, being Arabic and all. He's not a fundamentalist, though. I've had a beer with him on the dock before, and he likes the western chicks, if you know what I mean.'

Luke shared a laugh with the South African. 'So, have you seen Hassan's boat lately?'

'Matter of fact, I saw him pull in this afternoon.'

Luke scanned the waterfront, but saw no sign of the luxury vessel. 'Where does he moor his cruiser?'

'Just up there.' The South African pointed along the waterfront to the stone and concrete pier that marked the start of the main harbour. A high-speed ferry boat was pulling away from the dock. 'I'm heading into the harbour myself. It's where our office is. I've got to lock up all this stuff.' He gestured to the air tanks, wetsuits, fins and dive masks that littered the bottom of his boat. 'I don't know if Hassan will be there, but I can take you up there now if you like.'

'That'd be great. Can I pay you something?'

'There's an Indian restaurant across the road there. Go grab us some cold beers, man. Tell the oke running the place Piet will bring the empties back tomorrow. I'll be ten minutes paying off my touts and then we're off.'

Luke walked across the road to the restaurant and returned with a plastic shopping bag clanking with six bottles of Safari Lager. He marvelled at how often things fell into place once you did a bit of leg-work and got talking to the locals. Even if Hassan bin Zayid was not on his boat, Luke would at least get some extra colour and more of an insight into the man's life.

He introduced himself to Piet and handed the cargo of beer aboard. Piet started the outboard motor, jumped onto the beach again, untied his mooring line and tossed it to Luke as he pushed the boat away from shore. Piet navigated them between an elegant dhow and a Taiwanese container ship, its deck stacked five-high with steel boxes. Luke opened two bottles of beer, using the lid of a third bottle, held upside down, to prise the caps off the first two. He handed one to Piet and said, 'Does anyone else use Hassan's boat?'

'Not that I know of. Haven't seen him around for some time, but he definitely came in today.'

The sun was setting and it cast a warm, golden glow on the white-washed fort and the pale coral-brick buildings ashore. Soon the muezzin would be calling the faithful to prayer from the minarets of the island's mosques. Piet hugged the waterfront and swung the dive boat around to starboard, past concrete wharves lined with cargo ships, more dhows, and an assortment of commercial motor boats similar to his. Long, low warehouses, painted pale-green with orange rusted roofs, fringed the harbour foreshore. Ahead, Luke could see some luxury cruisers.

'Ah, shit, man.'

'What is it?' Luke asked.

'There he goes, see?'

Luke looked where Piet was pointing and saw a long, sleek cruiser coming towards them on their left.

'Listen, can you get closer to him for me?' Luke asked. 'While there's still a little light I'd like to get a picture of the boat, to use later with my story.'

Luke pulled out the camera and unscrewed his fifty-millimetre lens and replaced it with the larger telephoto.

'I'm just going to lie down in the boat so I can rest the lens on the side, OK?' he said to Piet. In truth, he didn't want to arouse the Arab's suspicion in case he was seen.

'Sure, I'll move a little closer.'

Through the viewfinder Luke could see the bridge of the cruiser as the auto focus whirred into action. Hassan bin Zayid leaped into focus, standing behind the wheel. Luke had the shutter release set to high speed motor drive and fired off three quick frames. Hassan turned and looked over his shoulder. Luke panned right with the camera and saw a woman climbing the ladder from the lower aft deck. He pressed the shutter release again.

Luke adjusted the lens and zoomed in tight on Hassan and the woman, who was now standing beside him. She put two drinks down on the dashboard in front of him and then rested a hand on his shoulder. The woman was young, blonde and pretty, dressed in a short black cocktail dress. He registered a glimpse of toned golden thigh above the cruiser's gunwale. Luke fired off another five shots and the camera stopped.

'Shit,' he said. 'Bloody memory card is full.' Luke ejected the full card, slipped it into the pocket of his shorts and found a blank card in the front pocket of the camera bag. He reloaded and refocused on the boat, which had now passed them.

Hassan turned to the woman and they kissed. A lingering, lazy kiss. The touch of lovers.

'That old dog!' Piet said. 'What did I tell you? That oke likes his *mzungus* – whiteys.'

185

'I wonder where they're heading?'

Piet cracked open two more bottles of Safari with his pocket knife. 'Hey, I know where I'd be heading with her, man. Somewhere quiet, under the moonlight, one of the islands maybe, or a romantic little cove. Some place where you will *not* want to be disturbed for a few days! Get up and drink your beer, man.'

'Thanks,' Luke said, sitting up now that the cruiser was nearly out of sight, around the point, heading towards the main channel between Zanzibar and the mainland. He checked the small camera screen and cycled through the images of the couple kissing. It was growing dark now and he didn't know if the pictures would be useable, or even how a picture of a half-Arab businessman and a European woman would fit into his story. Still, he had worked around photographers enough to know that when an opportunity presented itself you were better off shooting the shit out of everything rather than waiting for a posed photo opportunity. He took a last glimpse at the boat and saw that Hassan bin Zayid was now talking on a mobile phone.

The woman had moved to the back of the boat and was looking back, holding a wineglass as she leaned on the rear safety railing. It seemed to Luke she was staring directly at him. Bin Zayid, too, was looking pointedly at Piet and Luke.

'You're not snooping, are you, man?' Piet asked.

'No, no. But I know that sometimes people don't like to be photographed, particularly if they're heading off somewhere with a beautiful woman.'

'Well, I'll tell Hassan you were looking for him, next time I see him.' Piet put the outboard in neutral and they glided close into a berth at the dock, between two dhows.

'That'd be great, Piet. Thanks for the ride.' Luke thought his openness had put the South African at ease once more, now that he knew Luke wasn't hiding from the Arab.

'No problem. You OK to get back to town from here? Where are you staying?'

Luke gave Piet the name of a cheap hotel on Humzvi Street and the

South African snapped his fingers and said, 'Hey, man, can you do me a favour?'

'Sure, name it.'

'One of the tourists who came out diving with me today left his day-pack here. He's staying in the place just up the street from you – the fancy hotel. You know it?'

'Sure. I'd be happy to.'

Piet opened the daypack, giving Luke a quick inventory. 'Just a mask and snorkel, some sun cream, a water bottle and a dive knife. I've got to refill all the bottles tonight, so you're saving me a walk.'

'No worries.' Luke took the pack, which had clearly seen better days. It was crusted with sea salt on the front and sweat stains on the back, and the nylon fabric was so worn it had already started to tear in a couple of places. He had to push the sheathed dive knife back inside the bag, as the tip was protruding from a small rent. 'Happy to help.'

'Thanks, man, and good luck with your story.'

'Why don't you get us another drink,' Hassan bin Zayid said to the woman. He could still taste her white wine in his mouth from their kiss and was hungry for more of her. That could wait. When she drifted away he called his office from his cell phone.

'Zayid Enterprises, how may I help you?'

'Grace, it's Mr bin Zayid.'

'Yes, sir.'

'That journalist who called and left a message for me today, what did he look like?'

The African receptionist thought for a moment, then said, 'He was a white man, sir. Long hair. A small beard, you know, just the moustache and the chin. Blue shirt, too, I think.'

'Thank you, Grace. That will be all.'

'Oh, sir, please, one more thing.'

'Yes?'

'Mr el Mazri called. Sir, he said the journalist – it was the same man – visited him at his antiques shop earlier today. It was Mr el Mazri who gave the man the address of the office. He said he wanted to warn you that the reporter was asking questions about your brother.'

Hassan stared ahead into the growing gloom of the channel. News of his brother's death was known to the world and it would not be unexpected for a reporter to claim to be wanting information about a downturn in the tourism industry, while really seeking information about his family's links to a terrorist organisation.

'Thank you, Grace. You did well. Please call Mr el Mazri back and thank him for the information. You won't hear from me now for a few days, as we discussed before.'

'Very good, sir. Goodbye.'

No, the fact that a reporter was asking questions was not unusual – Hassan had half expected more journalists to come looking for the family once it was revealed in the American media that Iqbal had been born on Zanzibar. What was of concern to him was the fact that the reporter who had visited his offices was quite obviously the same man who had been taking pictures of him and the woman. The man had made himself even more conspicuous by trying to hide behind the gunwale of the dive boat.

Hassan weighed the risks in his mind. He had come too far. He could leave no loose ends at this critical stage of the operation. He dialled another number.

'Yes?' came a deep African voice.

'Achmed, it is Hassan. I have work for you.'

'Yes.'

'Go to the office. Ask Grace for the business card of the *mzungu* who visited her today. It will have all the information you need.' Hassan gave Achmed the rest of the detailed instructions, imagining the broad smile that would be splitting the man's scarred face at the prospect of the night's work ahead. Hassan had met some tough characters in Africa, but none, he thought, was quite so threatening as the tall African who had served his family's business interests so well and for so long.

'Here's your drink,' she said, returning to his side in the cockpit. 'Cheers.'

'Cheers,' he said.

There was no turning back now, he told himself. Not that there ever had been.

The centre of Stone Town was fully awake. The lanes and squares were alive with the sounds of music and chatter, the aroma of exotic foods and spice, and the sharp tang of sweaty bodies. Luke meandered his way through the throngs of tourists and locals.

He decided to get some food and maybe squeeze in a drink at the Africa House pub before delivering the diver's pack and turning in at his own hotel. Down on the waterfront, near the Old Fort, rows of vendors had set up their stalls for the evening food market. Luke's mouth watered as he inspected skewered prawns, fish, beef and chicken pieces sizzling atop smoky charcoal braziers. Pots of deliciously spiced curries simmered on gas burners, adding to the heady mix. He ordered two skewers of prawns, one of chicken and a couple of pieces of unleavened bread to wrap them in. From another vendor he bought a cold can of Coca-Cola, then found a space on a park bench overlooking the harbour.

After he had finished eating he headed off in the direction of the Africa House. Away from the waterfront the streets were quieter and he found himself alone as he cut through a narrow side alleyway. He admired the ornate doors on the ancient homes and wondered what it would be like living in a centuries-old house. His reverie was broken by the sound of hurried footsteps behind him.

His mobile phone rang and he scrabbled in his camera bag for it.

'Luke Scarborough speaking.'

The line went dead. Luke checked the screen of his phone, but no number appeared in the received-calls box. He heard the footsteps again, close now. He turned and saw a tall black man. The man was smiling, but his face was not friendly. A puckered scar ran from his right ear to the corner of his mouth.

'Hello, my friend,' the man said.

'Sorry, I've already got a place to –'

A blur in front of his face. The sound of his nose breaking. Blackness. Intense, blinding pain. Luke felt his body tumble backwards, onto the cobbled lane.

Achmed grabbed the Australian around the throat with one massive hand, lifted him to his feet and drove his other fist into the boy's belly. He glanced up and down the laneway, then dragged his victim into the deepest shadows. He grabbed the reporter's left arm and twisted it up hard behind his back. The backpack and camera bag slid from Luke's other shoulder to the ground. From his pocket, Achmed pulled a knife and held the point against Luke's throat.

'Lie down. If you make a sound I will kill you.'

When Luke was on the ground, face down, Achmed placed a foot on his back. He unzipped the camera bag, found the Canon and ejected the plastic memory card. He put it in his pocket, then grabbed the camera by its long lens and smashed the body against the stone wall of the nearest building. Its shattered innards rained down on the pathetic figure writhing on the ground. Achmed tossed the ruined camera aside. He retrieved the memory card from his pocket, folded it between his thumb and a finger until it snapped, then dropped the two halves next to Luke's face. Next, he methodically searched the camera bag's many pockets, looking for other memory cards.

Luke could not move his body, with the African's huge booted foot on his back, but his arms were still free. Slowly, he moved his hand across the cobbles. He felt jagged pieces of the trashed camera, the least of his problems. His fingers reached the daypack belonging to the absent-minded scuba diver. He traced the worn fabric of the pack and found the rent through which the knife protruded once more. Gently he eased three fingers inside the hole and then spread them, pleased as he felt the tear expand. Now he was able to get his whole hand inside the bag. Suddenly the other lens for his destroyed camera landed near his face and he stiffened, not daring to move in case the man looked down at him.

When moments passed with no further blow, Luke carefully ran his fingers along the length of the knife's scabbard until he was grasping the handle securely in his right hand. With his thumb he eased part of the blade from the sheath.

'Hey, what the fuck are you doing, boy?' Achmed said as he reached down for the daypack.

Luke felt the pressure of the foot ease slightly on his back. As the African tugged on the bag, the rip in the side expanded even further. The fabric snagged on the loosened scabbard, and when Achmed pulled harder, the bag and sheath came away, revealing the glittering nine-inch blade of the dive knife.

Luke rolled hard to the right and lashed out with all his might. The blade sliced through the leg of Achmed's jeans and the flesh of his calf. Achmed yelped and lost his balance as Luke followed the knife slash with a fist up into his opponent's groin. Achmed hit the building wall and fought for balance, lashing out with his own knife. Luke ducked the swing and lunged wildly with the bigger dagger. Achmed ignored the blood running down his leg and saw the clumsy thrust coming. The boy was no fighter. He sprang to his right. However, instead of landing on the smooth stone of the pathway, his right foot rolled on the cylindrical body of Luke's smaller camera lens. Achmed's ankle turned, and suddenly he was on the ground, falling hard on his right side, trapping his knife hand under his body.

Luke screamed, the sound animalistic, demented, and pounced on his fallen attacker. He drove his right arm forwards as he landed on the bigger man. There was a split second's resistance as the point of the blade pushed against the other man's skin, but with Luke's weight behind it, the knife broke through and slid up and inside the African's rib cage. Air hissed from the growing wound as the knife nicked a lung. Achmed's eyes bulged wide and he tried to scream, but no noise came from his mouth. Luke's right hand was suddenly wet, spray-painted red with the force of air from the dying man's lung. The reporter squealed as even more blood pumped from the wound. He wondered if he had pierced the man's heart.

Luke tried to free the blade, but found it was stuck. He rolled off the man, rocking back on his knees, and raised a bloodied hand to his mouth in horror as the body convulsed, then was motionless.

Luke looked around him. There was no one in the alleyway. He saw the broken memory card on the ground near the shattered remains of his camera and telephoto lens. This was no robbery. The man was after his camera gear, but not for resale. It was clear he wanted to destroy the images stored in the camera's memory and on the card. Fortunately, he had not had a chance to search Luke. The first memory card he had used when photographing Hassan bin Zayid and the woman was still in his pocket.

Luke stared at the body. He started to shake and couldn't stop. He dropped to his knees and wrapped his arms around himself to try to still the shivering. He did not want to touch the dead man, but he knew he had to. With a trembling hand he touched the corpse's arm. It was still warm. The smell of the spilt blood, and the contents of the man's bowels, which had been voided when he died, made Luke gag. He tried to gulp air and swallow, but couldn't hold back. He turned his head to one side and vomited on the ground next to the dead man. Tears streamed from his eyes as he emptied his stomach. The vile mix of smells around him made him dry-retch over and over again.

Finally Luke caught his breath and wiped his eyes. He summoned the courage to look at the corpse again. The pistol was tucked in the man's belt. Someone would surely come soon. He had to search the dead man. Clipped to the belt of the man's jeans was a cell phone. Luke knew he shouldn't touch it, but he wanted to confirm his suspicions. He eased the phone from the belt and scrolled through the menu. He checked the 'dialled calls' and was not surprised to find his own cell phone number at the top of the list. The man had called him just before the attack, and then hung up after confirming the identity of his victim.

His shaking calmed a little, now he was acting like an investigative journalist again. Luke had a very good idea how the man got his number, but selected the 'received calls' function to confirm his theory. The top entry read *Private number*; the next, however, he recognised as the office number for Zayid Enterprises. He wrote down the other numbers in the 'received calls' list in his notebook, and scrolled back and did the same for the dialled calls. He wiped the phone's leather case with his handkerchief to remove his fingerprints, then replaced it on the dead man's belt.

He searched the man's pockets but found no wallet or other identification. However, he did find a plastic bag filled with white powder. Whether it was cocaine or heroin he wasn't sure, but it seemed the would-be assassin was multiskilled in his life of crime.

The telephone on the dead man's belt started ringing.

'Shit,' Luke breathed. The tremor returned to his fingers. The chirping sounded fearfully loud in the confines of the alley. He picked the phone up and ended the call. 'Shit,' he said again.

The screen showed the caller had blocked his or her number from showing. It was probably the same person who had called before. Luke kept the phone and ran down the alley and back out into the broader laneway, towards the waterfront again.

A young African man wearing board shorts and a T-shirt, his hair a mass of dreadlocks, stepped out of a doorway and said, 'Hey, my friend, looking for a hotel? Some ganga maybe? What happened to you – been in a fight, man?'

Luke stopped and looked at the man, who stared back, uncomprehending. The phone rang again. Luke looked at it, then at the young African again. His voice was deep, just like the man who had attacked him.

'Want to make twenty US dollars?' Luke croaked, his throat raw from being sick. He coughed and spat.

The man looked wary. 'Hey, man, I'm no faggot.'

The phone kept chirping.

'No, no! I want you to impersonate someone on this phone, I'll tell you what to say. It's a joke on a friend. Twenty bucks – OK?'

'Sure, why not.'

'Hold the phone away from you – I want the caller to think it's a bad line, so he won't recognise you. Keep your answers short.'

Luke pressed the green key and held the phone out to the young man. Luke mouthed the word hello.

'Hello,' the man said hesitantly.

Luke brought the phone back to his own ear, motioning the man to stay where he was.

'It is me,' a male voice said on the other end of the line. 'Is it done yet?'

Luke covered the mouthpiece and told the young man what to say. 'It is done. This line is bad.'

Luke took the phone back. The voice said, 'Good. You planted the drugs in his bag, in the hotel room? A kilo, as we agreed?'

'Fuck,' Luke whispered, covering the mouthpiece. There was nothing like a kilogram of powder in the bag the man had been carrying. That meant he had already planted the drugs in Luke's pack.

'What?' asked the young man.

'Nothing, nothing. Just say, "Yes, it is done."' The young man did as ordered and Luke held the phone back to his ear.

'Good. I will have someone else call the police. They will be at his hotel in ten minutes from now. The drugs will make it look as though he died as the result of a deal gone wrong. Did you plant some of the stuff on him?'

'As ordered,' the young African man said at Luke's behest, bewildered at the game he was playing.

'Good. You will be paid the usual way.'

The phone went dead.

'What was all that about, man? Are you in trouble?' the young man asked.

Luke fished in the traveller's wallet hanging around his neck for a twenty-dollar bill. When he went to hand over the money he saw the young man was staring at his right hand and arm, which were covered in the dried blood of the dead man. The man started to back away from him.

'Here, take the money,' Luke said.

'I don't want no part of no trouble, man.'

'Don't worry, no trouble. I got into a fight with some other guys before. No problem. Want to make another twenty?'

The young man took the bill with the tips of his thumb and fore-fingers, careful not to touch Luke's skin.

'I've got to meet a girl. I need a shirt and don't want to go into a shop looking like this. How about selling me yours?'

The man thought about the odd request for a couple of seconds, then said, 'Thirty.'

'Shit. OK.' Luke peeled off three tens. The young man took off his Bob Marley T-shirt and handed it over. 'Thanks.'

'Can I go now?'

'Sure. You've been a big help.'

Luke hurried back into the alleyway. He took off his own blood-stained T-shirt and wrapped it around the hilt of the diving knife in the dead man's chest. If he was going to be framed for drug possession he didn't want to compound his troubles by having the police thinking he was a murderer as well. He yanked on the knife but was surprised at how firmly it was stuck in the dead body. He placed a foot on the corpse's chest, grabbed the knife and leaned back. Slowly, the knife came free with a sickening sucking sound and another gasp of putrid air. He had planned to leave the gun on the man's body, but now that he realised the extent of the plot against him he decided that he might need to even the odds. He pulled the pistol from the man's jeans and stuffed it in his own pants. He put on the African man's T-shirt and bundled the knife and bloodied shirt into the daypack, which he had to carry in his arms because of the tear. The camera gear, too, might incriminate him, so he scooped up the shattered body and lenses and dropped the mess into his camera bag. He jogged back into the main laneway and headed towards the busy waterfront.

In a small square he found a hand-operated water pump and a stone trough beneath the spout, half full of water. He rinsed the blood from his arms as best as he could and then winced in pain as he scooped warm water up to his throbbing nose. He stared at the mix of his own blood and that of the dead man's swirling in the water in the trough. From what the man on the phone had said, the police would beat him to his hotel room. If he fronted them he would be arrested, charged and locked in a Zanzibari jail until he could organise a lawyer. He had some numbers from a dead man's cell phone but, beyond that, nothing firm to connect the drugs planted in his room or the attempt on his life with Hassan bin Zayid. He was shocked at the reaction his simple request for an interview had provoked, although from the destruction of his camera gear it was also clear that bin Zayid knew he had been photographed. So what? Hassan was a native of Zanzibar, obviously well known within the tourism industry, who led a flashy lifestyle that included an ostentatious boat and a parade of western girlfriends. Why would he send someone to kill him for taking his picture?

'The woman,' Luke said aloud. He still had images of her stored on the first memory card, but he now had no camera on which to view them, and his laptop computer was in his hotel room.

He took a circuitous route back towards his hotel, on the off-chance that he might be able to beat the police. He was out of luck. As he peered around the corner of a decaying stone building he saw an African police-man holding an AK-47 assault rifle leaning against the wall of the hotel, smoking a cigarette and scanning up and down the laneway. Luke turned and walked quickly back into the bowels of Stone Town. He made his way back towards the dhow harbour. He needed a boat off the island – tonight, if possible. There were no embassies on Zanzibar, so he had to get himself to the mainland, to Dar es Salaam. There he would seek asylum in the Australian embassy and explain the extraordinary events that had led to him being framed on drugs charges. He would call International Press and ask them to arrange legal representation for him, and then file a story about the whole sorry mess. He knew he was taking a risk by evading the police on the island – if they caught him his attempted escape would brand him as guilty, no matter what story he came up with.

On his way to the docks he found a small convenience store and bought some bananas, a couple of big bottles of water and some cold chapatis from the Indian proprietor. He also picked up a copy of the *International Herald Tribune*. He would go mad on a boat trip without something to read.

It was late when he arrived at the harbour and most of the dhows were in darkness. He walked along the dock and stopped. On the night air he heard voices, and followed the sound. Further along he saw the pale glow of a hurricane lantern hanging from the mast of one of the wooden boats. Below it, three men were sitting on the deck around a pot balanced on a charcoal brazier. Luke's stomach rumbled with hunger at the smell of the spicy curry.

'*Jambo*,' the eldest of the three men said when he saw Luke on the wharf.

'*Habari*,' Luke replied, using the extent of his Swahili in returning the greeting. 'Do you speak English?'

'Of course,' the old man said. 'How can we help you?'

'I need a boat to the mainland, to Dar.'

'We carry cargo, not tourists.'

'That doesn't worry me.'

'It worries me. Tourists want the world but don't like to pay for it. I don't like the port formalities at the other end. I spend too much time leading westerners through immigration and customs.'

Luke stepped on board the boat, uninvited. 'What if you had a tourist who would pay you three times the going rate and who didn't want to bother you with customs and immigration?'

The old man put down his plate and narrowed his eyes as he regarded Luke. 'I would lose my boat if I was caught helping you avoid the authorities.'

'Which is why I am offering three times the normal fee.'

'Five times,' the old man said.

'Four.'

The man smiled. 'Very well. Cash up-front.'

'Half up-front, half when we get to Dar. I don't want to end up at the bottom of the channel halfway across.'

A younger member of the trio, an African about Luke's age, piped up. 'What's to stop that happening anyway?'

Luke yawned and lifted his arms high, slowly, as if stretching. The movement caused his T-shirt to rise up and all three men caught a glimpse of the pistol.

'I want no trouble on this boat,' said the old captain, addressing his two crewmen as much as Luke. 'The deal is done. I hope you do not mind, but there is no room on the boat for you to sleep tonight. We will leave in the hour before dawn. Meet us here then.'

Luke had wanted to leave immediately, but he guessed the sailors were reluctant to make the crossing in the dead of night without any navigational aids. He headed back towards town. He would try to find somewhere quiet to lie down, or maybe a bar where he could buy a couple of beers to ease the pain in his face. He left the dock and stopped when he came to a bench seat under a streetlight. The adrenaline had well and truly worn off and he was more tired than he could ever remember being.

He pulled the newspaper from the plastic shopping bag and idly leafed through it. On the fifth page was a story that caught his eye. The headline read: *MAN-EATING LION KILLED IN ZIMBABWE – HUMAN REMAINS FOUND*. Luke shook his head and rubbed his tired eyes. It was a follow-up story about Miranda Banks's disappearance. According to the report the remains of a Caucasian female had been found in Mana Pools National Park. Police in Kariba were speculating that the remains were probably those of the missing American woman, although further tests still had to be carried out. There was a quote from an American embassy spokesman, who had officially released Miranda's name to the press.

Beside it was a photograph.

He wore a black wetsuit and boot polish on his face and hands as camouflage.

He finned slowly, so as not to leave a visible wake. It was a long swim, more than half a kilometre, but he was fit and as at home in the water as a dolphin. The lights of Nungwi's beach bungalows twinkled ahead of him.

This would be the final nail in the coffin for the local tourism industry, but he cared nothing for the tens of thousands of US dollars it would cost him. Money was no longer important. Family and God were all that mattered, and his family was now all gone. He had been selfish, greedy, weak for so many years. It had taken Iqbal's death to teach him that. God had spared him for a reason.

Hassan bin Zayid took a deep breath and duck-dived as he neared the shore, coming into the steeply shelved shore underwater. Even two metres down he heard and felt the beat of the bass from the disco's speakers reverberate through his body. The tide was high and he surfaced under the overhanging rock that supported part of the terrace above him. The music was deafening now, assaulting his senses, insulting his reawakened religious sensibilities with its calls for the barely clad youngsters above him to gyrate against each other. He'd been seduced, too, danced to their tune for years, but he was turning his back on the west now, for good. He felt ashamed of his past weakness, for falling the same way as his father. But he would have revenge enough for both of them.

Hassan turned his head in surprise at a noise behind him. He followed the trickling stream with his eyes. A young white man was hanging his penis over the edge of the balcony and urinating. He was disgusted, and the thoughtless laziness of the boy steeled his reserve further. Even others on the island, like him, who had made their fortunes from the tourist industry, would not mourn the passing of people like these.

Avoiding the ripples caused by the cascading urine, he finned his way around the rock and under the bare wooden floorboards. Sand showered him and the water's surface as dozens of bare feet stomped above him in response to the primitive rhythm from the speakers. Hassan slung his spear gun over his shoulder and grabbed one of the deck's wooden supports. The pole was slick and he slid back into the water on his first attempt. On his next try he managed to hook one arm over a timber support and haul himself up. His face was only a few centimetres from the floorboards now and he peeked up through a crack. He smiled at the sight. A girl was standing astride the gap. She wore a red G-string under a printed Zambian and her legs were long and smooth. The whore would get more than she bargained for this night.

He sat on the cross-member and unslung the waterproof bag from his shoulder. From inside he withdrew the bomb and roll of wide black duct tape. The Semtex had come as part of the delivery he had taken from the man in Dar. The timing mechanism was a cheap digital travel clock. As he had to swim with the device, he had been limited in the amount of shrapnel he could place in it. The fifty or so nails packed along one side of the soft plastique hardly seemed enough. He wanted to wipe this cancerous growth off the pristine beach it sullied.

Further along the shore an inflatable boat was tied to the wooden handrail of a flight of steps that led into the water at high tide. On his way in he had given a wide berth to a gleaming white catamaran flying the French tricolour. He assumed the dinghy belonged to the cat. It gave him an idea about improving the bomb's effectiveness. He placed the explosives and tape back in the bag and wedged it into the gap between pillar and cross-member, then slid back into the water. Beneath the surface the music once more subsided to a dull throb. He swam to the moored boat and ducked under it, emerging on the far side, out of sight of any casual observer leaning over the railing of the deck above. He placed his hands on the rubber side of the craft and lifted himself up. As he'd hoped, the plastic fuel tank was sitting on the floor of the boat and it was not chained to anything. He reached into the water, drew the stainless-steel dive knife from its scabbard and slashed the fuel hose. He lifted the tank over the edge, clamped off the cut end of the hose with his fingers, and swam on the surface, the fuel container floating in front of him.

It was a delicate balancing act, getting the container up onto the wooden struts under the deck, and he spilled gasoline onto the water's surface in the process. It wouldn't matter. In his mind's eye he saw half-naked backpackers leaping into the water to escape the fire and carnage above, only to land in water ablaze with fuel. He hosed some more of it onto the greasy surface below him.

With the tape he fixed the bomb securely to one of the cross-members and, using the rubber hose, tied the plastic fuel tank through its carrying handle to a support post, above and to one side of the explosives. He set the clock for thirty minutes and slid back into the water, which now smelled strongly of gasoline. He dived deep for cleaner water and finned his way silently back out to sea, the sickening thump of the music getting softer with every powerful stroke of his legs. Sadly, the boat was out of sight of the shoreline when the red numerals on the clock reached midnight.

The resort, with its sun-bleached wooden decking and ageing thatched roof, was consumed by flames in a matter of seconds.

A German tourist, who had always wanted to make his living as a freelance news photographer, was in his bedroom when the bomb went off. He snatched up his digital camera and ran towards the inferno. He threw up after taking his first ten frames. What made him retch, and rethink his career options, was the sight of the badly burned torso of a girl, the charred remnants of a lime-green bikini top stuck to her body.

The media reports the next day listed the death toll as nine western tourists from nearly as many countries. Another nineteen were in hospital with severe burns. An African bartender, a Muslim Zanzibari dive instructor and a teenage girl who painted henna tattoos on the white hands and feet of tourists were also burned to death.

13

Jed stood on the upstairs verandah of the lodge in Mana Pools National Park watching a herd of buffalo through his binoculars. He was dressed for the bush. He wore a pair of dun-coloured fatigue trousers with baggy side pockets, a brown T-shirt and sandy suede desert boots. All of his gear had been issued to him for service in Afghanistan but it suited the dry African bush just as well.

Jed heard the rattle of a diesel engine as a vehicle pulled up behind the lodge, out of sight. The buffalo, sixteen of them by his count, were meandering slowly along the length of the narrow island in the middle of the river, munching away on the grass like big black cows.

'They call them black death, you know.'

Jed put the glasses down and saw Moses below him. He waved. Moses had brought Jed's hired Land Rover back with him from the staff village. The sun was not long up, still low over the hills at his back. The sharp-eyed tracker had seen where Jed was looking and had identified the buffalo immediately, even though Jed found it almost impossible to pick them up again without the binoculars.

'Why is that?' Jed asked, although he knew he would be told the answer in any case.

'The buffalo is the animal most feared by big-game hunters. They are unpredictable and will charge with no notice if you are on foot. If you wound a buffalo when hunting, then you had better put it down with your very next shot or run up the nearest tree, because if you don't, he will kill you.'

'I'll try to remember all that.'

'Good. The ones to fear most are the *dagga* boys, the muddy old male buffalos who are not part of a herd any more. Be especially wary of a lonely buffalo.'

Jed headed downstairs to let Moses in. Chris was at work on Miranda's laptop computer, which she had set up on the dining table.

'Coffee, Chris?'

She looked up. 'Pardon me? Oh, sorry, Jed, I was just reading something. No, I'm fine, thanks.'

She had already been awake and at the computer when Jed had woken at five, half an hour before the dawn.

'Good morning, Professor,' Moses said as he entered the lodge.

'Morning, Moses. I hope you got some sleep last night. Not too much partying?'

He smiled sheepishly. 'Of course not, Professor. I was on my best behaviour.'

'That's good, because we don't want to rescue you from any jealous husbands. What's the good word around the village?'

'As a matter of fact, there is some news from the staff. There is another person missing.'

'Really?' Jed asked, sitting on the carved wooden arm of a sturdy lounge chair.

'Yes. A young woman – a maid from one of these lodges.'

'What do they think happened to her?' Chris looked up from the computer screen.

'They are not sure. She went missing about the same time as Miss Miranda. This girl was bad sometimes – she used to visit a man in one of the hunting camps outside the park, so for some days they thought she had taken leave without telling anyone.'

'Which would explain why Ncube wasn't told about it, I guess.' Chris looked at Jed.

Moses continued. 'The warden checked the neighbouring camps when she did not return and she was not there. Some people think she may have been taken by a lion as well.'

'It's possible,' Chris nodded. 'The one I shot was stalking a female Parks employee.'

'But there were no other remains found in the lion you killed, apart from . . .'

All three let the statement hang, unchallenged, until Chris changed the subject. 'If she's dead it could also have been a crocodile. Maybe she was fishing or swimming.'

'Yes, that is very possible too,' Moses agreed. 'She would not be the first person in the valley to be taken by a croc. There is another thing I learned about the missing maid.'

'What's that?' Jed asked.

'Although it was not part of her duties, she used to work for your daughter.'

'Work?'

'She did her washing for her, her clothes, and sometimes cooked for Miranda if she was out late in the bush, calling the lions.'

'Calling?' Jed was trying to piece all this new information together in his mind.

Chris interrupted. 'She'd go out at nights, with an armed ranger as an escort and sometimes the park's ecologist, and play tapes to try to lure lions to her, so she could study them. The tapes are of other lions, and of dying prey. But, Moses, there are signs in all the lodges saying that washing up and cooking are not part of the maids' duties.'

'Exactly. This girl caused some resentment amongst the other staff. Jed, your daughter was very good to her, and paid her well, in US dollars, but the other staff say the girl was letting her normal duties slip. They were jealous of her, and of her clothes.'

'Her clothes?'

'Yes. It seems Miranda had given this girl some of her own clothes. The other staff think that maybe she was stealing things from Miranda's washing.'

Chris shrugged, not sure what to make of the new information, then had a thought. 'Maybe that's why we haven't been able to find any of Miranda's day-to-day clothes. It's possible this missing maid stole them and ran off.'

'Hard to say. I'd sure like to talk to her, though, if she isn't already dead,' Jed said. 'For now, I want to see Miranda's campsite. Do you want to come with us, Chris?'

'No, I think I'll keep going through these computer files. See what I can salvage. Miranda did some great work here and I want to make sure it's catalogued and maybe even published in a paper, with full credit, some day.'

Jed nodded. 'That'd be nice. Have you found anything else personal on the computer? Emails, a diary, that kind of thing?'

'I can't get into her email account because it's password-protected. I've tried everything I can think of, but I can't crack it. She's got a file marked personal, but that's blocked as well. I'm afraid I'm no computer hacker, but I'll find someone in Jo'burg who can get into this stuff and then I'll email it to you.'

'Thank you,' Jed said. He thought Chris looked fresh and lovely this morning, dressed in a sleeveless blue shirt with the top three buttons undone. He couldn't help but notice the swell of her full breasts as she leaned forwards to take a closer look at the computer screen. Her short cut-off jeans and brown ankle-boots showed off her golden legs to perfection. Her hair was piled high and he noticed she had put on a little makeup.

Last night, when he'd seen she had been crying, he'd had the urge to take her in his arms, to comfort her and to seek solace for himself, despite the arguing that had gone on between them beforehand. He'd seen soldiers hug each other after a dangerous mission or cry on each other's shoulders over the loss of a comrade. Wounded men needed friends to hold their hands. Humans often needed to touch as part of the healing process. He and Christine had both loved Miranda, and they were both grieving for her now.

Jed put a hand on her shoulder. 'Sure you don't want to take a break and get some fresh air with us?'

She placed her hand on his and looked up into his eyes, forcing a little smile. 'I'm OK, Jed. You go with Moses, see some of the bush. I'll fix us a salad for lunch and maybe we'll go for a drive and a sundowner together later.'

He felt his heart beat a little faster at the touch of her hand. He was experiencing stirrings in his body which had been dormant for six months during his time in Afghanistan. There was an old myth, common to all armies of the world, that the cooks put something in the food to suppress the men's sexual urges. In fact, it was just plain old hard work and lack of sleep that made life easier, in one respect at least, for soldiers away from home. Jed had done nothing physically strenuous since his fight with the burglar in Johannesburg, and there was nothing stopping him from feeling acutely aroused by the close presence of a beautiful woman.

He reluctantly removed his hand from her shoulder and asked Moses to help him with Miranda's folded safari tent.

'Are we going to camp now?' The tracker looked surprised.

'No. I just want to take the tent out and have a look at it. I thought that if I do that on the spot where Miranda was camped it might at least give me a feel for what her life here was like.'

'I see,' Moses lied. Death was a part of every African family these days, especially with the virus. In the old days families had grieved for days and days, the women wailing and the men drinking. Now it was not unusual for people in the towns to take an hour off for a funeral and then go back to work afterwards. Moses had lost many friends to HIV–AIDS and the cemeteries of Zimbabwe were overflowing with the bare earthen mounds of fresh graves. In most towns, new land had been acquired to meet the demand for more and more burial spaces. Kariba, where Moses lived, had been hit particularly hard by the disease. The town had a high population of prostitutes whose clientele included long-distance truck drivers crossing the border with Zambia, as well as the fishermen from the kapenta rigs – the floating fishing platforms that harvested tiny fish from the lake.

While Moses didn't understand a lot of what Jed was doing, he certainly knew what would make the man whole again. The best thing Mr Jed Banks could do right now was to get drunk, farewell his daughter for good, and sleep with the pretty, if skinny, lady professor. That was what a man needed to get his life back in order – beer and women – even if the combination occasionally caused as many problems as it solved. But Moses said none of this, keeping his wise counsel to himself as he loaded the truck with the dead girl's tent.

Chris waved Jed and Moses off as the Land Rover pulled out from under the fig tree behind the lodge.

'Shoo! Go on, beat it!' she yelled at four grey vervet monkeys sitting in the tree. She clapped her hands and shook her head in annoyance. Monkeys and baboons continually patrolled the area around the lodges and the park's camping ground during the day, seeking new ways to get to the hordes of food they knew waited inside human dwellings. Chris was aware from her studies that the primates were capable of devising elaborate plans of attack. Often, one or two of their number would act as highly visible decoys, trying an obvious method of entry to a building or tent, while the rest of the troop sought out less conspicuous routes to get to their booty. She had observed that the animals could tell the difference between men and women and generally seemed bolder when they thought there were only females present, especially a lone woman.

Chris picked up a rock and hurled it at a monkey that had climbed down out of the tree and was boldly approaching her. The stone only bounced off the juvenile male's arm, but the blow was enough to show him that she meant business. He scampered back up into the tree and Chris went back inside, shutting the screen door behind her.

She returned to the laptop and continued to read through the emails she had been checking before Jed had quizzed her on the contents. It was a small lie, telling him that Miranda's email folder was password-protected, but a justifiable one. There was nothing in the folder that would cast any light on what had happened to Miranda, and all the messages were business-related rather than personal. There was nothing that would tell Jed anything more about his daughter than he already knew. They were of little interest to Chris, either, as most of them were directed to her and she had read them long ago. She didn't really know why she was going over them.

Half-heartedly, she opened a recent message from Miranda to her mother.

Hi Mom. First off, I don't mean to sound rude but, as advised before, can you PLEASE PLEASE not send messages to this address any more – just use my Hotmail account instead. I know you had trouble accessing it the other day, but that was just a server problem, I think, so don't worry about it. Things are fine here and Chris passed on the parcel you sent to me, via South Africa, when I last saw her. Thanks for the sun cream – it's really expensive here and hard to find. Hopefully I'll get a chance to work on my tan soon and to see a little more of this continent. Love, M.

Chris rocked back in her chair, clasping her hands behind her head, and stared at the ceiling of the lodge. A gecko had crept into a far corner and begun its daily sleep.

What was all that about working on her tan and seeing more of the continent? Miranda had said nothing to her about taking leave or travelling anywhere other than Zimbabwe. It was another piece of information to file away, and a possible line of questioning for the man Chris knew she would have to confront at some time. How she did that, where and under what guise, were all serious questions she had yet to formulate answers to.

To continue her own investigation into Miranda's death – for Chris was sure she would never be found alive – she would need to speak to the man Miranda had farewelled from Marongora before her last trip to South Africa. The problem was, Chris knew Jed Banks would also want to track the man down, and she did not want him around for that particular interview. But then she didn't want him to walk out of her life either.

'Too bad,' she said aloud to herself. Jed had to go.

She pondered Miranda's references to some kind of holiday again. Her tenure in Zimbabwe was fixed but not inflexible. If she had wanted to get away for a break to a beach in, say, Mozambique, or any-where else in Africa for that matter, all she had to do was ask. However, Miranda seemed to be intimating to her mother that she was about to depart on a trip. Was it possible, Chris wondered, that Miranda had simply departed on an unannounced, spur-of-the-moment jaunt? Miranda's dedication to procedures and her unfailingly responsible attitude suggested otherwise, not to mention the remains in the belly of the dead lion. However, there was no harm in checking.

Chris went upstairs and opened one of her aluminium storage cases. From it she took a satellite phone and portable Trivec Avant tactical satellite antenna. The antenna had a number of pieces which fitted together to make an elongated, skeletal-looking structure. It was designed to go with the Lightweight Satellite Terminal tacsat radio transceiver in another case, but it also worked with her phone and gave her a more reliable signal. The Motorola LST-5C, like the antenna, was ex-military, and both Chris and Miranda had them as back-up, and in case they ever needed to contact aircraft or other assets. Chris positioned the assembled antenna on the verandah of the lodge, where it would have a clear line of sight at the sky and the satellites orbiting the earth. She connected it to the phone and, when she gained a signal, called a number in Pretoria.

'United States embassy, can I help you?' a male receptionist answered.

'Could you put me through to Mort Solomon in the trade secretary's office, please?'

'Certainly, ma'am.'

Chris drummed her fingers on the wooden balcony as she waited, watching a pair of elephants showering themselves with water in the shallows of the Zambezi.

'Solomon.'

'Mort, it's Christine. How's things?'

'Hi there, traveller. Long time no hear. When are you coming back to civilisation as we know it? I've found a great new bottle of Cape red we really should split sometime.'

God, she thought, Solomon was always on the make. 'One of these days, Mort.' In his dreams. 'Look, I need you to check some cross-border movements for me.'

'OK. I'll go secure.'

Chris waited a few moments while the embassy man pushed a button on his phone to enable a scrambler, which would ensure no one could eavesdrop on the call. She didn't think it was entirely necessary, but Mort, for all his flaws, was a stickler for rules. 'Who do you want me to check out?'

'Miranda.'

'Jesus Christ, Chris. The girl's dead. The case is closed. Just come back and file your report.'

Chris felt her cheeks colour. 'I haven't finished exploring all avenues, Mort, and this is some information I *need* to file my report!'

'OK, cool down, babe.'

'Don't fucking call me that, Mort, you know I hate it.'

He laughed. 'Sorry, *Professor*. Look, the kid had an unfortunate accident. If you girls want to work in the bush these are the risks you take. Anyway, shoot, what do you need?'

Asshole. Chris took a deep breath. 'I need you to check if Miranda, or anyone using her passport, has crossed the border from Zimbabwe into South Africa, Mozambique, Botswana or Zambia since her disappearance.'

There was silence as Solomon took down the details. 'OK. I take it you haven't recovered her passport.'

'That's right. No passport. Some other stuff's missing too.'

'Probably stolen. She might have had her passport on her when she . . . when the lion got her.'

'I don't carry my passport in my top pocket when I go darting lions, Mort. But yes, you're right, it's a possibility. Anyway, it's a loose thread that needs to be tied. I'm not saying she's still alive and, hell, I don't think she is anyway, but we should find out if her passport's in circulation.'

'Agreed. I'll get the bureaucrats onto it. Call me back this afternoon.'

'Will do. Thanks, Mort. Hey, what are you hearing about the bomb in Tanzania?'

'Jesus, what a fucking mess. You heard they evacuated the embassy?'

'I heard.'

'But hold on, there's more.'

'Not another one?'

'Yep. Just got a signal. A nail bomb with some gasoline to get things going at a disco on Zanzibar.'

'Bastards. Could be the same cell that planted the IED in Dar,' Chris said, thinking out loud. IED was the military acronym for an impro- vised explosive device. 'Are we helping out with the investigations on the ground?'

'The ambassador's sending some marines from the embassy in Tanzania to beef up security. FBI are on their way from stateside to help out the Dar locals with the bus bomb. The embassy threat could have just been some asshole pulling a prank, but no one wants to risk it. There were no Americans killed in the Zanzibar blast. Brits, Aussies, Germans and a couple of other Europeans. All kids.'

'What's it all mean for your part of the world?'

'They're sending a pick-up team from home, to be based here on stand-by, just in case the Feds or our guys turn up anything interesting. Also, our VIP, the one you disapprove of on animal conservation grounds, is going back to his original plans, so you might bump into him.'

Chris frowned. 'Because of the problems in Tanzania?'

'Yeah. State put the mother of all travel warnings out yesterday on mainland Tanzania and Zanzibar – too late for the victims of last night's bomb.'

'I'll be finished here soon. I don't like it that I haven't been able to find Miranda's body, but the forensic tests should be back soon on the remains they pulled from the lion. You read about that?'

'It's in all the papers down here, although they neglect to mention that you were the great white hunter that bagged the killer lion. Bet the local guys were surprised at a pretty white lady outshooting them.'

'Let's just hope my name stays out of the papers. I don't want to be known as a lion killer and I don't intend being within a hundred miles of that asshole VIP of yours who kills animals for fun.'

'Hey, you don't mince your words, do you? Just because we're on a secure line doesn't mean I'm not being taped.'

'What's it to me? I'm just a humble scientist, remember? Bye, Mort, I'll call again this afternoon, at four.'

'Yeah, I remember. See ya, babe.'

'Asshole.'

'Just wanted to make sure you still cared,' Solomon said, then hung up.

Chris shook her head, picturing his shit-eating grin. Grey hair, ponytail, tattoos. Old school. A knuckle-dragger who wore his political incorrectness on his sleeve and oozed macho bullshit every time he opened his mouth. Still, a lot of people, including her, forgave Mort Solomon an awful lot because he was a good operator and knew his business like no one else.

She repacked the tacsat antenna and phone and went back downstairs to shut down the computer. There was nothing more the machine could tell her about Miranda's last days.

'Do you think I'm crazy, Moses?' Jed asked as the Land Rover bucked and bounced along the road that paralleled the Zambezi River through the park.

'What do you mean?'

Jed drove while Moses navigated, scanning the bush to the front and sides, always on the lookout for game.

'Do you think I'm mad for wanting to believe my daughter is still alive?'

'Death is no stranger to me, to my people, to my country. It is to yours.'

'But I've been to war. I'm a soldier.'

'Even in peace, people here are better at dealing with death, because we see a lot of it. We have the AIDS virus, but even before that the people in this valley always lived with death – in childbirth, from wild animals, from disease, from war. You have seen other soldiers die, but you have not seen your own children taken from you. It must be hard for you to believe that this can happen.'

'There's a saying that humans are not made to bury their children.'

'Except in Africa. Jed, from what I know, your daughter is not the sort of woman who would run away without telling anyone. She does not sound like a foolish person.'

'She wasn't . . . isn't.'

'People get killed in this park. Even white people.'

'What do you mean by that?'

'The world doesn't care if an African child is killed by a lion or if a woman doing the family washing is taken by a crocodile. But if a European is killed, then all of a sudden it is big news. People are outraged and demand to know how such a terrible thing can happen in this day and age.

'This is very hard for you to accept, Jed, I know. But the fact is that no matter what you see in the glossy tourist brochures or on your television, Africa *is* a dangerous place and people get killed here. The sooner you accept this, and that your daughter is not coming back, the sooner your soul will heal.'

'I know,' Jed said, taking out a cigarette and lighting it. 'Still doesn't make it any easier, though.'

'It is not supposed to be easy. We are here.'

They had arrived at a picturesque grassy clearing with a panoramic view of the river and the escarpment on the Zambian side. The site was a stone's throw from the riverbank. Jed parked the car in the shade of a spreading Natal fig and got out. 'So this is where Miranda camped?'

'This place is the BBC camp. A British television crew lived here for a long time when they were making a documentary about the valley. It is a nice site.'

'It is indeed.' Jed walked towards the river, admiring the incredible view and the beauty of the lush green countryside around him. He tried to imagine Miranda walking to and from the river, sitting on the sandy bank or in a camping chair, enjoying the sunset. Living alone, in the middle of the bush. The images did not come easily. He had only known his daughter as a tiny baby, apart from the odd awkward meeting during her formative years as a college student. Aside from their few camping trips he had no frame of reference for her as an intrepid young scientist fending for herself in a wild continent.

'They liked her, the National Parks people,' Moses said, coming to stand by Jed.

'They told you that?'

'She liked talking to the women, and tried to learn some of the local language. They gave her a nickname, you know.'

'I didn't know. What?'

'*Mama Shumba*, the mother of the lions. The other women thought she was very brave.'

'And what did the men think of a woman out here alone, researching big cats?'

Moses smiled. 'The truth? They thought she was an idiot.'

Jed couldn't help smiling at Moses's candour.

'Do you know where they think she died?'

'The head ranger said it was on the track to the river, near where the sand starts. Come, we'll have a look.'

The two men walked closer to the sandy bank and Jed could see now where animals, either buffalo or elephant or both, had worn a clear trail to the water's edge. They found a spot where the dry grass on either side of the bare dirt pathway yielded to the river's sand. There was no sign of any human remains, not that Jed had expected there would be.

'They say they found some blood and pieces of bones and clothes here, but by the time the police and more rangers got here, the hyenas had removed all trace of the body. One of the rangers said he saw a blue hat, covered in blood, but that too was gone when they returned. The man said he recognised the hat as Miranda's as it had an American university's name on it.'

'I didn't read about the hat in the police report. Maybe someone souvenired it?'

'Stole it, you mean? Not all African people are thieves, Jed. But, yes, I suppose it is possible. In any case, it is not good.'

'No,' Jed agreed. One more piece of evidence, albeit circumstantial, that Miranda was dead, consumed by wild beasts.

Jed stared down at the ground, the spot where his only child's life had most likely ended. If he was a religious man, he would have prayed, but he was not. Instead, he knelt down on one knee and ran his hand across the ground, feeling the texture of the grass, the sand, the dirt of the track. The surface of the earth was warm in the morning sun. He scooped a handful of dark, rich, musty soil from the trail and let it run out, slowly, through his fingers. He smelled the river's dankness on the slight breeze, the dung and scent of animals that had passed to and from the water's edge, and the sweat of his own body. This was a place where man's impact was minimal and where humans took their chances with the animal inhabitants in much the same way as they had since their ancestors evolved from primates.

'I know where I would like to die, if I had a choice.' Jed stood and brushed the dirt from his hands.

'In battle, as a warrior?'

Jed smiled. 'No. In a wood cabin on the edge of the Great Lakes. With my boots off, and in bed, after a great day's fishing and drinking. I want to go peacefully.'

'Me, I also want to die in bed, after a great day's fishing and drinking. But I don't want to go peacefully – I want a young woman involved as well.' Moses grinned.

'I wonder whether Miranda would have wanted to stay here long-term, whether the place had got to her.'

'Africa? Maybe. People come to this valley for all sorts of reasons. Some to hunt animals, some to save them. Some come to commit crime, like the Zambian poachers, and some to stop crime. One thing that these people have in common is that they never leave, or never want to leave. Miranda was doing the work she loved. No one comes here thinking it is an easy life. It's hot and wet and muddy in the summer, and hot and dry and dusty in the winter; there are tsetse flies and malaria, and, yes, it can be very dangerous. But there is nowhere on earth more beautiful than this place.'

Moses helped Jed unload the tent from the Land Rover and said, 'Over there, under that tree, where the grass is yellow. That is where she must have had it set up.'

'We'll put it in the same place.'

Jed stripped off his shirt and laid it on the branch of a fallen tree. The sun and the temperature were climbing steadily and the sweat ran into his eyes and beaded on his chest as the two of them erected the canvas dome tent. The tent had collapsible metal poles and, when erected, would have been big enough to sleep a family of four in relative comfort.

'I never asked you, Jed, but why did you come looking for me? Who told you about me?' Moses asked as they worked.

'A lady called Eveline.' Jed looked up at the tracker for a reaction.

Moses gave a little smile. 'A good woman. A good friend. I saved her life, a long time ago.' His tone was matter-of-fact.

'What happened?' Jed asked as he hooked the canvas dome onto a bendy pole.

'Her husband had died and she came on a photographic safari with some friends. I was the junior guide. I got to carry the food and water, but no rifle. The senior man was *madala* – old. His eyes were not as good as they were when he was young. He saw some buffalo spoor on the trail but told the tourists it was old – more than a day. I checked it and said, no, it was fresh, because the ants had not crossed the tracks, no grass or leaves had fallen on them. Also, I saw that the buffalo was limping – he was favouring his right hind leg and the imprint in the ground was not as deep. The old man told me to be quiet, but I thought we were getting too close to a dangerous injured animal. Even if the senior man agreed with me, he could not back down in front of the tourists, you understand?'

Jed nodded.

'We passed a thicket of Jesse bush and this one old buffalo bull, he charged us. I knew we would come to him eventually. The main guide, he fired his rifle, but he didn't kill the buff. Just wounded him. The bull was heading right for Eveline, so I pushed her out of the way, then led her to a tree and helped her climb it. The buffalo turned on the old man and gored him. I got the rifle and killed the animal.

'Eveline and I stayed in touch. I worked for her for a while, on her farm, when the tourism work dried up. She was the madam, the one in charge, but we were friends. We came here to the valley often, before she had to leave the country.'

Jed wondered how deep the friendship went, but said nothing. 'I'm going for a piss.'

'Be careful, Jed,' Moses said.

'Sure.'

Jed walked to the edge of the clearing that Miranda's tent now stood in again. He started to unzip, then turned as he felt a hand on his arm. 'Hey, buddy!'

'Stand still. Don't move,' Moses said.

Jed turned. The guide had a rock in his hand. He drew back his arm and threw it. Jed followed the short, sharp trajectory of the throw and took a step back as he saw a flash of movement. A long, thin grey-green coloured snake rared momentarily, lifting its narrow, pointed head off the ground, rising to knee-height not three metres from where Jed had been about to relieve himself. The snake slithered off. 'Shit. Thanks,' he said.

'That was a black mamba – they call it that because the inside of its mouth is black,' Moses said, watching the reptile zip away, back into the long grass.

'Looks like you saved my life, as well as Eveline's,' Jed said.

'It is nothing. My job. However, if it had bitten you, there would have been little I could have done for you.'

'When did you see it?'

'I saw it when we stepped out of the Land Rover. I said nothing because I didn't want to disturb your memories. I've been keeping an eye on it while we were putting up the tent.'

'Eveline told me you were good.' Jed found he had lost the urge to urinate. He wouldn't have seen the snake until he trod – or pissed – on it.

'As I said, it is my job,' Moses said, shrugging his big shoulders. 'This is a nice tent. Good for hunting or photographic tours.'

Jed thought a moment, then said, 'Consider it your bonus.'

'What do you mean?'

'It's yours. You can have it. I don't need a tent – I hired one with the Land Rover. Besides, I spend enough time under canvas in the Army so I don't want to take it home.'

'But it was your daughter's,' Moses said.

Jed sighed. 'Everyone around me seems to be of the consensus that it's time for me to accept that Miranda is gone and to find some closure – to let go. I don't need a tent to remember what my daughter's face looked like or the way she laughed.'

'Thank you. It is a fine tent.'

'Well, let's see what's inside.'

Jed unzipped the large entry flap. The door was made of two layers, an exterior of canvas and an interior panel of closely woven green nylon mesh, which allowed air to get in while still affording some privacy. There was an identical door at the rear of the tent, or the front, depending which way it was erected.

'Both of these doors are intact. Strange.'

'Why strange?'

'Well, the police theory was that Miranda was taken by the lion

218

because she left the flap of her tent open, presumably because it was hot.'

'It wouldn't be the first time that's happened.'

'But why would she unzip the whole door? Why not leave the mosquito mesh zipped closed? She could have opened both the canvas flaps and allowed the air to circulate. Would a lion be able to see through this insect screen?'

'No. Some people sleep on the ground in the bush with just a mosquito net over them. The lion sees in black and white and has trouble with his . . .' Moses struggled to remember the English term, 'deepness?'

'Depth of vision?'

'Yes, that is it. To him even a mosquito net looks like a solid building or termite mound. However, if a door is open, and it can see movement inside the tent, a lion will enter.'

'So why would she have the whole door open?'

'Who knows? Maybe she was opening the door in the middle of the night for some other reason. To go into the bush.'

'To the toilet, you mean?'

Moses shrugged. 'It's possible.'

Jed stepped into the tent. It was a familiar smell. Damp, slightly moulding canvas, the distinctive odour getting stronger as the material absorbed the sun's rays. How many nights had he spent under canvas? Too many. He didn't like tents – they reminded him of base life on overseas operations. Waiting to go out in the field or coming back, dog-tired. He preferred spending his nights in the open air.

Moses followed him in and dropped to one knee. 'See here, Jed. Some dirt is left from the lion, I think.'

'The police report said they found fresh pug marks, muddy lion tracks, on the floor. I would have thought there would be some claw marks, maybe punctures in the floor?'

'The lion's claws are retractable. He keeps them inside his paw until they are needed. Only the cheetah walks with his claws out all the time.'

Jed ran a hand over the walls. 'No rips in the door or sides. No sign of violence. No blood.'

Moses surveyed the floor of the tent, his eyes sweeping left and right. 'Yes, you are right. No blood. There is nothing to suggest she was killed or attacked in here, although the lion has entered the tent at some time.'

'So you think she was killed outside the tent.'

'That would explain why the door was left fully open. She leaves the tent in the middle of the night – or day – for whatever reason. The lion takes her and later searches her tent, possibly looking for another victim.'

Jed walked outside into the sunshine and looked down at the river again. At least this theory indicated Miranda had not been completely reckless by sleeping with the tent flap open. Who knew why she had left the comparative safety of her tent and ventured out that night?

'When will you know for sure about the identity of the remains in the lion's belly?' Moses asked.

'Probably in a couple of days, but I'll have to get to somewhere with a telephone, or some place where my mobile phone works.'

'At least you will be prepared for the news, Jed. And you have now seen where your daughter spent her last days.'

'Yes. That's some comfort, I suppose.' Cold comfort, he thought to himself. 'I'm really beginning to see what brought her here. It is a magnificent place. Moses, I need your help with one more thing.'

'Of course, what is it?'

'I want you to talk to some of the women in the staff village – I understand you're good at that.'

Moses smiled at the compliment.

'I want to find out who the man was my daughter was seeing. I don't care what their relationship was, but I do want to talk to him, to meet him. I suspect the professor will try to find out this information as well. Has she asked you?'

'No, she hasn't.'

Jed nodded. 'Good. Now, I'd like a couple of minutes alone, down by the water. Do you mind staying here?'

'I don't mind. Go, say goodbye to your daughter, Jed. Just watch out for buffalo down there.'

Jed walked back along the animal track towards the river, past the spot where one of nature's superpredators had torn the life from his only child. As he placed one foot in front of the other he felt the emotion well up inside him. By the time he reached the sandy riverbank he was finding it hard to breathe. He started to retch, as though he was going to vomit, but only a cry escaped his lips: a guttural moan, like the sound of a dying animal. He bit his lip to stop the noise, but couldn't stop the tears that flooded his eyes, obscuring his vision. He sank to his knees in the hot white sand.

He saw the face of a tiny baby, him standing over her in his camouflage fatigues, Patti smiling, but her eyes silently reproaching him for missing the birth. The eight-millimetre film of a little blonde girl taking her first wobbly steps – he'd watched the home movie over and over again when he returned from an exercise in Egypt, hoping he could make up for not being there in the flesh. He saw the chubby little hand waving at him as he left the family home for the last time, bags packed. Patti not crying, just hating him. He saw the beautiful young woman who had done well at school and college and who had sought him out and let him back into her life, even though it proved too little, too late.

He had failed his child. Completely and utterly. He had given nothing to her development as a person except for alimony cheques and Christmas presents, and birthday gifts when he'd remembered. Despite all that she had turned into a fine young woman. Or was it because of his absence that she had done so well?

Jed wiped his eyes with the back of his hands and took a deep breath. He told himself he must cling to the memories of their reconciliation and to his pride in all she had achieved in her short life. He stood and brushed the sand from his knees and stared out at the shimmering river. The sun's reflection off the water hurt his reddened eyes and he held a hand up to shade them.

'Goodbye, baby,' he said aloud. 'I hope I can see you again one day and tell you how much I loved you.'

The two men returned to Chris Wallis's lodge around lunchtime and the three of them dined on salad, cold meats and colder beers.

'We'll go for a drive this afternoon to one of the waterholes I know,' Chris told Jed as they cleared the plates from lunch. She could tell from his red-rimmed eyes that he'd been crying, but she knew that this emotional release was an important part of finally letting his daughter go. 'You're welcome to join us, Moses,' she added.

Moses knew women and he caught the unstated 'but' at the end of her sentence. 'No, thank you, Professor. If you don't need me I have some people to see at the staff village.'

Jed walked Moses out to the Land Rover and, out of earshot of Chris, said, 'You won't forget to ask around about Miranda's friend, will you?'

'Leave it to me, Jed. I will find out the information you need and give it to you tomorrow. Will we be leaving then?'

'Unless what you find out gives me a reason to stay longer.'

Moses climbed into the truck and, as he started the engine, leaned out the window and said, 'Oh, and Jed, one more thing.'

'What's that?'

'Good luck tonight.'

'What do you mean?'

'You'll see.'

Jed shook his head in bewilderment and waved Moses off.

Chris carried the satellite phone and the tacsat antenna downstairs and out of the lodge towards the riverbank. She kept an eye out for game, but nothing was stirring in the early afternoon heat, and predators tended to sleep at this time of the day. She walked until she found a large tree which would shield her from sight of the lodge if Jed woke. He had said he was bushed and had gone to lie down for a while. He would not hear her from this range either. Once she was set up, sitting behind the collapsible antenna, she put a call through to Mort Solomon.

'Hi, Chris,' he said.

'Hello, Mort, what did you find out?'

'And a good afternoon to you, too. Never mind, I'll keep it short.'

'So?'

'So, nothing. No one by the name of Miranda Banks, Miranda Banks-Lewis or Miranda Lewis exited Zimbabwe or, for that matter, entered any of the neighbouring countries in the last three weeks. The last record they have of her was crossing into South Africa a few weeks ago and then back into Zimbabwe a while later.'

'That was when she came to see me, in Kruger.'

'Only means one thing, kiddo,' Mort said.

'I guess so.'

'Miranda hasn't run away and joined the circus, Chris, and you'd better start getting used to the idea.'

'I guess you're right. See you, Mort, and thanks.'

'Don't mention it. I'll buy you a drink when you get home. Ciao, babe.'

Chris hung up and dismantled the antenna. Another door had closed. She trudged back to the lodge, secured the phone in its case and walked to Jed's room. She stood in the doorway and looked down at him. His face was peaceful in sleep, his lips parted a little. He was shirtless, dressed only in boxer shorts. She appraised his well-defined, tanned body. There was not an ounce of fat on him. He was not overly hairy, either, which pleased her.

'Jed,' she whispered.

He didn't stir, and she wondered for a moment if she should leave him be for the rest of the afternoon. Still, she had packed the cold box with beer and crackers and cheese and fruit. This would probably be his last sunset in the bush and she wanted him to go home with at least one pleasant memory of Africa. In fact, she wished the same thing for herself. Even before Miranda's disappearance, a cloud had been hanging over her position and the funding for her lion research was in danger of being redirected to projects of more interest to the organisation that paid her. Who knew where she would end up next? She'd been offered a teaching job in the States and wondered once again if she should make the decision to leave Africa before someone else made it for her.

She moved to the bed, and placed a hand on his shoulder and gently shook him. 'Jed,' she said a little louder. 'Jed, wake up.'

He opened his eyes, a little confused at first, then saw her and smiled. 'What time is it?'

'Ten after four. You still want to go out?'

'Sure. Do you?' he asked, rubbing his eyes.

'Definitely. I'll leave you to get dressed. I've got everything packed.'

Jed pulled on a khaki T-shirt, trousers and his boots and met up with Chris again downstairs. 'Good to go, ma'am,' he said as he closed the back door and got into her vehicle.

'Don't call me ma'am. It makes me sound like either an old lady or an officer, and I'm neither.'

'I wouldn't be sitting here if you were,' he said, and they both laughed. 'Where are we going?'

'It's a surprise.'

They headed east along the river road and took a right when they came to the crossroads near the park headquarters.

'We're heading away from the river now. That's Long Pool, on the right, the biggest of the five permanent waterholes.'

Jed saw a herd of zebra filing towards the expanse of brown stagnant water, the stallion in the lead nervously looking around him for crouching killers. They passed through an open plain of golden grass dotted with impala, waterbuck and comical little warthogs, whose tails stuck up like radio antennae when they took flight at the sound of the Land Rover. Chris took a left turn off the main road onto a badly rutted track that climbed and dipped over a series of dry creek beds. Jed gripped the dashboard in front of him as the vehicle bounced and swayed. 'Quite a road.'

'You should see it in the rainy season.'

'This must be a pretty special place we're going to. I didn't think there'd be anything to top the view of the river at sunset,' Jed said.

'Just let me know what you think when we get there.'

A few minutes later Chris eased the vehicle off the road into the shade of a clump of trees. 'Come with me. It's just on the other side of these bushes.'

Jed was speechless. Unlike the other waterholes he had seen in the park, the water here was a deep blue. It covered an area about half the size of a football field and a big tree dominated the left side. Its massive branches were so heavy with giant birds' nests that they drooped almost to the surface of the water. The setting sun was like a huge fairytale pumpkin suspended above the trees and its reflection was captured perfectly on the mirror-smooth surface. The combination of water, trees, sunset and a lone bull elephant that slowly approached the far side of the life-giving reservoir captured Africa's beauty in a single vista.

Chris opened the back of the Land Rover and pulled out a picnic blanket and the cold box. She laid the blanket down and they sat close to each other.

'Miranda told me in an email once that this had become her favourite place,' Chris said.

'I can see why. Thanks for bringing me here.'

'In return you can open us a couple of beers.'

'A small price to pay.' Jed knocked the caps off two ice-cold Zambezi Lagers and handed a foaming bottle to Chris.

She raised her hand to her mouth and licked off the spilled froth. Jed realised he was staring at her.

She smiled. 'Can't waste a drop.'

'Here's to Africa,' he said, raising his bottle.

'No, here's to Miranda,' she countered.

'To Miranda.' They clinked bottles and Jed looked out over the peaceful waterhole. 'I said my goodbyes to her today, Chris.'

'I know. I think it's for the best, Jed. It was good you came all this way, that you found out how she lived and what she was doing.'

'I still don't know a hell of a lot about either of those things, but I don't regret coming.'

'Neither do I – I mean, I'm pleased you're here, even though I may have seemed a bit defensive at first.'

'I know it's been hard for you too, Chris.'

'She was my friend. No, more than that. Miranda was . . . well, if I'd married and had a child, I would have wanted her to be just like Miranda.'

Jed noticed Chris blinking and wondered if she was fighting back tears. He placed his beer on the ground and put his hand on her shoulder.

She leaned closer to him and he put his arm all the way around her. Chris rested her cheek on Jed's shoulder, staring at the waterhole for a few seconds. When she turned her face to him he kissed her tenderly. She put her arms around his neck, drew him closer, and parted her lips as he kissed her again.

Jed felt her tongue darting into his mouth. His body stirred as he breathed in the scent of her. It had been months since he had been with a woman and he found himself desperately wanting to consume every inch of Christine Wallis as soon as he possibly could. He lay back and she allowed herself to be drawn down onto the blanket with him. His hand caressed her neck, then moved to her breast. She did not resist, so he undid her shirt buttons, sliding a hand inside. He felt her heart racing as his callused palm brushed her hardening nipple. Jed looked around, and over his shoulder. 'Will anyone come here?'

'Only me if you keep going like this,' she giggled.

Jed smiled and kissed her again. She moved her hand to his trousers, clutching, hooking her fingers in the waistband. Jed had been led to the waterhole. He didn't need to be shown how to drink. He undid the rest of her buttons, freed a breast from her bra and sucked greedily on a nipple.

Chris closed her eyes and revelled in the feel of him, the smell of him. Jed undid the belt on her shorts, then the button and the zip. She raised her hips off the ground to allow him to slide her pants down.

She kicked them off over her boots and he kissed his way down over her smooth, tanned belly. Chris tried to roll over, but Jed placed a restraining hand on her belly and moved between her thighs. She drew her knees up and ran her hands through his hair as he pulled the triangle of her thong to one side and parted her swollen lips with the tip of his tongue.

'Oh, God,' she breathed as he found her clitoris.

It had been so long since he had tasted a woman that he found the musky tang of her almost overwhelming. His erection strained at his trousers, longing for release. Chris ground herself against his tongue and face and he felt her thighs start to close around him.

He raised his head and saw her eyes were closed tight. Sensing his stare she opened her eyes and looked down at him across her body. Jed rolled onto his side and slithered up the blanket, replacing his tongue with his fingers, but she gently took his hand and moved it away. She reached for the zipper of his fatigues and freed him, staring wantonly into his eyes as she stroked him. 'I want you,' she said, then lowered her mouth to him. It was his turn to lie back in ecstasy.

When he felt himself nearing his climax he drew her up beside him on the blanket. He moved between her legs, spreading them wide, touching her, rubbing her, then stopped. 'Damn,' he said.

'What is it, Jed?'

'I don't have any protection.'

'I don't care, Jed.' She wasn't taking any contraceptive pill as she always practised safe sex, but she could not remember wanting a man so badly. She was willing to risk it.

Jed was aware of the risks the simple act of sex carried with it these days, but he, too, was blind to his desire. He moved to her and entered her in one long, smooth stroke. Chris gasped as he filled her, excited by the swift way he had taken her, knowing she would yield to him. The feeling of his bare cock inside her heightened her arousal. She raised her bottom and ground herself against him. She wrapped her legs around the small of his back, drawing him deeper inside her.

He drove harder and faster into her body, kissing her mouth, her neck, her cheeks. When he again felt himself close to finishing he paused, wanting to delay their climaxes as long as possible. 'Get on top of me,' he commanded her.

Chris straddled him, locking eyes with him as she slowly lowered herself down on his shaft. 'God, you feel good,' she said. She hiked up his T-shirt and placed her hands on his chest, her fingers clawing at the golden hair as she rode him. Jed thrust himself up into her, moving his hands to her breasts and sucking on each nipple in turn. Their bodies were slick with sweat, their coupling as raw and natural as that of any other two creatures in the African wilderness.

'I'm going to come,' he warned her, in case she wanted to move off him.

Chris was breathing faster now. 'Inside me,' she whispered.

Afterwards, they lay still and spent on the picnic blanket, the soft evening breeze cooling the perspiration on their bodies. Jed reached over and brushed a damp strand of hair from Chris's face. 'I've got to leave soon, probably tomorrow,' he said.

'I know.'

'Our lives . . . It's hard to know when we'll meet again.'

'When, or if?'

'I'd like to see you again, if we can manage it.'

'I've been approached about a teaching position in Virginia. It starts next fall.' Chris lay with one leg hooked over his, unwilling to break contact with him.

'Virginia? I've had some people at Langley after me for a while.' He laughed a little at the revelation.

'CIA?'

'Other Government Agencies, as we used to say in Afghanistan. The agency's always looking for ex-military people. Building up their own little private army again, just like in the sixties.'

'How would you feel about leaving the Army?'

He laughed again. 'I've been in more than my fair share of wars, Chris. A little time back home wouldn't hurt me at all. Also, I'd like to think I can pass on a trick or two that might save some rookie in the future.'

'I think you'd be a great teacher,' she said.

'Would you want to see me again, if we were both living in Virginia? Or is this just the time, the place, the circumstances coming together?'

'You tell me.'

He looked thoughtful for a moment. 'I can't forget what happened here, how we met, but in a funny way that would be OK. I didn't know Miranda for very much of her life and I don't want to forget my daughter. You would remind me of her every day – in a good way, I mean.'

'Go home, see your ex-wife and lay Miranda's memory to rest properly. After that, send me an email and tell me if you're going to end up in Virginia. We could see each other back in the States and work out where we go from here. I'm ninety-nine per cent certain I'm going to take that teaching job.'

'What would it take to make you a hundred per cent certain?'

'This,' she said as she encircled him with her hand and rolled on top of him again.

14

'Your itinerary is confirmed, General. You'll be leaving from Dallas on Tuesday, as planned.'

'Thanks, Janey,' Lieutenant General Donald 'Crusher' Calvert said to his civilian personal assistant. He had given up the fantasy that his staff might get used to calling him by his first name now that he was retired. 'Anything in the papers today?'

'The press clippings are in your email inbox, sir. The one from the *Post* is interesting.'

'Interesting?'

She pulled a print-out from a sheaf of other papers in the crook of her left arm and said, 'The headline is MR CRUSHER GOES TO WASHINGTON, question mark.'

'Very funny. What else does it say?'

'*Retired general Donald "Crusher" Calvert is being promoted as a potential congressional nominee by senior unnamed Republican Party sources in the lead-up to next year's election. Calvert, fifty-four, a Vietnam combat veteran, former commander of the 18th Airborne Corps and, most recently, Coalition forces in Afghanistan, caught the public's eye and imagination as the fast-and-hard-talking Pentagon spokesman during the invasion of Iraq and subsequent operations against Islamic extremist terrorists around the world.* Should I start calling you "congressman" now, sir?'

'Don't believe everything you read in the papers, Janey.' For now, the behind-the-scenes machinations of the Hill could wait. He was going hunting. He leaned back in his leather office chair and eagerly opened the folder Janey had placed in front of him. This was a holiday, his first in three years. 'I see we haven't lost any time on safari by changing countries,' he said as Janey cleared a pile of files from his out-tray.

'No, sir. I was quite adamant with the travel people that the new arrangements shouldn't eat into your time on the ground.'

'Good, good.'

'I'm still worried for you, sir.'

'Oh, don't fret, Janey. Zambia may not be the safest place in the world, but it's one of the few places where I can still hunt big game. The area I'm going to is about as remote as it gets in Africa these days, so there's no risk of political agitation or anything like that.'

'I know, sir. I've read the security assessments – they're in the folder too, by the way – but I can't help thinking you'd be better off in the Bahamas or maybe Australia.'

He laughed. 'I'd be mobbed in places like that, and probably for all the wrong reasons. No, this is my chance to get away from it all and to hell with anyone who tries to stop me.'

'Yes, sir. Do you think the bombings in Tanzania will have any repercussions elsewhere on the continent?'

'That's the thing about terrorists, Janey, you never know where they're going to strike. There's no rhyme or reason to it, but we can only go on the CIA and State Department assessments. There's no way I could flout the current travel ban on Tanzania – that would undermine the present administration and send the wrong message to American tourists.'

The irony of the situation was that the lodge in Zambia had been his first choice for this coming trip. Botswana, where he had first hunted in Africa, was now off his list of possible safari destinations, as the government there had recently banned commercial hunting of dangerous game – opting instead to concentrate on tourism only.

231

He had hunted in South Africa, but been unimpressed with the lack of sport involved in the lion hunt he had been taken on. While the animal had a decent mane, it was so old and slow it looked as though it might have had a heart attack or died of other natural causes if he hadn't put it out of its misery. Despite the denials of the owner of the lodge, he suspected the animal had been drugged prior to his arrival. It had all gone a little too smoothly. He knew some South African hunting ranches had been exposed in the media for staging 'caged' hunts, in which the animals had no chance at all of escaping the hunter. What he wanted was a true test of wits, stamina and courage between man and beast, and he needed somewhere wild for it.

Wylde Heart Safaris in Zambia had been recommended to him by a retired admiral at a cocktail party. A booking had been made, but later cancelled after a telephone call from the Secretary of State. The Secretary, a one-time brother officer with whom Calvert had served in Vietnam, and who knew of his impending retirement, had asked him if he would accompany him to a regional security conference in Dar es Salaam.

'You can still go on safari, Donny, after the conference,' the Secretary had assured him. 'I need you there as an adviser to brief the delegates on our worldwide operations against Al Qaeda.'

'Yes, sir,' Calvert had answered respectfully, then added, 'I'm honoured, but surely you know as much as me about our current efforts.'

'You want me to spell it out for you, Crusher, you old dog? You're the public face of the war on terror these days. The other politicians and soldiers there will respect your view, plus the exposure won't hurt you. Do your hunting for a week after the conference and you can fly back with me after I finish some gladhanding in Kenya and Uganda.'

His staff had made the changes, but now, just a few days short of the conference, had cancelled them. State and the CIA had briefed him on a plot to shoot down the Secretary's jet in Mombasa. He'd been told that a recently captured Pakistani prisoner at Guantanamo Bay had revealed details of a terrorist plan to conduct coordinated attacks on aircraft in Afghanistan and Africa, with up to six shoulder-launched surface-to-air missiles. The aim was to show that the terror organisation could conduct simultaneous operations in different parts of the world. The intelligence had led to the US Special Forces raid on the compound in Afghanistan, which had netted two of the missiles. A further two missiles, and two more terrorists, had been destroyed in an attack on a dhow off the coast of Mombasa, by a CIA-owned Predator Unmanned Aerial Vehicle armed with a hellfire missile. Despite the victory, which had still not been made public, several of the African heads of state who had promised to attend the conference had pulled out and the whole thing had been called off. Calvert thought the fact that two of the anti-aircraft missiles which had left Pakistan were still unaccounted for, and were possibly somewhere in Africa, probably added to the African politicians' nervousness.

At first Calvert had fumed at the cancellation, and the loss of the opportunity to be seen on the world stage as something other than the be-medalled front man for other soldiers' deeds on the battlefield and the guy who had to explain the rising body count in Iraq. However, his disappointment had been softened by the knowledge that he would have more time to spend hunting, and that he could now pursue his preferred choice of a Zambian safari.

He smiled as he flicked through the revised itinerary in the folder. He would fly to Lusaka, the capital of Zambia, and pay a private courtesy call on that country's president on his first day. Once his official commitment was over, his safari would begin in earnest, with a flight in a light aircraft to Willy Wylde's private hunting concession, located on the edge of the Lower Zambezi National Park in the south-east of the country.

He perused a colour brochure which showed pictures of satisfied hunters, many of them American, sitting beside or, in some cases, astride their slain trophies. He was going for a bull buffalo and a leopard on this trip, two of the big five that had eluded him on his last couple of safaris. He gazed enviously at a photo of a doctor from New Jersey who knelt next to a solidly built leopard. He decided that if he got his hunting quota out of the way early he would try his hand at catching one of Africa's other great and wily predators, the hard-fighting tigerfish.

'This is going to be great. I'll have a leopard skin and a stuffed tiger to show you when I get back!'

'A tiger?'

'It's a fish.'

'Yes, sir.' The secretary frowned at her boss's enthusiasm. As much as she admired him, she violently disagreed with killing animals for sport.

'Aw, Janey, I know you don't like hunting, but it's not as bad as the goddamned bunny-huggers make out.'

She couldn't resist rising to the bait. 'Tell that to the leopard you're going to shoot, sir.'

He shook his head. 'Hunting is the lifeblood of some struggling communities in Africa, Janey. By managing their wildlife in a sustainable way they can keep hard currency coming into the country and provide wealth and jobs for local people.'

'Yes, but it's not *their* wildlife to manage, sir. The world's wildlife belongs to all of us.'

He had had the debate with many people in the past and, if the truth be told, had always shied away from stating his case too forcefully. He knew that if he wanted to pursue a career in politics he would have to keep his passion to himself for fear of alienating too large a chunk of the voting public. Still, he persisted in stating his case to his feisty and not unattractive assistant. 'Janey, without hunting we wouldn't have the great game parks of the world. Big reserves like the Kruger National Park in South Africa were started by governments that realised they needed to protect and conserve wildlife for future generations.'

'But, sir, it was the hunters who nearly wiped out all the wildlife in the first place.'

'Irresponsible hunters, Janey. Poachers. People who would kill any-thing that moved for money and hang the effect on the future of the species. Today, hunting is also important for wildlife management. Animals such as elephants have to be killed in some reserves because there are too many of them. Controlled culling helps manage animal populations and provide income for people who need it.'

'They're all good arguments, sir, but you know that there's a large proportion of the community who will never agree with you. The press won't like it either, General. You know they've criticised your previous safaris as sending the wrong message to the rest of Africa.'

'I don't give a damn what the press thinks, Janey.'

'Yes, sir,' she said, realising she would gain nothing from prolonging the argument. 'Did you see that State has assigned two secret service agents to you for personal protection during your safari? I heard the Secretary of State made the order himself.'

'Yes, I saw it and I'm not happy about it.' He did not want anyone else tagging along on his trip, but he was astute enough to realise that as a public figure he warranted protection. Perhaps, too, it was the Secretary's way of telling him that he should get used to the trappings of high office, no matter how inconvenient and intrusive they may be.

15

C hris didn't know how she felt about Jed Banks, and that annoyed her.

She raised a hand to her eyes to shade them from the bright morning sunshine that streamed in through the louvred windows. She could smell him on the pillow next to her, on the damp sheets, on her, in her. She had let him into her body, but he had also invaded her mind, and it made her angry. He was leaving, and it made her sad. She had never fallen for a man so quickly, so completely, and she felt lost, out of control, angry, happy and confused, all at the same time.

He had not used a condom. She hadn't wanted him to, not even once they got back to the lodge, where they made love again after dinner, and once more, half an hour ago, in the morning. That made her feel stupid. She didn't expect he was carrying any sexually transmitted diseases – although you never knew with soldiers – but she wasn't using any other form of birth control. What if she became pregnant? The idea didn't repel her as much as it once did, and that was totally weird.

'Christ, get a hold of yourself,' she whispered. Outside, somewhere in the river, a hippo mocked her with a call that sounded like a fat man's big belly laugh.

She screwed her eyes tight against the merciless, revealing sunlight and tried to work out why she had told him she was considering the job in Virginia, and why she had all but invited him to shack up with her. She could hear Jed in the next room packing his rucksack. He was leaving her, which would make things easier for a time, although she knew she would miss him. She wanted to cry and hated that he had made her feel so screwed up.

Chris stood and felt his wetness and hers, still hot inside her. She was a mess, mentally, emotionally and physically. She needed to shower and get back to work, not lie around thinking about a man. She pulled on a T-shirt and denim shorts and grabbed a towel.

'Hello, beautiful,' he said, turning at the sound of her footfall on the wooden balcony outside his door.

He moved across the floor, took her in his arms and kissed her. She rested her head on his shoulder and hugged him, her body moulded against his. They fitted together so well. He kissed her hair. Her heart and her resolve melted.

'Moses will be here in a minute,' he said.

'I can do quick,' she said, laughing at her own lasciviousness.

'I doubt I can do anything after last night and this morning,' he said, although they both felt him stir through his jeans. She looked up at him and smiled. 'Enough, enough already, I've got to get the four-by-four back to Harare today.'

'I've got to get organised myself, and start heading back to South Africa.'

'Wish I could stay with you longer.' He brushed a wisp of hair from her face.

'So do I, but maybe this is for the best.'

'You're dumping me so soon?' he asked with mock seriousness.

'More like a raincheck. I don't know what I'm feeling right now, Jed.'

'Me too, but it's all good.'

'Same here,' she lied.

They heard the clatter of the Land Rover's engine downstairs as Moses pulled up, then the slamming of his door.

'Tell Moses goodbye from me. Say I'm still asleep. I don't want to see him like this – I feel like a tramp.'

'Don't be silly, you look beautiful, and you could never look like a tramp.'

She leaned closer and whispered in his ear, 'I'll be whatever you want me to be, soldier.'

He smiled. 'OK then, be my email buddy until you get back to the States, OK?'

'Deal,' she said. 'I'll miss you.'

'Me too.'

They kissed, passionately, and finally it was Chris who broke contact.

Jed shouldered his pack and the narrow wooden stairs down from the verandah creaked with the extra weight. He looked back over his shoulder when he was halfway down, and saw she stood where he had left her, outside his room.

Images of their lovemaking flashed through his mind, visions of her face contorted in pleasure, the sounds she made, the taste of her. He had been in this situation before, more than once. In every case, except with Patti in the early days, he had turned and walked away, and never seen the girl again. He enjoyed the company of women, but his lifestyle and career were not suited to long-term relationships – he'd learned that the hard way with Patti and Miranda. In his younger years he had enjoyed the thrill of the chase, of getting a woman into bed, but his days as a Lothario were long gone. He'd met more than a few women since Patti who were just after sex, with no strings attached, and that had been fine with him, but the encounters had left him feeling hollow, unwanted.

Did he really want to see Chris Wallis again? Yes, he was sure he did. Certainly the sex had been fantastic. Their bodies and minds had seemed perfectly attuned, anticipating each other's needs and preferences intuitively. Also, he hadn't been lying when he said he wanted to stay in touch with her because she provided a lasting link to Miranda. That was no basis for a relationship, of course, but he wanted to let her know, up front, that he no longer held her responsible for Miranda's death.

He smiled at Chris and said, 'I'll be checking my emails as soon as I get home.'

'Check when you get to Johannesburg: I'll send one tonight.'

He paused on the stairs. Mobile telephones didn't work in the Zambezi Valley and there was no conventional telephone line into the lodge. 'You didn't tell me you had a satellite phone.'

She tried to hold back the blush but couldn't. 'You didn't ask. Don't miss your ride. Get out of here before I rip your clothes off, Jed Banks.'

He laughed and waved again, but he could tell she had made the joke to cover her embarrassment. 'Hi, Moses, how was your night?' he asked when he saw the guide in the living room, but he only half listened to the man's answer. He might have fallen for Chris, in a sexual way and maybe something deeper, but he still had the feeling she was holding something back from him.

'Fine. Are you all packed?'

'Packed and ready to go home,' Jed said, loud enough for Chris to hear upstairs.

Chris gave herself a mental kick as she showered, and again as she changed into clean clothes. Jed had caught her out in a lie and she was a fool for allowing it to happen. Her feelings for him were affecting her work.

She rummaged through her bag for her diary and looked up the number of British Airways in Johannesburg. She flew frequently enough to need the reservations number on hand. She set up the portable satellite antenna and phone again and dialled the number.

When the woman answered, Chris said, 'Good morning, I'm calling on behalf of my husband, Mr Jed Banks. He wanted me to confirm his booking from Harare to Johannesburg tomorrow, please.' Chris guessed that Jed would be flying on the Comair flight, a subsidiary of British Airways, rather than the less reliable Air Zimbabwe.

'One moment, madam,' the reservations officer said. 'Oh, I'm sorry, there must be a mistake, Mr Banks is not booked on tomorrow's flight.'

'Oh, silly me, I mean the day *after* tomorrow,' Chris said.

'No, nothing on that flight either. Perhaps you could get Mr Banks to call us back and we'll clear this up.'

Chris hung up feeling a little better about concealing the fact she had a satellite phone from Jed; after all, he had lied to her about his departure date. She wondered what he was up to, and sincerely hoped he wasn't going to do the same thing she was. She flipped through a sheaf of print-outs of emails that Miranda had sent her during her time in Zimbabwe and found the one on which a telephone number had been marked with a yellow highlighter pen. She dialled the number, prefixing it with the international code for Zambia.

'Crescent Moon Safari Lodge, good day,' a male voice answered.

'Good morning, may I speak to Hassan bin Zayid, please?' Chris asked.

'I'm very sorry, but Mr bin Zayid is not here right now.' The man sounded African, the voice deep.

'Can you tell me when he'll be back?'

'Who is calling, please?'

'I'm a friend of Miranda Banks-Lewis, the American woman who was researching –'

The man cut in, 'Ah, we were all very sorry to hear about the death of Miss Miranda, madam. She visited us often.'

'Yes, so she told me. I'm a friend of hers and she told me of her acquaintance with Mr bin Zayid and his help with her research work. I wanted to thank him in person, if possible, for all he did for Miranda and to pass on my sympathy. I understand they were close friends.'

'Indeed they were. Miss Miranda was very popular here. However, I am sorry but Mr bin Zayid is in Tanzania on business. He was most distressed by what happened.'

'I see. When will he be back?' Chris asked again.

'We do not expect him for two, maybe three, more weeks, madam. If I could have your name, I will pass on a message to him. Perhaps he can call you back.'

'No, it's OK,' she said. 'I have the number for his office in Zanzibar. I'll try him there.'

'Very well, madam, but Mr bin Zayid will be travelling around Zanzibar and Tanzania inspecting his other properties, so he may be hard to get hold of. Are you sure you don't want to leave a message?'

'No, but thank you for your help anyway.'

'A pleasure, madam. Goodbye.'

It was still a loose end. She would have liked to interview bin Zayid in person, to find out how close he and Miranda were. She wondered when exactly the wealthy hotelier had left the valley. Mort Solomon would be able to check his movements from Zambia to Zanzibar. She hated calling in another favour from the creep, but she had no choice. She dialled his number.

While she waited to be put through she thought about Jed. She wondered if a relationship between two people who could lie to each other so easily could really mature, especially after they had just made passionate love. She was willing to give it a try, she thought. Maybe.

'What?' Jed exclaimed.

'Hassan bin Zayid, that is the man's name.'

'Jesus Christ, an Arab?'

'What's so bad about Arabs? I myself was a Muslim for a while.'

Jed ignored the braying zebra filing down to drink at Long Pool as the Land Rover juddered along the corrugated dirt road. 'What do you mean, you were a Muslim?'

'Muhammad Ali, the fighter, was a hero of mine. I converted when I was a teenager, but gave up when I discovered alcohol.' Moses laughed.

'Aw, hell, I don't want you to think I'm racist or prejudiced, I'm just surprised, is all. I spent six months in Afghanistan hunting for Arab terrorists and now I find out my daughter was dating one.'

'Not all Arabs are terrorists, Jed.'

'I know that. I didn't mean that this guy was a terrorist. Well, what else did you find out about him?'

Moses had spent much of the night drinking with the head warden and two of his rangers and, between them, the three parks officers seemed to know quite a bit about Hassan bin Zayid. One of the rangers was certain the Arab had been sleeping with the young American woman, but Moses decided to leave that piece of information out, in deference to Jed's feelings. 'They say he is a good man,' he said instead.

'What the hell does that mean?'

'He owns a game reserve on the Zambian side of the river a couple of kilometres downstream from here. He's into wildlife conservation. This man spends a lot of money on captive breeding of rare species. They say he has some black rhino and cheetah over there which he is going to release into Lower Zambezi National Park.'

'Good for him. What was he doing over here?'

'The warden said Hassan was funding research in Lower Zambezi into the number of predators there – lions, hyenas, leopards – and that he wanted to get similar figures for the Zimbabwe side, in Mana Pools National Park. He comes to meet with the researchers on this side every couple of months to compare population numbers and trends. They say that is how he met your daughter.'

Jed pondered the information. It seemed innocent enough. 'How often did they meet?'

'I asked the men this and the warden did not want to say. Afterwards, one of the rangers told me that this man did not only come on his official visits.' Moses stopped the Land Rover to let a big bull elephant cross the road in front of them. The massive creature shook its mighty head as it passed and flapped its ragged ears. Moses left the engine running in case the elephant decided to charge.

'So what, there were unofficial visits?'

'The man has a boat and he used to cross the river illegally sometimes to visit your daughter.'

'And did she ever travel across the river illegally?'

'The one ranger I spoke to, he said yes, that he suspects she did sometimes cross the river in Mr Hassan's boat. The warden would not want to say this because it is very illegal, Jed.'

'Shit, so she was hopping borders as well.' Jed shook his head. 'What else did they say about him?'

'He is very wealthy. His family is from Zanzibar. He owns a lot of hotels, they said.'

'When was the last time anyone saw or heard from him, either officially or unofficially?'

'The ranger said he thinks the last time he was over this side of the river was about a week before your daughter was taken by the lion.'

No one, Jed noticed, not even himself, was keeping up the pretence that Miranda might simply be missing. It seemed the verdict that she was dead had been reached. He felt the need to meet this Hassan bin Zayid, if only to find out what Miranda saw in him, but what good could possibly come from such an encounter? He wondered whether the man even knew Miranda was gone and, if he did, why he hadn't crossed the river to find out for himself what had happened.

'Did you get an address and telephone number for this guy?' Jed asked abruptly.

'I did.'

'Sorry, Moses, I don't mean to be rude.'

'I understand.'

Once through the last of the national park's gates they turned left onto the main tarred road and climbed out of the Zambezi Valley. Jed took a last look at the wide expanse of bush below the heat haze. For him the beauty of this place would always be tinged with the tragic memories of his loss.

They drove in silence along the top of the escarpment to Makuti and then down the winding road that led back to Kariba and Nyamhunga township. As Moses's home town came into sight Jed reached into his daypack, pulled out his cell phone and switched it on. At last, the thing would be of some use.

The phone's screen showed it had picked up a local telephone service provider and, after a few seconds, it beeped, signalling Jed had received a message. He had to dial the States to check his messages. The recorded voice on the other end of the line told him he had three. He played them back.

'Hi, Jed, this is Patti. Call me when you can. I'm not holding out hope for any miracles, but I do want to know what you've been able to find out. How was Professor Wallis? If I ever meet her I'll kill her for sending Miranda to that place. Oh, by the way, Miranda's name is public knowledge now and I've had a few people from the press calling me. One even came to the door. Just thought you should know in case they try and track you down as well. Hope you're OK. See you.'

He deleted Patti's message, intending to return her call soon, and the next message played.

'Jed, it's Hank Klein. I got that information you asked for, but it took a little longer than I thought. Goddamned system was shut down for a day. Fucking computers. Anyway, the lady you asked for, Wallis, Christine – here it is. You were right, she served in the 82nd Airborne from 1989 to 1994. Meritorious Service medal, Army Commendation medal. Made it to sergeant and, oh yeah, she was recommended for Officer Candidate School but took an honourable discharge when her service was up. Must have got a better offer. Good soldier, according to her jacket. Well, that's about it, except you got one thing wrong, buddy, she was C-2 not C-1. Hope this helps. You owe me a beer, you son of a bitch. Keep your head down, wherever you are.'

Jed deleted the message. Interesting, he thought. The third message on his phone began with a loud burst of static. The connection was obviously a bad one.

'Jed, it's Luke Scarborough, I don't know if you remember me . . .'

How could he forget him? The kid had nearly got himself and Jed killed when he fell out of the Chinook.

'I'm in Africa, in Zambia right now. I understand you're in Zimbabwe – I'll be crossing at Kariba on Tuesday. I need to talk to you, urgently.'

Scarborough rattled off the number of his cell phone but Jed did not bother to write it down. Instead he punched the number in the keypad that deleted messages. The kid's call had wasted enough of his money already. Jed knew what Luke Scarborough wanted to talk about – Miranda. Patti's message had said she was being pestered by reporters and he imagined this was more of the same.

He took out the piece of paper Moses had written Hassan bin Zayid's number on and dialled.

No one answered the phone at Crescent Moon Safaris, so Jed left a message, asking for bin Zayid to call him back.

'No one there?' Moses asked.

Jed shook his head. 'I'm going to cross the border into Zambia anyway, Moses, as soon as I drop you off.'

'I thought you might. I would offer to come with you, at no cost, but I don't have a passport.'

'I appreciate the gesture, but this is something I've got to do on my own.'

Jed didn't feel at all bad about lying to Chris about his departure date, not in the light of her revelation that she had a satellite phone stashed away. It would have been nice of her to offer to let him use it, given that there was no other way of making a call from the national park.

'You won't make it to the lodge today,' Moses said. 'It's not far in a straight line, but it's a very bad road into the Lower Zambezi. You should take a detour and stay in Lusaka tonight, but don't hang around that country too long. All Zambians are thieves.'

Jed smiled. 'I'll try to remember that. Can I drop you at your house?'

'No, the shebeen is fine.'

Jed raised his eyebrows but said nothing. When he pulled up at the bar he peeled off three one-hundred US dollar bills.

'This is too much, Jed. Take a hundred back. It's what we agreed.'

'I don't want to fight off the debt collectors next time I need a safari guide. Try not to spend it all on beer and women, although, come to think of it, that's what I'd do.'

'Thank you, Jed. Let me know if there is anything I can do for you on your way back from Zambia. This money will keep me out of trouble for a while. My kid will get some of it too.'

The two men shook hands and Jed waved farewell as he turned back for the road into Kariba. In town he bought fuel, and some more food.

He passed through the border formalities without delay and crossed into Zambia along the top of the mighty concrete wall that held back the man-made sea of Lake Kariba. Once he cleared the Zambian post, at Siavonga, the Land Rover's diesel engine lowered as the vehicle climbed sluggishly up the escarpment.

Zambia, he noticed, seemed more run-down and untidier than even trouble-plagued Zimbabwe. Unlike the other side of the border, there was no sign of any naturally occurring wildlife, save for a couple of scrawny guinea fowl being held up by skinny teenage boys looking for a roadside sale, and a man brandishing the tanned skin of a python.

Sixty-five kilometres from Siavonga he turned right, towards Chirundu. The town, if the cluster of shanties, brothels and bars could be called that, was another border crossing point, this time on the Zambezi River below the damn wall. He didn't stop, and trundled along the worsening pot-holed road past a billboard that shouted *Speed Kills, Condoms Save.*

Bad tar gave way to rutted dirt as he followed the river's course towards the Lower Zambezi National Park and the private game lodges that bordered it. He crossed the sluggish brown Kafue River on an old hand-cranked punt, its operator's skin glistening with sweat in the low afternoon light. Just on nightfall he called it quits and pulled into a quiet campsite with manicured lawns and permanent safari tents overlooking the Zambezi. Fortunately, sleep came to him quickly after the long journey and a few beers.

The next morning he rose at four-thirty, and was showered and on the track again by five. The bush closed in around the Land Rover as the road narrowed and it took him more than an hour to cover twenty kilometres. An increasing number of signs to private lodges told him he was getting closer to his destination. He took the next lodge turn-off he saw, in order to ask for directions.

The sign said *Wylde Heart Safaris, one kilometre.* He found the driveway much smoother than the main route. No doubt the lodge maintained the access road itself, rather than relying on the Zambian Government or a local authority. At the entrance gate he stopped beside an African worker in overalls, who was slashing long grass with a sharpened piece of iron bent into a scythe. The man directed him to the main building. A tall white man – Jed guessed he was in his early fifties – raised a hand to his eyes to shield them from the sun's glare and then waved.

'Morning, can I help?' he said as Jed pulled up.

'Morning, sir. I'm hoping you can. I'm looking for a place called Crescent Moon Safaris, and all I know is that it's somewhere in this area.'

'Hassan's place?'

'That's right. You know him?'

''Course I do. We're practically neighbours. He's a champion fellow. Willy Wylde is the name, by the way.'

'Jed Banks.' He shook Wylde's offered hand. 'Yes, Hassan is a great guy,' he ad-libbed.

'You're a client?'

'No, a friend of a friend.'

'Are you a bunny-hugger too?' Wylde asked.

'Excuse me?'

'A conservationist, like Hassan. I'd have picked you for a hunter – most American chaps who come to this part of the world on their own are.'

'Nope, just an acquaintance.'

Jed looked over at the reception building. There was a man painting the walls with fresh whitewash and another on a step ladder patching a worn section of thatch. A woman wearing a starched white pinafore over her green maid's uniform was mopping the painted concrete floor of a wide shady verandah.

Wylde noticed the direction of Jed's glance and said, 'We're giving the place a bit of a spruce-up. Got a very important client coming in soon. *Very* important.'

'The rich and famous coming to town?'

247

Wylde tapped the side of his nose with his index finger. 'Sorry, mum's the word. This chap guards his privacy for very good reasons. Now, I can draw you a quick map to Hassan's place. Come inside for a moment and I'll get some paper. It'll only take you about another twenty minutes to get there, but I have to warn you that I did hear that Hassan was out of town.'

'I've tried calling a few times, but only got a recorded message. I was in Lusaka on business and thought I'd give it a try anyway.'

Wylde nodded and started to draw on the back of a discarded envelope on the reception counter. 'Well, there are worse places in the world to potter about. I'd offer you a room myself, but I'm expecting my client at any time.'

'He's booked the whole place out?' Jed asked, seeing at least four separate bungalows around the main building.

'Brings a bit of an entourage with him. Already had a couple of chaps on the advance party check the place out. But as I said, I can't go into details. There you go.' Wylde passed the envelope to Jed. 'Out the gate, turn right and follow the map. You'll see a sign about five kilometres down the road. Can't miss Hassan's place.'

Crescent Moon Safari Lodge was clearly aimed at an upmarket clientele. The guard on the gate was immaculately turned out in a khaki uniform bearing the lodge's embroidered logo, a rampant lion superimposed over a red crescent. The man spoke into his radio and then directed Jed up a track to the main lodge. The lawns around the building were lush and manicured, despite the dryness of the surrounding bush.

Jed parked the Land Rover and walked across stone pavers to a thatch-roofed lodge. The common area, which was open on two sides and took in an uninterrupted view of the river, was decked out with dark wooden furniture and an eclectic mix of expensive antiques, all designed to re-create the feel of a romanticised nineteen-twenties safari camp. Jed picked up a pair of binoculars that looked as though they dated from the First World War. When he heard footsteps he replaced them next to the old-fashioned gramophone.

'Good afternoon, sir, how can I be of assistance?' The young African man was dressed in the lodge uniform. His lips were curled into a smile that showed even white teeth, but there was no warmth or greeting in his eyes.

'I'm looking for Hassan bin Zayid.' Jed was not in the mood for pleasantries.

'I'm sorry, sir, but he is not here just now. Do you have a booking with us?'

'No. I called, but all I got was the answering machine. My name is Jed Banks. Did you get my message?'

'Ah, Mr Banks. I was so sorry to hear about Miss Miranda – we all were shocked to hear of her passing. Please accept my condolences.' The man clasped his hands in front of him and lowered his eyes a little.

'Thank you,' Jed said.

'I'm sorry, also, that no one has replied to your message, but the lodge is closed right now. I have referred all messages, including yours, sir, to our reservations office.'

'Where is that?'

'Zanzibar, sir. The head office of our group is located there.'

'That's a long way from here?'

'Nearly all of our clients come from overseas, sir, on packages booked through our head office. We don't rely on what Americans call, I think, passing trade.'

'So not many people just drop in, like me?'

'No, sir. As you would have seen, the road is not good and we are off the beaten track.'

'When will Mr bin Zayid be here again?'

'Ah, I don't know for sure, but not for at least another two weeks. He will be in Zanzibar and elsewhere in Tanzania on business.'

Shit, Jed said to himself. 'Do you have a number for him?'

'I can give you the number of our head office, sir, but I understand

Mr bin Zayid is moving around a lot. He has been very hard to contact lately.'

'I see. Well, I'll take the number anyway. Mind if I look around the lodge while I'm here? I'm trying to get a feel for the places my daughter stayed, the places she liked and the people she met.'

The man hesitated for a moment. 'Well, since you have come all this way, sir, please feel free to look around. However, as I said, the lodge is closed for the time being.'

'I understand, I won't be long.'

Jed wandered around the lodge. There was a wooden dining table surrounded by ornately carved chairs, and a lounge area with wicker armchairs and couches topped with plump cushions. Mahogany book-shelves were lined with field guides to African animals, birds, reptiles and trees, and a selection of novels in a wide variety of languages, including Arabic.

The lodge looked over the Zambezi River and somewhere in the distance Jed heard a hippo snort, a sound he would forever associate with this part of the world. Paved pathways led to the individual accommodation bungalows. He walked around one of the huts, dodg-ing a spitting water sprinkler, and found a gravelled car park behind the main lodge. An open-topped Defender pick-up was parked by the rear-access door to the main building.

Jed wandered over to take a closer look at the vehicle. It was fitted out for hunting, with the back empty except for a bench seat across the open tray and a roll bar across the top, with gun racks welded to it. Interestingly, an expensive-looking hunting rifle was cradled in the rack. The weapon was topped with a telescopic sight that made Jed even more curious. It was a night sight, similar to the one he had used himself in Afghanistan. He moved closer and peered into the rear tray of the pick-up. In the back were two green canvas rucksacks and two AK-47 assault rifles. The weapons looked clean and well cared for. As well as the packs there were two matching hunter's vests, civilian versions of military-style web gear. In the chest pouches on the vests he counted ten additional magazines for the assault rifles. That was a hell of a lot of firepower for a safari lodge dedicated to conservation rather than hunting – more than three hundred rounds apiece, including the magazines fitted to the rifles. He was tempted to look inside one of the bulging packs, but he heard the crunch of footsteps on the gravel behind him and turned.

'Can I help you?' This man was taller, older than the African Jed had met in the lodge. His face bore the scars of smallpox. He looked like a man of the bush, a tracker maybe.

'I'm just looking around. I came here hoping to find Mr bin Zayid.'

'He is not here. He will be gone for some time.' The man's voice was stern, as hard and unwelcoming as his face. He carried four two-litre water bottles in green canvas pouches, which he slung into the truck.

'So I heard. Going on a hunting trip?'

'Yes.'

'Funny, I got the impression you guys didn't shoot animals here at Crescent Moon.'

The man frowned, looking to the lodge in apparent annoyance. 'I am hunting men.'

Jed raised an eyebrow. 'I would have thought there were laws against that, even in Zambia.'

'I am hunting poachers.'

'I'd have assumed that anti-poaching patrols were the responsibility of the Government.'

The man exhaled, as though he was annoyed at having to justify his activities to an uninvited foreigner. 'The Zambian Wildlife Authority is responsible for anti-poaching patrols in national parks, but the lodge owners support them. We help train the rangers and conduct our own sweeps for snares and poachers' camps on our lands.'

'So it's not a search-and-destroy operation.'

'I hunt these men, but I didn't say I kill them. Landowners don't have the right to shoot poachers on sight.'

'Then why all the hardware?' Jed gestured at the assault rifles and magazines crammed with copper-jacketed bullets.

'The poachers are heavily armed. Sometimes we have to shoot back in self-defence.'

'I see,' Jed said, thinking that three-hundred rounds per man was quite a defence.

'Anyway,' the man said with an air of finality, 'I am sorry that you travelled all this way to see Mr bin Zayid. If you give me your name I will make sure Mr bin Zayid is told of your visit.'

'Banks, Jed Banks.'

'You're related to the girl?'

Jed was taken aback to hear Miranda described as 'the girl'. Everyone else had spoken of her in fond terms.

'Yes, I'm *the girl's* father.'

'Forgive me,' the man said hurriedly. 'I am sorry for your loss. She was very much appreciated here.'

Appreciated? An odd choice of words.

'I would have thought Mr bin Zayid would have stayed in Zimbabwe when he heard the news, to find out what happened,' Jed said.

The man's face betrayed no emotion. 'Mr bin Zayid has been kept up to date with all the details of the investigation.'

Jed noticed again the man didn't use Miranda's name. 'How much time did she spend on this side of the border?'

'I really can't say. I manage the game reserve and am out of camp often. I spend a lot of time in the bush.'

'Hunting poachers?'

'Amongst other things. Mr Banks, again I am sorry you have wasted your time by travelling all the way here. I assure you I will relay our conversation to Mr bin Zayid, but there is really nothing more I can do for you now.'

The man climbed into the pick-up and backed out of the car park, along with his two packs, two combat vests, six-hundred-odd rounds of ammunition and three guns.

Jed Banks was alone in Africa. His daughter was dead and her boyfriend was nowhere to be found. There was nothing more he could do. He walked back to his Land Rover and started the long journey home.

16

'Solomon.'

'Mort, it's Christine again.'

'Hey, babe. Did you get my message?'

'Don't call me that. And no, I haven't checked my emails today.' Chris stood on the verandah of the lodge at Mana Pools.

'I'm going secure, OK?' he said.

'Whatever.' Chris drummed her fingers on the balcony railing as she waited for the scrambler to kick in. Two saddle-bill storks were standing in the shallows of the Zambezi, their striking red, yellow and black bills poised above the water's surface. The female of the pair – Chris could tell the sex from the markings beneath the bird's eyes – shot her beak into the water and returned with a small, squirming silver fish. Her mate looked on enviously.

'OK, that's better,' Solomon said. 'Well, you should have checked your messages. Remember how I told you our VIP visitor had changed his plans and was reverting to plan A?'

'What's that got to do with me?' Chris already knew General Crusher Calvert had changed his hunting plans from Tanzania to Zambia because of the heightened security threat in East Africa and the cancelled security summit.

'He wants a briefing on the work you've been doing in Africa – all of it.'

'What? You have got to be fucking joking.'

'Yeah. I know, it's probably a little out of your way. He gets in day after tomorrow.'

'It's a two-day drive for me to get there, Mort! How did he find out about my work?'

'It seems one of his security people was talking to our security people here and it came up that you were working in Africa in lion research. The general's security guy knew how keen the big man is on conservation – well, almost as hot as he is on killing – and passed on the news.' Solomon chuckled. 'Now the crush-man wants to meet you. We've sent a message back saying you happen to be in the general area and that you'd be delighted.'

'Thanks a lot, Mort.'

'Like I said, Chris, we want you to brief him on everything.'

'So he knows who I am, what I do?'

'All of it, babe. He could be a lot more than a retired general in the near future, so it behoves us all to start kissing his ass.'

'Dammit. Email me the latest summaries so I can pretend I know what I'm talking about. I've been a little out of the loop up here in the bush, you know.'

'You got it.'

'When does he want to see me?'

'He wants a few days first up to shoot the shit out of some of God's furry creatures, kind of blow off some steam, I guess. His people say you should head over to them and give your briefing on the fourth day. Why don't you take a couple of days R and R in Kariba beforehand?'

'OK. I'll be there,' she said without enthusiasm. 'Oh, and Mort, the reason I called . . .'

'Yes?'

'I need you to check some more border movements for me.'

'Not for Miranda again.'

'No, for Hassan bin Zayid.'

'I thought we were finished with him. What gives?'

Chris detected the note of alarm in his voice. It was understandable. 'Don't panic, Mort. I just wanted to get in touch with him and I've been told he's in Zanzibar.'

'It's my job to panic. You know what I always say: panic now and avoid the rush later. Any reason to doubt that he's in Zanzibar?'

'Not really, but I want to find out if I'm being strung a line by his people.'

'Why do you want to talk to him?' Solomon asked. 'What's he got to do with you?'

'He knew Miranda. They turned out to be friends in the end.'

'Friends! For Christ's sake, Chris, I didn't think you were running a dating agency up there. Was he screwing her?'

'Mort!'

'I'm not joking, Chris. Jesus H Christ. She was up there doing *research*. That was supposed to be all. Now you've got me very worried and very pissed.'

'Cool it, Mort. These things happen. He turned out to be a good guy. Funded her research, helped her out a lot. And if they were doing anything more, it was definitely without my sanction. That's one reason I wanted to talk to him, to close the book.'

'OK, OK. I'll run a check on him – I spend half my life checking things out for you, babe. But in the meantime, you get your ass across the border and fix your hair and nails for the big man.'

Chris ignored his sexism because she needed information from him, but she was growing increasingly weary of the whole charade. More and more she wanted to go home to the States now – maybe to make a home. 'OK, Mort. I'll be a good girl and put on a nice show for the general. Don't forget to send me the summaries I asked for.'

'Yes, ma'am, at your service.'

'Where is Crusher staying, by the way?'

'Place called Wylde Heart Safaris,' Solomon said, then spelled out Wylde's name. 'Cute, hey?'

'Very. Where is it?'

'In the Chiawa Game Management area, on the border of the Lower Zambezi National Park. You know it?'

'Know of it. Bin Zayid's place is in the same general area. It's upriver on the opposite side to where I am now, no more than a kilometre or two as the crow flies.'

'I thought you said it would take you two days to get to that part of Zambia.'

'It will, Mort, by road. You can't just zip across the river – it's against the law.'

'Wouldn't have stopped me when I was your age,' Mort said.

Chris laughed. 'The world was a very different place when you were my age, Mort.'

'Yeah, and I miss it sometimes.'

She was sure he did and, for a second, even felt pity for him, stuck in his airconditioned office. He was probably as envious as hell of her and people like Miranda Banks-Lewis.

'Let me know about bin Zayid, OK?'

'Sure. He'd better be where his people say he is. I don't want any surprises in the next few days, Chris.'

'No one does, Mort.'

Mashumba's brother watched from the shadows. He had travelled far away from the two-legged creatures, along the river, to evade the noisy machines full of the upright animals. There were fewer and fewer machines now. His brother was gone, killed by the terrible noise, and that had seemed to placate the hunters.

He was hungry. His time downriver had not been good. Without his brother, hunting was harder than ever before. He had tried to catch an impala, but the little antelope was too fast for him. He had stalked and pounced on a zebra, but the animal was too big for him to bring down himself and it had kicked him hard in the face with its hoof, knocking two teeth from his jaw. If he were not hunting right now he would have moaned because of the constant pain.

Returning to the stretch of river where the two-legged ones lived was risky. He knew the danger. But he had to eat. He watched this one walk from the machine to the huge anthill – for that was how he perceived the lodge, in his monochrome vision. When she appeared again she was moving slowly, burdened with something. His golden eyes tracked her as she disappeared into the machine, then reappeared empty-handed. The time to strike was when she walked to the machine from her lair, when she was carrying something.

He crept closer, tail down, ears back, keeping his tawny body as close to the ground as possible. He darted from behind a dirt mound to a bush. He watched. Listened. Waited. Judging it safe to move again he slunk closer, to the base of a mopani tree. His nose twitched, for he was now close to another strange structure that smelled of rotting food.

Chris wrinkled her nose at the smell of the rubbish dump behind the lodge. When the National Parks lodge attendant emptied the trashcans she did so into a brick structure about as tall as a man, which was at the rear of the wood-fired hot-water boiler behind the lodge. Chris supposed the set-up had been designed so that some of the rubbish could be shovelled into the fireplace and burned as fuel. In these days of polystyrene containers and plastic wrap, however, it was impractical and harmful to the environment to burn such disgusting products. The problem was that the staff only cleared out the rubbish once a week, shovelling it into a cart towed by a trailer. It was near the end of the week and the pile stank to high heaven.

Solomon's request was an inconvenience, but not an insurmountable one. She could use a couple of days' rest in a hotel in Kariba, she realised, although she didn't relish the long drive to the safari lodge on the other side of the river. She hefted her backpack into the Land Rover and turned back to the lodge. She would leave all of Miranda's equipment here, and take her own computer and communications gear with her to Zambia. Her Glock would have to stay in the lodge as well, as she didn't have a permit to carry the pistol in Zambia. She was sure the weapon and the expensive stuff would be safe until she returned. She would pay for the lodge for another week at least, and spend a couple of relaxing nights back in Mana Pools after she had finished her political duties across the border.

A light breeze rippled the shimmering surface of the Zambezi and carried on over the hot sands of the shoreline. It caressed the leaves of the big Natal mahoganies close to the river as it headed across the bend in the river. By the time the zephyr reached the lodge it had almost exhausted itself. Chris was perspiring from her efforts and the slightest puff of this wind on the back of her neck brought a tempting promise of relief from the heat. The breeze also carried away the smell of rotting refuse; however, it brought with it a new scent.

Chris went back inside and fetched her laptop, in its bulky protective aluminium case. As she walked out of the kitchen towards the Land Rover the breeze stirred again. She froze.

Slowly she turned. There it was. Unmistakable. The smell of damp fur, like a dog that's just come in out of the rain. Except the musty odour was sharpened with the tang of feline urine. Her heart thumped in her rib cage.

Around her the bush had gone silent. The little yellow weaver birds had stopped chattering; the woodpecker had given up his tireless attack on the leadwood; the cicadas in the trees had ceased chirping. Even the omnipresent hippos weren't snorting. There wasn't a monkey or baboon in sight and that alone should have told her long before the smell that something wasn't right. Chris fought to control her rising panic. She scanned the bush as she judged the time it would take her to reach the swinging screen door of the lodge's kitchen. Too long. She started to back towards the rear hatch of the Land Rover. The hair stood up on the back of her neck.

'*Wah-hoo*.' A baboon's warning call from a nearby tree broke the silence. Chris felt her knees go weak.

*

Mashumba's brother flinched at the annoying bark of the detestable baboon. He tensed for his final dash towards the woman. It was no more than a few steps, then a leap and he would be on her. He, too, had felt the breeze ruffle his shaggy mane and he twitched his tail involuntarily in annoyance. The creature had turned and was looking right at him. He would be discovered any second now. He knew he could lie low and then retreat. That would be the sensible thing to do. But his empty belly growled and his shattered jaw throbbed. The muscles in his legs twitched and his powerful shoulders knotted as he summoned his remaining reserves of energy. Like an arrow released from a longbow, he was on his way.

Chris knew lions. She had studied and lived amongst them for years. She knew the worst thing she could do when faced with one of the superpredators was to run. She knew the best thing to do was to stand rock solid still and wait for the beast to decide she wasn't a threat. Ninety-nine times out of a hundred, the old Africa hands said, the lion would back down. She had seen it happen herself, in the Kruger Park. Of course, that theory went completely out the window if a lion had started its charge. Once a big cat was in full flight nothing short of a well-aimed heavy-calibre bullet or a tight burst of automatic-rifle fire would stop it. The other thing she knew she should do was stay silent.

Chris screamed, a piercing primal shriek, as the huge head erupted from behind the tree near the water heater, not ten metres from her. Great padded paws the size of bread plates made clouds of dust rise as they thudded into the ground. Soon the hooked, yellowed claws would be extended in preparation for the ripping of flesh. She half ran, half fell backwards into the open rear of the Land Rover. The cat had crossed the distance between them in less than a second. She flung the heavy aluminium case containing her laptop at the lion and the box glanced off his snout. The edge of the floor bruised the back of her thighs as she slammed herself backwards inside the truck. She bent her knees and raised her feet to ward off the lion as she dragged herself further inside with her elbows. Her head banged against another storage box.

'Back, get back!' she screamed.

He shook his head and bellowed in agony. The metal box had connected with the pus-filled sockets where his two missing teeth had once been.

Chris felt her body vibrate with the force of the deafening roar. The lion reared up on his hind legs, too close for another pounce, but he swiped at Chris's booted feet with his paw.

Chris grabbed her backpack and swung it into the lion's path as she arched her back and threw herself up and over the top of the rear seat. The beast's claws tore into the nylon rucksack and for a moment became entangled in the fabric. He shook it free and his massive claws found purchase in the heavy rubber mat of the four-wheel drive's cargo compartment. He pulled his whole body into the cramped vehicle and lunged forwards again.

Chris screamed in pain as the lion swiped once more and connected with her leg, just above the ankle. She felt her flesh rip. She rolled and propelled herself between the Land Rover's front seats. The lion's body smell and the fetid odour of his breath filled the cab. He was half stuck – his rear legs in the cargo area of the truck and his front paws on the back seat. He roared and tried to push himself forwards.

Chris reached for the keys in the ignition and grabbed the battery-operated alarm activator on the key ring. She pressed the button in and set off the panic alert.

Mashumba's brother bellowed at the terrible sound that pierced his ears. All thought of his hunger and the easy meal in front of him disappeared in the cacophony that invaded his pain-wracked head.

Chris leaned on the horn as well as she cowered in the front passenger seat. She saw the lion was trying to escape now, but having trouble extricating the front half of his body from the back seat compartment of the truck.

Leaving the alarm still screaming she opened the front passenger door and tumbled headfirst out onto the ground. The lion spared her a glance as he, too, tried to exit, his stinking breath fogging the passenger's window as he bellowed at her. Chris slammed the front door closed and sprinted for the lodge, ignoring the pain in her leg.

As she ran she looked back over her shoulder and saw the lion had managed to rock back on his haunches and fold his huge body into the cramped rear of the Land Rover. Chris didn't see the raised edge of the concrete slab which provided the lodge's foundation. She tripped and fell forwards, grazing her knee and outstretched palms. Her wounded leg was afire with pain as it, too, connected with the concrete.

Mashumba's brother jumped down out of the back of the four-wheel drive and looked around. He saw her, now, lying on the ground, and lunged forwards, covering metres with each outstretched bound. He would have her, after all.

Chris crawled, tried to stand and fell again as her injured leg crumpled. The lion was almost on her. She summoned the last of her energy and dragged herself into a crouch. Terror and adrenaline gave her new strength and she half ran, half fell through the swinging screen door into the kitchen. She grabbed the heavy wooden door, which had been propped open, and swung it, pushing against it from the inside with her back.

The lion stopped and nudged the door with his huge snout, preventing her from closing it fully. The door bashed against its frame as the confused beast reared up and slashed it with his claws. One huge paw slipped along the painted planks and popped through the narrow gap. Chris shrieked in fear at the sight of the hooked claws so close to her body, and pushed hard again with her back. The lion roared in pain and dragged its paw out. Chris fastened the bolt on the door and sank to the floor.

The windowpanes rattled at the sound of his roar. She dragged herself to her feet and watched through the window as the lion turned and flicked his tail in anger, his pendulous testicles swinging as he trotted back off into the bush.

Suddenly feeling sick, Chris leaned against the kitchen sink, one hand supporting her weight. Her other hand covered her eyes. 'Oh, poor Miranda. Poor baby,' she sobbed. 'My God, what did I do to you?'

Outside the car alarm had stopped. She looked down at the blood pooling on the floor and it took a moment for her to realise where it was coming from. She brushed the tears from her eyes with the back of her hand and examined the wound. It was a fifteen-centimetre gash down the outside of her left calf. She raised her leg up high onto the kitchen sink and turned on the cold tap. She picked up a measuring jug, filled it and then tipped the water straight into the wound, biting her lip to stifle her cries. The wound was not as deep as she had first feared and there appeared to be no damage to muscle or ligaments. However, she knew the real danger was infection. A lion's teeth and claws were forever coated with bacteria from the flesh and blood of their prey. Though primarily hunters, the big cats were also opportunistic scavengers and would feed almost as readily on days-old rotting carcasses as on fresh meat.

She wrapped a tea towel around the wound and hobbled into the lounge room of the lodge, where she had left her daypack. Inside was her first-aid kit. She opened it and drew out a phial of saline solution, a plastic bottle of iodine, some butterfly sticking plasters and a US Army field dressing. She had thought the three field dressings she carried were probably overkill – they were designed for use on bullet and shell wounds.

Chris snapped off the cap of the saline solution and doused the open wound. While this hurt, she knew the pain was only a prelude for what was to come. She thrust the unbloodied corner of the tea towel into her mouth and bit down hard on it as she emptied the little bottle of iodine into and around the cut. Tears welled in her eyes again. Once it was done she spat out the towel, ripped open the field dressing and dried the wound with the big sterile pad. Before the blood could well again she placed four butterfly sticking plasters across the gash as makeshift stitches. She thought she probably needed sutures, but the plasters would hopefully hold until she could get to Kariba and a doctor. Next, she wrapped the field dressing around her calf to further stem the bleeding and tied it on with the attached bandage.

Chris activated the car alarm again from inside the lodge and let the siren wail for half a minute before she hobbled out and slammed the door of the building closed. She retrieved the now-scuffed carry case holding the laptop and hurled it in the back of the truck, not caring how it was stowed, slammed the rear door and jumped into the driver's side. Only then did she deactivate the alarm.

She wondered if the lion was related to the one she had shot. It was not unusual, she knew from her own research, for pairs of lions to turn into man-eaters. As the animal that had just tried to kill her was a male, she wondered if it was the brother of the dead one. They appeared to be the same age, old men who had probably been kicked out of their pride by younger, stronger cats. Maybe this one had fed on Miranda as well. She pushed the terrible thought from her mind.

Chris drove the short distance to park headquarters at Nyamepi, and hobbled into the office.

'You know, Professor, that I am obliged to keep the lodge vacant until five-thirty p.m. each day in case someone has made a booking from Harare,' the warden said when she asked him to reserve her accommodation for another week, even though she would be out of the Park.

'And you and I both know, Warden, that it is very unlikely anyone will be booking a lodge here in the next week because of the current lack of fuel in the country. We both also know the political situation is keeping foreign tourists and tour operators out of this park. Here's enough money to pay for the next seven nights,' she said, pushing a wad of cash across the counter.

He smiled but studiously avoided discussing politics. 'We will keep the lodge for you, Professor.'

There were two rangers lounging around the office. One of the men asked her why she wore the bulky dressing on her leg.

'Stupid, really. I scalded myself with hot water when I dropped a pot. Nothing to worry about.'

'You should get that seen to when you are in Kariba,' the warden said.

As she turned to leave, a sound far off, but nonetheless distinct, made them all turn and look downriver.

'Lion,' said the warden.

'A long way off,' said one of the rangers.

'Maybe two kilometres,' the other said.

'Strange for him to be calling so late in the morning,' the warden said. All in the room knew that lions generally called at dawn and dusk, either to bring other members of the pride together or to warn other pride males that they were entering another group's domain.

'Maybe he's just plain angry at something,' Chris ventured.

'Perhaps he was annoyed by the sound of your car alarm going off earlier. Did you have a problem with it?' the warden asked.

Chris felt her cheeks start to redden. 'Silly me, I get the remote-control buttons mixed up sometimes. It took me a long time to shut it off.'

'I think in the future we will keep all researchers either in the lodges or in the main camp ground here at Nyamepi,' the warden said. 'I fear that leaving people out by themselves in the remote campsites is too much of a temptation for the lions. Also, and forgive me for saying this, but maybe people sometimes get careless when they live alone in the bush for too long.'

Chris thought about Miranda. Had she just grown careless? She had got close to Hassan bin Zayid, and that was not part of her brief. 'Maybe you're right,' she said to the warden.

She would miss Africa, she realised as she passed Long Pool and the open vlei where the zebra grazed. It was a hot, dusty and bone-jarring eighty kilometres out of the park on a corrugated dirt road. She thought of the things she would not miss – the tragic, pervasive evidence of the AIDS pandemic; man-eating animals; suicidal drivers; carjackers in Jo'burg armed with AK-47s; corrupt politicians; petty bureaucrats; poachers; and arms traffickers. Then she considered what she was leaving behind – sunsets that made one believe in God; the birth of baby animals with the coming of the summer rains; the smiles on the faces of African schoolchildren seeing an elephant for the first time; cold beers on hot, cloudless days; and the wonderfully comforting knowledge that in some out-of-the-way corners of this overpopulated, heartless world, paradise still existed.

But leave she would, she decided as she left the valley behind her. As soon as she had briefed the general on the local situation it would be time to move on and, in all likelihood, face some kind of penance back in the States over the death of Miranda Banks-Lewis. She felt she deserved that. There would be an enquiry, above and beyond whatever the local police had done in Zimbabwe, conducted by the people who funded her work in Africa. It would find that Miranda was sent to do a job; she completed that job and then died by accident. It happened. But people would ask, behind her back, why Chris Wallis had recruited a science major fresh out of college to go alone into a country whose security situation was parlous at best to do a job some would say Chris should have done herself.

It was a good question. The answer was that Miranda wanted the assignment in Zimbabwe more than anyone back home could really imagine. Chris thought Miranda had the right attributes to carry it off successfully, and she couldn't be everywhere at once. Chris wiped her eyes with the back of her hand and blinked away the tears as she slowed for the turn-off to Kariba. She'd had such high hopes for Miranda, imagined her taking up her line of work as a full-time career some day. There would be plenty more time to think about her own future in the coming days, but first she needed to find a doctor and get the wound on her leg properly dressed.

She smiled grimly at the thought of what she would say when the doctor asked her, 'What seems to be the problem?'

17

Luke Scarborough woke to the sound of his own snoring. He had never been so exhausted in his life. The breath whistled through his broken nose. His eyes watered with pain as he blew a clot of dried blood from one of his nostrils into his palm and wiped it on his filthy T-shirt.

The exhaust-smoke-shrouded office buildings of Lusaka were on either side of the bus, a stark change from the flat plains they'd been travelling through for hours. The driver called out something in Swahili, then, looking at Luke, the only white man on the bus, said, 'Rest break coming up. Don't go far from the bus, it's only fifteen minutes.'

He had been travelling for three days straight. The first leg had been the unnerving boat trip from Zanzibar to the mainland, with the roguish band of Arab sailors casting nervy sideways glances at the bruised and bloodied passenger throughout the three-hour voyage. The pungent odour from the sacks of cloves he lay against, so intoxicating on dry land, added to his queasiness on the open water. He had been sick over the side of the leaky dhow so many times he had lost count, and arrived on a deserted beach north of the port city of Dar es Salaam dehydrated, unsteady on his feet and green in the face. He'd flagged down a passing *matatu* minibus cab on the main road between Bagamoyo and Dar and headed for the latter.

He was desperate to get in touch with Jed Banks. He had tried several times from mainland Tanzania, but received no reply. He had wheedled Jed's mobile phone number out of the man's ex-wife, Patti, whom he had called from Dar, just before boarding the train to Zambia, the Tazara Express. She had not been happy when he called her at home for the second time.

'Mr Scarborough, I must have had fifty calls from press people since I spoke to you about Miranda. Your story identified us to the rest of the world and I've had television crews on my doorstep and calls from radio stations at all hours of the morning. I don't think I can take much more of this,' she had fumed.

'I'm sorry, Mrs Lewis, really I am, but I need to get in touch with Jed urgently.'

'I've spoken to him and told him I've been bothered by reporters and that he should probably expect more of the same. Why can't you people let us grieve in peace? Why can't you let her rest?'

He understood her bitterness. Dealing with grieving relatives in the wake of tragedies was part and parcel of a journalist's life, and even the most cynical could not help but feel bad sometimes about the way the media intruded on people at the worst time of their lives. 'I apologise again, Mrs Lewis, but this is something different. I think your ex-husband may be in grave danger.'

'What are you talking about?'

'I tried to interview the brother of an Al Qaeda terrorist Jed killed in Afghanistan and, as a result, I was attacked and nearly killed myself. Your husband needs to know this man is on the loose in Africa and that he may be looking for revenge against Americans and US interests over here.'

'Slow down. Why should I believe you?'

'Jed saved my life in Afghanistan, Mrs Lewis. I'm only trying to repay the favour.' There was more he could tell her, but he needed to see Jed in person first, to confirm his theory.

She was silent for a while and Luke covered his free ear with his palm to shut out the honking of traffic and shouts of Dar es Salaam's market vendors, in case he missed her reply.

'OK,' she said. 'But don't give this number to any other reporter or else no one will save you from me.'

'You got it,' he said, and she gave him Jed's mobile phone number.

'Where was he when you last spoke to him?' Luke asked before she could hang up.

Again she hesitated, but having revealed the phone number, saw no harm in telling him. 'Still in Zimbabwe. God, I even hate the sound of the name of that damn country. He said he was in a place up north, near where Miranda lived. Kabira or somewhere like that. Only place his phone has worked in the last few days.'

'You mean Kariba. Thanks, Mrs Lewis. Did he say when he was leaving?'

Her patience was wearing thin. 'He's booked on a flight from South Africa next Thursday, I think, but he doesn't tell me everything, Mr Scarborough. Never has. That was always the problem with being married to a Special Forces guy. They never tell you squat.'

'Thanks again for all your help. I'll call back and explain some more if I can, when I can.'

'No offence, Mr Scarborough, but I hope I never speak to another reporter as long as I live.'

He'd got what he wanted from her, but having Jed's number was no use if the man never answered his bloody phone.

The Tazara Express was an express in name only and made interminable stops during the forty-five-hour trip from Dar to its terminus at Kapiri Mposhi, about two hundred kilometres north of Lusaka. At Kapiri Mposhi station Luke had to push away a pickpocket. He was petrified he would lose the camera memory card with the pictures of Hassan bin Zayid and his companion. After the encounter with the Zambian thief he stuffed the card into his underpants, paranoid that he might still lose his daypack on the remainder of his journey.

He suffered attacks of nausea every time he recalled how he had killed the man in Zanzibar, the sight of the body and the smells of death. However, his stomach was empty and he knew he had to eat. He crammed a gristly meat pie into his mouth and downed a litre bottle of water before heading to the bus station. He found a coach bound for Lusaka and jumped aboard just as the driver was shutting the door. Sleep-deprived and filthy, he drifted off into a fitful doze, waking twice when the African businessman sitting next to him politely but firmly removed his head from his shoulder.

The coach pulled up at the Lusaka terminal. Luke staggered out into the harsh sunlight and joined a queue for the reeking men's toilet. Afterwards he tried Jed Banks's number again. Once more, all he got was the soldier's recorded voicemail message. He screwed his eyes shut and fought back a terrible urge to start sobbing. He took a deep breath. He realised he was probably suffering from shock and fatigue, but he had to keep it together.

Luke tossed up whether to go directly to the United States embassy in Lusaka, wherever that was, or to press on to Kariba, in Zimbabwe, in the hope of tracking Jed down there. First, however, he knew he had to call his chief of staff in London and explain what had happened to him.

'Let me get this straight,' Bernie said, incredulous, 'you killed a man in self-defence. Fucking hell, Luke!'

'Yes, Bernie. I was mugged in Zanzibar, but it wasn't a coincidence, he was after my camera and –'

'It's an expensive camera, but you should have just given it over. You're insured, for Christ's sake.'

'Let me finish, Bernie!' Luke talked his chief of staff through his theory about Hassan bin Zayid and the link to Jed Banks. At the end, he said, 'So, what do you think?'

'I think you've had a bad experience, and that you should probably find a lawyer. Better still, let me get our legal people onto it. I'll get them to see if they have a contact in Tanzania and we'll get this mess sorted out.'

The driver of the bus was honking the horn, signalling passengers he was ready to depart. Africans loaded with snacks and drinks lined up to board. The bus carried on to Harare, Zimbabwe, via the border crossing at Chirundu. Once across the border, Luke figured he could hitchhike or take a minibus to Kariba.

'I'm not in Tanzania any more. I'm in Zambia,' Luke shouted above the bus station's din.

'Fucking hell, Luke! You mean you left the country without telling the police or *anyone* you were involved in the death of a local citizen? Where are you now? Exactly? I'll have one of our lawyers call you back as soon as possible and give you advice.'

'I've got a bus to catch, Bernie. I'll email you the pictures as soon as I can download them onto a computer. You judge for yourself.' Luke knew this was a career-making news story, one worth risking imprisonment over.

'I don't care about the bloody pictures. The story's no good to me with you rotting in an African jail, Luke.'

'Bye, Bernie. I'll call again once I've found Banks.'

'Luke, wait, I'll –'

Luke ended the call and sprinted for the bus, which had started to move. The driver opened the door for him and he jumped aboard. He reclaimed his former seat, squeezing in next to the disappointed-looking businessman.

Luke dialled Jed Banks's phone again. He heard the same message. 'Shit!' he said out loud, and thumped the window with his fist.

The businessman started and then stared at him.

'Sorry,' Luke mumbled. He began to shake, as he'd done after the killing, and wrapped his arms around himself. Despite his bravado on the phone to Bernie, he was scared. Eventually, he calmed himself and fell asleep against the window, waking a little while later once the soothing hum of the coach's big diesel came to a halt. Luke wiped his eyes and pulled back the curtain. 'Where are we?' he asked the man next to him.

'This is the border. We will be here for some time.'

It was an understatement. For two hours they sat in a queue of long-distance lorries. Children sold corn cooked on charcoal braziers to the passengers. Prostitutes in gaudy miniskirts and low-cut blouses, some reed thin with the virus, sold themselves to the truck drivers. African music blared loud from car radios and battery-powered boom boxes. Luke walked up and down the line of vehicles to stretch his legs and try to clear his head. The sun's rays felt as though they were singeing his scalp and he regretted the loss of his hat, amongst the rest of his possessions. He took out the phone and saw he had no signal and, of more concern, the battery indicator showed he was nearly out of power. Even if he could have found a power point he had left his charger at the hotel.

The coach passengers joined a long queue of travellers seated outside the Zambian customs and immigration offices. Luke had switched from his Australian to his British passport – the latter a legacy of having an English-born father. He thought that if the Tanzanian police had put out an alert for him they would have used his Australian passport number, which he had declared to the owner of the hotel he had stayed at in Stone Town. When he finally made it inside the building and fronted the immigration clerk, the bored woman barely gave him a second glance as she pounded his passport with a worn stamp.

The bus crossed a new-looking bridge over the wide Zambezi. The Zimbabwean border formalities were a little quicker, but by now Luke was losing what little reserves of patience he had. 'Come on, come on,' he fumed under his breath as the last of the passengers ambled over to the bus. Africans, he had noticed, never seemed in a hurry to do anything.

Chirundu, on the Zimbabwean side, from what Luke could see of it, consisted of a few official buildings, a seedy-looking hotel and a general store. As the bus rolled past a line of lorries Luke was surprised to see a lone bull elephant standing between two of the trucks.

The man next to him noted his wide-eyed look and said, 'You often see elephants around here. They come sniffing around the trucks at night, looking for those transporting maize and other food. They wander from the bush and through the township on the way to the river to drink.'

The border-town squalor of Chirundu quickly gave way to thick bushland. The coach had to stop after a few kilometres for three big black Cape buffalo that were ambling across the road.

'I didn't see any game on the roads in Zambia,' Luke said.

'You slept most of the journey, remember? But no, you're right, there are virtually no wild animals left in Zambia outside of their national parks. They have all been poached. The Zambians are all criminals, you know.'

'So I've been told.'

The road came to a T-junction and Luke saw a sign that pointed to Mana Pools National Park on the left. The bus went right, climbing slowly up the Zambezi escarpment, and Luke was treated to a grand view of the national park where Miranda Banks-Lewis had supposedly been killed by a lion.

The bus stopped at the service station at Makuti, where a sign pointed down the hill to Kariba, seventy-three kilometres away. Luke waved goodbye to the businessman and found a shady tree to sit under while he waited to hitch a ride into town.

He felt better being out of the confines of the coach and another step closer to his quarry. He forgot his tiredness and rank smell and the fact that he was wanted for trumped-up drug offences and, possibly, murder. He sniffed the warm, heavy air of the Zambezi Valley. He was on the scent of a story that would probably make the newspapers in every country in the western world, and then some. There could even be a book in it.

He would not stop until he found Jed Banks. He owed Banks for saving his life in Afghanistan and, if things panned out as he hoped they would, the news he had for the Green Beret master sergeant might just settle that debt – if he wasn't too late.

18

The Tanzanian customs man was impressed by the luxury motorboat. Boats of all sizes came and went from Bagamoyo Harbour, from leaking dhows to cargo ships, but the cruiser, with its sleek modern lines, polished chrome fittings and impressive array of radar and radio masts, was a thing of beauty. It was registered in Zanzibar, he saw from the writing on the stern. It had to be owned by an Arab.

He was right.

'*Jambo*,' the Arab said as he stepped onto the dock.

'*Habari*,' the customs officer replied. 'You are coming from Zanzibar?' he continued in Swahili.

'Yes. I have some very sad duties to perform here. Two of my most trusted workers are returning home,' the Arab explained. 'Come aboard, fetch them now,' he said to two African men in the uniforms of bell-hops from a hotel in town.

'Sad?' the customs officer asked as he accepted an expensive foreign cigarette from the packet proffered by the Arab.

The man gestured back to the boat's gangway with his glowing cigarette tip. It was early morning and the light was still dim, thanks to the overcast sky which masked the rising sun.

The customs officer shook his head as the first of the two coffins was carried down the gangway, the Africans struggling under its weight.

'The virus,' the Arab said, shrugging his shoulders as if there was nothing anyone could have done. 'Would you like to look inside?'

The customs man was a good Muslim. He did not drink and he led a relatively pure life. He was young, twenty-five, and he had his whole life ahead of him. He had listened to the advertisements, seen the billboards and read the pamphlets about HIV–AIDS and he was determined to stay healthy. He rarely cheated on his wife and when he did use the services of prostitutes he always took up the offer of a condom. He knew the risks of transmission other than by the exchange of bodily fluids was minimal; however, he did not want to take any risk that was not absolutely crucial to the performance of his job.

'No, I do not need to see the bodies,' he said.

The Arab handed over the two death certificates, and the customs man scanned them. They appeared to be in order. 'Why weren't these men buried on Zanzibar?'

'They were from the same village, here on the mainland. Their last wish was to be buried with the other members of their families.'

'It is good of you to go to this trouble.'

'These men served me well. This is the least I can do for them.'

The customs officer felt bad. He had assumed he would dislike the rich Arab, simply from the look of his new boat and the cut of his tailor-made clothes. This was a good man. He wrote down the name of the Arab – *Hassan bin Zayid* – and the description of cargo – *human remains* ×2 – on his log sheet.

Hassan climbed into the passenger seat of the minibus and the second African slid shut the rear door and sat on one of the two cheap coffins. Hassan smiled. One type of cargo that did not raise eyebrows in Africa these days was human remains. Coffins were for sale at roadside carpentry stalls and in hardware stores and it was not unusual to see them being carried, full, on the backs of pick-up trucks. The virus had taken the mystery, the ritual, the strangeness and even the solemnity out of death. Disposing of human beings had become big business in Africa.

'Where to, boss?' the driver asked.

'To the ranch,' bin Zayid said, referring to a game farm owned by the family. The manager, a white Kenyan who had moved to Tanzania to run the property, was away on holidays with his young family. Hassan's private aircraft, a Cessna 208, was parked there.

They drove fast and in silence and eventually the driver turned onto a potholed secondary road.

'Careful,' Hassan barked as the two coffins bounced and slammed into the metal tray of the van.

The man in the back, who had bumped his head on the roof when the caskets bounced, turned away to hide his smile. What difference did a few bumps make to people who were already dead?

'Where are you taking these men to be buried, boss?' the driver asked.

'I'm going to fly them to the village where they came from. It is near Arusha.'

'Ah,' said the driver. 'That is far.'

'Yes, that is why I am flying there.'

'Will you be wanting us to pick you up again, from the ranch, when you return the aeroplane?'

The answer to that question, Hassan thought, was very much in the hands of Allah the all-merciful. And hopefully he would be merciful. Still, he was not afraid, nor was he excited. This was business, in a way. He was going to settle a debt, nothing more, nothing less. The risks were high, but he was not scared of death. The only thing he feared was failure.

At the homestead, ostriches ran up and down the fence line, craning their long necks for a view of the vehicle as it trundled along the dirt road. The driver stopped the van by the wooden doors of an aircraft hangar on the edge of the property's airstrip. A windsock hung limp in the warm morning air. It was muggy and Hassan had to wipe tiny beads of sweat from his top lip as the driver opened the hangar door.

'The aeroplane has been checked and the tanks are full, as you ordered, boss,' the man said.

'Good,' bin Zayid said. 'Load the plane.'

The two Africans sweated freely as they carried the heavy coffins into the hangar and slid them awkwardly through the aircraft's side cargo hatch. The roomy single-engine Cessna 208, also called the Caravan, had been designed to transport up to ten people or the equivalent amount of cargo. Hassan had removed the passenger seats long ago, as the aircraft was usually used only to transport cargo around the various bin Zayid properties.

'Well done,' Hassan said when they had finished. 'Close up the hangar when I've taken off.'

Hassan taxied to the far end of the strip, the aircraft trailing a plume of grass and dust as it went. He applied the brakes, then squeezed his way between the pilot and copilot's seats. From the briefcase, the only piece of luggage he had brought with him from the boat, he took a screwdriver and proceeded to unfasten the lid of one of the coffins. He wiped the sweat from his brow and opened the casket a little. He felt inside and disengaged the wire. He lifted the cover completely.

She looked so peaceful, and still so beautiful. It was a shame that her death was so necessary. Hassan returned to his seat, strapped in, and released the brakes. He wanted to be able to keep an eye on her as he flew. He needed to remind himself of her deceit as he prepared to settle the debt owed to his family. During the long flight he would have time to recall every detail of how she had come to his bed, how they had made love, how she had lied to him. He increased the engine's speed and the Cessna hurtled down the strip and into the grey sky.

The sun broke through the cloud as the aircraft cleared the horizon. The driver of the van that had transported Hassan and the coffins had to shield his eyes as he watched his employer disappear.

'Funny,' he said to the sweat-stained man who was hauling the doors of the hangar closed.

'What is?' the man asked. He saw nothing funny about rising at four in the morning to drive the cranky Arab boss-man and two disease-ridden stiffs out to the countryside.

'He's heading south.'

'So?'

'Arusha is north-west of here.'

Hassan flew due south in order to skirt Dar es Salaam, and then he banked south-west across the wilds of Tanzania. He kept the main road connecting Dar with Mbeya, the last big town before the Zambian border, in sight and on his left.

As well as Miranda he thought of Iqbal and the divergent paths their lives had taken during their years at university. Hassan wondered if it was fear that had kept him on the safe path of pursuing the family business in idyllic, fragrant Zanzibar. He had opted for paradise on earth – money, women, alcohol. It was an easy life. He had told his peers that it was his duty to continue the family's presence on the island, but in the last few days he had come to the conclusion that he had simply been afraid to let his brother lead him into his world, the world of the *mujahideen*.

Hassan had known fear, walking in the bush. There was the time he had stumbled upon a pride of lions on a kill in Tanzania's Selous Game Reserve, but that was nothing compared with living through a rocket barrage or fleeing from the buzz of an approaching helicopter gunship's chain gun, as Iqbal had in Chechnya. He wondered if his twin had been scared when he died, if he had run from Jed Banks or if he had looked him in the eye and died like a man. War had been declared a long time ago, but Hassan had sat quietly on the sidelines, lapping up his earthly delights while others fought for their beliefs. He was ashamed, but now he was taking a stand.

He looked back over his shoulder at the still body of Miranda Banks-Lewis. Her face looked serene. He recalled the feel of her skin, her scent, the exquisite softness of her lips on virtually every inch of his body. The memory of the joy of entering her, and her surprise when he had despatched her prior to lifting her into the coffin. The thought of their final confrontation made him smile and he noted he was becoming physically aroused – not a comfortable sensation on a long flight.

The reporter's intrusion into his affairs on the island had worried him, but he believed he had dealt with the man in good time. The fact that he was dead did not worry Hassan. In the past he had disapproved of violence towards westerners on Zanzibar. It was bad for business and drew unnecessary outside attention to the Arab community on the island. But things were different now. He had, as he reminded himself once again, joined the war. There were no rules in war.

He looked at the other coffin and mentally checked over the contents – the casket certainly did not contain a dead African worker. The success of his mission depended on everything in there working properly – and on the plans he had made with Juma.

Hassan was confident Miranda had not learned anything that would incriminate him, but he had taken her with him to Zanzibar to make doubly sure. Making her death appear to be the result of a man-eating lion had been a nice touch. Had she simply vanished, there would have been too many questions asked. Her disappearance had to look like an accident. Juma had told him that the staff at Mana Pools believed there was a man-eater in their park. While he was aware her death had been reported as sensational news around the world, it had not unduly aroused the suspicions of the authorities on the ground in Zimbabwe. Keeping the news of Miranda's own 'death' from her had not been hard. He had instructed his people in Zanzibar to remove the television and radio receiver from his motor cruiser prior to her arrival.

'When I'm on my boat I like to be a million miles from the world's cares,' he had lied smoothly. 'We've no need for satellite news channels or the BBC World Service here. I've got some music CDs and a few DVDs if you get bored.'

She'd smiled back at him and given him a mischievous wink. 'I've got a feeling we'll be able to make our own fun, Hassan.'

After they had flown to the ranch near Dar es Salaam they'd taken a waiting car to the port and had boarded his boat. They'd cruised for the rest of the day and made love that night, as though nothing were the matter. The next morning he had taken the Zodiac inflatable back to Dar on the pretext of a business meeting, and to pick up spares for one of the game reserve's Land Rovers.

His meeting with the travel agent a few days earlier, in the beach bar of the resort he had very nearly bought, had signalled his crossover from civilian to warrior.

'I wondered if you would come, Hassan,' the man had said. He was overweight, sweating in the sun in his western business suit.

'I am ready to help, in whatever way I can.'

'Why the change of heart? Your brother, I suppose.'

'My reasons are my own.'

'If you had come to me a week, a month or half a year ago, Hassan, I would have told you to go away. I would have said I knew nothing about what you are offering, that we never had our previous conversation.'

'I understand the need for secrecy,' Hassan assured him.

'You understand nothing of our world, your brother's world. You talk of secrecy in the way a cheating husband lies to his wife. I talk of secrecy in terms of life and death. You are here because two of our number are dead.'

'How –'

'There, you see? You want details about things that do not concern you. But I will tell you, because you met these men. The two who came to your lodge two months ago, the ones I booked. You remember them?'

'I do.' He remembered the two young Arabs well. He had wondered about the real purpose of their visit. They had rented a boat from him and cruised up and down the Zambezi. They had carried binoculars and field guides, but had known nothing of African birds or mammals when Hassan had tried to strike up a conversation with them. He remembered, too, how Miranda, who had been visiting the lodge at the time, had seemed curious about the men.

'They knew the value of secrecy. They travelled with false passports, but forgeries of the highest quality. They were not identified through their documents, I am sure of it, nor from careless talk on mobile telephones. Someone saw them, perhaps photographed them, and from these images, or this chance sighting, they were recognised as men wanted in other parts of the world. I had thought they would be anonymous here in Africa. I sent them to your lodge on a reconnaissance mission. Did someone there see them, photograph them?'

Hassan felt his pulse start to quicken. 'No, of course not. Who would have seen them at my lodge? You know that I had no other bookings when these men arrived. You made sure of that by paying a premium price for their accommodation.'

The travel agent regarded him through heavily lidded, suspicious eyes. 'I don't know, Hassan. I will be honest. I would not ordinarily trust a man who has undergone such a sudden conversion as you, who approaches me and asks to join me. This, I think, is dangerous. However, with the martyrdom of my other two men I have no choice. If you are a spy, Hassan, if you are working for the crusaders, then I will know soon enough and I will go to God knowing I have done my duty and that I was betrayed by you.'

'I am not a spy. I swear on the graves of my father and my martyred brother.'

'Your oaths don't concern me, Hassan. Your actions do. I will give you a task so that you might prove yourself worthy of more.'

Hassan had taken delivery of the bomb in the backpack there and then, and been sent to the centre of town. The travel agent knew of the departure time of a coachload of a American tourists. Even Hassan, who knew nothing of military operations, thought it madness to undertake such a mission with no planning or surveillance of the area.

The bus was where the travel agent said it would be, outside the four-star hotel that was part of an American chain. The guests were filing out of the hotel. Elderly, mostly, corpulent in the main, loud, laughing. Bellboys were piling suitcases and packs on trolleys in the foyer and wheeling them out to the coach. Hassan walked into the hotel and no one gave him a second glance. He'd pulled his cap down low, in order to shade his eyes, in case cameras were watching him.

He walked into the hotel's men's room. In a cubicle he unzipped the pack and set the timer on the digital alarm clock as the travel agent had instructed him. He flushed the toilet, part of the charade, walked out, set down the pack and gripped the washbasin. His heart pounded in his chest. He splashed water on his face to wash away the sweat, to calm his nerves, then walked out. A man and a woman in matching polo shirts and baggy shorts were piling their bags onto a trolley. Hassan waited a few paces behind them and, when they left, added his pack to the pile. The bellboy took no notice of him. He walked out into the sunshine, hailed a taxi and left. It had been as simple as that. The first radio reports of the carnage had reached him in a room at the beachside resort. The travel agent had shaken his hand.

Next the travel agent had briefed him on the two missions that were to have been undertaken by the martyred Arabs. The first was a bomb to be planted in a nightclub at Nungwi. That would be Hassan's next task. The second would be closer to Hassan's home, on his doorstep, in fact, in the Zambezi Valley.

After Hassan overflew the grubby scar on the open landscape that was Mbeya he deviated west of the main road to avoid being seen by anyone at the border post at Tunduma. He doubted the sight of a light plane would arouse suspicions, but his registration letters were clearly visible under the wings and he didn't want anyone remembering them if questions were asked later.

Hassan's plan was to remain alive at the completion of his mission, but he knew his chances were slim. He wondered what paradise was really like. If it was sumptuous feasts on the shores of azure waters, surrounded by beautiful houris, then it would be just like Zanzibar. He was sure Iqbal was enjoying himself, but Hassan could have all that without dying.

Below him the empty plains and bushland of Zambia stretched forever. The English even had a phrase for it – MMBA, miles and miles of bloody Africa. Development, such as it was, was concentrated along the main road. People walked, cycled and drove in an endless parade below him. The sight reminded him of a line of tireless, unstoppable Safari ants. Soon those people down there would be talking about his deeds. The war was about to come to this struggling African nation. And why should it not? The one advantage he and his newfound colleagues still possessed, despite the array of technology and weaponry the Americans had brought to bear against them, had always been the most crucial of all – surprise. The crusaders, as Iqbal and the travel agent called them, would always be on the back foot. What he was about to do was primarily for Iqbal. He had taken up his brother's fight. Glancing back again at Miranda in her coffin he recalled the time they discussed the day Osama bin Laden had become a household name. It had been in the lodge, in Zambia, sitting in the deep-cushioned wicker armchairs after dinner, listening to the Zambezi's nocturnal chorus.

'What did you think about nine-eleven?' she had asked him without preamble.

They had been discussing the politics of Zimbabwe. It was before they first slept together and he wondered, later, if it was part of a quiz he had to complete correctly before she awarded him first prize – herself. However, at the time, he had answered immediately, and from the heart.

'It was a horror. It was a cowardly, senseless attack which brought discredit to the whole Arab world. I am ashamed of it.'

He had believed his words then, and still did. The attack had polarised the world. People like him, the moderates who had been cocooned from armed struggle, had been forced to take a side, and there were only extremes left in the war between Islam and America and her allies.

'Do you think we can all ever live side by side, in peace?' Miranda had asked him.

He had found her naivety appealing, her innocence refreshing. Until he found out the truth about her, of course.

In the distance Lusaka rose in all its ugliness from the dry brown plains. Hassan turned the aircraft's nose to the west. Soon he could see the mighty Zambezi below and he started his descent. In an ideal world, he thought, he and Miranda Banks-Lewis could have lived side by side. He was sure a psychiatrist would have told him his fixation with blonde Caucasian women had something to do with his mother, but he didn't really care. No matter how many western women he bedded, how much alcohol he drank, how much money he made, or how much of Africa he owned, he would never truly find paradise on earth. Here, in this life, man was destined for war, not peace, and he, Hassan bin Zayid, had been brought into the fray, courtesy of the father of the woman he had loved. Also, she had deceived him, cynically and maliciously.

It was time, as the Americans would say, for some payback.

19

It was a rutted, bone-rattling dirt track, but it was still the closest thing to a main road in this part of the Zambezi Valley. That was why the tree across the left-hand lane aroused Jed's suspicion immediately.

He didn't want to slow down, but he was travelling at close to seventy kilometres an hour, the maximum he dared try on the loose surface. He changed from fourth down to third. Jed scanned the thick dry bush on either side of the road as the speedometer wound back to thirty. As he slowed he looked at the base of the tree. The stump was close to the edge of the road and he could tell from the bright orange-red of the wood it was still wet.

'Motherfucker,' he spat, and planted his foot as he rounded the tree.

The rear of the Land Rover swung out sharply to the right and Jed swore again as he heard one of the tyres blow. He fought the steering wheel and kept the vehicle on the road. A less experienced driver would have overcorrected, but that was dangerous in a four-by-four like this one. With its high centre of gravity, a wrong turn of the wheel at speed on a gravel road would send the vehicle into a roll.

There were two types of ambush drill. In a vehicle, you just kept on going. On foot, you turned and faced the bullets and charged through them in the hope of taking your enemy by surprise. That kind of gutsy move was OK if you had a gun in your hand. Jed figured the roadblock had been placed to force him to run over whatever it was that had punctured his tyre. He was then, according to the thinking of whoever had cut down the tree, supposed to stop, get out, kick the tyre and then try to remember where the jack was.

Fortunately, it felt like the rear tyre was only punctured, and not a complete blow-out. Although there was no air in the tube there was still enough rubber to give him some traction. He knew, however, that the metal rim of the wheel would soon cut through the tread. Jed turned and looked back over his shoulder. The rear window disappeared in a spray of crystalline glass and he ducked as the air parted on the left side of his head. The aluminium roof of the Land Rover clanged as though someone had hit it with a sledgehammer.

He lay as low as he could while still watching the road and steering, resting the left side of his torso on the cubby box between the two front seats. The truck shuddered and bounced and he smelled burning rubber as the wheel rim chewed and burned through the last ply of the tyre. The vehicle slowed as the hot, sharp metal edges of the wheel ploughed the dirt road.

The Land Rover came to a halt, its engine still ticking over. Jed turned off the ignition and pocketed the keys. The bastards wouldn't get this prize so easily. He popped the hood, found the fuel filter and, using the Leatherman tool on his belt, undid the drain plug underneath it. Hot diesel fuel spilled over his hand and then onto the dusty ground below. The fuel system would need to be primed manually before the vehicle would start again.

Jed grabbed his water bottle and jogged into the bush to his left. He ran through the trees about forty metres, then stopped. He began to walk backwards, slowly, carefully retracing his steps until he was almost back at the road. On his first sprint into the bush he had spied a toppled power pole lying rotting in the bush, parallel to the road. He walked along it now, as though on a balancing beam, and then leaped as far as he could off the other end. Now he ran alongside the road, just a couple of metres off it, for near on a hundred metres.

The Land Rover was still in sight. He watched the road for a couple of seconds and, satisfied no one was in sight, darted across to the other side. He looked around for a weapon and found a stout section of deadfall about a metre long. It wasn't much against a rifle, but it would do. He crouched low and watched his stranded vehicle. Jed wiped his forehead with the back of his arm. He was sweating from the run but his heart rate was fine. He realised he was almost enjoying this. He had evaded an ambush and was now turning the tables on his attacker. Some two-bit Zambian carjacker was about to get an ass-kicking, US Army style.

He thought about Hassan bin Zayid's hard-faced game manager and his truckload of weapons and ammunition. Someone had just shot at him – the missing rear window and hole in the roof of his rental vehicle were proof of that – but Jed had no reason to think the man, no matter how surly, would be out to kill or rob him. More likely it was one or more of the poachers the man had spoken of. Men who were desperate enough to hunt game in woods patrolled by heavily armed landowners would probably think hijacking a shiny new rental car was an easy way to make a year's pay. He reckoned he had been observed driving into the reserve and, as there were so few ways into and out of the place, it was a pretty safe bet he would be coming out on the same road.

No one walked down the road to the Land Rover. That figured. He put himself in the criminal's shoes. He would approach the vehicle through the bush, then give it a quick check to assess the damage. Next, he would try to find the driver. Jed would have killed for a pair of binoculars. He thought he saw a tree move on the right-hand side of the road, near the vehicle. That meant the man, or men, had approached on the same side that Jed had exited. He hoped the would-be thief would pick up his false trail. He gave his pursuer a few minutes. The man did not emerge from the bush. Presumably that meant he was following the blundering, obvious path Jed had made through the undergrowth.

Jed moved quickly, quietly, back down the other side of the road, towards the Land Rover. If it was only one man, he would take him. He would wait until he was checking the wheel or trying to start the engine and then hit him with the tree branch. If there were two or more he would lie low and wait until they left. He was brave but he wasn't stupid. The truck was insured and he was not going to get himself killed for sport.

Juma scanned the road, the bush and the ground in front of him. He moved carefully but rapidly. He was disappointed the ambush had failed. The mopani trees in this area were too short to block the whole road – they were young regrowth after last year's fire – but he was pleased he had had the presence of mind to bring the home-made caltrops. The devices were simple – three six-inch nails hammered at odd angles into offcut lumps of soft wood from the workshop. He and Hassan had used them to ambush a poaching gang's car six months earlier. Juma had covered the gap between the fallen tree and the far side of the road with the pointed booby traps and they had done their job once again.

However, since the man had not stopped immediately to repair his punctured tyre, Juma would now have to track him down to finish off the job. He knew the girl's father was a soldier, but Juma had no doubt who would come off the better in this game of wits. It was imperative that he kill the American. Back at the lodge the man had been too nosy for his own good.

Juma saw the Land Rover. He smelled the hot, burned rubber where the metal rim of the wheel had sliced through the tyre. He crouched and watched. The vehicle was empty. The man was not there, attempting to change the wheel, as he had hoped. He waited, in case Banks was hiding in the bushes nearby. Nothing happened. Juma edged forwards, quietly and carefully. He watched where he placed each footfall, avoiding dead branches and piles of dried leaves that would crackle a warning to his prey. He kept looking back at the Land Rover and scanned the ground for spoor – footprints and other telltale signs of his two-legged quarry.

There it was. As clear as a white line down the centre of a road. The man had careened through the bush, probably in panic. Branches were broken or bent at waist and chest height on the mopani trees. The ground was scuffed and, where the floor of the forest was free of dead leaves, his boot prints showed clearly. A woodpecker tapped away incessantly somewhere. Juma stopped and listened for other sounds. There were none. He followed the trail, slipping off the safety catch on the right of the assault rifle. The weapon's barrel was still hot from the bullet he had fired earlier, and he was disappointed there was no blood spattering the well-defined tracks in front of him. He raised the butt of the rifle into his shoulder, ready to squeeze off a shot at the first sign of the target.

Juma stopped. The hair on the back of his neck stood up. He licked his lips and stared hard down at the ground again. The spoor had stopped. He scanned around him, three hundred and sixty degrees. Nothing. The man was smarter than he had guessed – and that worried him. He turned around, back towards the road, and moved to the last clear print. How had he missed it? The slight overlapping of the imprint was as clear as a newspaper headline to him now. The news was that Juma had made a cardinal error. If the American had been armed, and Juma fervently hoped he was not, then the hunter would have become the prey by now. His quarry had retraced his steps. Juma heard a noise and froze. He eased the safety on the AK-47 to automatic, curled his finger around the trigger and prepared to fire.

On the other side of the road, beyond the Land Rover, Jed lay on his stomach in a thicket of long grass and watched the back of the man who was tracking him disappear into the bush, following the false trail. The man had a dark-green shirt on. A pretty common item of clothing in the bush, Jed supposed. He was a black African. A lighter green bush hat prevented him from seeing if the man was bald or how he wore his hair.

Jed's knuckles showed white as he gripped his primitive club. He

288

knew there would be a wheel brace somewhere in the truck, but he didn't want to lose his advantage by clanging away inside the vehicle. He rose to his feet and ran, bent at the waist, to the side of the Land Rover. He paused briefly in the shadow cast by the vehicle, then peered up over the hood and scanned the bush on the other side. There was no sign of the man. He moved again, finding a shady tree on one side of the pathway he had made earlier. He would ambush the African on his return.

Far off, down the road in the direction he had been travelling, Jed heard the noise of a motor. The sound grew and he recognised it as the rumbling of a diesel. Soon the vehicle came into sight. It was a police Land Rover. Jed was almost disappointed.

He was a citizen of the United States, alone in an African country, stalking a local resident with the intent of doing him grievous bodily harm. He *assumed* the man he was now tracking was the one who had laid the ambush and fired on him. But what if he wasn't? He realised his instincts and training had taken over from his common sense. Perhaps it had something to do with the helplessness he felt over Miranda's death. He wanted to *do* something, to take some action to get him out of the funk he was in. Was killing a suspected carjacker the right thing to do?

He stepped out into the middle of the road and waved the branch over his head, flagging down the policeman. The white truck had already slowed, the driver no doubt curious about the similar vehicle stopped dead in the centre of the road.

'Good afternoon. What seems to be the problem?' the lone Zambian constable asked as he wound down his window.

'Flat tyre, but that's the least of my troubles,' Jed said, then explained about the ambush.

The policeman got out of his truck and inspected the bullet hole in the roof of Jed's hire car and the shattered rear window. 'Please, get into my vehicle. I will radio for assistance. These people are very well armed – they may be poachers. I don't think they will try to take on the police, but you never can tell.'

*

Juma stared down the barrel of the assault rifle and placed the fore-sight on the centre of the policeman's back as the man bent inside the Land Rover's cab to inspect the bullet hole in the roof. The American was on the far side of the vehicle, out of Juma's line of sight. He took up the slack in the trigger. The sight rose slightly as he inhaled, then returned to the original aiming point as he released his breath.

Juma cursed. It was not worth the risk. He could kill the policeman, but then the American soldier would take immediate evasive action. The policeman was armed with an automatic pistol, and who knew what else was in the Land Rover. He released the pressure on the trig-ger, lowered the rifle and reapplied the safety catch. The American had been lucky. That was all. Better, in any case, that he lived and carried the wound of his daughter's death for many more years. Juma did not know if the boss had anything special in mind for the American – now or in the future. He decided he would say nothing of the ambush to Hassan. Bin Zayid was not a man who liked to learn of failure. 'Bring me solutions, not problems, Juma,' he was fond of saying.

The Zambian policeman drove west, back towards Chirundu, at a speed fast enough to scare Jed half to death. At times all four wheels of the police vehicle were off the ground as they sailed over ruts and wash-outs.

A nerve-jarring half-hour later, still on the eastern side of the Kafue, they met up with the reinforcements Jed's saviour had radioed for – a Land Rover crammed with eight officers in riot gear. They were dressed in dull blue-grey fatigues and carrying a mixture of weapons, includ-ing AK-47s, shotguns and even a bolt-action Lee Enfield rifle. With them was a snarling German shepherd.

Jed's police companion turned the vehicle around and led them back to the disabled Land Rover, which still sat forlornly in the middle of the road.

'It is strange that they did not try to change the tyre and drive away once we left,' the policeman said. 'I was sure the vehicle would be gone.'

'Maybe they figured it wasn't worth the risk,' Jed said, but he doubted his own words.

The policeman helped Jed change the ruined wheel for the spare. Once they were finished, Jed reprimed the fuel filter. 'Try the ignition now,' he said to the officer. The engine rattled to life.

The commander of the riot squad, a sergeant, emerged from the bush, followed by the German shepherd and its handler. The rest of the policemen lounged in the shade of a tree, smoking cigarettes and drinking from their water bottles.

'It was one man only,' the sergeant said, removing his cap and wiping the sweat from his brow. 'The dog wanted to follow the trail, but I think this man is long gone. He used this to puncture your tyre.' He showed Jed the home-made caltrop.

Jed fingered the nail-studded piece of timber. He got the feeling the riot squad's hearts were not really in their job. To be honest, the thrill had worn off for him too. Now that the adrenaline rush brought on by his potentially deadly game of tag had dissipated, Jed just wanted to get on the road again. 'Thanks for trying anyway, Officer.'

'This ambush technique is not all that unusual, I am afraid to tell you,' the sergeant said. 'Out here these criminals think they can get away with anything.'

'Somebody told me to be careful in Zambia. Said the place was full of criminals.'

The sergeant laughed. 'Ah, yes, that is true. But it's not as bad as Zimbabwe.'

Jed smiled. He took the tyre lever and knocked out the remaining shards of glass from the rear window before stowing the iron bar with the ruined rear wheel rim in the back of the Land Rover. He would have some explaining to do when he got the vehicle back to Harare. It seemed an age since he had picked the truck up. Now, at last, his mission was nearly over. In a day or so he would be on an aircraft, sipping Scotch, watching in-flight movies and thinking about the next posting in his military career.

Jed got into his vehicle and followed the policeman who had first come to his rescue to a police camp. Except for the charge counter and the presence of a few bored-looking uniformed cops, the station was unlike any other Jed had ever seen. It was a mud-brick building with a tin roof and, judging by the old-fashioned hurricane lanterns on the counter, no electricity. Somewhere out back goats bleated and hens clucked. The policeman took out three forms and two pieces of well-worn carbon paper and rolled them into a manual typewriter that reminded Jed of one he had seen in the Smithsonian in Washington. It was a long, slow business, filling in the details of what had happened, but Jed knew he would need an investigation report to get him off the hook with the car-rental company.

He didn't get to Chirundu until four in the afternoon and then had to queue behind a long line of coach passengers. He cursed his timing.

'Did you enjoy your stay in our country?' the immigration clerk asked when Jed finally presented himself at the counter in the airless building. The man thumbed through the pages of his passport.

'I met a very unhelpful man who hunts other men for a living, then I was ambushed and shot at by someone who was trying to kill me. The beer was quite nice, though.'

The man smiled politely. 'Ah, yes, the beer is good in Zambia. Do you have a cigarette for me?'

'No.'

The man frowned and thudded the stamp into the passport.

Jed crossed a new bridge over the Zambezi. A party of tourists was pushing off from Chirundu in six Native American-style canoes. He supposed they were headed downriver to Mana Pools National Park. He thought of Christine, of the taste of her mouth, and the rest of her. When he came to an intersection that led to Mana Pools one way and Kariba the other, he was half tempted to turn left and go look for her. However, he had a plane to catch and a life to get on with. His leave was almost up. As it was, he would arrive back at Fort Bragg jet-lagged and with no time at home to decompress. That was OK. He figured the sooner he immersed himself in work the better. It would help him deal with the loss of Miranda. Also, he wanted to talk to some people about that job in Virginia.

He wondered if the CIA really was his bag. The Agency had been recruiting ex-military people in droves since September 11 and he knew that even if he didn't leave the Army and apply for a job as a spook, they might second him in any case. Better, he reasoned, to go across with spy pay and conditions than do all that dirty work on a master sergeant's wage.

It was odd, but when he had mentioned the prospect of CIA work to Chris, she had hardly raised an eyebrow. That was peculiar, given what his buddy in personnel back at Fort Bragg had told him about her background. They both had a lot to discuss next time they met – if there was a next time. A picture of her straddling him, her breasts swinging enticingly in front of his eyes, filled his mind. He smiled. She was pretty, sexy as hell, great in bed, intelligent and mysterious. There would be a next time.

The road snaked up and out of the Valley and the last of the sun's rays were slanting hard through the Land Rover's side windows when Jed finally reached the top of the escarpment. He checked his watch and did the calculation. He would be lucky to make Harare by midnight, and the thought of driving through the African night and then trying to negotiate a strange city in the dark did not appeal to him. Besides, he was beat after his eventful day. A road sign told him he was at a place called Makuti. Of greater interest was the next billboard, which pointed to a motel. That would do just fine.

Jed rose early the next morning and drove the Land Rover down to the filling station in front of the Makuti Motel.

'Do you sell Cokes here?' he asked the attendant.

'In the shop,' the man said, gesturing with a thumb.

Inside the kiosk Jed bought a Coke in a glass bottle and a chicken pie for breakfast. The shopkeeper told him he wanted the bottle back, so Jed stood outside to consume the pie and soft drink. He brushed some flaky pastry from his beard and with his hand shielded his eyes against the glare of the sun. A young white man carrying a tattered daypack was walking up the hill from the Kariba turn-off towards the gas station. Jed vaguely recalled seeing a person sitting under the road sign pointing towards Kariba. He walked back inside and handed over his empty bottle.

'That man has been awake since five o'clock. He wants a lift to Kariba,' the shopkeeper said, pointing out the window. 'He has been trying for two hours with no luck. I think it is because of the way he looks.'

'Well, he's still out of luck. I'm headed for Harare.'

Jed returned to his Land Rover, got in and started the engine.

'Hey!' called the young man.

'I'm headed south, sorry,' Jed yelled over the noise of his engine. He saw the guy was young, bedraggled, with an unkempt goatee beard, stubble and dirty clothes. He wasn't surprised the kid had failed to get a lift. He looked like a bum. Jed put the car in first and started to roll forwards.

'It's you! Hey! Jed Banks!'

Jed looked back over his shoulder at the sound of his name. He was at the edge of the gas station's driveway, waiting for a lorry to pass. He gave the young man a closer look.

'Goddamn reporter,' he said under his breath, shaking his head. He recalled the message on his cell phone, the Australian accent. It was the kid he had met in Afghanistan. The one who nearly got him killed and the one who had been pestering Patti. Part of Jed wanted to stop and be hospitable, but the rest of him wanted to get away from Africa, from the questions that would yet again dredge up the horror of Miranda's death. Jed floored the accelerator and pulled out onto the highway.

Jed looked in his rear-view mirror. The kid was running down the blacktop after him, waving his arms like a madman. This was embarrassing. He knew reporters could be tenacious, but this was a joke. The damned fool was going to get himself killed carrying on like this. Jed stopped the truck.

'I told you, I'm headed south, not to Kariba. And I don't want to be interviewed about Miranda, Afghanistan or any other damn thing,' Jed said as Luke arrived, panting, by his window.

Luke coughed and grabbed the door handle on Jed's side, in case he made to leave again. He fought to regain his breath.

'What is it, kid?'

'Miranda . . .' he gasped.

Jed stomped on the clutch and rammed the gearstick back into first. 'I fucking told you, Scarborough. I'm not going to –'

'No, wait . . . She's alive.'

'What?'

'Miranda's alive, Jed.'

20

J ed's heart raced, but he could hardly comprehend the news. If this was some ploy by the reporter to make him stop and spill his guts, he swore he would kill the man and leave his body by the side of the road for the hyenas.

As he turned the Land Rover around and headed back to the filling station, he said to Luke, 'I swear to God, I'll gut you if you're lying to me, kid.'

Luke nodded. 'Stop so I can get my backpack. We can talk here.'

'OK.' Jed ran a hand through his fair, sweat-dampened hair. He had a million questions, but he held back. He would not play into the kid's hands. He would listen to what he had to say first.

Luke picked up his backpack and Jed parked the Land Rover under a tree behind the gas station. He killed the engine. 'OK. Shoot.'

'I wanted to thank you, first, for what you did for me in Afghanistan,' Luke began.

'Cut the crap. We can swap war stories later.'

'OK. Sorry.'

'My daughter's remains were found in the belly of an adult male lion, shot here last week. If this is some kind of con, I'll –'

'Yeah, yeah, kill me. Look, do you want to know what I found, what I saw, or not?'

Jed nodded. 'I'm listening.'

'I was in Zanzibar a few days ago. I was trying to track down a guy, the brother of the man you killed in Afghanistan, in fact.'

Jed shrugged. He had left Afghanistan too soon after the firefight to read the after-action reports. He had no wish to know the name of the man he had shot.

'Who told you his name?' Jed asked.

'Centcom released it a few days afterwards. It was Iqbal bin Zayid. He was in all the newspapers. Didn't you see the stories?'

'Bin Zayid?' The name hit him like a punch in the chest and a terrible feeling of dread swept over him. He hadn't seen any news reports of the action he'd been involved in. He was too busy catching military transports to the States and then flying to Africa.

'Yeah, bin Zayid. Anyway, his brother –'

'Hassan.'

'How did you know the brother's name? You didn't even know the name of the dead guy until a couple of seconds ago.'

'We'll get to what I have to say soon enough. Keep going. You haven't told me anything I want to know yet,' Jed said, stone-faced.

'Anyway, I tried to track down this Hassan bin Zayid. A millionaire businessman, up to his arse in hotels and money, but he proved very hard to find. I was given the run-around by his office and then, by chance, I got a lead and found out where he kept his boat. A cruiser. Real flashy.'

'What about my daughter?' Jed interrupted.

'I think she was on board bin Zayid's boat.'

'You *think*?' Jed said. 'I need more than *think*.' There was no vehemence in his words, though, for a half-dozen different explanations were already forming in his mind. He let the reporter continue.

'I saw a woman on the boat, with Hassan bin Zayid. They kissed. She was dressed up to the nines. Attractive, blonde, young.' She was more than attractive, she was a knockout, Luke recalled, but he reminded himself he was probably talking to her father.

'And?'

'And I took her picture. Bin Zayid must have seen me – I was on another boat. Later that evening I was mugged by a guy I'm certain was sent by bin Zayid. He smashed my camera and destroyed the memory card inside it. Then he tried to kill me.'

'To kill you?' Jed suddenly thought of his own near-death experience on the dusty road out of Zambia. Too many possibilities and impossibilities clouded his mind.

'Yeah, but I fought him off. I . . . I killed him, in fact.'

Jed was surprised. He looked at Scarborough again, saw the red eyes, the dishevelled state of his hair and clothes, the dark stains under his fingernails. Dried blood. Luke was staring out over the tree-covered African hills. Jed had seen that look in men's eyes before. He knew the kid had been to a bad place and was revisiting it in his mind. Jed had been there himself a few times lately.

'It's OK, kid. Keep talking.'

'I couldn't work out why the guy tried to waste me just for taking a picture. I mean, Christ, nobody ever tried to *kill* me for doing my job.'

'Welcome to my world,' Jed said. 'What makes you think the girl you saw was Miranda? You've never met her before and I didn't have a picture of her the night we met in Afghanistan, when you were asking about her.'

'I know, I know. Well, bin Zayid also set me up, big time. Planted a load of heroin in my room and sent the cops around to pick me up. I guess the idea was to discredit me first so when my body showed up no one would worry too much. I had no idea who the woman was. But later on, after it was over and I was trying to get off Zanzibar, I found an international newspaper. There was a story on your daughter's death in it and a picture of her. I'm sure it was her I saw on the boat and that's why bin Zayid tried to kill me.'

'Slow down. How did my daughter's picture get in a newspaper?'

'It was a file picture taken by her local paper when she first set off for Africa. I passed on her name to some colleagues in the States and they tracked down the picture. But that doesn't matter now.'

'The fuck it doesn't.' Jed was angry at the way the reporter thought he could ignore the wishes of a grieving family and publish his daughter's picture despite the fact Patti had wanted it kept private. This wasn't the time to lose it, though. 'How can we be absolutely sure it was her? You said your camera and pictures were destroyed by the mugger.' Jed wanted so much to believe the odious specimen in front of him, but did not want to raise his own hopes.

'I can't. Only you can. I had a couple of shots on a second memory card which the guy I killed never got his hands on. I can show them to you and you can tell me if it's her or not.'

'OK then, let's see them.'

'We need a digital camera or, better still, a computer to download the pictures onto. My laptop and all my other gear was in my hotel room in Zanzibar. The police have it all now.'

Jed nodded. If what he was saying was true, Scarborough was on the run and had crossed several international borders in order to get this information to him. His attitude towards the younger man softened. 'I know where we can find a computer.'

'Where?'

'A friend of mine, working in Mana Pools National Park. We can be there in a few hours. That's if she hasn't left already.' A friend? He realised he suddenly needed to ask Chris Wallis a whole lot more questions.

'Cool,' Luke said. 'Let's go.'

Jed tried to collect his thoughts. There were several explanations, ranging from innocent to evil, for how Miranda could have turned up alive on Hassan bin Zayid's boat. The first, and most benign, was that the whole thing had been a terrible mistake and she had left for a holiday with her rich Arab boyfriend and neglected to tell anyone she was going. That did not sound like Miranda. News of her death had been reported around the world and, surely, once she learned of it she would have contacted her mother and, presumably, the authorities in Zimbabwe to set the record straight. Maybe they had been out of touch with the news media? A more sinister scenario was that bin Zayid, unlike Jed, had made the connection between his family and hers. Had he kidnapped her in order to wreak revenge on Jed for killing his brother? But how would the guy know who had shot Iqbal bin Zayid?

'Was my name mentioned in the stories about Iqbal bin Zayid's death?' Jed asked Luke, as he started the engine.

'No. The public affairs people stopped using the full names of American servicemen in stories in order to protect their security.'

Jed remembered reading the new policy. The CIA had learned that Al Qaeda operatives were trying to identify the addresses of soldiers serving in Afghanistan, possibly with a view to targeting their families. It was also why troops serving in the terrorists' former base country had to burn the return addresses on letters and packages sent to them. Afghans had been seen rummaging through the trash dump early on in the campaign looking for old mail and, in the States, terrorist sympathisers combed local and national newspapers looking for servicemen's names and home towns. If a soldier had an uncommon surname it needed little more than an internet search or a telephone book to find out where his or her family lived.

'But,' Luke added, sheepishly, 'I did name you as Master Sergeant Jed in the story I filed.'

Jed nodded, angry, but resigned to the ways of the new media-driven defence force. If Miranda had mentioned his Christian name to bin Zayid, and that he was serving in Afghanistan, it would have been possible for him to make a connection, but there were a lot of Jeds in the Army.

Luke took a deep breath. 'Um, I also mentioned in the story you had a daughter working on lion research in Zimbabwe.'

'Tell me you didn't,' Jed said.

'I'm afraid I did.'

That did it. If bin Zayid had seen Luke's story he would have known immediately that Jed was the man who had killed his brother. Sinister pieces started to fall into place. The surly reception he'd received at bin Zayid's safari lodge; the attempt on his life. Had he stumbled too early into a kidnap plot?

'You said when you saw her on the boat she was dressed up and they kissed?'

'That's right. She didn't look like she was there against her will, Jed.'

Jed swore to himself again. There were still too many questions and not enough answers. He needed to see these pictures. If it was her, he had to see Hassan bin Zayid immediately – and screw the efforts of the man's flunkies to head him off. If it came to another visit across the border, he would take some additional muscle with him. Jed braked at the driveway of the filling station, then switched on his right-hand indicator and headed down the hill towards Kariba.

'Hey, isn't that the wrong way, man? I thought Mana Pools was to the left,' Luke said.

'It is. We're going to pick up a friend first.'

Jed strode into the shebeen in Nyamhunga township where he had first met Moses. The woman behind the bar screwed up her eyes to get a better look at him in the gloom.

'Hey, I remember you, mister. I don't want trouble in here again. You can please leave.'

Jed held up his hands, palms out. 'Relax, I'm just looking for someone.'

'Moses?'

'Yes.'

'Ah, he is a reformed man now,' she said, then laughed. 'Probably been to church this morning.' Again the cackle.

'Can you give me his address?'

'Sure why not. Tell him to come back – my profits have been down this past week.'

Moses was standing on a rickety wooden ladder, replacing a shingle tile on the roof of a dreary-looking house. The whitewash was peeling from the cheap cinderblock bricks and the lower third of the home's façade was spray-painted a natural red-brown where last season's rains had splashed up mud from the grassless yard. A small boy in ragged overalls with short-cropped curly hair and arms as thin as twigs craned his neck to watch the big man at work.

Moses came down the ladder and wiped his hands on a grimy white singlet, then turned. 'Jed! How are you? I didn't expect to see you again so soon.'

Jed opened the rusty gate and shook Moses's hand. 'I need help. Again. Miranda may still be alive. She may be in trouble.'

'What?'

'I'll explain in the truck. Can you come?'

Moses scratched his chin and looked back at the little boy. A woman, young and pretty but tired in the eyes and mouth, walked from the house, drying her pink-palmed hands on a tea towel. 'What is it, Moses?'

'Miriam, this is Mr Banks. I told you about him.'

The woman offered her hand. Jed was impatient but said, 'How do you do, ma'am.'

'I don't know what happened, but this one came back from your trip a changed man,' Miriam said. 'I was sorry to hear about your daughter. You have my deepest sympathies.'

'Thanks, but that's the point. I think she may still be alive, and I need Moses to help me look for her again.'

The woman's eyes widened. 'I was never going to let this man out of my sight again, but if what you say is true . . .'

'I'll get my things,' Moses said.

'There isn't any danger, is there?' Miriam asked Jed as Moses disappeared inside the modest house.

'No more than usual.'

'He can't afford to lose his licence as a guide, Mr Banks.'

'I understand.'

'I pray you do. I wish you well.'

Moses ran his fingers through the little boy's short hair and kissed Miriam. 'I will be back,' he said.

'I hope so, but I will believe it when I see it.'

*

Jed introduced Moses to Luke and filled him in on the reporter's findings as they drove. Moses listened to it all and, at the end, had no questions, just a statement.

'If you go after this man, Hassan bin Zayid, it will not be straight-forward for me to accompany you. I will not be able to cross into Zambia easily. I'm not a licensed safari guide in that country – just another unwelcome Zimbabwean.'

'I'm not asking you to break any laws, Moses.'

'I will do what I can for you, Jed,' he said.

The three-hour drive to Mana Pools gave Jed a chance to brief Luke on what he had been up to during his investigations into Miranda's disappearance.

'What I don't understand,' Luke said, 'is if Miranda is still alive, whose remains were found in the belly of the lion?'

'That's been puzzling me, too,' Jed said. 'There can't have been another European woman killed in the area, not without it being reported.'

'Why do you assume the remains belonged to a European woman?' Moses asked from the back seat.

Jed thought the guide had been dozing. 'Because they were white.'

Moses looked puzzled.

'Any other white women gone missing in the Mana Pools area?' Luke asked.

'No, though one of the National Parks maids has gone missing. The word was that she had run off, maybe with some of Miranda's things. But she was African.'

'Black, you mean?' Moses asked.

'Yes, I suppose so,' Jed said.

'Well, you're wrong,' Moses said. 'She was white.'

'A European maid working for National Parks?'

'No. When I was asking in the staff village about the maid, one of the rangers said she was *musope*.'

'What does that mean?' Luke asked.

'*Musope* is the Shona word for albino. Her skin would have been whiter than yours. Much whiter, in fact.'

Jed and Luke looked at each other. The only shred of physical evidence that Miranda was dead had suddenly been called into question. Jed's excitement that his daughter could still be alive was tainted by his fear about what had become of her.

'Surely the medical examiners would have been able to tell the difference?' Luke said.

'Tissue from the remains was being sent for DNA testing in South Africa. I'm supposed to get the final results – and pick up the remains for burial back in the States – when I get back to Harare,' Jed said.

'So we can't tell for sure, just yet,' Luke said.

'Which is why I need to see those pictures you're carrying,' Jed said.

When they stopped at the National Parks office to get their permits to enter Mana Pools National Park, the officer on duty remembered Jed.

'Back so soon?' he asked.

'I need to see Professor Wallis again. It's urgent. She hasn't left the park yet, has she?'

The man stamped their permits, handed them across the counter and said, 'Ah, she has gone to Kariba.'

'Kariba? Is she coming back?'

'Yes, but she said she will be gone for four or five days.'

'Shit.' Jed ignored the look of shock on the ranger's face. If Luke was right about Miranda he would have to track Chris down. He needed answers and couldn't wait five days. They headed back outside to the Land Rover. 'Let's carry on,' he said to the other two. There was nowhere else they could go that afternoon. He silently fumed for most of the remaining eighty kilometres into the park.

'Leave me to check in with the warden,' Moses said as they neared the turn-off to park headquarters. 'You go on ahead. I'll visit my friends in the staff village and see if there is any new gossip, then join you at the professor's lodge later.'

'Thanks, Moses.' Jed stopped the Land Rover. The vehicle rocked as the big African got out.

'Good guy to have on our side,' Luke said as Jed drove off again.

Jed slowed and looked at the Australian. '*Our* side? I don't think so. Look, I appreciate you coming here with the news, but we're in this mess mostly because of you and your kind. Anything I do as a result of this information is a matter for me and, if he can help, Moses. We're not in this together as one big happy family, buddy.'

'Jesus!' Luke exploded. 'You'd be on a bloody plane back home with some albino chick's hand in a wooden box if I hadn't shown up! Cut me some slack, man. OK, you saved my life in Afghanistan, but that doesn't give you the right to treat me like shit all the time. What do you think I'm going to do – phone in reports on the hour to CNN?'

'You tell me what you're going to do.'

'If Miranda's alive, it's news. I can't ignore that and you can't either.'

Jed knew the boy was right. 'So, what will you do, if we – I do find her alive?'

'All I want is the chance to break the story. A one-on-one interview if she'll give it. Nothing more. If she says no, I walk, but I want your word and hers that she won't talk to any other journalists if she turns me down.'

Jed thought about the proposition for a few seconds, then nodded. He supposed leaving the matter up to Miranda – if she were alive – was the fairest thing to do. However, he still felt angry at Luke for putting enough information in his article about the firefight in Afghanistan for Hassan bin Zayid to make the connection between Jed and Miranda. 'Whether Miranda speaks to you or not, I want my name left out of your story. Are we clear on that?'

'Crystal,' Luke said, turning away to stare out the window.

The Zambezi shimmered in the golden rays of afternoon sun as they pulled up behind the lodge.

'Nice spot,' Luke remarked.

Jed grunted. At this moment he cared nothing for the spectacular vista in front of him. He strode inside and took the stairs two at a time to the upstairs bedrooms. Luke trailed behind him.

'Most of Chris's gear is gone, but it looks like she's left Miranda's stuff.' He wondered what had delayed Chris's departure for South Africa and diverted her to Kariba.

'Which one of these cases has the laptop?' Luke asked.

'I don't know. They all look alike.' They were confronted by a pile of aluminium transit cases.

'They've all got these little padlocks on them.' Luke fingered one of the small brass locks.

Jed walked down the stairs and outside to the Land Rover. Behind the passenger's seat was a canvas roll of tools. He undid it and took out a long-bladed screwdriver. Back in the room, he threaded the shaft of the screwdriver through the first of the locks and twisted. The padlock, which was more a visible deterrent than a serious security measure, popped open and Jed twisted the latches on the case. Chris must have had spare keys to each of the locks, Jed thought. He stared at the contents. It wasn't a laptop computer.

'What is all that stuff?'

Jed didn't say, but he recognised it all immediately. State-of-the-art image intensification night-vision goggles, auto-focus binoculars that calculated range and heading through a light-up display, and a GPS unit. Expensive, sophisticated gear. Exactly the same makes and models as issued to United States Special Operations Forces – people like himself.

'Just stuff for tracking and researching animals,' he said, only realising the irony of his words as he spoke them. He hoped Luke didn't catch on.

'Oh,' said Luke.

Jed stuck the screwdriver in the lock of the second box. 'You thirsty? I could really use a drink,' he said to Luke, looking over his shoulder.

'No, I can wait,' he said.

Jed didn't want to make a big deal of his growing suspicions. The second lock popped as easily as the first. Inside the case was a dismantled tactical satellite antenna and an LST-5C radio. Not only did Chris and Miranda have satellite phones, they had a field-portable tacsat communications system capable of sending encoded burst transmissions of voice, pictures and video at high speed and high resolution.

'What's that? A radio?' Luke said.

'Must be for radio-tracking animals,' Jed lied.

He checked the outside of the case for any giveaway markings, bar codes or serial numbers. There were none. He directed his attention back to the first box and picked up the GPS unit. He directed it over. There was a dark space where a sticker might once have been, but no serial number or identifying marks on that, either. He felt sure people with expensive equipment in a poverty-stricken continent such as Africa would engrave or otherwise mark it in some way in case it was stolen. The hairs on the back of his neck bristled. He'd seen unmarked gear like this before. The third case yielded a new-looking Nikon digital SLR camera with a suite of lenses.

'That's professional quality gear,' Luke said. 'It's pricey stuff.'

Jed had used similar cameras on reconnaissance missions and didn't need to be told that this was top-drawer equipment. The contents of this case alone were worth the same as a new car.

'Hey, there's a reader for camera memory cards. We're almost in business,' Luke said.

Jed snapped the lid of the case closed. 'Fourth time lucky,' he said, shattering the lock on another case.

'Bingo,' Luke said. 'Do you know her password?'

Jed hadn't thought of that. 'Let's hope she doesn't use one.' He carried the case downstairs and Luke followed. There was no electricity in the lodge, he remembered. 'I wonder how she keeps the batteries charged?'

'Probably has an inverter to run it off her car's cigarette lighter. That's what I do – or did – with mine.'

Jed switched the computer on and they both stared at the start-up screens, impatient for the operating system to kick in.

'Looks good so far,' Jed said. They had not been prompted to enter a password. He scanned the desktop icons on the screen, making sure there was nothing sensitive the journalist would be tempted to click open. 'No peeking at her files, OK?' Jed would do his own checking after they had viewed the photos.

'Of course not,' said Luke, offended.

'Over to you, kid.'

Luke took Jed's seat, acutely aware of the big American soldier leaning close over his shoulder. Outside he saw herons flying low up the river, heading for their evening roosts. He connected the memory-device reader to the computer. He took the card from his pocket and slid it into the reader.

Luke double-clicked on the first of the picture icons that appeared in a box on the screen.

'Shit,' he said. The first image was badly out of focus. He could make out a man and woman standing on the bridge of a white boat, but that was it. No details of the faces were clear, although the woman was obviously blonde and slender. 'I snapped these pretty quickly. I'm sure the others are better.'

Luke closed the picture and put the cursor over the second icon. He licked beads of perspiration from his upper lip.

'There! That's better, what do you think?' he said as the picture appeared.

The detail of the man's face was sharp. He had his head back, laughing at something the woman had said. She was half turned away from the camera, although most of the profile of her face was clear.

'No. I can't tell for sure, but I don't think it's her,' Jed said. His voice was soft.

'No way!' Luke said. 'Are you sure?'

'If it was my daughter I'd know immediately. But she's half turned away. Do you have a clearer shot?'

Luke was mad, and confused. He'd nearly been murdered for these pictures, and he'd crossed two countries to get to Jed, but now his theory was crumbling. Why the set-up in Zanzibar if bin Zayid hadn't been concerned with him seeing the girl on the boat? He began to feel sick with doubt. Maybe Hassan bin Zayid was simply playing around with another man's woman. But, if so, was the threat of him being exposed serious enough for him to try to frame and murder an innocent journalist? No way.

'I hope this one's better,' Luke said, bitter.

The third picture flashed up on the screen. Bin Zayid was in profile now, but the woman had turned and was facing directly into the camera, smiling. Her features were perfectly focused.

'I can zoom in, make the face bigger, if you like,' Luke said. He did it without waiting for Jed's answer.

'It's not her,' Jed said. He turned and walked across the room, staring out at the majestically languid Zambezi which burned red with the last light of the dying sun.

'What? Come on, take another look, man!' Luke was livid. He had risked his life – and taken another man's life – over these pictures. He pulled the newspaper from the torn daypack and fumbled through the pages to the story on Miranda's death. Luke strode across the room and held the picture to Jed's face. 'Take another look. It's her! The girl in the pictures is the same as the one in this newspaper!'

Jed shrugged. 'I think I know my own daughter.'

'Bullshit. You hardly knew her. You told me yourself in Afghanistan. You spent most of your lives apart. She probably changed her hair or something since you last saw her.'

Jed turned and gave the Australian a hard, cold stare. 'Be careful what you say. I knew my daughter; you didn't. She's dead and I have to come to terms with that. I'm sorry you went to such trouble to get these pictures to me. I wanted to believe you. I really did. But it's just not her.'

'Well, where does that leave us?' Luke pleaded.

'Us? There is no us. Time to go back to where we belong. I'm sure the professor won't mind if you stay here the night. You can hitch out tomorrow.'

Luke felt utterly deflated. The American hadn't even offered him a ride out of the park. He put his head in his hands and sat there as Jed walked outside into the gathering gloom. He felt like crying. It was partly the exhaustion, but he could also feel the greatest story of his life slipping slowly out of his grasp.

21

It was a good site for the kill, Hassan bin Zayid told himself one more time. Everything was going to plan, but still his stomach churned. It was just nerves, he supposed. He had arrived at the dirt airstrip with time to spare. Juma had been waiting with the Land Rover and their kit, as planned.

'Help me with these boxes,' Hassan had said, pointing to the back of the Cessna. The engine ticked as it cooled down. The stillness and quiet assaulted Hassan's ears after the noisy hours in the air. 'The hole is dug, for the woman?' he asked as they lifted the cheap coffin out of the plane.'

'Yes. At the bush camp.'

Good old Juma. Reliable and unquestioning as ever. But Hassan noticed the man was avoiding his eyes.

'What is it?'

'Nothing.'

'I know you too well. What's gone wrong, Juma?'

'The girl's father . . .'

'What about him?' Hassan snapped. He knew the man had called the lodge and been told Hassan was unavailable.

'He came here.'

'He *what?*'

'He came, boss. But I sent him away. I told him you were in Zanzibar.'

'What did he see?'

Juma shuffled from foot to foot.

'Out with it!' bin Zayid barked.

'He saw this Land Rover. The packs, the weapons.'

'And what did he ask? What did you tell him?'

Juma faced up to the Arab. 'I told him I was going on an anti-poaching patrol.'

'And he believed you?' Hassan fought to control his rising panic.

'I think so.'

'And that was it? He left?'

'Yes.' Juma did not dare tell his employer about the failed ambush.

'Very well. Let's get the other box loaded.'

They pushed the Cessna into its wooden hangar. Inside the building, perched like a resting dragonfly, was an ultralight aircraft. 'It is fuelled? Ready?'

'Yes, boss,' Juma answered.

'Good. Let's go.'

Juma drove the Land Rover down the dirt road that led to the airstrip. When they were almost in sight of the river he turned left onto a rutted, rarely used track. The trail led to a small satellite camp, a remote outpost two kilometres along the river from the main lodge. The bush camp consisted of a thatch-roofed timber hut, a pit toilet concealed by a reed screen, and two round concrete slabs, each about two metres in diameter. One stand was for making a campfire and the other was the base for a bush shower. A canvas bucket dangled from a tree branch above. When small groups of clients used the secluded bush camp, Juma and two African servants went ahead of the main party and erected canvas tents for the clients and bin Zayid to sleep in, and a canvas screen for the shower. The hut was used to store food and a gas-powered deep-freeze, and was safe from marauding baboons, monkeys and hyenas. Now the camp was deserted.

Juma stopped the vehicle and they got out. Hassan leaned into the back of the truck. He looked at Miranda's motionless body. There was no going back now. He closed the lid. They lifted the casket out of the truck and lowered it into the shallow hole Juma had dug.

'Cover her,' Hassan said, and turned away as he heard the first shovel-load of sandy earth spattering the lid.

As Juma worked, Hassan took up his AK-47. He removed the magazine, checked it was full and replaced it on the rifle. He pulled the cocking handle and let it fly forwards, chambering a round. He checked the webbing vest and rucksack Juma had prepared for him and nodded his approval. He leaned back into the rear tray of the Land Rover and removed the lid of the other coffin. From inside he removed two loaded HN-5 surface-to-air missile launchers from the straw packing. He placed them gently on the floor of the Land Rover, snuggled between the two packs to stop them bouncing around too much.

After successfully planting the bomb on board the tourist bus in Dar es Salaam, the travel agent had handed over the prize in his cache of arms – the two anti-aircraft missiles – and briefed him on the plan. He'd shown Hassan a video filmed in Afghanistan on how to operate the missiles. 'A crash course at best,' Hassan had remarked.

'These things were designed to be operated by illiterate Russian conscripts. Afghan tribesmen who'd never seen anything more technologically advanced than a bolt-action Lee Enfield were able to shoot down Russian helicopter gunships by the score using this weapon. I'm hoping you, a university-educated man, can hit one unarmed civilian aircraft, Hassan,' the travel agent had replied caustically. Along with the missiles, he had given Hassan three hand grenades and the explosive device he'd used to bomb the nightclub in Zanzibar.

The missiles were Chinese copies of the Russian SAM 7, often referred to by its NATO nickname, the Strela. The Chinese version, known as the Red Cherry, was exactly the same in its look, feel and operation. The missile was old technology – its design dated back to the late sixties – but the two Hassan possessed would be more than adequate for his mission.

Juma joined him beside the vehicle, brushing the dirt from his hands on his green fatigues. 'Let us go,' Hassan said. He took a small GPS from a pouch on his webbing and turned it on.

They drove the rugged four-by-four back out to the dirt road leading to the airstrip, and then followed that road for a few hundred metres. Juma engaged low-range four-wheel-drive and turned onto a trail in even worse condition than the one that led to the bush camp. They headed west, towards the boundary of the bin Zayid concession. Hassan kept an eye on the GPS as they bumped over rocks and exposed tree roots. The Land Rover bucked sickeningly as Juma climbed out of a dry creek bed. The watercourse marked the boundary between bin Zayid's land and the property of his neighbour, Willy Wylde. Hassan was not worried that Wylde or one of his scouts would chance upon them. He guessed, correctly, that Wylde and most of his staff were waiting on the edge of their own airstrip, anxiously expecting the arrival of their most important hunting client ever.

Eventually they arrived at the killing ground. 'It is a good position, boss,' Juma said, sensing the Arab's nerves as he scanned the sky.

'That it is, Juma. That it is. Camouflage the vehicle.'

Lieutenant General Donald 'Crusher' Calvert, retired, shook hands with the President of Zambia and smiled for the camera.

The US military had well and truly recovered from its post-Vietnam hatred of the media and now actively courted it. Media representatives had ridden into Baghdad in American tanks and helicopters, and had been a constant presence at the Coalition base at Bagram, Afghanistan, when Calvert had commanded the forces there. As a former Pentagon spokesman he had held court at more than his fair share of press conferences, but any commander worth his salt these days knew that one had to be a good media performer to win and keep the top jobs. As an aspiring politician, he knew he was in for even more exposure. It was only a local newspaper in a Third World African country, but his smile was no less broad, his eyes no less steely than they would have been for the *Washington Post* or the *New York Times*.

The visit hadn't been as bad as he had feared. The new president displayed all the vigour and foresight that had recently carried him to victory against an incumbent who had presided over the country's steady and seemingly unstoppable downward economic spiral during his decades in power.

'One more picture, please, Mr President.'

Both men smiled. It was a closed photo opportunity. The pictures were being taken by a Government-paid photographer and, by mutual agreement, would not be released to the local press for a couple of days in order to give the high-profile American time to reach his hunting destination unmolested by the media. The name of the lodge, and the real purpose of his visit, would also be withheld. The press release would say the American dignitary was 'taking time to enjoy Zambia's unique wildlife'. It wouldn't fool the American media, he realised as he held the handshake and smile. The US press knew he was a sports hunter, and while Pentagon correspondents couldn't have given two hoots about his chosen sport – some of them hunted themselves – he knew the Washington press gallery and animal rights groups would be incensed. Sooner or later he would have to face a barrage of questions about the ethics of hunting. But, for now, the hell with them. He was here to enjoy himself.

'I wish you good luck and safety on your hunt, General,' the Zambian head of state said.

'It was good to meet you, sir, and I wish you and your country well with the outstanding economic and developmental initiatives you're working on.'

'We have a long way to go, but we are getting there,' the African leader said.

The general smiled and nodded. Things appeared to be looking up for the poverty-stricken country. Tourism in Zambia was moving ahead in leaps and bounds and the Europeans were pouring aid money into rebuilding the country's road and rail network.

That was the funny thing about Africa, Calvert mused. Yesterday's political and economic basket case was today's powerhouse – and vice versa. Mozambique had been plagued for years by civil war, with warring factions propped up by neighbouring countries with vested interests, but now the shattered country was back on its feet with its tourism and farming sectors booming. Zambia was the same. He would get a more detailed briefing on the situation in sub-Saharan Africa in a couple of days. A female operative would be delivering it, he had noted from his program, and he genuinely looked forward to learning more about the current state of play on the continent – but not as much as he looked forward to tomorrow's hunt.

He waved goodbye to the President, saluted the smartly turned-out honour guard of tall African soldiers lining the driveway, and climbed into the shiny black American embassy four-by-four. The airconditioning inside was a relief from the early afternoon glare.

'We're moving,' the secret service agent said into a microphone taped to his wrist.

'That we are, Johnny, and not before time,' Calvert said to the tall, broad-shouldered bodyguard. With his aviator sunglasses and blond crewcut he was every bit the Hollywood stereotype of his profession.

Calvert loosened his tie and shrugged off his sports coat. 'This is your first time in Africa, isn't it Johnny?'

'Yes, sir,' Agent John Wozak said from the front seat of the SUV.

'What do you think so far?'

'Airports, hotels and presidential palaces all look the same, sir, but I'm looking forward to getting out into the bush.'

'There's nothing like it. The colours, the sounds, the smells – it gets to you.'

'Yes, sir.'

'Ever hunted?'

'Deer when I was a kid.' John Wozak practised once a week on the pistol range and was trained to use lethal force to protect his charges. He often wondered, though, how he would feel if he had to kill a human being. The thought of killing an animal for fun just left him cold.

'Nothing like it. God, I'm looking forward to this.'

Their aircraft, a twin-engine Piper Comanche, was waiting on a quiet apron on the edge of Lusaka Airport. An escort of two police motorcycles and a patrol car, all with flashing lights, led Calvert's party through a private entry gate on the airport perimeter, well away from the main passenger terminal. The three policemen on duty at the gate saluted as the motorcade covered their starched uniforms, oiled weapons and spit-polished shoes in a thin layer of African dust.

'Good morning, General, I'm Rob Westcott. I'll be flying you this morning,' a tall grey-haired man said as Calvert strode up to the aircraft.

Calvert extended his hand in greeting. 'Pleased to meet you, Rob. Mind if I sit up front with you?'

Westcott shook the hand and said with a grin, 'I wasn't sure whether to salute or not.'

'I'm done with saluting. Are you ex-military, Rob?'

'Rhodesian air force. I was a pilot during our bush war. You mightn't have heard of it.'

'Matter of fact, I had a couple of friends from my Vietnam days who signed up to help you guys out. One of them didn't make it back.'

'I'm sorry to hear it. We all lost friends. It was a long, bloody fight. You were best out of it, General.'

Calvert smiled. 'Oh, I've ducked my share of lead over the years. But it's good to know I'm in the hands of a combat pilot – even if you were air force.'

'Well, it'll be a pleasure to have you up front, General. But, as I always used to tell the army guys, touch any of the pretty buttons and I'll shoot you.' The two men laughed in instant camaraderie.

'I want to see as much of the bush as I can while I'm here, even if it's from the air,' Calvert said as he climbed into the aircraft and took the seat next to Westcott.

'The best way to see it in my book, General,' Westcott said, as he showed Calvert how to attach his safety belt.

'Don't like it on the ground?'

'I was shot down by anti-aircraft fire over Mozambique in seventy-nine. Spent a day and a night eating dirt and trying not to get killed. I've tried to stay above the trees as much as possible ever since.'

'You'll be at dinner with us tonight, Rob?'

'I'll be staying at the lodge, yes, General. I've been booked to be on stand-by the whole time you're on safari, in case . . .'

'Don't worry, Rob, I know what it's in case of. If my staff can't have me stay five minutes away from a hospital they at least want to know that someone can fly me to one. Please make sure you join us for the meal this evening. I'd like to hear some of your stories from the bush war, if you don't mind telling. And stop calling me General. It's Don, if you must, but everyone calls me Crusher.'

'Well, Crusher, I'd be happy to swap war stories with you tonight.'

Wozak, another secret service agent, Stu Wardley, and the general's aide, Mike Treble, took their seats in the back of the aircraft.

'Mike, when's that lady coming to brief me?' Calvert asked over his shoulder as the pilot began his pre-flight checks.

'Day after tomorrow, sir.'

'Good, good. What do you know about her?'

'Ex-military, degree in science with a major in zoology, respected in her academic field and a real asset according to the embassy people in Johannesburg. Oh, and they also tell me she's a looker.' The aide smiled.

'Sounding better all the time,' Calvert called over the engine noise.

'Clear skies and very little turbulence all the way,' Rob said as they left the grey-brown scar of Lusaka behind them. 'It's only a short flight, but you'll get a good view of the Zambezi before we land.'

Calvert scoured the landscape below him, revelling in the vista of untamed expanses. 'Do you fly down to the valley often?' he asked the pilot through his headphones.

'Once a month or so. I've been into Willy Wylde's place quite a few times. Plenty of game down there. I usually have to buzz the strip to clear the animals off. One time there were four lion on a zebra kill in the middle of the runway. I buzzed them three times, but they weren't moving for anyone.'

'What did you do in the end?'

'Landed at another strip nearby. Place is owned by an Arab chappie.

317

Hell of a nice guy. He drove the tourists to Wylde's place and they were treated to a close-up view of the lions.'

And that was why Calvert loved Africa. Where else in the world would an airstrip be closed because of the presence of man-eating predators?

'That's the Kafue River below us now,' Rob said, dipping the wing slightly so the general could get a better view.

Calvert stared down at the dry bush flanking the river. The nose of the aircraft started to dip.

Westcott continued his commentary. 'That's Kanyemba Island in front of us. Zimbabwe is on our right, on the other side of the river. We're passing over the Chiawa Game Management Area now – some tribal lands and a few farms and villages, but you'll see fewer people and more game as we get closer to the Lower Zambezi National Park. We should start seeing some animals soon.'

Juma pointed skywards.

'I hear them, but I can't see them,' Hassan whispered.

'At ten o'clock, boss,' Juma said, trailing his finger across the clear blue sky.

'Got them.' Hassan lowered the binoculars slung around his neck.

He picked up the first of the missile launchers, which he had readied for firing. He quickly checked again that the covers were off each end of the tube and the conical-shaped combined battery and gas unit was screwed in tightly under the front of the launcher.

Given the abundance of game on Willy Wylde's well-managed ranch, Hassan assumed the pilot would overfly the airstrip to ensure it was free of game and other obstacles. Hassan's firing position was roughly a kilometre east of the end of Willy Wylde's landing field. He would fire at the Comanche as it passed over his head, after the pilot had made his inspection but before he began his turn to come around again. The best position for firing the surface-to-air missile was from the rear, so that the heat-seeking warhead could get an unobstructed fix on an engine's exhaust.

Juma stood by Hassan's side, the other missile launcher ready in his hands in case of malfunction. They could have fired both missiles simultaneously, but Hassan was sure he could bring down the light aircraft with one. Also, he wanted to keep the second in reserve. The spare warhead would not go to waste if the day unfolded in the manner he assumed it would.

Hassan rested the long, tubular tail of the missile launcher on his shoulder. 'Remember, don't stand behind me when I fire, Juma.'

'Yes, boss.' He was not stupid. He had fired RPG 7 rocket-propelled grenade launchers during a brief stint in the Tanzanian army and knew full well not to get caught in such a weapon's back blast.

Hassan pointed the missile towards the approaching aircraft. He thumbed the switch which energised the launcher, activating its battery and, at the same time, allowing a stream of Argon gas to cool the infra-red seeker unit. With its temperature much lower than the air around it, the seeker would be better able to lock onto the inviting infra-red emissions from the approaching aircraft's hot engine exhaust ports. He tracked the Comanche through the crude optical sights on the exterior of the tube.

Immediately, he heard the tone in his right ear which told him the missile had locked onto the aeroplane's engines. He could have fired now, but then the pilot would have seen the missile coming towards him and might have been able to outmanoeuvre it. He resisted the urge to send the rocket on its way and run from this place. He drew a deep breath and turned to track the aircraft as it approached.

'Looks clear below, General,' Westcott said. 'That's Willy Wylde's landing field ahead.' The pilot pointed to a dirt airstrip carved out of the virgin bush.

'Just a couple of vehicles on the side,' Calvert said.

'That'll be Willy and his troops. They'll probably have an honour guard and red carpet laid on for you.'

'That I don't need.'

'Willy's all right. He'll be all nerves for the first day, but once you get him out into the bush you'll see why he's rated the best hunter in these parts.'

'I'm counting on it.'

'I'll take her down a bit, see what we can see before I turn back for the landing,' Westcott said into his headset microphone.

'Buffalo!' Crusher Calvert exclaimed, seeing a stretch of verdant flood plain peppered with black dots.

The animals started to run at the sound of the droning engines. 'Big herd. Maybe three or four hundred.' Rob levelled out and banked away so as not to disturb the animals overly. 'Black death, they call them.'

'So I understand. I'm gunning for one on this trip. A big bull.'

'Good for you. I'd rather face down a lion than be charged by one of them. Elephant in the river, over there.'

Calvert nodded as the wide, silvery expanse of the Zambezi came into view. Four elephants – all mature bulls judging by the length of their tusks and big rounded heads – were grazing on a reedy island near the Zambian shore.

'That's all hunting concessions you can see across the river in Zimbabwe. Mana Pools National Park is on the opposite bank to where we're heading. You're much better off on this side of the river these days, General.'

'So I've heard.'

'Yes, you're safe as houses over here, Crusher.'

Hassan released half of the deep breath he had drawn. He felt the adrenaline surge through his veins. He would remember this moment for the rest of his life. The rest of his life, of course, might only be a matter of hours.

The tone was loud and strong in his ear. He aimed for the port engine. He squeezed the trigger and felt the heat on his cheek, heard the roar of the launch motor. The missile sprang from the tube.

*

John Wozak bumped his head on the little Perspex window at the back of the aircraft as he flashed his head back around. Something on the ground had caught his eye. He pressed his cheek against the Perspex to peer down at the stretch of riverbank they had just over-flown. It had looked like a puff of dust. But now he saw a streaming tail of smoke led by a fiercely burning bright light as the missile's motor ignited.

'Missile!' he screamed.

Westcott had been preparing to turn to port, to head back for his run-in to the airstrip. Someone yelled something from the rear com-partment. Most likely one of the secret service types had seen his first elephant in the bush below. He looked back over his shoulder.

The agent was yelling at him and pointing out the rear window.

'It's a fucking missile!' the man screamed. 'Left-hand side!'

Westcott caught a glimpse of the smoke trail through the rear passenger window. He had been fired at before by a surface-to-air missile. That telltale stream could be nothing else. He cut the throttle and stamped hard on the left rudder pedal, pushing it to the bulkhead.

The Comanche rolled on its back. Westcott ripped back the control wheel and the plane dropped sickeningly.

Calvert's head slammed into the window on his left. 'What the . . . ?'

'Brace yourselves!' Westcott bellowed. He pushed the wheel full for-wards, steepening the dive angle. It was a dangerous move, even at two thousand feet above the ground, but he had no alternative. By turning left, towards the oncoming missile, Westcott hoped he would mask the heat signature from the engine on that side of the aircraft.

'He has seen the missile,' Juma said, observing the violent manoeuvre through his binoculars.

Hassan was not in the mood for pessimism. 'He's too late.' However, he held his breath as the missile slowly came about and followed the aeroplane down. Had the pilot been flying a jet fighter his instinctive actions might have saved him, but the Comanche was a commuter.

'It is going to hit!' Juma cried.

'Yes,' said Hassan.

The control wheel shuddered in Westcott's hands as the missile warhead, a payload of more than a kilogram of high explosive, detonated just short of the hot exhaust, sending thousands of tiny shards of metal into the engine, wing and fuselage. A flash of brilliant light seared the white-painted aluminium skin of the aircraft. Arms went up in front of faces in a vain attempt to ward off the heat and deadly shrapnel. The boom of the detonation over the screaming whine of protesting engines assaulted the passengers' eardrums. Shrapnel and pieces of the port engine burst out, as the ragged remains of the metal cowling peeled away in the slipstream. Most of the debris went aft, but splinters of aluminium, nuts, bolts and tiny components blew every which way at the moment the grenade-sized warhead at the tip of the missile erupted.

Stu Wardley, John Wozak's partner, had left his seat and was leaning over the other man trying to see the missile. A dislodged bolt shot through the skin of the aircraft like a bullet and continued flying and tumbling through Wardley's right eye and out the back of his skull. Wozak reeled to one side as Wardley's body bounced off him, brains and blood gushing from the empty eye socket and grotesque exit wound as the man crashed into the carpeted floor of the aircraft.

Mike Treble had been sitting in front of Wozak. A piece of aluminium cowling the size of a man's hand sliced through the fuselage and tore a furrow across Treble's dark-blue business shirt, laying open his heart and lungs. He died a few seconds later.

John Wozak felt for a pulse on Wardley's blood-drenched neck. There was none. The agent's brains covered the floor of the aircraft, which was also slick from the massive volume of blood that had gushed from Treble's wound. Wozak swallowed rising vomit. He took the Glock nine-millimetre pistol from his shoulder holster and pulled back the slide, cocking it and chambering a round. Someone had killed his partner and had attempted to assassinate the man in their charge. He would be ready for the bastards if they showed up to finish the job they'd started.

'I'll go back and help the guys,' Calvert yelled to the pilot above the tortured whine and thump of flapping metal. The aircraft was vibrating so much he could barely get the words out.

'Sit down!' Westcott barked. It was an old tradition, founded in common sense, that on board an aircraft the pilot outranked any passenger. 'Strap into your seat, as tight as you can. Brace for impact! There's nothing you can do back there until we land.'

Calvert took another look out the window and nodded. He fastened the lap and shoulder straps of the inertia belt into the housing below his belly and said a quick Hail Mary.

The warhead had taken off the left aileron and a sizeable chunk of the wing. Westcott turned, but was gentle on the rudder. Too much and he would create a spiral dive from which there'd be no recovery at their height. He checked the airspeed again and fought to keep the fine balance between stalling and losing too much altitude. He pulled back on the wheel a little and kept his right foot down hard on the corresponding rudder pedal, to compensate for the massive torque being created by the remaining engine. He kept the power up and set the right propeller pitch to full fine. Westcott had to find somewhere to land and it was clear to him now that he wouldn't make the airstrip. That left only the river.

Westcott keyed the microphone switch on the wheel and said, 'Mayday, mayday, mayday, Comanche niner-juliet, delta-alpha-romeo, sierra-oscar-alpha. Engine failure. Ditching in the Zambezi River, thirty kilometres east Chiawa. Five souls on board. Hit by a surface-to-air missile. Repeat . . .' He reiterated the call as he busied himself for the landing. He would have to glide in. He went through the checklists. Before shutting down the fuel and electrical systems, he lowered the flaps. 'Brace yourself, General. We're going into the drink.'

'You're doing fine, Rob. What are our chances?'

A stupid question, the pilot thought. 'I'll get us down in one piece, Crusher. Let's just hope someone gets to us before the hippos and the crocs.'

'We'll make it.' Calvert forced a smile. Under his breath, he said, 'Glory be to the Father, the Son and the Holy Spirit . . .'

'Stop!' Hassan yelled to Juma, pulling out his binoculars from the pouch on his web gear.

He and Juma had run for the concealed Land Rover as soon as they saw the missile strike the engine of the Comanche. As planned, Juma had followed the track away from the launch site down towards the river. The private road paralleled the riverbank and afforded good views up and down the Zambezi from a number of carefully chosen lookout positions.

Hassan caught sight of the stricken aircraft. 'He's making for the river. I *knew* he would.'

Hassan had thought through what he would do if he found himself in the pilot's unenviable position. The turn back to the original landing strip would be too tight – impossible to make with the destroyed engine and damaged controls. Unless the pilot located Hassan's own airstrip and made for that, he would probably try to ditch in the river. In either case, he would deliver General Donald Calvert, dead or alive, into Hassan's waiting hands. In the case of a third eventuality – the aircraft crashing somewhere in the bush – Hassan's plan was to return to his own airstrip and take off with Juma in his ultralight. Using a GPS, he would mark the position of the downed aircraft, land, and drive or walk to the crash site.

'Back to the bush camp. Quickly!' Hassan ordered. 'We'll pick them up in the boat.' His flat-bottomed game-viewing boat, equipped with two forty-horsepower outboard motors, was fuelled and waiting at the satellite encampment.

Time was of the essence now. Hassan assumed the pilot would have got a mayday message away and that rescuers would soon be on the way, by boat and, probably, by helicopter. He figured he had an hour, at the most.

Rob Westcott took a final glance over his shoulder into the cabin. 'Get that man strapped in!' he yelled at John Wozak, noticing the other agent lying on the floor.

'He's dead,' Wozak called back. He had to yell to be heard over the incessant noise of wind whistling through the punctured fuselage. 'So's Treble.'

'Strap them in anyway,' Westcott shouted over his shoulder. The last thing they needed was a couple of hundred kilograms of human flying around the cockpit when they hit the water.

'Mother of God,' Calvert muttered.

They were headed down the centre line of a straight stretch of the river. Westcott eased back on the wheel. He'd kept the airspeed a little high, conserving some energy for the flare so that he could control the point of impact with the water rather than simply smacking the aircraft down.

The surface of the river rippled from the slipstream of the aircraft as it raced along, metres from the water. A flock of herons took flight as the shadow loomed over them, and a startled bull elephant wallowing in the shallows flapped his ears and trumpeted loudly in a show of mock anger. The pachyderm decided this was one intruder not worth taking on and hastily ran away.

From his military training, Westcott knew it was too risky to bring the aircraft down tail first, as doing so would either bring the nose down too hard, causing them to submarine, or would make them skip like a stone across the water's surface. 'I'm going to dig the right wing into the water to slow us, General,' he said to Calvert. 'Hold tight – it's

going to be hard on your neck when we hit. We'll spin hard on impact.'
Westcott was thankful now he'd gone to the expense of installing
five-point harnesses for both pilot and front-seat passenger. They'd
need all the restraint they could get.

'Brace!' he called again over his shoulder into the rear cabin. It was
the best he could do. He registered the sight of blood on the ceiling and
carpet. No time to think about that now.

Westcott brought the aircraft down a little fast, flaring it several
metres above the water. Luck hadn't deserted him completely. There
was a straight stretch in the river around five hundred metres in length
filling his windscreen. The controls were getting heavy. He allowed the
Comanche to sink towards the water. His airspeed was just above the
stall, the control wheel shuddering. The water whipped past his side
window, sun flashing off the ripples. The plane was still travelling at
a hundred and forty kilometres an hour. He sideslipped the aircraft,
trailing the right wing, lowering it towards the water. It skipped once,
striking the ripples. The impact rang through the airframe like a
sledgehammer. The leading edge of the wing hit again and dug into the
water. The aircraft spun through two hundred and seventy degrees,
partially ripping the right wing away.

Crusher Calvert felt as though his neck had snapped as the aircraft
slammed into the water. His body was flicked like a bullwhip, his head
smashing into the window again and then flicking forwards, stopping
just inches from the instrument panel in front of him as the safety
harness cut painfully into his shoulders and belly.

A bow wave surged up beside them and then washed back over the
nose of the Comanche. Suddenly the aircraft was still, the tail rising up
as water covered the front. With a sickening lurch the aeroplane righted
itself again, the tail splashing back down into the river. They were level
and floating – for the time being. Westcott shook his head. His mind
reeled. He realised the tremendous G-forces created by the spinning
landing had caused him to black out for a few seconds. He tried the radio
again but it was dead. His shoulders and gut hurt where the seatbelt had
dug into him on impact, but other than that, he seemed all right.

'General! Crusher, are you OK, man?' Westcott was shocked at the red smear on his passenger's temple.

'I'm OK,' Calvert said weakly. He wiped the stickiness from his head and inspected his fingers. 'Banged my head against the side door when we hit. Neck's a bit sore, but I'll be all right. How you doing, John?' he croaked back into the cabin.

'I'm fine, sir. Where's the raft, the lifejackets?' Wozak demanded of the pilot.

'We don't carry any. We don't fly over the ocean so there's no requirement.' Westcott was not apologetic. He didn't need a security guard taking over now – he was still the captain of the aircraft. 'General, I'll get out and test the depth of the water. I'd like you to wait outside on the wing with Mr Wozak. Can you swim, sir?'

'Yes, I can swim.'

Westcott undid his harness, opened his door and stepped out onto the wing. The Comanche dipped with the sudden transference of his weight, but it still seemed to be floating. He heard the drone of a motor and raised a hand to his eyes to cut down the afternoon glare off the water. 'It's a boat!'

'Hallelujah,' Calvert said, undoing his harness.

'Sir, I think you should wait there a second until we see who it is. Someone was shooting at us, and we don't know if these people are friendlies or not,' Wozak said, squeezing between the general and the empty pilot's seat to follow Westcott outside. He held his loaded Glock in his right hand.

Calvert frowned. He wanted to get out of the damned aircraft before it sank or caught fire. He looked out the side window, which had been painted with droplets of brown water, and saw a low-slung speedboat slicing its way towards them. There were two men in green uniforms on board.

'They look like National Parks guys,' Westcott said, noticing from a distance that both were African and dressed alike.

'I'm not taking any chances,' Wozak said grimly.

*

Hassan bin Zayid had pulled a black ski mask over his face and placed a floppy green bush hat on his head, the brim pulled low over his eyes. To complete his rudimentary disguise he wore a pair of black leather gloves. He sat behind Juma in the ski boat, an AK-47 and a hunting rifle loaded and cocked at his feet. Also in the bottom of the fibreglass hull was the second, unused HN-5 surface-to-air missile, a five-litre tin can of gasoline and two marine safety flares. In his right hand he held an automatic pistol with a silencer screwed onto the barrel.

Juma waved from the boat. 'Hello! Hello! Are you all right, sir?'

Westcott cupped his hands around his mouth and called, 'Who are you? Where are you from?'

'Zambia Wildlife Authority,' Juma called back. 'How many of you are there? Do you have any injured?'

'Two dead, three of us OK,' Westcott replied.

'Shit,' Wozak hissed. 'Let's wait until he comes alongside before giving the whole the game away, OK?'

Hassan bin Zayid's right index finger curled around the pistol's trigger. The pilot had told him what he needed to know. Juma's questions were part of their plan, and it had worked. They now knew exactly how many people were on board. Calvert would have one or more hunting rifles, probably stowed in the aircraft's cargo compartment, and his bodyguards would be armed. Hassan peered around Juma's muscular bulk to see if he could determine who was alive. He saw the pilot and another man, presumably one of the secret service agents, on the starboard wing. There was a face in the copilot's window. Even from a hundred metres away he recognised it from scores of televised press conferences, and as many newspaper photos.

Juma cut the boat's engines and allowed the craft to drift silently towards the aircraft. 'Where can I tie up?'

'To the prop, or what's left of it,' Westcott replied. He moved to meet the boat, blocking bin Zayid's view of the young bodyguard.

Hassan bent forwards, pretending to look for something in the bottom of the boat, so as not to show his masked face just yet.

'Keep your hands where I can see them, buddy,' one of the Americans drawled.

'We are here to help you, sir,' Juma said.

'Let's see some ID before you tie up. You in the back, stand up.'

Hassan bin Zayid rose to a crouch, Juma's body still shielding him from full view of the bodyguard, and anything else he might try. The man was too damn suspicious for his own good.

'For God's sake,' Westcott moaned. 'Let's get off this bloody plane before –'

Bin Zayid's arm flashed up and his pistol coughed twice, both bullets thudding into the pilot's chest. Blood sprayed across the other man's body, but the agent raised his arm and instinctively squeezed off two shots from his pistol as the pilot's body was punched back onto him. The aircraft rocked as Westcott landed on his back on the wing, then slid headfirst into the river. A smear of red on the bright white aluminium skin marked his body's passage.

Hassan saw Juma clutch his neck and stagger. He fired another two silenced shots before the American bodyguard could regain his footing and aim again. One missed, but the other drilled through the man's belly. The agent sank to his knees and dropped his pistol, clutching his stomach with both hands.

The speedboat, which had still been travelling under its own momentum, thudded into the aircraft and Hassan leaped aboard. The agent coughed blood down the front of his bush shirt and slumped to one side in a vain attempt to reach his pistol, which had landed just out of reach, on the wing. Bin Zayid straightened his arm and fired one shot between the American's eyes. The man's head snapped back and struck the aircraft's skin with a dull clang.

'General Donald Calvert, come out and you will live,' Hassan called into the aircraft. The man whose face he had seen at the copilot's window was no longer in the cockpit.

Juma stepped onto the wing, covering his employer with his assault rifle. His neck and the collar of his green shirt were drenched in blood, but he seemed alert and ready for action.

Unless the pilot had lied to them, Hassan assumed that the second secret service agent was one of the dead men he had referred to. The general, he presumed, had scuttled into the main cabin of the aircraft. The danger was that the old soldier was right now searching for a weapon of some sort.

'General Calvert? I'll give you ten seconds to surrender. After that I will torch this aircraft. You may stay where you are if you wish. My mission will still be accomplished if you die here.'

From his position on the wing, Hassan fired two shots at random through the skin of the rear cabin.

Lieutenant General Donald Calvert, once the commander of nearly nine thousand Coalition soldiers engaged in the global war against terrorism, cowered on the carpeted floor of the cabin, his cheek sticky from the spilled blood and brains of his dead bodyguard.

'God have mercy on me, and on you, Stu,' he whispered to himself. His hands groped inside the dead agent's sports jacket. He'd taken part in many conflicts in his thirty-five years in the military, but he hadn't touched a dead man, hadn't smelled the metallic stench of copious amounts of fresh blood, since he was a young platoon commander in Vietnam. He'd survived the North Vietnamese Army's rocket and mortar attacks, been wounded when his signalman had lost a leg to a landmine, and faced down massed infantry attacks when a firebase he'd been defending had nearly been overrun. He held two Bronze Stars and a Silver Star, all for valour. He would not let this pissant African terrorist get the better of him. The history books would show he went down fighting, or killed a terrorist and lived. A win-win scenario either way, but he wasn't ready to die yet. He cursed himself for not keeping his hunting rifle with him in the cabin of the Comanche, but consoled himself with the realisation that Wardley would have a weapon on him. His fingers found the nylon holster under the agent's stiffening arm. Calvert swore a silent oath. Empty. Wozak must have taken Wardley's pistol. The general weighed his choices. He could be

330

burned to death or he could give himself up. Never in his life had he known the shame of surrender, but there was still a chance while he drew breath. When the time was right, he would kill one or both of these men, even if it meant his own death.

'Get the gasoline and the flares. Douse the aircraft. We'll burn him alive,' Hassan said to Juma.

The African did as ordered, unscrewing the cap from the metal can and tipping a third of the contents into the cockpit.

'Smell the gas, General. I'm going to burn the aircraft now. I'm happy for you to die inside it. The choice is yours. Come with me and you will live,' Hassan taunted. 'Give me a flare,' he said. He took the cylinder from Juma, pulled the cap off and placed it on the bottom of the tube. A sharp tap with the heel of his hand would send the incendiary flying into the aircraft.

'I'm coming out,' Calvert said. His voice betrayed him, escaping as a whimper.

'Very sensible, General. Three seconds only. One . . . two . . .'

Calvert held his empty hands before him as he emerged at a crouch from the cockpit.

'On your knees, hands behind your back.' The politeness was gone.

Calvert knelt on the wing and Juma tied his wrist bitingly tight with a length of plastic cable.

'Up!' Hassan commanded. He pulled the once powerful man up by his bound wrists, gaining satisfaction from the little yelp he emitted as his shoulders took the strain. He put a foot on Calvert's rear and kicked him forwards, headfirst, into the boat. Calvert landed hard and groaned aloud in pain.

Hassan tossed the can of gasoline into the carcass of the aeroplane, picked up the flare and punched the firing pin in the cap into the base of the cylinder, igniting the projectile inside. Incandescent red light glowed through the portholes and the spilled gasoline ignited with a crump. He stepped onto the boat and pushed away from the burning wreck. On the far side of the wing he noticed a ripple in the water's surface, then the momentary appearance of one and then two pairs of beady eyes reflected in the glow of the flames. The crocodiles had been drawn by the scent of blood.

Hassan started the engine in neutral and let the big outboard idle.

'How bad is your wound?' he asked Juma.

The African felt the side of his neck. 'He nicked me. It is nothing.'

'Where are you taking me?' Calvert asked.

'Telling you would ruin the surprise.' To Juma, Hassan said, 'Gag him.'

Juma picked up a roll of black duct tape, tore off a strip and sealed their prisoner's lips. Calvert stared hard into the African henchman's face as though he were committing every feature, every blemish, to memory.

Hassan thrust the engine throttle forwards and the bow leaped into the air as the boat cleaved the Zambezi. They raced back towards the hunting camp on the Zambian side. Hassan cast a glance over his shoulder. The red glow of the flare was still bright inside the aircraft and flames were now licking out of melted windows, scorching and blackening the once white exterior. The aircraft seemed to jump out of the water a little as pieces of metal burst from the port wing. The noise of the explosion followed a split second later. The fire had spread to the fuel tank in the wing and a greasy black mushroom cloud stained the clear sky over the water.

Hassan looked back up the river and turned the steering wheel hard to starboard to avoid a pod of curious hippos. The big beasts had raised their little eyes and waggling ears from the water, curious about the cause of the noise. Hassan's evasive move caused the general to roll to one side and bang his head on the gunwale of the boat.

'Sorry,' bin Zayid said, smiling.

He pushed the throttle wide open and moved close to the high undercut banks on the Zambian shore. There were still no other boats or aircraft in sight, but they would come soon enough. Wylde, and possibly some of the other land-holders, would have already mounted a rescue, and the Italian doctors at the hospital in Chirundu would have been told to stay at work. He guessed a Zambian air force helicopter would soon be on its way.

However, night would settle on the Zambezi in a couple of hours and Hassan bin Zayid was already within sight of his secluded camp. No one else except Juma knew the details of this phase of the plan. As far as the other staff at his lodge knew, their employer was still away in Zanzibar on business. In time, people would come to his lodge and ask questions – it was only natural that as an Arab and a Muslim he would attract attention – but by then he would be long gone.

22

'Tell me what was going on between my daughter and Hassan bin Zayid,' Jed demanded. He stood next to the driver's door of Chris's Land Rover as she turned off the engine. His face was clouded with barely suppressed rage.

'What?' she asked, as she switched off the Land Rover's headlights.

She got out of the vehicle and tried to brush past him. He put an arm either side of her and rested his hands on the warm hood of the truck. Her face was white. She held a portable satellite phone loose in her right hand and stared out into the gathering gloom of the night. She didn't seem to have heard a word he had said.

'My daughter, goddamn it! What the fuck were you and she up to here? The truth, Chris, all of it.'

'Jed, I can't do this right now. Something else has come up.'

'What else? What can be more important than finding out what happened to my daughter? She's *alive*, Chris.'

'Alive?' She doubted it very much.

'I've got an Australian journalist inside who's got a picture of her with Hassan bin Zayid in Zanzibar taken only a couple of days ago. Now I want you to level with me and tell me what kind of game you two were running up here.'

'Jed, like I said, something else has come up. Get out of my way. I've got to go upstairs and pack.'

He continued to block her, even though she gripped his forearm with one hand. 'No way. Answers first. And what are you packing for? I thought you were gone for a week. Why are you back so soon?'

She closed her eyes in frustration. 'Jed, I can't explain right now. But I *have* to pack some things and go somewhere. Something terrible has happened.'

'Yes, Christine something very terrible *has* happened. My daughter has been kidnapped by an Arab and is still alive somewhere in Africa.'

'Jed, an airplane crashed somewhere near here in the Zambezi River less than two hours ago. There are Americans on board and they need help. I've got to get out there and find the crash scene. I've got to get equipment, a boat and first-aid gear. This is serious.'

Now Jed was confused. 'How do you know, did you see it crash?'

'I got a call on my satphone. I was about to cross the border at Chirundu. Please get out of my way, Jed. I've got work to do.'

'Work? You're a zoologist, aren't you? What use is a scientist on a search and rescue mission?'

'Jed, I've got to get my things, please let me . . .'

He reached behind him and pulled an automatic pistol from the small of his back, where he'd tucked it into his jeans. 'Got to go get this, huh?'

She looked at the Glock in his big hand. He held it close to her face. 'What's this, Professor? The serial number of this pistol seems to have been filed off. Tut-tut, Chris. I know you had a pistol, but is this an illegal weapon, or was it issued like this?'

'You've been going through my things.'

'So, what do you need, Chris? This, or maybe your military tacsat radio and your night-vision goggles. Is it a rescue mission you're going on or a search and destroy?'

'I don't know what you're talking about.'

'Oh, yes you do. Teaching job in Virginia, my ass. Where, at Langley?'

'No.'

'Don't lie to me, Chris. You're CIA, right?'

She said nothing, just stared hard into his eyes. 'Get out of my way.'

'You're a spook, aren't you?'

'Keep your voice down, Jed. What was that about a journalist inside?'

Jed took a step closer to her, so close now his chest was almost brushing her breasts. The smell of her threatened his resolve. He took a breath, through his mouth. 'I made a call. Checked you out with an old friend at the 82nd.'

'Been spying on me?'

'Spying? Well, that's rich, lady. You told me you were a clerk in personnel during your time in the Army.'

'I was.'

'Yes, I know, but you left out the bit about transferring to C2. Military Intelligence, Chris. That part slip your mind?'

'It's none of your business what I did in the Army,' she said, unable to meet his accusatory stare any more.

He reached out and grabbed her chin between his thumb and fore-finger, turning her face towards him. 'Look me in the eye and say my daughter was not involved in any intelligence work up here.'

Chris closed her eyes again. 'Jed, we're wasting time, here. There could be people dead out there in the river. *Americans*. I've got nothing more to say to you right now.'

'Was having sex with me part of the plan, Chris?'

She shook her face free of his grip, drew back her arm and slapped him hard across the face.

He was taken aback by the force of the blow but didn't flinch. He wasn't ready to let up on her just yet. 'You couldn't stall me at Johannesburg with that planted magazine of ammunition, couldn't stop me from coming here and investigating. So what was plan B, Chris? Give me a good time and send me away with a smile on my face and a spring in my step?'

Tears welled in her eyes. For a moment Jed felt his resolve weaken. 'If that's what you think, then –'

'What I think doesn't matter. I'm tired of trying to figure you out, to second-guess you.' He held the pistol in front of her face again. 'What's this for?'

'Protection,' she whispered.

'My ass. No serial number, Chris, like the rest of your gear. I worked with Company guys – and women – in Afghanistan. Now, give me the truth or you're going nowhere. One way or another you're going to tell me about my daughter.'

Jed could see she was angry, was weighing up the need to get moving with the need for secrecy.

'All right,' she hissed. 'Yes, I'm CIA, a nonofficial cover agent. There, I've said it. I used my degree in zoology as a cover for fieldwork in Africa and Asia and ended up head of the Africa desk back at Langley. I retired from the Agency in 2000 to do my PhD and get into animal research full-time – turned out I liked my cover a lot more than my real job. After September 11, though, they came looking for me and I volunteered again. A lot of us came back after that.'

He nodded. It was the same in the Army. Plenty of guys had gone back onto active duty after the horror of the attacks on the World Trade Center and the Pentagon. 'So where does Miranda fit in?'

'She was a volunteer on a research program I was running. She'd also been assessed by the Agency as possible career trainee material. I was told to watch her, talk to her, and initially recruit her as a civilian asset. The idea was to put her on the payroll if she did well.'

'Jesus Christ. An *asset*? So you sent her to this place to do your dirty work.'

'There were legitimate reasons for sending her, both from a wildlife conservation point of view and for intelligence-gathering reasons.'

'What's the connection with bin Zayid? Did you send her up here to spy on him?'

'That's a crude way of putting it . . .'

'I'm a fucking crude guy when I want to be, Chris.'

'We've been monitoring Islamic fundamentalist groups and certain individuals in east and southern Africa since the bombings of the embassies a few years ago in Kenya and Tanzania. He came up on our radar because of his brother.'

'Don't talk to me about his brother.'

'What do you mean?'

'I killed him in Afghanistan, apparently.'

'You what? This is too weird. When did you find all this out?'

'A little while ago, from my reporter buddy inside. As usual they seem to know more than you spooks or the intel people.' His remark was not as glib as it seemed. More than once in the tactical operations centre in Bagram he'd seen a room full of staff officers glued to CNN to find out the latest about some incident or other. Nothing beat real-time news, and some reporters were as good as or better than intelligence analysts at putting together the pieces of a complex puzzle.

Chris let the insult slide. 'We were looking for some terrorist suspects that I believed were based in Zimbabwe. I figured Hassan bin Zayid had the money and motive to be the cell's financial backer.'

Jed took a pace back, easing the physical and psychological pressure on her, and lowered the gun. He rubbed his eyes. 'So you set my daughter up to get friendly with him.'

'It wasn't like that, Jed. Not what you think.'

'Not what I *think*! How the hell do you know what I think? The ranger up at Marongora said they were kissing, Chris. Was that *all*? Did she fall in love with the fucking target?'

'We don't use the honey trap, Jed. That was for the Russians, and James Bond. Miranda wasn't sent up here to sleep with bin Zayid. But I'm not sure what her feelings for him were – and that's the truth. I had my suspicions, but she wouldn't give anything away when she last came to see me. You found out about her trip down to South Africa a couple of weeks ago. It was a debriefing, both on her lion research work and on what she'd found out about bin Zayid.'

'And what did she find out about him?'

'Her assessment was that he was clean. He espoused no fundamentalist Islamic beliefs; he drank alcohol and liked to party; he had had relationships with western women in the past; he seemed genuinely shocked by September 11 and generally had a pro-western outlook on life and politics,' Chris explained. 'There was one other thing . . .'

'What?'

She looked as though she were weighing up whether or not to tell him. 'Miranda got hold of bin Zayid's brother's phone number. I heard Langley was putting an EW trace on him.'

'Jesus. So it was probably information gained by Miranda that helped the electronic warfare guys pinpoint Iqbal bin Zayid's terrorist cell and the surface-to-air missiles in Afghanistan.' The revelation stunned him for a second. He didn't know whether to feel proud of Miranda, angry at Chris, or to blame himself for the chain of events that was unfolding before his eyes. The dread pumped through him like snake venom.

'It's no one's fault, Jed. Don't waste time trying to pin this on some-one. Miranda did a job I assigned her and did it well. She also got pictures of two other men who passed through bin Zayid's place. They were subsequently identified as terrorists and terminated.'

He rubbed his eyes. Chris was right. Miranda had done her job. Chris had done hers, and he had done his. Even the reporter, Luke, had only been doing what he'd been paid to. 'There were some things at bin Zayid's place that didn't add up. Now they're starting to.'

'What? You went to bin Zayid's game reserve?' Chris asked.

'Yeah. They said he wasn't home, but he had a henchman who seemed to be hiding something. The guy had a Land Rover packed with enough guns and ammo to take out an infantry company. There were two of everything – packs and weapons – but only one goon. Maybe he was waiting for his boss to return. Also, someone tried to car-jack me on the way out of Zambia – maybe they thought I'd seen too much. If bin Zayid's turned, then it could have been because of his brother's death. There was enough information in the media to link me – and Miranda – to the killing.'

Chris nodded. 'Where are these pictures of Miranda, Jed?'

'They're on a photo memory card. I looked at them on Miranda's laptop, but I don't want to arouse Luke's suspicions by viewing them again.'

'Luke?'

'The reporter. He tracked me down halfway across Africa, from Zanzibar.'

'Gutsy.'

'I told him it wasn't Miranda, but it was, no doubt about it. I'm not sure he bought it, though.'

'Why lie to him?' Chris asked.

'I don't want any more publicity about this at the moment.'

'And I don't want him finding out about the plane crash yet either.'

'So, why was Miranda with this bin Zayid guy on his boat? Did she run off with her boyfriend and forget to tell anyone, or has he made the connection between her and the Company?'

Chris pondered the question, chewing on her lower lip. 'I got our people in the US embassy in South Africa to trace his movements, and Miranda's. They had records of him leaving Zambia and arriving in Tanzania – in Zanzibar. But there are no records of Miranda leaving Zimbabwe or Zambia, or crossing any other borders, for that matter.'

'So he got her to Tanzania illegally. The confusing thing is that in the pictures it doesn't look like she's being held against her will, and Luke said he saw the two of them kissing.'

Chris spoke her mind. 'Maybe he wanted her out of the way – out of the Zambezi Valley. He didn't want her dead, but he wanted it to look like she'd been killed by a lion. By presenting himself at customs and immigration he left a paper trail that showed he was in Zanzibar – legally. A good alibi.'

'An alibi? For what?'

'Nothing.'

'OK, then how come there are records of him crossing all the borders, but not Miranda? How do you smuggle someone against their will? How do you get in and out of an airport unseen these days?'

'He has a private plane and a luxury boat. If she's on board all he needs to do is get her to give him her passport so he can look after the formalities. It happens all the time over here. Tour operators take in a dozen passports at a time, for all their clients, and the immigration guys just stamp away. It's not like the States, Jed – there's no retinal scans or electronic fingerprint checks.'

'Yeah, so I've noticed. So, he's got her, illegally, out of the country, and made it look like she's dead. That doesn't sound good to me.' The pieces started to fall into place in Jed's mind. 'This plane crash . . . who was on board?'

'I've got to go, Jed,' Chris pushed past him. 'Time's wasting.'

He grabbed her again, by the shoulders. 'Chris, I'm in this up to my neck already. Miranda's alive and you're talking about alibis. Level with me. What happened with this plane crash and who was on board?'

'Please, Jed. Just give me the pistol.'

'Why? Worried about crocodiles?'

'I don't have time for smart-ass remarks.'

He dropped his hands to his side and looked into her eyes. 'Neither do I. I'm coming with you if it's dangerous enough for you to need a pistol. I don't want to see anything happen to you. Not now I've found you.'

He couldn't blame Chris for lying to him – he'd have done the same in her situation. His feelings for her were too deep for him to let her go now.

Chris took a deep breath. 'Lieutenant General Donald Calvert was on board that aircraft. It was shot down by a surface-to-air missile. There's a CIA pick-up team – hard asses from Special Operations Group – flying from South Africa to Lusaka by Lear jet as we speak. The Zambian army has scrambled a helicopter to bring them down here. I've been ordered to cross the border by boat and see if I can work out what's going on.'

'Holy shit.'

'Exactly.'

'And you think bin Zayid's involved? He's kidnapped Miranda as insurance and made it look like he's in Zanzibar.'

She nodded. 'I can't be a hundred per cent sure, Jed, but the last thing I heard, when I got the news about the missile hit, was that bin Zayid was on the move again, in his boat.'

'On his way to where?'

'This morning he docked at Dar es Salaam from Zanzibar. From Miranda's early reports we know he's got a ranch with a private airstrip just out of Dar. He could have flown there.'

'Was he alone on the boat? Luke saw Miranda with him on his cruiser.'

Chris took another deep breath and put a hand on his arm. 'As I said, there's no record of Miranda crossing any borders. Tanzanian customs have a record of bin Zayid entering the country alone, except for . . .'

'Except for what, Chris?'

'Two coffins.'

Jed turned, shaking her hand off him, and stared out towards the river. A row of lights glowed on the Zambian shore. The light of the explosion further upriver had died away. He felt nauseated. 'Who was in them?'

'The paperwork said two African males. I'd be surprised if the customs guys inspected the bodies. There's a plague in this part of the world, called AIDS.'

He was helpless. His daughter had disappeared again. Maybe she was dead for real this time. He couldn't stand around all night tormenting himself with myriad gruesome scenarios. What he needed now was to do something. Anything.

'One thing at a time,' he said. 'Let's go see if we can find Calvert. After that I'm going back to bin Zayid's safari camp. This time I'm going to get answers.'

'OK.' Chris hurried into the lodge to collect the rest of her gear.

Jed followed her. He heard the shower running and was pleased that Luke Scarborough was out of their hair for a while. The last thing they needed now was a reporter nosing about.

Jed, Chris and Moses had assembled in the lodge's downstairs living room. Jed, who had changed into black jeans, combat boots and a dark-green T-shirt, outlined his simple plan, quickly and quietly, worried that the reporter would catch them. His strategy had more holes than a poster of Saddam Hussein after the fall of Baghdad. Jed had briefed Moses on the crash and told him it was the work of terrorists. He'd also let on that Chris was a part-time US government employee, as well as a wildlife researcher. The tracker had nodded his understanding.

'Moses, I'll give you a chance to back out. You know we can use your help, but we can't order you to break a dozen local and international laws,' Jed said to the tracker.

'You are going to look for your daughter. You don't want to be eaten by a lion or killed by a hippo on the way. Without a trained guide you will be blind in the African bush.'

'OK, you're in, Moses. Let's do it,' Jed said.

They filed out of the lounge room and Jed and Chris paused by the concrete barbecue outside. Jed fished a half-burned stick from the ashes and rubbed black charcoal up and down his bare arms. He smeared more on his face, then anointed Chris with the rudimentary camouflage.

'I'll pass,' Moses said, and they all laughed. It did a little to ease their nerves.

They had decided the quickest way to the crash site was by boat. Moses had told them of a canoe safari operation that was currently set up at Nyamepi Camp, the main camping ground near Park head-quarters. The safari clients were not due for another two days and Moses was sure the operators would be in bed early.

Jed checked his watch, and the rising moon. As well as a boat he needed a weapon. Chris had tried to protest and Moses had looked doubtful, but he was not crossing an international border in search of terrorists armed with surface-to-air missiles while they had one pistol between the three of them.

A dull light glowed in the window of the headquarters building. Moses led them in a dogleg behind the building, close to the river, and they came to a wire fence, holed and sagging from past incursions by elephants. They followed the fence until they found a gap large enough for all of them to climb through without rattling the strands.

'We are in the staff compound,' Moses whispered.

Jed had a basic memory of the layout of the settlement. He recognised the low tin-roofed workshop building, with two partly disassembled Land Rovers resting on axle stands outside. Moses led them through a thicket of trees to the grey-painted storeroom where Miranda's possessions had been kept.

'Well, here goes the first crime of the night,' Jed whispered to Chris.

'Second. We're not even supposed to be out of the lodge after dark,' she corrected him.

Jed advanced, armed with a long-bladed screwdriver from the Land Rover's tool kit. He had told them that he alone would break into the storeroom. If he was discovered, then Chris and Moses could at least carry on undetected, while he faced the warden's wrath. He moved forward at a crouch, pausing behind a low shrub to look and listen. There was the faint sound of tinny music from a battery-powered radio in one of the staff houses. Paraffin lanterns burned warm and orange from a few windows. Chickens clucked somewhere nearby. He smelled wood smoke from a cooking fire and human excrement from the communal toilet block.

Jed sprinted for the storeroom building and, once he reached it, pressed his back flat against the asbestos sheet wall. He edged around the corner of the building to the door and scanned the courtyard and vegetable gardens between the housing blocks. There was no sign of movement. He moved to the door and placed the screwdriver under the padlocked hasp and staple. The lock itself looked secure, but the wooden door and frame were fringed with cracks from a mixture of damp and termite attack. He levered the screwdriver up in a sharp motion and felt the screws securing the lock start to wriggle free from the decaying doorframe. He put his weight under the screwdriver and the fitting popped out and clattered against the padlock. He looked again, wondering if anyone had heard the noise, and retrieved one of the dislodged screws from the ground and put it in his pocket. No one emerged from the houses. Jed pushed open the door, wincing as it squeaked on rusty hinges, entered the darkened building and closed the door behind him.

On his head was a harness of nylon webbing supporting a night-vision monocle. He reached up and flipped the black metal tube down and switched the device on. It was pitch-black inside the building, so he also turned on the infra-red illuminator, which cast an invisible beam the image intensifier could pick up. The interior was lit up for him in a wash of pale-green light. From outside, an observer would see nothing.

He turned his head from side to side, sweeping the walls until he found the gun rack. A chain ran through the trigger guards of all five rifles and around the solid wooden rack itself, the free ends joined with a heavy padlock. Jed had remembered the rudimentary but effective security and planned for it. From his belt he took his Leatherman and unfolded a small flat-head screwdriver. Years previously he had taken part in a NATO exercise in Arctic warfare with British Royal Marines and Norwegian Special Forces. A British soldier had shown him how the Belgian-designed Fabrique Nationale Self-Loading Rifle, known as the SLR, could be modified for a firer wearing thick snow gloves. The trigger guard was easily removed with a small screwdriver and Jed found the screws in an identical rifle in the rack. He removed them and the metal guard and this freed the rifle from the chain. He did the same with a second SLR.

Further along the wall he found a cardboard box full of assorted magazines for the SLRs and the AK-47s also used by the Parks service. He located only six of the metal, twenty-round magazines for the SLRs. The long-barrelled weapon was more accurate than an AK but, unlike the Russian assault rifle, could not be fired on full automatic. Jed and Moses would be a long way short of the firepower carried by their enemies, but it would have to do. Near the magazines was an already open wooden box of 7.62-millimetre ammunition. Jed knelt on the rough wooden floorboards, placed a magazine between his legs and filled it with twenty of the brass and copper-jacketed rounds. He repeated the exercise for all six magazines.

In another cardboard box was a pile of web gear which smelled of mould and damp. It was probably reject equipment, damaged or superseded by newer issues. For himself he found a chest rig with a broken buckle, but fixed that by knotting the shoulder strap to the waistband, and a belt and two ammunition pouches for Moses. Chris had agreed that she would carry only her pistol.

Jed shrugged on the chest webbing and put all six rifle magazines in the pouches. He fastened the belt for Moses around his waist, slung one of the rifles over his shoulder and carried the other at the ready position. He moved back to the door and switched off Christine's night-vision device to conserve its battery. Outside he paused to reaffix the hasp to the doorframe with the screw he had saved. The screw was loose in its hole and the whole lock would fall off the door again at the slightest touch, but to a casual observer it would look as though the building was still secure.

Jed stepped back out into the yard and a rooster crowed nearby. He dropped to one knee behind a rusted two-hundred-litre drum. The bird continued its alarmed call and a shaft of lamplight shot from one of the staff houses as a door was opened.

A man wandered out into the beam and called out something in an African tongue. Jed heard his heart beating in his chest. The rooster settled and the ranger took a couple of paces from his home, scanned the yard, then returned indoors. Jed sprinted back to the thicket by the fence where he had left Moses and Chris.

He handed one of the rifles, the belt and pouches, and three magazines to Moses. The African silently, expertly, cocked the weapon, checked to see if it was clear, fired the action and fitted a full magazine. Jed did the same. Moses nodded and they moved on.

Moses led them back out of the fence and around the staff village to the Nyamepi camping ground on the other side. Fortunately the ground was nearly empty. A party of two South African four-wheel-drive Toyotas was parked at one riverside spot, the occupants already asleep in foldout rooftop tents on each vehicle. The three of them crept inland, around the ablution blocks, to stay out of sight of a second campsite, where a Zimbabwean family had erected a nylon dome tent beside their truck. A man and a woman sat silhouetted against the moonlit Zambezi, savouring the last of their drinks beside a dying fire.

'The canoe operators set up at the far end of the camp, out of sight of the other campers,' Moses whispered. 'Watch out for buffalo. They favour these open flat areas beside the river.'

They skirted a green canvas dome tent and heard a man snoring inside. Jed smelled the cooling embers of a cooking fire. The canoes were lined up on the sandy bank of the Zambezi, tethered by ropes to hefty iron pegs to stop them drifting away if the water level rose unexpectedly during the night. The Zambezi was not tidal, but its level and speed were affected by the periodic release of water from the mighty Kariba dam upstream. Each canoe was about five metres long. They were painted dark-green and had the same shape as Native American canoes familiar to Chris and Jed from the Western movies of their childhood.

Moses launched a canoe into the river and jumped into the bow. Jed motioned Chris to sit in the middle, between him and Moses. He passed his rifle to her and pushed off from the bank. Moses was already paddling as Jed found his oar in the bottom of the craft.

'What about me?' Chris whispered.

Jed took the SLR back from her, grasped the foldout cocking handle on the left side and yanked it back. He let the handle fly forwards again, chambering a round. 'Take this,' he said to her. 'You never know what we'll bump into out here.'

She checked the safety catch was still on, and rested the long gun across her lap. 'The last reported position of the aircraft was near the western border of the Lower Zambezi National Park,' she said, leaning forwards so Moses could hear her.

The guide nodded. 'Not far. Less than a kilometre from here, but the going will be hard.'

They rounded the grassy island in front of the Mana Pools campsite and struck out into the main channel of the river. Here the faster flowing water snatched the long canoe and tried to turn it side-on to the direction they were heading. Jed dug the paddle in deep and hard, attacking the current like it was a living thing. Droplets of water splashed Chris's face as Moses's arms dipped and rose like pistons.

They approached another island and its width acted as a brake against the current, allowing Moses and Jed to ease their efforts for a few moments. Moses lifted his paddle out of the water altogether and Jed mimicked him, unsure why the tracker was stopping. Moses tapped three times on the side of the canoe with the blade of his paddle.

Chris leaned back and looked over her shoulder to explain. 'He's seen some hippos up ahead. Tapping on the boat lets them know we're coming and gives them time to move out of the way. We don't want to surprise them.'

Jed nodded. There would be enough danger in store for them without having to contend with a two-tonne territorial beast capable of biting their fragile craft in half. They left the shelter of the island, the hippos visible to Jed now as dark humps in the water. A few more had already waddled up onto shore to start their evening feeding, huge heads lowered and jaws chomping rhythmically.

The paddling was hard again back in the channel. After half an hour of more back-straining work Moses pointed ahead. 'Smell the smoke?'

They rounded a point a few minutes later and saw high-powered flashlights sweeping the water. The beam of one settled on an unnatural mound in the middle of the river. A boat was tied to the incongruous island and another motored slowly around, back over its shiny wake that had transcribed a circle around the scene at least once before.

Moses held up a hand to his eyes as a light stabbed his face.

'Who goes there?' a voice called, accompanied by the metal snicker of a rifle being cocked.

'Americans,' Jed called. 'Come to help.'

'I'm a US Government official,' Chris said.

The man was still wary. 'One man paddle. The other two keep your hands high, where I can see them.'

Jed paddled from the rear of the boat and Moses and Chris complied with the order. The man standing on the wing of the downed aeroplane had a rifle pulled firmly into his shoulder, the barrel pointed at Jed's chest.

'Where have you come from?' the man called. Jed picked up the accent of a European born in either Zambia or Zimbabwe. The man wore khaki shorts and shirt. An African in a matching uniform kept a hand-held spotlight trained on them.

'Mr Wylde?' Chris said.

'Who wants to know?'

'I'm Christine Wallis. I've been in Zimbabwe on some other business but the US embassy had instructed me to come across to your camp and brief Lieutenant General Calvert on regional security matters in two days' time.'

Willy Wylde nodded. 'I remember your name. The security people told me you'd be joining us soon. Have you got some ID on you?'

Chris reached into the concealed pouch hanging around her neck and under her shirt and found her passport. She held it up as Wylde's employee reached forwards to grab the bow of the canoe. Willy reached for the passport and compared the photo with her face. The picture didn't do her justice.

'I won't ask what your real job is or your branch of service, Ms Wallis, but I'm grateful you got here so soon. And who are your companions?'

'Moses is our guide, from the Zimbabwe side, and this is Master Sergeant Jed Banks, US Army Special Forces.'

Willy cocked his head and inspected the American. He was quite a sight, face and arms blackened with camouflage. Wylde saw the two SLR rifles as well. 'Well, I won't ask what you were doing on the other side of the border, or where you got your weapons. You all know you're breaking a half-dozen laws just crossing the river like this, I suppose?'

'That's the least of our worries now,' Chris said, businesslike. 'Where is . . . ?'

'There's no sign of the general, I'm afraid. Dead or alive,' Wylde said. 'There are two dead men inside the cabin – one's a secret service agent, according to his ID. His face and arms were badly burned, but it looked to me like he was either shot or hit by a blast fragment. The other man was cut quite badly. You can see the holes in the aircraft where shrapnel entered it. It was last light when we got here and the place was already swarming with crocs. They were falling over each other feeding.'

'My God,' Chris said.

Wylde nodded. 'There were blood smears on one wing and muddy bootprints. I'd been told that the general and his bodyguards were coming direct from a meeting with the President of Zambia and that they shouldn't be asked to do any walking over rough ground until they'd had a chance to change into their bush gear.'

'So the bootprints didn't belong to them,' Jed said, pre-empting the hunter but impressed with his quick deductions. 'How about the pilot?'

Wylde shook his head. 'Rob Westcott would have been in a starched uniform and spit-polished dress shoes for this flight. Bloody air force types always like dressing for the occasion.'

'So at least one other person was on the wreckage,' Chris said. 'Presumably one of the people who shot the aircraft down.'

'I suppose so,' Wylde shrugged. 'Whoever did this came to the boat and tried to set fire to it. I also found an empty distress flare canister near the cockpit door, and the whole wreckage still smells of petrol. These things run on aviation gas – kerosene, not gasoline. The blaze must have been extinguished when the aircraft settled further into the water and the cabin started to flood.'

Jed jumped onto the aircraft and made his way into the cabin. He recoiled momentarily at the stench of burned flesh.

'I've had four of my guys patrolling in Land Rovers since it happened, but I don't have an army of staff here. I'm doing everything I can,' Wylde said.

'That's good, Mr Wylde. I'm sure you've done all you can for the moment. We've got a team of agents en route from South Africa right now and our embassy in Lusaka has called the Zambian Government for help,' Chris said.

'I received a radio call from the police at Chirundu. They're sending a boat. It should be here soon,' Wylde said.

Jed poked his head out of the blood-spattered cabin, glad of the fresh air after the stench of the dead men. 'This guy's pistol is gone.'

'So, what now?' Willy Wylde asked Chris, clearly eager that she, as the only quasi-official representative of the US Government present, should take charge now.

'Have your men crossed into Hassan bin Zayid's property yet?' Jed butted in.

'Now I remember you. I thought you looked familiar,' Willy said. 'You were over here the other day looking for directions to Hassan's place. He's in Zanzibar, as I told you the other day.'

Jed repeated his question.

'No, my men haven't got to the boundary of my property yet, not that I've heard. I suppose you suspect Hassan because he's an Arab.'

Chris spoke up. 'Mr Wylde, you'll agree, I'm sure, that we have to consider all possibilities at a time like this. New information has come to light that sheds some doubt on Hassan bin Zayid's whereabouts. We'll need to search his ranch. When was the last time you spoke to Mr bin Zayid, Mr Wylde?'

'He called me last week, from Zanzibar.'

'What was the call about?' Chris asked.

'He wanted to know if I could take a party of tourists for him.'

'And you told him you were busy.' Chris looked at Jed.

'What else did you tell him?' Jed asked.

Wylde felt the hot colour rising to his cheeks. He swallowed hard, aware that people would remember whatever he said next well into the future. 'I told him I had an existing booking.'

'Bin Zayid knew about the booking,' Jed gave Wylde an accusatory stare, 'somehow. He called to confirm it was still going ahead.'

Wylde started to protest his innocence, but Chris cut him off. She did not need the two men fighting at this crucial time. 'Mr Wylde, no one is blaming anyone for anything. We've got some doubts, though, about Hassan bin Zayid and we have to see if he's returned.'

Jed said, 'His staff told me he was in Zanzibar as well. I had a look around his lodge and the place seemed empty. Does he have another house on the property?'

'No,' Willy said, shaking his head. 'He sleeps in the main lodge when he's there.'

'Is there anywhere else on the property he could be hiding?'

Wylde scratched his chin. 'There's a bush camp further down the river. It's rarely used. Most of Hassan's clients are rich Arabs who don't like to stray too far from soft beds and satellite TV. There's just a hut and a *braai* site at the camp, from what I remember. Probably a pretty good place to hide up.'

'Can you show us on a map?' Jed asked.

'Better than that, I can give you the GPS coordinates for it. Most of us landowners got together to mark out the main camps and points of interest in the valley a while ago. It helps us give references for anti-poaching patrols and our own guides in case anyone gets lost in the bush.' Wylde pulled a GPS unit from the pouch at his belt and scrawled through the pre-set waypoints.

Chris gave Jed her GPS and he copied in the point that Wylde had listed as 'cresbc'.

'Crescent Safari bush camp,' said Wylde, explaining the abbreviation.

'I'm going, Chris,' Jed said.

'You know you should stay here, Jed. You have no jurisdiction whatsoever in this country. I have to stay here and wait for the pick-up team to arrive, and I suggest you stay with me.'

'Moses?' Jed looked at the tracker.

'I am going with Jed,' Moses said to Christine.

Chris bit her lower lip. 'Be careful.'

'I will,' he promised her. 'You too.'

'I'll radio my guys and tell them to sweep through Hassan's land as well and to converge on the hunting camp. Leave your canoe and take one of my two motorboats,' Wylde said.

'Thanks,' Jed said.

'Good luck.' Willy offered a hand to Jed. They shook, the tensions of the previous minutes forgotten. 'If he's here he probably flew in.

I'd check the hangar at the airstrip north-west of the main lodge if I were you.'

Jed nodded.

Willy asked the tracker next to him to hand over his walkie-talkie and he passed it to Jed. 'Stay on our frequency. We'll let you know if anything turns up at this end.'

Jed said to Moses, 'Let's go.'

Chris was scared for Jed's safety, and for Moses. She wished she'd had time, even just a few seconds, to farewell Jed in private.

She took her portable satellite phone out of her daypack and turned it on. She flipped up the aerial and gained a signal. The phone beeped with a message. She dialled the message bank number and pressed the keys to start the playback.

'Chris, it's Mort.' He was shouting to be heard over the whine of a jet engine. 'We're at Jo'burg airport, about to board the Lear. I've got the team. We'll be in Lusaka by nineteen-thirty your time. Call me then with an update – I hope you're on the scene by now. We're R-Ving with a Zambian military helo when we land. Should be in your location no later than twenty-thirty. Have some good news for me when you call, Chris.'

Chris swallowed rising bile – the stench of the dead men inside the plane was becoming overpowering. She doubted she would have any good news in the next half-hour.

23

'Cut the engine: we'll drift with the current,' Jed said to Moses. The tracker nodded and there was silence. Moses kept a hand on the boat's steering wheel, ensuring the rudder was straight as they approached a bend in the river.

Jed checked the GPS again. The distance to the waypoint was two hundred metres and closing. Jed pointed to the riverbank and Moses turned hard on the rudder. The fibreglass hull of Wylde's boat made a shushing noise as it docked with the sandy bed of the river. Jed stepped over the side of the boat into water up to his knees and pulled the craft onto dry land. He scanned the tree line through his night-vision monocle. Moses knelt beside him. 'Clear,' Jed said. He checked the GPS and pointed across the jutting spit of land. 'Camp's on the other side of this point.'

Moses nodded and started to stand.

'I'll lead,' Jed said.

Moses shook his head. 'You brought me along because I know the bush. Let me do my job.'

Jed was reluctant to place the tracker in any greater danger, but he conceded the big man was right. 'Do you want the night-vision device?'

'I've been walking in the dark since I was a child.'

Moses moved off, pausing every ten metres or so to listen and peer into the engulfing gloom. The vegetation became thicker as they proceeded through the middle of the spit of land, alternating between thick riverine bush and huge, isolated Natal mahoganies that had weathered countless floods.

The guide stopped and studied the ground. Jed closed on him and looked over his shoulder. 'Leopard,' Moses whispered. The tracks showed the cat had crossed their path, following a well-trodden game trail to the river.

'Wrong killer,' Jed said. It was a timely reminder, though, that as well as the terrorist, or terrorists, there was the ever-present threat of running into dangerous game.

Moses resumed his careful pace. A few minutes later he held up a hand. Jed dropped to his knees and crawled forwards. 'The camp,' Moses mouthed.

Jed scanned the outpost. A thatched hut with a closed door. A barbecue area and woodpile. There was no light or sign of habitation that he could make out. He was almost disappointed. He had hoped to find bin Zayid holed up here. Still, he knew the man could be hiding anywhere. 'Let's circle around and check the hut. I'll go left, you right, OK?' he whispered, his lips pressed to the African's ear.

Moses nodded and the two men headed in opposite directions. Jed crept slowly, checking the ground in front of him before each careful placement of his foot. After every two or three steps he stopped and scanned the clearing and hut. There was still no sign of movement in the otherworldly, glowing green vista presented by the night sight.

It took Jed ten minutes to complete his measured sweep around the campsite. He stopped and knelt in the grass at the edge of the clearing, at the rear of the hut. He checked the bush to his left and saw Moses dropping to a crouch. He gave a thumbs-up and the African returned the gesture. Jed held his rifle to his shoulder and pointed it at the hut, waving the weapon from side to side. Moses gave a thumbs-up and raised his rifle to cover Jed.

Jed stood and darted across the five metres of beaten earth to the hut and flattened himself against the wall. He slowly moved his face to a shuttered window. There was no glass behind the wooden slats, just chicken wire and gauzing to keep out mosquitos and vermin. He smelled the hut's dank, stale interior. Through a broken louvre he could see into the room. There was no one inside, only a few storage boxes, including one behind the door, and a gas-powered freezer, whose hinged lid was open. He raised a hand and motioned Moses to join him. Moses crept to the hut then started to circle it. Jed met him on the far side, near the door, and saw he had picked up a shovel.

'I found this behind the hut.' He turned the tool in his hands and held up the blade of the shovel for Jed to see. He rubbed his fingers along the edge. 'There is damp earth still on the blade. Someone has been digging here recently.'

Jed started to look around the clearing, but turned as Moses said, 'The door is not locked, the padlock is just hanging here.'

Jed felt the hairs rise on the back of his neck.

'Moses, NO!' Jed hissed.

The explosive force of the grenade blast knocked Jed on his back and the shock wave threw a cloud of dirt and dust into his face, temporarily blinding him.

Moses had started to side-step away from the door, but much of the left side of his body took the full force of the grenade's fragments, shielding Jed, saving his life. The guide landed a metre from the American, also on his back. Jed coughed and spat dirt and rubbed his eyes with the back of his arm. Through involuntary tears he saw the state of his friend. Smoke rose from his shredded shirt and trousers. Jed got to his knees and crawled to Moses. He was a mass of blood and burns. The skin had been flayed from his left arm and leg and parts of his torso. Amazingly, though, the African was not dead.

'Moses, hang on, buddy,' Jed said. He grabbed the walkie-talkie slung over his shoulder and barked into it. 'Wylde, Wylde, this is Banks! I've got a man down. Repeat, man down, do you copy?'

Jed pulled his T-shirt off and wiped Moses's face while he waited for a reply. Blood oozed from a hundred tiny shrapnel holes across his body, and here and there splinters of wood from the shattered door poked out like obscene thorns, but the worst wound was to his chest. Moses tried to talk, but all that came out was a ragged, gurgling choke.

It was a sucking chest wound. Jed reached into his trousers and pulled out his wallet. It was a cheap waterproof plastic sheath stuffed with money and credit cards and then folded closed. He opened it and, using his teeth, tore off the first fifteen centimetres of plastic. He pressed the plastic down over the hole in Moses's chest and felt the lung sucking against the airtight seal. He wrapped the T-shirt around the guide's torso and tied it tight, holding the wallet section against the wound.

'Wylde, Wylde, this is Banks, answer, damn it!' he said into the radio.

'Wylde here, over.'

'Moses is hit. Grenade. Booby trap. He's bad. Tell Christine Wallis that there's no doubt at all now bin Zayid's our man. We'll need people to go over this place with a fine-tooth comb. Send the local bomb squad if there is one. He was here, but there's no sign of him now. I'm bringing Moses back in the boat. Got that?'

'Affirmative. I'll call the Italian hospital at Chirundu on the Zimbabwe side. They're already sending a boat. Chris says to tell you her people will be here in a helicopter any minute.'

'Roger that. On my way. Out.' Jed slung Moses's rifle around his neck and said, 'Come on, buddy, you're going home.' He lifted the bigger man across his shoulders in a fireman's carry and picked up his own rifle. Moses groaned in agony as Jed set off at a trot.

'Hold on, Moses, hold on. I'm sorry, man, but we've got to get away from this place.'

When they reached the boat Jed felt as though his legs were ready to give way. He lowered Moses in as gently as he could, but the tracker still cried out. 'At least you're conscious. Don't let go, man. Hold on for Christ's sake.'

Jed pushed the boat out into the channel, put it in neutral and pressed the starter. The engine caught first time and he backed out, turned, then opened the throttle full forward. The nose lifted high and he raised a fantail of water as he roared up the still moonlit river.

'Almost there, buddy.'

Moses opened his eyes and stared at Jed. He opened his lips to speak.

'What is it?' Jed leaned over and took Moses's hand in his.

'You asked . . .' the tracker croaked.

'What?'

'The most dangerous animal . . .'

'Doesn't matter now,' Jed said. 'You'll be fine, buddy. Doctor should be there when we get back to the crash site.'

'The most dangerous animal is the one with two legs. Be careful, Jed. Find your daughter . . .' Moses coughed, his whole body shaking with the painful effort.

A flashlight beam swept the water ahead of them. 'Over here,' called Willy Wylde.

Jed could see another silvery wake beyond the crash site. He prayed this was the hospital's speedboat, travelling from Chirundu.

'Bloody messy,' Wylde said, noticing Moses as Jed bumped the boat against the crashed aircraft.

'Jed, are you hit?' Chris cried in alarm.

Jed shook his head and looked down at his bare torso. He realised he was covered in Moses's blood. 'No, I'm fine. Is that the hospital boat coming?'

'Yes,' she said. 'How is he?'

Moses coughed again and bright blood spewed from his lips. He tried to sit up, then he thudded back into the hull.

'We're losing him,' Jed said, dropping to his knees. He scooped blood from Moses's mouth with his fingers, tilted his head back, pinched his nose and pressed his lips to the African's.

Jed blew five quick breaths into Moses's lungs and looked up. Chris was by his side and started compressions on the unconscious man's chest. Her hands were red and slippery in the moonlight. They continued CPR, her five compressions to every one of Jed's breaths, until the boat rocked under the weight of another person. 'Move aside, please, I am a doctor,' the man said with a thick Italian accent.

An African nurse and a younger man, a local intern, Jed guessed, carried on the mouth-to-mouth while the doctor injected Moses with morphine and set up an intravenous drip. Jed and Chris stepped back onto the wing of the aircraft. Wylde offered Jed a cigarette and he gladly accepted, spitting Moses's blood from his mouth first, then drawing hard on the nicotine to kill the bitter metallic taste.

'We heard the blast and I thought the worst,' Chris said.

'There was no sign of Miranda or Calvert, but the bastard had used the place as a base. We've got to get back there, quickly.'

'I agree, Jed,' Christine said, 'but let's wait for the team to arrive. We'll have back-up and the chopper. We'll find him if he's still in the area.'

'We're losing him,' the doctor yelled at his colleagues. He pushed the intern aside and started thumping Moses's chest. Chris turned away at the sight of blood being forcibly pumped from the man's many wounds by the doctor's ministrations.

Jed led her across the cockpit to the far side of the gutted aircraft. 'Miranda's alive, Chris, I know it. I can still feel her, in here,' he said, tapping his heart.

'How can you know?'

'Don't ask me how. Call it father's intuition or some crap like that. We know bin Zayid's involved in this now. We know Miranda was with him . . .'

Chris saw the longing in his eyes. 'He was seen with two coffins, Jed.'

Jed turned away from her and looked upriver. He tore the cigarette from his mouth and threw it into the water. 'Oh no,' he breathed.

'What is it?'

'Something you just said.'

'What? About Miranda?'

'The coffins! The bastard had been digging at the hunting camp. Moses found a shovel with fresh earth on it, just before the booby trap got him. I forgot about it while I was treating him. That's it. I'm going back.'

'Wait, Jed.'

'No.'

'Listen! It's the helicopter.'

Jed heard the distinctive *thwop-thwop* of a Huey and saw the reflection of the lowered landing light as it raced up the Zambezi River. He looked down at Moses, whose face looked peaceful as the morphine kicked in. From the beam of a medic's flashlight he could see Wylde's boat was awash in pink: blood mixed with river water.

'Your friend is stable, but I can make no guarantees. He must go into surgery – now,' the doctor said as he stood and peeled off bloodied rubber gloves.

Jed felt the wind from the chopper's rotor blades and looked up. The light blinded him. 'Stupid bastards,' he said out loud. There was enough moonlight to fly by and the landing light only made them all a better target. He looked away from the bright beam and turned on his night-vision sight again. He scanned the river.

There was a movement.

'Chris, get away!' Jed shouted. 'Wave them off!'

'What?' Chris could see Jed yelling but couldn't hear what he was saying.

Jed waved at the descending helicopter as it approached them. The copilot waved back and Jed cursed.

The man was standing on the riverbank, in the open, not more than a hundred metres from him. He was holding something long in his arms. Jed flicked his SLR's safety catch to fire and turned and pointed the rifle towards the helicopter. He aimed off and fired three warning rounds. He saw the shock in the pilot's and copilot's eyes and the aircraft bucked as the pilot flinched at the brilliant muzzle flashes and sound of gunfire.

Jed turned back to the shore and looked down the barrel of the rifle. The man had raised the long object onto his shoulder. Jed fired instinctively at him, one, two, three shots, but he lost sight of his target in a blinding flash of light that whited out the night-vision monocle's view.

He heard the missile's scream and, as his sight returned, saw it heading towards them. He turned and ran for Chris, who was now only a few paces from him, along the wing. He hit her in a flying tackle and they fell, entwined, into the river.

The Agusta-Bell 205, an Italian-built version of the ubiquitous Huey helicopter of Vietnam fame, had started to climb, away from Jed's warning shots. The projectile lit the night sky as it closed in on the chopper at a speed of five hundred metres per second. The missile veered slightly upwards to compensate for the change in its target's altitude and buried itself, exactly as its makers had intended, in the hot, inviting orifice of the helicopter's jet engine exhaust. The high explosive detonation destroyed the whining turbine immediately.

Jed held Chris close to him as she coughed river water from her lungs. He dragged her under the comparative safety of the aeroplane's wing. They watched as the helicopter rocked in the air like a bucking bronco.

Someone inside the stricken aircraft wrestled with the rear cabin's sliding door and Jed saw at least three people either jump or fall out of the hatch. Shattered engine parts sprayed the river surface on the way down, and Chris and Jed ducked as metal pieces ricocheted off the wing above them. A wave washed over their upturned faces as the chopper flopped, belly first, in the river.

The rotor blades, which had still been spinning, sheared off when they touched the river's surface and careened into the night in two different directions. Fire flared in the helicopter's cabin, and Chris and Jed heard tortured screams. Hippos started a panicked chorus up and down the river, and flocks of birds, alarmed by the chaos of the rocket and the exploding helicopter, erupted noisily from their roosts.

'Let's save who we can,' Jed said, half wading, half swimming.

Willy Wylde, who had sheltered behind the aeroplane's cockpit as the rocket hit, called out to Jed. 'Watch out for the crocs!'

'No,' Jed answered, looking back over his shoulder, 'you watch out for the goddamned crocs.'

'Grab a torch – a flashlight,' Wylde ordered Chris.

Chris spotted a light used by the medical team, who were all now cowering in the bottom of their boat. A nurse was bent over Moses, protecting him. 'Give me that,' she yelled at the doctor. He tossed the spotlight to her.

'Rake the water with the beam. You'll see their eyes soon enough,' Wylde said. He had picked up Jed's SLR and was watching the water intently. 'See? There! Hold the light steady.'

Chris saw the glowing, beady red eyes in the water and followed them with the bright beam of the battery-powered spotlight. The beast was about five metres behind Jed, who had nearly reached the downed, smoking wreck of the helicopter.

Wylde fired twice. 'Got the bastard. Find me another target.'

Chris saw the water roil as the crocodile rolled in its death throes. She swept the beam of light back and forth behind and around Jed. 'There's another!' she cried.

Wylde swung and fired. 'Two down.'

Jed was guided to the wreck by a burning object inside. When he reached the chopper he saw it was the body of the copilot. The pilot was in the back, unbuckling the harness of an injured man.

'This one is unconscious but alive,' the African pilot said. 'This other one here is dead. Broken neck. The others fell or jumped as we came down.' The man gagged at the smell of his dead comrade's burning body, but kept at his work.

Jed could not help but be impressed by his bravery. 'Let's get you out before the whole thing goes up in flames,' he said as the pilot passed the unconscious man through the cargo hatch.

Together, they dragged the man into the water. Wylde had started his second boat and motored out, with Chris, to meet them. They dragged the wounded man aboard, then helped Jed and the pilot in.

'Mort!' Chris said.

'You know him?' asked Jed, wiping water from his face.

'He's kind of my boss. He was the team leader.'

'Looks like he's hit his head, out cold,' Jed said. Blood welled from a cut on Solomon's temple. 'Might not be serious, but he's no use to you now.'

'I'm afraid it's back to us,' Chris said.

'And them?' Wylde interrupted.

Two men were swimming towards the boat, waving. Jed could hear their calls now. 'Thank God for small mercies,' he said.

Wylde turned the high-powered flashlight on the men.

'Turn that light out, for Christ's sake!' Jed yelled.

They all heard the shot from the riverbank and ducked low into the boat.

The head of the man caught in the spotlight snapped back and his body floated motionless.

'The shooter's still out there,' Jed hissed. 'Bastard.'

'Oh my God, I didn't realise . . .' Wylde began.

'Quiet,' said Jed. 'It's not your fault. Let's pick up the other guy and get these boats out of here. We can't land here.'

'We can go back to my camp, set up a base there,' Wylde said.

Jed guessed that Hassan bin Zayid – he was certain that was who was doing the shooting – wanted them to do exactly that. 'I think bin Zayid's left something behind at the hunting camp. I'm going back,' he said to Chris as Wylde hauled the survivor from the helicopter crash over the gunwale of the boat.

'That's crazy, Jed. I won't let you go alone.'

'Ms Wallis?' the bedraggled man said from the floor of the boat.

'Yes?'

'It's Jones, ma'am, from the embassy security detachment.'

'Oh, yeah, right. Harvey?'

'Harold, ma'am. If this guy's going after the bastard who did all this then he's not alone.'

'You still armed?' Jed asked him. He suddenly realised he had seen the man before. It was the intruder he had fought with at the hotel in Johannesburg, the man who had tried to delay his trip to Zimbabwe by planting the bullets in his bag.

Jones reached around behind his back and shifted a squat black submachine-gun back in front of his chest. 'Still got my MP-5 and two hundred rounds of ammo.'

'Good. Dry and clean your weapon as best as you can. We'll forget the ass-kicking I owe you,' Jed said.

'You hit me pretty good, too, Sarge.'

Jed gave the man a quick smile then said to Wylde, 'Willy, I want you to let us off onshore a couple hundred metres downriver, once we're out of sight of here. Me and Harold are going hunting.'

The hospital's motor boat chugged towards them and slowed beside Wylde's craft. The doctor's face was white with fear. 'How many more are wounded? We have to get this man to the hospital or he will bleed to death,' he said, nodding towards Moses, who had passed out.

'We've got one unconscious guy here, but he can stay with us. We might want him when he wakes up. Take him – Moses – back to your hospital, but come back or send another boat as soon as you can. We might need you again before the night's out.'

The doctor told his staff to sit tight and he gunned the boat's engine.

Chris spoke up. 'I'm going with Jed and Harold, Willy. Look after the casualty. His name's Mort Solomon.'

'Chris, you've got to stay with Willy,' Jed said.

'Says who? You've got no standing here, Jed. By rights I should be sending you back across to Zimbabwe before you trigger a major international incident.'

'It's a little late for that.'

Chris picked up Moses's rifle from the bottom of the boat and shook the bloody water from it. 'Think this thing will still work?'

'Only one way to find out. You got a weapon, sir?' Jed asked the Zambian helicopter pilot, who sat silent in the rear of the boat, staring blankly into the night. 'Sir?' Jed said again, louder.

'No, sorry. I think I should go back to the base camp, if that's all right with you, and make my report,' he said in a plummy, British-educated voice.

'Fine, sir, we understand,' Chris said. 'Maybe you can get us some more people from the Zambian armed forces. Another helicopter or two would help.'

'I doubt we have enough helicopters to waste on a foe armed with surface-to-air missiles,' the pilot said candidly. 'But I'm sure the army and police will be here in force later this evening. I'll call headquarters and make sure of it.'

'OK,' said Harold Jones, 'payback time?'

'If we're not too late,' Jed said.

24

Miranda Banks-Lewis woke up and screamed.

Her world was pitch-black. She scratched at the fabric lining of the box centimetres above her face, kicked her legs and banged on the wooden wall beside her. Her hands were tied in front of her with plastic cable and her ankles felt as if they were bound with rope. As her mind cleared she suddenly realised exactly what kind of box she was imprisoned in.

A coffin! She screamed again, a high-pitched, animal shriek that no one heard. As a child, she and her friends had read with morbid fascination horrific tales of people who had mistakenly been buried before death. Ever since then she had nursed an irrational, but all-consuming fear of being buried alive.

Miranda breathed deep and felt the plastic oxygen mask covering her nose and mouth. She traced the tubes from the mask to a steel canister between her legs. The cylinder was cold between her thighs. Her head ached and her back and bottom were slick with her sweat. She forced herself to stay calm and remember. She was wearing a dress, one of only two she had brought to Africa. She touched the thin straps on her shoulders, felt for the hem. Her feet were bare but she remembered she had packed her heels. Especially for him. She almost cried now at her own stupidity.

Hassan. The boat. Zanzibar. She realised now that she had been drugged. She recalled, with vivid clarity, the last thing he had said to her. She saw again his smile as he reached under his jacket and withdrew the pistol from his waistband. Her initial thought was that he was going to kill her, that he had found out the truth about her. Then she had seen it was a gas-powered tranquilliser gun, the kind he used on his cheetahs at close range. She closed her eyes and remembered the sting of the dart. She felt her belly, where the projectile had hit, and noted it was still tender. How long had she been out? A day, maybe two? That really didn't matter now. The important thing was that he had kept her alive. But for what purpose?

She felt around the casket again, looking for some kind of weapon. Shit. She wasn't trained for this sort of thing. Not trained for intelligence work at all. Miranda thought of Chris Wallis. Funny, pretty, intelligent Christine. Her mentor and role model in the field of scientific research and animal conservation. How thrilled she had been to receive the email from Professor Wallis inviting her to take part in her predator research in South Africa and Zimbabwe.

'Welcome to Africa. Every day's an adventure here,' Chris had said to her as she greeted her at Johannesburg airport. Miranda smiled in the dark confines of her underground prison, pleased with herself that she could laugh at the irony of those first words.

Miranda had worked with Chris for a month before the academic had let on that her work involved more than studying animals. Ostensibly Chris was researching the prevalence of man-eating lions in the Kruger National Park, in the areas bordering Mozambique.

'I guess it's not just immigrants who are crossing the border,' Miranda remarked one day as they drove along a dirt road in search of a collared female lion and the rest of her pride.

'What do you mean?' Chris replied.

'Well, if you were organised, and armed in order to protect yourself from the lions, this would be a pretty good smuggling route for drugs or diamonds or stolen goods, as well as people.'

Chris nodded. 'You're right, of course. What fences there were along the border are coming down with the development of the new trans-frontier conservation area that links Kruger with a neighbouring reserve in Mozambique. This new peace park has allowed animals to re-establish their traditional migration routes, but it's also made life easier for criminals . . . and maybe others.'

'Others?'

'Other people who want to cross international borders without being noticed. People who want to move weapons and explosives.'

'Terrorists?'

'Let's take a break here.' Chris stopped her four-by-four under the shade of a marula tree.

'There are things we can learn here other than how many people are killed by lions, Miranda.'

'Like?'

'Like more about the people who try to cross, those who succeed and those who don't. By talking to the rangers who find the bodies, and to the survivors. We're concerned when, say, a large number of Muslim Africans start crossing borders illegally.' Chris let her words hang in the air.

'We?'

'America. Our allies. The South African Government.'

'Are you out here for America, Chris? I thought we were here for the wildlife.'

'Both.'

'What do you do? Who do you work for?' Miranda asked, her mind racing.

'I observe, and I record my observations, the same as any other scientist.'

'You're ex-military, aren't you?'

Chris shrugged. 'You've read my bio, you know I was in the Army.'

'Are you still working for the Government, Chris?'

'Would it bother you if I was?'

Miranda thought for a few seconds before answering. 'My dad – my real father – is in Afghanistan. He's with Special Forces.'

'I know.'

She was surprised. 'How? I never told you. It's not in my bio. He even has a different name to me. I use my stepfather's name.'

'His name is Jed Banks. He's a good soldier by all accounts. Probably approved of you joining the Young Republicans at college.'

'You checked up on me! My politics is nobody's business and, for the record, my dad votes Democrat.'

'Now that I didn't know, but I check up on all my research students.'

'Including their politics and their father's military records?'

'Where necessary, yes.' Chris held her eye and Miranda did not want to break the stare first.

'Why are you telling me this, Chris?'

'You tell me.'

'What makes you think I'd want to help you?'

'I have no idea whether you would want to help me or not. But you're smart, you're fit, you've got a good eye for detail and you're mature. We're in the middle of a war, Miranda. Your dad's doing his bit . . .'

Miranda laughed. 'You almost had me then, right up to the part about "doing your bit".'

'But you will, won't you?'

'Are you CIA?'

'I could tell you who I work for, but then I'd have to kill you.' They both laughed.

There were no miniature cameras, no bugs, no poisoned lipstick or concealed weapons. But the job was real and Miranda took to it with the same dedication and professionalism that she had applied to her research work. Chris was pleased. In time, she revealed her real life story to Miranda.

'All I wanted to do when I left the CIA in 2000 was go to Africa and study wild animals full-time. But the government came looking for me again,' she explained to Miranda over a drink one night as they staked out a waterhole near the Mozambican border. Night birds called and in the distance they heard the mournful rumble of a male lion's roar.

'In the same way you came looking for me?'

'Pretty similar, Miranda. One of the Company guys in the South African embassy – Solomon, a real jerk – tracked me down out here in the bush. He wanted me to look at some satellite pictures of a vehicle that had been taken by one of our birds.'

'What were the photos?'

'They were of a pick-up truck. In the back was an RPG 7 – a Russian-made rocket-propelled grenade-launcher. It was kind of hard to make out as it was partly covered by a tarpaulin. The wind must have loosened the covering as it drove along. Solomon wanted to know what I could tell from the photo.'

'Surely they had someone who could identify a grenade-launcher?'

'That was the easy part. Solomon told me that the CIA badly needed to track down this vehicle, but the satellite had been unable to get a clear shot of the vehicle's licence plate. They needed any information that would help them place its owner. I identified straightaway that the truck was parked a couple of blocks from the US embassy. I'd been there a few times before to meet with USAID people about funding for my research.'

'Were they expecting an attack on the embassy?'

Chris nodded. 'Anyway, in the back of the truck there were three other things that the Company guys hadn't picked up on. First, there was a two-hundred-litre drum. Second, a coiled length of plastic hose, and third, a pair of red plastic triangles. What would that tell you?'

Miranda hadn't expected to be asked a question. She thought about the clues. 'The triangles are for Mozambique. I remember you told me that when I first saw them on the front and rear bumpers of your truck. You need them as warning signs in case you break down, right?'

'Correct.'

'So the vehicle was either from Mozambique or had been there recently. The drum is interesting. For fuel, I guess. That probably indicates the vehicle was passing through or coming from somewhere where fuel is a problem. Zimbabwe?'

'That's what I thought. The only vehicles I've seen in southern Africa that carry their own drums of fuel are Zimbabwean. The plastic hose –'

'Is used as a siphon.'

'Bingo. The Agency guys thought the drum was to turn the vehicle into a car bomb, in case the terrorists missed their target with the RPG.'

'So did they track down the truck?' Miranda asked, fascinated.

'The CIA got the South African Police to issue an all points for a red Zimbabwean-registered pick-up carrying a fuel drum. Two days later the vehicle was stopped in Pretoria. The driver was a Muslim Mozambican who had been living on a remote game ranch in south-eastern Zimbabwe. He was charged with possessing an illegal weapon – the grenade-launcher. He rolled over eventually and told the cops he and three other men had been training in Zimbabwe and planned to attack US diplomats in Harare and Johannesburg. His accomplice was picked up in Pretoria, but the Zimbabwean police were too slow to catch the other guys. By the time they finally got around to investigating the camp the place was empty.'

'Were they Al Qaeda?'

'A locally grown splinter group. There are still enough weapons kicking around Mozambique as a result of their civil war to arm a terrorist group with the basics. What worried us more was that one of the men hinted that they had been trying to organise supply of more sophisticated armaments – like surface-to-air missiles.'

'And you've got no leads as to where the other men went to?'

'Well, now that you mention it . . .'

By that stage Miranda was hooked. She found she desperately wanted to prove herself to Chris, to show her that she, too, could play an active, effective part in the war that had escalated with the destruction of the World Trade Center's twin towers.

Chris had a theory that the missing terrorists were still in Zimbabwe. 'Because of our government's frosty relationship with the regime we only have a very small diplomatic presence in the country. The Zimbabwean intelligence organisation, the CIO, watches our people and the Brits like hawks. They're paranoid that we'll try to covertly support their opposition party to overthrow the government.'

'So terrorists – even if they're not supported by the State – can pretty much do as they please,' Miranda said.

'That's right. As long as they're not breaking any local laws they can virtually carry on with impunity. Mozambique's a different story. The government there is doing everything it can to get back into the international community. The downside for Islamic fundamentalists in Zimbabwe is that there isn't a big Muslim community for them to blend in with. The vast majority of Zimbabweans are Christian.'

'I guess that makes it easier for you to look for supporters. Terrorists have to have money, right? Zimbabwe's economy is not strong, so they'd need a contact with access to foreign exchange, and maybe someone in the transport business or import–export who could move people and arms across borders quietly.'

'Good thinking,' Chris smiled, but then stopped.

'Chris, what is it? You look worried.'

'No, nothing. You know we can end all this right now if you're having second thoughts.'

Miranda bridled. 'I'm not the one having second thoughts. I'm ready to help in any way. I'm a big girl, you know, Chris.'

Chris nodded. 'You've just about nailed the profile of the guy I want to take a closer look at, only he's not in transport or import–export. He's into tourism in a big way.' Chris reached under the driver's seat and pulled out a large buff-coloured envelope.

'My secret orders?'

'Very funny,' said Chris as she removed a sheaf of papers. 'His name is Hassan bin Zayid. He's a Zanzibari–Omani or, to be precise, he's half Omani–Arab. His father started with a cafe and guest house on Zanzibar and expanded onto the Tanzanian mainland. The old man married an English flight attendant. The son inherited his mother's good looks and his father's taste in western women.'

'How do you know something like that about a person?'

'He made a pass at me the first time I met him. When the old man died, Hassan took over his tourism empire and expanded it even further, this time into Zambia, where he set up a luxury private game reserve. He's passionate about wildlife conservation and is breeding cheetahs in captivity with the intention of releasing them into the Lower Zambezi National Park. I met him at a Worldwide Fund for Nature conference here in South Africa. That's when he invited me up to the Zambezi Valley for a weekend. I got the impression straightaway that he wanted to show me more than his big cats.'

'Men. What a sleaze,' Miranda said.

'On the contrary. I very nearly accepted!' Chris flipped through the papers till she found a print-out from an internet website. 'That's him accepting an award for his conservation work from the Zambian Government. As you can see, he's very handsome. He's charming, has a great butt, and he's a multimillionaire who's nuts about saving endangered species.'

Miranda gave a little laugh. 'Well, when you put it that way, he sounds like quite a catch, except for him being an international terrorist and all.'

'Don't jump to conclusions. I've got nothing concrete on bin Zayid and there's no suggestion that he's ever broken a law either in Zambia or anywhere else. The thing that set the alarm bells ringing was his brother. Hassan has a twin, Iqbal, whose name came up in some intelligence we obtained from the Russians. Iqbal was on a list of Arabs who had been recruited to serve with the Chechens. Moscow suspected Iqbal of being the shooter who downed a heavy-lift helicopter full of soldiers near Grozhny.'

'I remember that incident. That was a dirty war, by all accounts.'

'There's no such thing as a clean one. Funny thing is that if the Chechens had started fighting for independence twenty years ago, America probably would have been in there supplying them with Stinger missiles. Don't forget that we helped give Osama bin Laden his big break in Afghanistan. The fact that Iqbal served with the *mujahideen* in Chechnya doesn't make his brother a terrorist.'

'But you're suspicious.'

'Hassan travels a lot between Zambia, Zanzibar and mainland Tanzania – he has his own aircraft and a luxury cruiser. He has money and maybe motive. On the plus side, he's a hedonist who likes wine, women and the good life – hardly your stereotypical Islamic fundamentalist. Still, I want to know more about him – who visits his game reserve, where his sympathies lie.' Chris handed over the envelope to Miranda. 'The print-outs are background on bin Zayid, his business interests and his conservation work. Amazing what you can find on the net these days.'

'*Amazing what you can find on the net these days.*' Hassan had said virtually the same thing just before he fired the tranquilliser dart into her.

It had been easy for her to strike up a friendship with Hassan bin Zayid. Christine had organised the visas and work permits she needed to establish a lion research project at Mana Pools National Park in Zimbabwe, just across the river from Hassan's lodge. Lower Zambezi National Park in Zambia and Mana Pools existed as a continuous ecosystem in all but name, and researchers and National Parks staff often hopped the river with the same impunity as elephants and other game that crossed the border when the water was low.

True to form, Hassan had welcomed the blonde, attractive Miranda into his world. Miranda had never used her feminine charms for trickery, but she surprised herself at how easily she could play the tease. She actually enjoyed the flirting and, as Hassan made no attempt to overstep the bounds of decency, she found herself looking forward to her regular visits across the river. He was as charming, smart, wealthy and good-looking as Chris had said. Miranda reported back to Chris via secure email that Hassan entertained clients from around the world, including some from the Gulf States. The Arabs who came to his lodge were not the wild-eyed fundamentalists she had at first expected, but rather corpulent sheikhs and wealthy businessmen with the same weaknesses as Hassan for good Scotch, fine cigars and, occasionally, western flight attendants from an Arab airline.

One night, while sipping a gin and tonic on the shaded deck overlooking the Zambezi, Miranda found that she was actually jealous of the attention Hassan was paying two attractive English women of about her age. The entire crew of a Gulf-based 747 was staying at the lodge as the guests of a millionaire friend of Hassan's, who had been a passenger on the flight to Lusaka.

'Gosh, who does a girl have to sleep with to wind up with a gaff like this?' one of the women chirped.

Hassan smiled. 'The owner might be a good start.'

'Ooh, you're a cheeky sod, aren't you,' the girl replied.

'Hold on, Jen, I saw him first,' her friend said, clinging theatrically to Hassan's right arm, nearly spilling his drink in the process.

Miranda caught Hassan's eye and he gave her a little smile and shrugged his shoulders. His message was clear. He had tried to woo her, but she had pointedly resisted his advances, while, in his view, seeming to lead him on. He was too much of a gentleman to push the issue with her, but too much of a man to resist the attention of the tipsy flight attendants.

Miranda retired to her room early and the shrieking laughter of the aircrew as she climbed the stairs to bed only made her angrier. She knew then that she was falling for the handsome target she had been sent to spy on. So far she had learned nothing about him that pointed to his involvement in any terrorist organisation. He had openly volunteered information about his brother and confirmed that Iqbal had served in Chechnya. During the discussion they had had about September 11 he had seemed genuinely appalled at the direction Islamic fundamentalism had taken.

'It's one thing,' he had reasoned, 'to support Muslim people who are fighting for an independent homeland in Chechnya, but no one can justify the indiscriminate slaughter at the World Trade Center. The people responsible make me sick.'

Despite her feelings about Hassan, and his apparent innocence, Miranda had felt duty-bound to find out all she could about Iqbal. Hassan had told her that he was currently studying at a university in Pakistan and teaching part-time in a *madrassa*, a school for Muslim boys. Hassan had said nothing about Iqbal being involved in the fighting in neighbouring Afghanistan, and Miranda sensed that he preferred not to know too many details about what his brother was doing.

Miranda had arrived early for a meeting with Hassan one day and, while she waited for him to return from the cheetah enclosures, she had taken his portable satellite phone from the battery charger on his office desk. She had scrolled through the numbers in the memory and found one with no name but with a country code prefix that she did not recognise. She had jotted down the number and had just stuffed the scrap of paper she had written on into the pocket of her khaki skirt when Hassan walked into the office.

'Sorry I'm late. Trying to steal my phone?' he had said with a laugh.

'Sorry, just admiring it. I've been meaning to upgrade.' She had felt her face redden, but he had said nothing more.

Miranda tossed and turned in her bed after the dinner party with the aircrew. That night she dreamed of Hassan making love to her. She awoke aroused and even more confused. The next morning, while the other guests took an early, hungover game drive, Miranda confronted Hassan on the deck.

'I haven't had a hangover like this since I was a teenager,' he said, sipping a tomato juice.

'You looked like you were enjoying yourself – you and your two friends.'

He laughed. 'Surely you weren't jealous?'

She shook her head. 'Don't be silly.'

'Of course, silly me, thinking you might care what I did, or who I slept with.' The smile had left his face.

'You're a grown man. You can do whatever you please, have whomever you want.'

'Yes, I can, but who I get is not always who I want.'

Miranda felt the anger rise in her. 'Well, which one did you sleep with last night?'

He smiled. 'Would it shock you if I said both of them?'

'No, Hassan, and neither would it surprise me.'

'Don't be a prude, Miranda. This is hard for me to say . . .'

She glared at him.

'It's you I care about, Miranda, but you don't seem to be interested in me, not romantically anyway. We have fun together, enjoy each other's company, and then when I think we're close to becoming intimate you turn your back on me. Is it because I am half Arab?'

'Oh, God, no, Hassan! Of course not. It's just that . . .'

'What?'

She could see confusion and maybe pain in his dark, soulful eyes. She didn't want to hurt him, but couldn't possibly tell him the truth. What truth? she asked herself. She couldn't tell him that she was spying on him, but there was another truth. 'I care about you, too, Hassan.'

'Maybe we need to get away from here, from the valley and your work. Maybe I need to get away from the lodge and the guests,' he said, smiling at his own joke.

Miranda took a deep breath. There was nothing more she could learn about Iqbal, and as far as she was concerned Chris's suspicions about Hassan had been unfounded. He was no terrorist, just a rich, gorgeous, sensitive heterosexual man who cared about endangered animals and loved life. Miranda knew she would have to go a long way to find another like him.

'Yes, maybe that would be a good idea.'

'We can take the plane, perhaps fly to Mozambique or even Zanzibar for a few days. I'd love to show you the beach, the place where I grew up. I'll sort some things out here later today. You go get squared away on your side of the river and I'll call you with the details tomorrow.'

Miranda did not call or email Chris Wallis and tell her Hassan was taking her to Mozambique. Her decision to keep the journey a secret flouted everything Chris had told her about the need to keep her informed of her movements, and of Hassan's.

They took off for Mozambique in Hassan's Cessna the following day. Miranda was concerned that they had not filled out any customs or immigration clearances in either Zimbabwe, for her, or Zambia, for him. Also, when they landed at the coastal town of Inhambane in Mozambique there was no sign of border officials and Hassan made no attempt to find them. He seemed to treat Africa as his personal playground.

'We're doing nothing illegal, Miranda, not running guns or drugs! Who cares if we fly over a couple of border posts?'

Miranda's worries about Hassan's disregard for international law melted away over a holiday cocktail of cold beers, grilled lobsters and the warm azure waters of the Indian Ocean. Hassan had booked two rooms at the four-star coastal resort, but after dinner and dancing Miranda lingered outside his door.

The kiss was meant to be goodnight, but it was the first time their lips had met and neither of them wanted the moment to end. Miranda found herself hungry for Hassan and opened her mouth to him. She let him lead her into his room, raised her arms as he lifted her top over her head, ran her fingers through his dark hair as he freed her breasts from her bra, and tumbled backwards onto his bed as he moved between her legs.

Afterwards, when she returned to Zimbabwe, she was too racked with guilt over her secret love and the pleasure he had given her to tell her CIA controller about the affair. When she met with Chris in person she let on nothing about her blossoming relationship with the man who was her target, or her illegal trip into a neighbouring country. Miranda became very good at concealing the truth.

After Miranda returned to Zimbabwe, she and Hassan made love every time she crossed the river to visit him. She had given up trying to find information to incriminate him and she was satisfied there was nothing more she could discover about Iqbal. Chris had seemed impressed and pleased with her discovery of the telephone number, however, which turned out to have the international dialling prefix for Pakistan.

'We'll track this number down. I'm betting that it's brother Iqbal on the end of that line and, if it is, there will be a lot of people interested in following this up. You've done a good job, Miranda,' Chris said.

Two weeks after her visit to South Africa Miranda was in Hassan's lodge when he surprised her with an invitation to fly to Zanzibar, to see the island where he had grown up. They would leave the next morning. They crossed the river in a rush, gathered some travel clothes and left everything else locked. There was no time to email or call Chris – not that Miranda would have anyway. She felt guilty, but she also realised her double, double life excited her, maybe even aroused her.

On the boat, off the coast of Zanzibar, Hassan told her of the death of his brother in combat in Afghanistan.

'It's amazing what you can find on the net,' he said to her. 'A friend called me in Zambia and alerted me to a feature article in a magazine about the death of a wanted terrorist. The action happened on the day my brother was killed. The American Special Forces team that killed him took along a wire service reporter with them. The man who killed my brother, who saved the reporter, is identified only by his Christian name, Jed. That's your father's name, isn't it, Miranda?'

She swallowed hard and felt the instant perspiration on her hands, the pounding of a vein in her neck. 'It could have been anyone, Hassan.' She realised now the stupidity of opening up to him as they shared their life stories in the way that new lovers do.

'It said in the article that this brave American soldier was more scared for the safety of his daughter, who was researching lions in Africa, than he was for his own wellbeing.'

'No!'

'The story speculates that the *terrorist* targeted in this raid was located by scanners that tracked his satellite phone signal. You liked my satellite phone so much, didn't you, Miranda? The day I caught you looking at it you said you wanted to upgrade. But when I checked your tent – yes, I crossed the river while you were playing with my cheetahs – I found that you had an American military tactical satellite system in your tent, along with various other sophisticated surveillance toys. I don't know any wildlife researchers in the world who would use their funding to buy a communications system that is designed for soldiers and spies to send encrypted messages.'

'Hassan, it's not what you think. I can explain everything.'

'You don't need to explain, Miranda. It's very simple. You hurt me, and now I want to hurt you. I tried the other day, when I fucked you like a whore.'

'Hassan, please, don't do this,' she begged.

'But you enjoyed it, didn't you? Moaned like a bitch in heat when I used you. It must have been as easy for you to play the virtuous little academic as it was the slut. Did the CIA teach you how to fuck as well as how to spy, Miranda?'

She backed away from him, tried not to think about her shame and to come up with a way to escape.

'Forget it, Miranda. There's nowhere to go on this boat. No one knows you're here. You and your father were doing your duty. Now, at long last, I must do my duty, to my brother. I would say that your father has every reason to be more concerned for your safety than his.' Hassan drew the dart gun, pointed it at her and pulled the trigger.

In the all-consuming darkness of the coffin, Miranda started to cry.

25

The adrenaline surged through Hassan bin Zayid's veins as he piloted the open-top Land Rover at high speed over a bump that caused all four wheels to leave the ground.

Iqbal would have been so proud of his work, he thought. 'You will be avenged,' he said aloud to himself. The rear of the vehicle skidded and Hassan wrestled with the steering to keep the four-by-four on the corrugated track. He ducked to avoid a low-hanging branch, taking heart from the fact that the bough indicated he was once more close to the bush camp. He turned off the engine as he crested a low rise and coasted down the opposite slope towards the Zambezi. He stopped the vehicle a hundred metres from the camp.

There was a light breeze from the river and he smelled the lingering remains of acrid smoke. He had heard the low crump of the exploding grenade as he waited with the surface-to-air missile for the rescue helicopter he knew would come. He smiled at his own cleverness. Nonetheless, he moved slowly and cautiously as he approached the camp. The American would probably come back here looking for him but, while Hassan had taken the longer route back to the camp by land, he doubted his enemies would have organised themselves in time to return just yet. Hassan heard a softly whistled bird call and froze in his tracks. Juma dropped from the branch of the tree above him, landing with the grace and surefootedness of a leopard.

'Two of them came, boss. One black, one white. The African opened the door of the hut and the grenade caught him.' Juma smiled as he relayed the story.

'Killed?'

'Wounded, but bad I think. Either way, he is one less to worry about.'

'But they came quickly. That means they are onto us. I see they haven't disturbed the coffins.'

When Juma had collected Hassan from the airstrip they had driven to the bush camp, with Miranda sealed in her coffin, alive but still drugged and on oxygen. They had buried her in the pit prepared by the African. It was a time-consuming but necessary part of Hassan's plot. He realised that with only him and Juma to execute the mission on the ground they would need a totally secure area in which to hold their captives during the operation. The coffins had seemed appropriate, not only for transporting Miranda and the surface-to-air missiles into mainland Tanzania, but also for hiding the hostages. If he and Juma had been killed during the inevitable rescue mission, which had arrived on cue after the general's plane was shot down, Calvert and Miranda would have slowly died in their wooden cells as their oxygen ran out. Whatever happened, the world would be rid of a military enemy of Islam and the bitch who had betrayed Hassan.

After capturing Calvert they had returned to the camp by boat and buried the general in the other box on top of Miranda's coffin and then covered him up before heading back down the river, by vehicle, to ambush the helicopter. Hassan's head told him that the reason for keeping Miranda alive, and not killing her outright, was so the organisation could use her as a second bargaining chip, in addition to Calvert. But in his heart, he knew he wanted to prolong her suffering, and exact his revenge on her, mentally and physically, over time.

'No, boss, they didn't find where the hostages were buried. But they found the shovel. I should not have left it out.'

Hassan nodded in agreement, noticing the spade against the wall of the hut. 'It doesn't matter. Soon we'll be gone. Dig them up.'

'One more thing, boss.'

'What is it, Juma? We can't waste time.'

'The white man, boss . . .'

'Yes?'

'It was the father of Miss Miranda. The man who came to the lodge.'

Hassan smiled. 'Don't look so worried, Juma. I'm pleased you didn't kill him before. I want him to live with the pain of his daughter's death. We will send her back to her father a piece at a time. Now, to work!'

Bin Zayid lit a cigarette while Juma dug. He was elated Jed Banks was in the game. In his wildest, sweetest fantasy of how this adventure would unfold he saw his brother's killer in tears as he realised that his actions in Afghanistan had been directly responsible for the death of his only child. Miranda deserved to die. It had been her information, he was sure, that had led the Americans to his brother.

There was only one shovel, but the coffins were not buried deep and Juma worked furiously. Hassan checked his watch. Both of them should still be unconscious, although if his calculations were correct Miranda would be coming to within the hour. That was fine by him. He wanted her awake when they arrived in Mozambique so he could use her. He was on the edge now, a freelance soldier in a war without boundaries. He would probably never return to his life of spoiled leisure, but he was free to indulge new passions, new vices above and beyond the laws of men. He had allowed himself to experience real intimacy with Miranda and then found out she had been spying on him, using him. His weakness had cost his brother his life. Hassan would seek retribution in the same way that Iqbal would have. He remembered his brother's stories about how he had tortured Russian prisoners for information during the fighting in Chechnya. Hassan had been shocked, but also surprised to find himself fascinated and excited. Iqbal had spoken of the experience in the same way that a boastful man recounts his sexual conquests.

As he imagined the degradations he would submit Miranda to he found himself becoming physically aroused. In his mind's eye he saw the final flash of the knife and felt her body spasm one last time.

'Faster, Juma,' he said, checking his watch again.

The plan, at least his part in it, was going more or less according to schedule. He was annoyed that Banks had made the connection between him and the attack on Calvert's aircraft so quickly, but he had left the booby-trapped grenade in the hut in case of just such an eventuality. As far as he knew, the man still believed his daughter had been killed by a lion. Hassan smiled to himself. The father's pain would be even greater when he learned that she had been alive and within his reach, possibly even under his very feet, and he had failed to save her.

Once Juma had finished they would load the coffins into the Land Rover and then drive to the airstrip. With Miranda and the general on board they would take off for a remote airfield in Mozambique, on the edge of Lake Cahora Bassa, where they would be met by two locally born members of the organisation to which Hassan now belonged. They would video General Calvert and Miranda, proving they were alive, and send the tape to an Arab-language satellite television station, along with a demand for the American Government to release all the remaining Al Qaeda and Taliban prisoners still held at Guantanamo Bay, in Cuba. Hassan realised that the parading of Calvert, as a well-known public figure, would generate media coverage for the cause, but that the Americans would not free anyone in order to save him. He was an ex-soldier, and the Americans would probably accept his death and try to glorify him as a martyr to their cause. Miranda, however, was a pretty young woman. After they had beheaded Calvert and released the tape of his execution, they would release a video of Miranda, alive and crying. Public opinion in America and elsewhere in the world might just turn at the prospect of a young woman being dismembered on television or the internet. But, even if the Americans did release some or all of the prisoners, Hassan had no intention of letting Miranda live.

Hassan had originally planned to weather the storm and continue to hide behind the fiction that he was still in Zanzibar. However, he realised that somehow the Americans, including Miranda's father, had

384

linked him to the attack much sooner than he expected. So what? he mused. He was committed to the fight now and he would continue his jihad until he died. Africa was a big continent and he had cash enough in his pack to last a couple of years at least. He had withdrawn a hundred thousand US dollars from one of the family accounts before leaving Stone Town.

'Finished, boss,' Juma said. The back of his fatigue shirt was black with sweat and his face was streaked with dirt.

When she heard the digging start, Miranda scratched harder, ignoring the pain and the blood on her fingertips.

After her tears had subsided she had resumed her blind search of the interior of the coffin. Inside the casket, about halfway along on the right-hand side, was a metal orb around the size of a tennis ball. On top was a smaller metal cylinder. It was fastened to the wall of the box with a band of thin, flexible metal, which felt as though it had been nailed to the wood. Her first thought was that the nails would make a weapon of some sort if she could remove them. As her fingers moved higher, to the top of the ball, she felt a metal handle, a small device of some kind on top and a ring that jangled when her fingers brushed it. She gasped. Forget the nails, she had seen enough action movies to realise she was sharing the box with a hand grenade.

Miranda snatched her hands away in panic. She took a breath and forced herself to think calmly. She touched it again, gently, in case her actions somehow set it off. Attached to the pin was a length of cord, which she carefully followed. At the end of the string was a loop attached to a hook that had been screwed into the lid of the coffin.

A booby trap. She knew enough about grenades to know that when you pulled the pin a lever flew off and the thing detonated a few seconds later. Exactly how long it would take, though, she had no idea. She supposed the fuse could be altered, so that the grenade exploded sooner. Miranda guessed that Hassan had rigged the simple activation device of string and hook so that in the event that she was rescued, whoever opened the coffin first would accidentally pull the pin from the grenade and kill both her and her rescuer. She shook her head in disgust at his deviousness. If, however, Hassan got to her first – and she assumed he wanted her alive for a little while longer for some purpose – he could easily disarm the trap by lifting the lid a few centimetres and unhooking the string before it became taut.

Miranda unhooked the cord herself and set to work trying to loosen the grenade from the band holding it to the coffin wall. Screw him. One way or another he was going to be on the receiving end of his own cleverness. The risk was that if she pulled the pin on the grenade and threw it at him then she, too, would be blown up instantly. However, she realised that if Hassan got to her before anyone else it would only be a matter of time before he killed her anyway. Better to die on her own terms than allow him to torture or abuse her. Her calmness surprised her.

She lay still for a second then realised that she could not waste any more time. She wobbled the grenade backwards and forwards, using its bulk and weight to loosen the nails that held it secure. She hooked her fingers into the edges of the banding, wincing as the jagged-edged sheet metal sliced the skin underneath her fingernails. The digging noises were getting louder now and her whole body shuddered in fright when the blade of the shovel clanged on the lid above her.

Gambling that the noise of the digging would muffle her work, she pulled again on the grenade, as hard as she could, and felt one, then the other nail on one side of the band pop loose. She bent back the metal strip and the grenade dropped with a thud on the floor of the coffin beside her. Miranda screwed her eyes shut, fearing the thing would go off. It just lay there, though, cold and hard beside her forearm. She reached across her torso, awkwardly because of her bound hands, grabbed it and deposited it between her legs. The shovel grated back and forth across the lid now and she heard muffled voices.

Miranda realised that if it was Hassan, the first thing he would do after opening the lid would be to unhook the booby trap. She fumbled with the grenade and, after several attempts, managed to untie the string from the pin.

Suddenly she was jolted. As the coffin was lifted her head flicked forwards and banged painfully on the lid. The grenade rolled along the floor between her legs, but she trapped it under her calves before it reached the other end of the box. Carefully, so as not to make a sound, she tied the free end of the string to the metal band, which was still fixed to the wall of the casket. She slipped the loop of the cord back onto the hook in the lid.

Hassan moved to the edge of the shallow grave and grabbed the carry handles at the head of the coffin. 'One, two, three! She's a heavy bitch.'

Juma lifted the foot of the coffin and, between them, they raised the box out of the ground and dropped it on the edge of the grave.

'Shall I disarm the grenade, boss?' Juma asked.

'We haven't time now. We can do that once we get them into the aircraft. Hurry, let's get her into the Land Rover.'

The two men lifted the coffin again and, backs bowed with the weight, carried it to the open tailgate of the four-by-four. 'Right, let's get the VIP,' Hassan said.

Miranda strained to hear their brief exchanges. Juma had always given her the creeps. She was surprised that Hassan mentioned another person. A VIP? She had the grenade tucked between her thighs now, her hands down over her crotch. When he eventually opened the lid it would take him only a second to notice that his trap had been disarmed. She would have to strike immediately.

At first, as Miranda thought in the coffin about the chain of events that had led to this, she had cried. Afterwards, as she worked on unfastening the device he had set to kill her, she became angry at what he had done to her and mad at herself for falling for him. Miranda wondered if he intended to use her for propaganda or ransom purposes. Also, she thought of her father. Was Hassan gunning for him as well? She tried to put herself in Hassan's shoes, to imagine how she would feel if he had used her to get information that eventually led to the death of her dad or mom. She had been so eager to follow in Chris Wallis's footsteps and to succeed as an 'asset' that she hadn't thought through all the possible consequences of her decision and the tasks she had carried out. Now she just felt stupid and afraid.

There was a scraping noise next to her and something bumped against the box. A vehicle engine started and she felt the vibrations of the motor through her back and bottom. She rocked from side to side as the vehicle started to move along a bumpy track.

If there was another person in the same predicament as she, a second prisoner in a coffin, then his or her casket would probably be rigged to explode as well. She needed to find a way to warn any potential rescuer, in the event that she was killed in her bid to thwart Hassan and Juma. She felt for the metal banding again and slid out one of the nails that held it in place.

After a while – she couldn't tell how long – the vehicle turned off the track onto smoother ground. It came to a halt.

'Open the aircraft up. I'll check on the pair of them. I don't want them waking up in midflight,' she heard Hassan say.

They must be at an airstrip. Inside her coffin Miranda reached between her legs and picked up the grenade. She tugged a little on the pin, testing its resistance. As her hands were tied she worried that she would be unable to pull it all the way out. Again she recalled an old war movie and slowly moved her hands to her mouth.

Hassan took his Leatherman from its belt pouch and flipped out a screwdriver blade. He crouched over the casket and undid the screws fastening the lid of Miranda's coffin, then hooked his fingers under the lip of the cover. Gently, he raised it a few centimetres.

Miranda had pulled the oxygen mask from her face. She smelled the sweet, dry night air. Even though it was dark outside she still had to blink a couple of times to get used to the comparative brightness cast by the moon and stars. A hand moved under the lid, feeling for the string. She felt the free end of the cord brush her torso as he unhitched it. Miranda tensed and, clutching the grenade, pressed her knuckles against the lid.

She heard Juma say, 'Ready here, boss.' His voice sounded muffled. Perhaps he was inside the aeroplane.

'OK. I'll just check on the girl,' Hassan replied.

This was it. She pressed her hands against the coffin lid, and when she felt Hassan start to lift it, she shoved up as hard and as fast as she could. She glimpsed the moment of shock on his face and heard him yelp as the edge of the wood slammed into his nose. Then he was gone, tumbling back over the edge of the pick-up's tray, to the ground.

Miranda sat bolt upright and looked either side of her. She blinked again and saw Juma, wide-eyed, inside an aircraft – bin Zayid's plane. Of Hassan, there was no sign, although she had heard him cry out. She raised the grenade to her mouth again, bit down on the pin with her teeth and yanked the device away from her. She swung her bound hands to the right, then back to the left, letting go of the grenade at the end of the movement, sending it straight through the open door of the Cessna.

Hassan dragged himself to his feet. He moved to the back of the four-by-four, his face clouded with confusion and shock at the sight of her sitting up in the coffin staring at him.

'Grenade!' Juma yelled.

Miranda had no idea how long it would take for the bomb to go off. She lay back down inside the coffin and prayed it would be soon.

Hassan, blood pouring from his broken nose, started to turn to escape the blast. Juma was too far back inside the aircraft to get out in time. He groped blindly around the floor of the aircraft looking for the grenade. It was within his reach, only a few centimetres from his face, when the blast hit him.

The metal casing of the device and the crimped coils of wire wound around the explosive core were designed to shatter on detonation. The flying shards and the force of the blast took off most of the African's head.

Hassan dived for the ground, but the fuse had been set to three seconds: not enough time for him to reach the comparative safety of the dirt. While Juma, the Cessna and the side of the Land Rover absorbed most of the blast and the fragments, Hassan's left arm and the exposed side of his torso suddenly felt as though they had been pierced by a dozen red-hot needles. He fell and writhed in the dust, his ears ringing from the blast.

Miranda felt the Land Rover rock as a spray of metal projectiles thudded into its side panels. The tray of the pick-up and the thick wooden walls of the coffin saved her from the shrapnel, but the blast temporarily deafened her.

After a moment she pushed open the lid of the coffin, which had been blown closed, and sat up once more. She brought her knees up and tried to stand, but her limbs were tired and cramped and she fell on her first attempt, landing sprawling across the coffin next to her. She smelled fuel and saw aviation gas draining from a dozen holes in the high wing of the Cessna. Good, she thought. The interior of the aircraft was a gory mess of blood and chemical-smelling smoke. The seats and part of the instrument panel had been peppered with shrapnel, and Juma's blood and brains coated the cabin walls and windows.

She turned away quickly, shaking her head to clear her hearing. Behind her, in the back of the Land Rover, was a pack. Strapped to its side was a hunting knife in a sheath. She crawled across the unopened casket and reached for the weapon. She slid it out and began sawing through the rope binding her ankles. As the strands parted, the blood returned to her numbed feet, stinging them.

She looked up and saw Hassan staggering to his feet. He lunged for her, but she leaped over the opposite side of the vehicle. She winced and cried out as her feet hit the ground. She dropped to one knee and rammed the knife into the front driver's-side tyre. The air exploded with a loud hiss.

'Bitch!' Hassan cried.

'What do you want with me, Hassan?' she said, brandishing the knife in front of her with her bound hands.

'You'll pay for this,' he said.

She bobbed her head up and looked in the front of the vehicle. There, between the seats, was an assault rifle with a curved magazine. She dropped the knife and reached for it, but Hassan, despite his wounds, was quicker than she. He leaned across the passenger's seat and grasped the stock of the AK-47 just as Miranda's fingers reached it. He cocked the rifle and pointed it at her.

'Don't move and don't say a word.'

He walked around the front of the vehicle, all the while keeping the barrel pointed at her. Miranda looked around her, but she was trapped again. At least I got one of them, and disabled his vehicle and aircraft as well, she thought.

Hassan looked inside the Cessna and up at the leaking fuel tank. He shook his head. 'Think you're clever, don't you?'

She smiled at him.

Hassan drew back the rifle, reversed it and lashed out at her, catching her in the stomach with the butt. Miranda gasped, doubled over in pain and dropped to her knees. He grabbed a fistful of her hair and dragged her to her feet again. Tears streamed from her eyes.

'Don't dare mock me, Miranda, or things will get worse for you.'

'Can't . . . get . . . much worse,' she stammered.

'Oh, yes it can, baby. Just wait and see.'

Miranda fought to regain her breath and watched as Hassan inspected the Land Rover. The vehicle had taken a load of shrapnel but would probably still start. He swore, however, when he examined the spare tyre. As with many safari vehicles the fifth wheel was mounted inside the rear cargo area for easy access, and bolted to a sidewall. The top third of the tyre protruded above the top of the wall and this had been riddled with shrapnel. It was soft to the touch. With two flat tyres the vehicle was virtually useless. She was proud of how she had stopped him, but very scared. It wasn't over yet.

'So, now we walk,' he said. 'But first I need to shut that pretty mouth of yours.' He pushed Miranda to the ground, on her back, and planted his boot on her belly to stop her from moving. He reached into his pack and pulled out a roll of duct tape, laid down his rifle, tore off a strip of tape and fastened it across her mouth. He leaned close to her, until his lips were only a few centimetres from her face. 'Pull it off and I'll shoot you, understand?' She nodded.

He looked at the second coffin and raised the butt of the AK-47 to his shoulder, aiming at the head of the box. Miranda looked up and saw what was happening. Hassan was going to kill whoever was in the second coffin. She rolled onto her side and managed to stand. She started to run.

Hassan noticed her movement with his peripheral vision and turned and pointed the rifle at her back. 'Miranda! Stop or I'll kill you now!'

Miranda sprinted as fast as her stiff legs and aching feet would allow. She expected the bullet to ram into her any second. She wondered how much it would hurt, and if she could survive it.

Hassan heard the sound of an approaching vehicle. Miranda was in the trees now on the edge of the airstrip. He had to catch her. Cursing himself for hesitating, he set the selector switch on the AK-47 to automatic, aimed at the head of the coffin again and pulled the trigger. One shot rang out, then the weapon jammed. He grabbed the magazine to remove it and noticed the metal was hot. He held it up to the moonlight to inspect it and saw for the first time that the rifle had been hit by three fragments of metal from the grenade. The shrapnel had probably severed the spring inside the magazine that fed bullets into the chamber. More bad luck.

He tossed aside the useless magazine and snatched up the canvas chest rig containing his spares. The vehicle engine noise was louder now. He had to run if he was going to catch Miranda. He hoped that either the one shot he had fired or the booby-trapped grenade still inside the coffin would finish off the general.

The pain in his arm and side was becoming more intense. He tried to wiggle his fingers and found that, while he still had full mobility, the action made his wounds hurt more. Blood oozed from the holes in his side, staining his ragged shirt. Painful as they were, the fragments were just below his skin and had not come close to any major organs. He shrugged into the chest rig and ran after Miranda.

26

Jed crouched by the open grave and waved to the others to join him.

'They've gone,' he said, 'by vehicle. Tracks of two men, by the look of it.'

Chris and Harold Jones, the surviving CIA agent from the downed helicopter, stood at the edge of the hole.

'Only one hole, Jed,' Chris said, stating the depressing fact that was on Jed's mind.

'He could have had both coffins buried in the one grave,' he countered. 'It's deep enough.'

'I hope you're right,' she said.

'What now?' asked Jones.

'We follow the tracks. Wylde said there was an airfield on the ranch. I'm betting these tracks will lead us there.' Jed pulled Wylde's walkie-talkie from the pocket of his fatigue trousers and called the lodge owner's head scout, who was driving a Land Rover onto bin Zayid's ranch. 'Do you know where the airfield is on this ranch, over?' he said into the radio.

'Yes, sir. The road back to the lodge goes via the landing strip,' said the scout above the noise of his Land Rover's engine.

'Meet us there. We think the suspects are headed that way. Be careful. Out.'

They moved as fast as they dared, at a slow jog. Jed kept his rifle up high, the butt on his shoulder, his thumb on the safety catch, ready to return fire immediately. He figured bin Zayid was on the lam now, and that the terrorist's top priority would be to get off the ground. Still, he looked down every few steps in case a trip wire had been strung across the road.

'Down,' Jed hissed when they heard the crump of an explosion.

'Grenade?' Chris asked.

'Yeah. Not too far ahead, maybe three hundred metres or so. You ever been in combat, Jones?'

'No, sir.'

'Well, it's game on, son. Stay low, pick your target and aim low. Remember, he's got hostages with him,' Jed said. 'If you shoot my daughter, I'll kill you. OK?'

'Yes, sir.'

They pressed on, faster now. Jed's heart belied his calm exterior. It felt as though it would burst from his chest. A vein throbbed hard in his neck. He tried not to think the worst.

The crack-thump of a gunshot. 'AK-47,' Jed said. 'Close. Don't worry, Jones, it wasn't fired at us. Not yet, at least. Fan out, line abreast, on my left and right. Don't get ahead of me, though. That looks like the airstrip ahead.'

From his pocket he heard the radio break squelch. 'One this is two, over,' the African voice said.

'Go, two.'

'Explosion and gunfire on the airstrip. I'm in the trees at the north end. I can see an aircraft and a vehicle. Some smoke drifting this way. No sign of any people, though.'

'Hold where you are,' Jed ordered. 'We're moving in from your right. Be prepared to put down covering fire on my command, over.'

'Roger, one. Two, out.'

'OK, showtime,' Jed said. They ran across the width of the airstrip. Jed motioned with his hand for Chris and Jones to hold and cover him once they were a hundred metres from the aircraft and Land Rover. He moved forwards alone.

The smoke had cleared, but the smell of fuel was still strong. Jed saw the punctured wing tank, the flat tyre on the Land Rover and the ruined spare. He smelled blood and saw the ghastly spatters on the interior of the damaged Cessna. He steeled himself for what he would see inside. The sight was shocking, but he breathed a sigh of relief that the body was not Miranda's. He waved for the others to join him and called in Wylde's scouts on the radio. He peered into the rear tray of the Land Rover pick-up and saw the two caskets – one open and one closed. He didn't move.

'Shit, let's get that coffin open,' Jones said, climbing into the truck. 'There's a bullet hole in it.'

'Wait!' Jed barked. 'I've lost one man to a booby trap already tonight.'

'Jed, there's blood on the inside lining of this one,' Chris said, leaning into the back of the vehicle so she could better inspect the empty coffin. 'It looks like an arrow, painted in blood.'

Jed pulled out his Leatherman. With the penknife blade he lifted a flap of torn cloth lining at the tip of the bloody arrow. 'Anyone got a flashlight?'

'Here,' said Jones, taking a small torch from his pocket.

'There's something scratched in the wood.' Jed focused the beam of light and read aloud: '*Grenade inside. Lift lid two inches and unhook string. Am alive. MBL.*'

'Miranda!' Chris said.

Jed didn't know how to feel. He had been mentally preparing himself to find Miranda's body in the unopened coffin. Now it looked like she was missing again, and probably wounded. 'She must have disarmed her own trap and killed the other guy.'

'Gutsy lady,' Jones said.

Wylde's two scouts pulled up in their vehicle and inspected the shattered aircraft. 'It is hard to tell, because of the wounds to the head, but by his build I would say this is Juma. He works for Hassan bin Zayid,' one of the men said.

'Same guy that tried to kill me, probably, but he's history.' Jed rapidly unfastened the screws in the closed coffin lid with his Leatherman. 'Stand back, all of you.'

When the second screw was out he lifted the lid just wide enough to get his hand inside. He felt the lanyard attached to the grenade and unhooked it from the lid. It was a simple but effective trigger. He hoped there were no more surprises inside. Jed raised the lid. He recognised the face immediately.

'It's Calvert. He's been shot.'

Branches whipped Miranda's face and thorns scored her arms and legs as she blundered through the thick bush. Her bare feet were studded with prickles, but she ignored the pain. She had no idea where she was heading. Her only aim was to outrun Hassan and find somewhere to hide. A tree would be the safest place, from him and from the wild animals that lived on his reserve.

She came to a narrow creek and splashed into it. The muddy bottom of the watercourse sucked at her feet, but the cool slime temporarily soothed her punctured soles. Behind her, she heard twigs snapping under his heavy footfall.

Miranda followed the creek around a bend. She thought that running through it would throw him off her trail. She left the smelly water and scrambled up a bank. The spoor of zebra and various antelope species were clearly embedded in the grey mud. This was obviously a favourite spot for game to drink. She noticed a beaten path through the grass, a trail probably made by elephant and now used as a highway to and from the water by other creatures. It would be harder for Hassan to pick up her tracks on the beaten pathway. She started to run, then pitched forwards into the dirt, letting out an involuntary yelp as she fell. Someone or something had grabbed her around the ankle.

*

Hassan was not an expert tracker, but Miranda was leaving a trail even a novice could follow. Long yellow grass was flattened, and here and there branches hung loose where her passage had bent them. She was barefoot, too, whereas he had on stout hiking boots. He would find her. Whenever he came to a tall tree he scanned its branches. That's where I would seek shelter, he thought to himself.

Hassan saw how Miranda's footprints disappeared at the edge of the creek. She had run along the watercourse. He looked left and then right. He took a chance and followed the creek to the right. He paused when he heard the short, sharp cry. It was unlike any animal he had ever heard in the bush. Hassan charged along the creek bank. On the far side he heard something rustling in the long grass at the edge of a game trail. He raised his rifle to his shoulder.

Tears of pain and pure frustration welled in Miranda's eyes as she scratched at the wire noose that had pulled tight around her ankle. To have escaped from the coffin and made it this far, only to be brought down by a poacher's snare. She felt like screaming at the injustice of it. The thin strands cut into the skin of her leg, and her fingers were sticky with blood from her torn nails and the effects of this latest wound.

'Ah, poachers, the archenemies of people like us.' Hassan laughed. 'It is our fate to be together to the end, Miranda. Don't fight it, my darling.'

'He'll make it, but he'll have a hell of a scar,' Jed said as he tied the free ends of the crepe bandage together. 'Won't hurt his political career either.'

General Crusher Calvert had been lucky to escape death or paralysis. The bullet from Hassan bin Zayid's AK-47 had carved a deep and ugly furrow down the right side of his neck. The wound had bled profusely, but the projectile had missed his windpipe and carotid artery.

'Lucky we got to him when we did,' Chris said. She checked the general's pulse. It was strong and regular. 'The lethabarb will wear off, but there's no way of telling how much he was given.'

'Lethabarb?' Jones asked.

'It's a common tranquilliser used on animals. Bin Zayid runs a cheetah-breeding and research program here. He would have had easy access to the stuff and known how to use it, so I'm betting that's what he used.'

'Well, it looks like Miranda's must have worn off sooner than he expected,' Jed said. 'Chris, you stay with Calvert. Get him back to hospital with Wylde's men. I'm going on.'

'Who made you the boss?' she asked, hands on hips. 'Miranda is as much my responsibility as yours. Harold, what was your mission?'

'To rescue General Calvert, ma'am.'

Jed noted the way Jones addressed Chris. He realised he still didn't know what position she held in the CIA. It was academic, anyway – no one was going to tell him what to do.

'Right. There's your general, Jones. Go with Mr Wylde's men and see that he gets to hospital safely,' Chris said.

Jones looked at Jed.

'He's not in charge of you, Jones. Now get out of here!' Chris snapped.

Jones and Wylde's men slid the coffin from the back of bin Zayid's Land Rover. Jed motioned with a flick of his head for Chris to move away from the others. 'Listen to me. I may have lost Miranda already. I don't want to lose you too.'

'Cut the crap, I'm coming with you,' Chris said.

'OK,' said Jed. 'We don't have time to argue. Now, bin Zayid's got no aircraft, no vehicle . . .' They rejoined the others.

'There's an ultralight parked in the hangar. Why didn't he take that?' Jones asked.

'It could be because it doesn't have the range to get where he wants to. It might have been part of a fall-back plan in case he had to go looking for Calvert's plane if it crashed in the bush,' Chris said.

'He could still have used it to escape the immediate area, but only if he had Miranda with him,' Jed said. 'That means she could be on the loose. What's the best way out of here, if not by air? The road's too obvious, it's too easy for him to get caught at a roadblock.'

'He'll head for the river,' Chris concluded, finishing Jed's thought. 'He must have a boat hidden near the bush camp – that's how he got Calvert off the plane in the first place.'

By the time Hassan reached the river he was almost dragging Miranda through the bush. She was hobbling, thanks to the deep cut inflicted by the snare, and her bare feet left bloody smears on the dry grass. He cared nothing for her pain, but he needed her alive as a hostage. She fell in a heap when they reached the muddy bank of the Zambezi.

Hassan moved the branches he and Juma had used to camouflage the boat and tossed them into the bush.

'Get up, you bitch,' he panted. He, too, was exhausted, but he could not afford to rest. He dragged Miranda up by the hair, but her scream was muffled by the tape he had fixed to her mouth. He pushed her into the boat and she fell on her side.

Her bloodied feet stained the deck as she pulled herself into a sitting position. She looked up into his eyes, determined not to show him fear. Hassan had to admire her spirit.

'This is so you don't try any more little tricks, or think about jumping out,' he said as he looped a length of rope around the bindings on her wrists and tied the free ends around the pole supporting the plastic seat next to his. 'Now, stay down,' he ordered, pushing her back onto her side.

The boat was powered by a big outboard motor, which was fed from a tin gasoline tank that could be removed when the boat was not in use. Hassan squeezed a bulb in the middle of the rubber hose that connected the tank to the engine. Miranda knew from her own trips back and forth across the river that this was to pump some fuel into the engine in order to prime it. Her face was a few inches from the tank and the gasoline fumes stung the inside of her nose.

Hassan started the engine and put the throttle into reverse. The boat glided away from the bank.

'Jed, look!' Chris whispered.

'I see one man, at the helm,' he said. He crouched low in the boat and rested his left hand and the wooden stock of the SLR on the gunwale of the boat. 'I don't see Miranda, though.'

When they had reached their boat, Chris and Jed had rowed silently away from the main riverbank to a reed-covered island in the middle of the Zambezi. Rather than motoring up and down the Zambian shore looking for where bin Zayid had hidden his boat, they had decided to wait, and watch and listen for him.

'Give me the night-vision monocle,' Chris whispered. Jed handed the device to her and she peered through it. Bin Zayid was bathed in a watery green light. 'It's him all right.'

Jed put the monocle back on and swung the rifle a little to the left. He lined up the iron foresight of the old rifle on the man's torso. He estimated the target was about two hundred metres away. The Arab's boat was moving backwards, slowly, away from the shore. 'I'm going to take the shot.'

Chris stayed perfectly still.

Jed raised the rifle slightly to compensate for the bullet's fall. It was a long time since he'd fired a rifle without the benefit of a state-of-the-art telescopic sight, but he had always been a good marksman. He took a deep breath then let half the air out of his lungs. He followed the slowly moving figure, aimed off ever so slightly to compensate for the movement of the target's boat, and squeezed the trigger.

The shot split the peace of the night and half-a-dozen startled waterbirds erupted noisily from their night roosts. A hippo grunted angrily nearby.

'He's down. You got him!' Chris said.

'Start the engine!' Jed ordered. He kept the rifle trained on the boat. Jed wasn't so sure it was a clean shot. The target had moved as he fired, as though he was bending down for something in the bottom of the boat.

Hassan bin Zayid pitched forwards and landed between the boat's two seats. Miranda kicked at him with her aching feet. He moaned in pain. He was not dead, but she was overjoyed that someone was out there looking for them – someone who was prepared to shoot first and ask questions later.

Hassan yelped like a dog as Miranda's foot connected with his left forearm, which was hanging by his side with white bone protruding from one of the two holes. He kicked back at her and reached for the AK-47 with his good hand. He rolled into a sitting position and cradled the rifle in his lap. With his right hand he pushed the selector down two notches to automatic and lifted the weapon by the pistol grip. To their left, from the direction where the shot had come from, Miranda heard a marine engine roar to life. Hassan leaned the rifle's barrel on the edge of the boat and squeezed the trigger.

The shots went wide, but Chris and Jed both ducked instinctively. Chris eased off on the throttle. 'I don't want to shoot in case Miranda's down there with him out of sight,' Jed called above the noise of the engine. 'We've got to get closer to them, Chris. Faster!'

Chris knew he was right, but she was terrified. She opened the throttle.

Hassan dropped the AK-47 and pushed his boat's throttle forwards. He steered from a crouch. With the extra jerry cans of gasoline in the bottom of the boat he had enough fuel to reach Mozambique. He doubted his pursuers had such reserves. It was not over yet, but he would need medical attention as soon as possible. His shattered arm was bleeding profusely. He would splint and bandage it as soon as he lost the other boat, then call his comrades by satellite phone and arrange for them to meet him somewhere on the shores of Lake Cahora Bassa, across the border near the town of Zumbo. It might take them a day or more to reach the rendezvous point, but he had the will to survive.

A hippo broke the surface of the river in front of him, its huge jaws wide in surprised anger. Hassan swung the helm over hard and Miranda was thrown against the side of the boat. A collision with one of the huge beasts at the speed he was now doing could kill him as sure as any bullet. Hassan reached again for his rifle and fired another wild three-round burst at his pursuers.

Chris jinked to the left to avoid the fusillade, but realised she had turned the wrong way when she felt the thump of displaced air as a bullet tore past her head. 'That was too close!' she cried.

'Stay with him. That's about ten or twelve rounds he's fired. It'll be hard for him to reload and drive, especially if he's wounded,' Jed yelled.

Great, Chris thought. Only eighteen or twenty more shots she had to survive. The two boats were equally matched in horsepower – as well as the need to avoid mammalian obstacles – and Chris found she was not able to close the gap between them, which now stood at about a hundred metres.

Jed grabbed the side of the boat and stood. 'Pull over, bin Zayid, you're finished!' he cried, and fired two shots high over the other boat.

'Are you crazy?' Chris shouted.

Jed dropped down again to a crouch in front of Chris as Hassan answered with a long burst of rifle fire. None of the bullets came near them.

'Don't tell me you're deliberately trying to get him to shoot at you?' Chris asked.

Jed looked her in the eyes, his stare cold and hard. There was not the slightest inkling of fear or panic in his eyes. 'If I get hit, promise me you'll kill him.'

Miranda wriggled in the bottom of the boat as hot, spent bullet cartridges rained down on her. Her face was next to the fuel tank and suddenly she had an idea. The tape on her mouth had been splashed with bilge water when Hassan turned to avoid the hippos. Miranda found that by moving her jaw she was able to stretch and loosen the dampened gag. She pushed her face into the putrid water, which was mixed with the mud and blood from her feet. She glanced up to see if Hassan was watching, but his concentration was alternating between the river ahead and the people following them. She worked her lower jaw furiously and the sodden tape began to fall away. She rubbed her face against the side of the boat and peeled off more of the tape until she was able to open her mouth completely.

Miranda rolled back onto her other side and craned her head back until she could get her mouth around the rubber fuel hose that fed into the gas tank. She bit down hard and pulled on the hose, worrying it as viciously as a dog with a rat.

To his right, on the Zimbabwean side, Hassan could see the twinkle of hurricane lanterns at the Mana Pools campsite and staff houses. Ahead of him the Zambezi glittered wide and clear in the moonlight. Now that he was in the middle of the river, there was less chance of him running into a hippo pod. The throttle was wide open and the other boat was no closer. He laughed and turned and fired three more shots. Hassan didn't notice the leak until the engine coughed.

The outboard chugged twice then suddenly cut out. Hassan wiggled the throttle and looked around him. Seeing the severed fuel line he raised his good hand and slapped Miranda hard across the face. He knelt and fumbled with the free end of the hose, trying awkwardly to reconnect it.

Miranda leaned over and head-butted his shattered arm. Hassan bellowed in pain and fell to his knees. Even in his agony he realised that the other boat's engine sounded very close now.

Eventually, Hassan managed to drag himself back into his seat. With his good hand he swung the wheel and pointed the still-coasting boat towards the shore. He would land on the Zimbabwean side, just down-stream of the main camp in Mana Pools National Park. The rangers would be alert now, wakened by the gunshots, and the Zambian police would be on their way from the other side soon. He needed to get hold of the boat that was pursuing them. He had lost his prime hostage, but he still had Miranda. If the man following him was who he thought it was, then he still had a chance to complete the part of this mission that mattered to him most.

'Stop cowering, Miranda, I am not going to hit you again,' he said, his voice calm now. He reached down and grabbed the fuel tank. He unscrewed the cap, one-handed, then lifted the can and tipped the remainder of its contents over the prone woman.

'No!' Miranda screamed and coughed as gasoline soaked her hair and eyes, and filled her mouth. The cold fuel drenched her breasts, her arms and her dress. 'I'm sorry, Hassan.'

'Sorry! My God, Miranda, what a pathetic thing to say. You spied on me, you lied to me, and you and your father caused the death of my only living relative. You think that if you say "sorry" this will all go away?'

'I never meant to hurt you, or your brother, Hassan. I thought you were a good guy, that they were wrong about you.' She coughed and retched as the gasoline fumes invaded her lungs.

'A good guy? There's no such thing in the world we live in these days, Miranda. You're about to find that out the hard way.' He grabbed a handful of her hair and lifted her up. 'Is that your father following us, Miranda?'

She looked at the other boat, which had also cut its engine and was now gliding closer to them. Miranda gasped as she saw Christine Wallis and her father.

'Well, is that Daddy, come to rescue his precious little lying bitch?'

Miranda said nothing, but Hassan saw the look on the man's face.

'Miranda!' Jed cried out.

'Ah,' said Hassan, 'I knew it. Keep your distance, Sergeant Banks. You know I'll kill her if you try anything.'

'Let her go, you sick fuck,' Jed yelled back.

'Oh, I will, Jed, let her go that is. Surprised?'

Jed held his tongue, and brought the SLR up into his shoulder.

Hassan's boat touched the shore first. He pulled the knife from his belt and slashed the tie binding Miranda to the seat pole, though her hands were still bound. He hauled her to her feet and held her tight against him, his bloodied, painful arm across her breasts. In his right hand was the AK-47, the tip of its barrel resting on Miranda's shoulder, the muzzle against her right ear.

'Drop your weapon,' Hassan shouted.

'Take the shot, Daddy. Kill him,' Miranda called out.

Jed looked through the circular rear sight of the SLR and lined it up with the blade of the foresight. The heavy rifle wavered in his vicelike grip. It was the rocking of the boat beneath his feet that was spoiling his aim. He blinked the sweat from his eyes. It was too risky. 'Let her go and I promise you one thing, bin Zayid.'

'What's that?'

'That I'll kill you quickly.'

Hassan laughed. 'You make your stupid macho jokes while your daughter's life is in the balance? You don't scare me. I'm offering you one chance, and one chance only to save her,' bin Zayid said as he pulled Miranda off their boat and back up the sandy riverbank. In the distance was the sound of a vehicle engine.

'Talk,' Jed said, lowering the rifle a little. To Chris, he said, 'Turn to the right, bring us in about sixty feet from him.'

She complied and their boat touched the shore a few seconds later.

'I want your boat; you want your daughter. Not much of a trade, I'm sure you'll agree, but I can make this all go away. Too bad you lost the general, but then, so did I. This way you get your little girl back and I get a chance at freedom.'

'Let her go. You can have the goddamned boat, bin Zayid,' Jed said.

'Throw your weapons into the river,' bin Zayid called, jamming the barrel into Miranda's soft, pale neck hard enough to make her cry out.

'Why? So you can kill us all in cold blood?' Jed replied. 'You have my word we won't fire on you once you're in the boat.'

'Your word? A minute ago you were promising to kill me quickly. No deal, soldier. Throw the rifles in the river.'

Chris looked at Jed. He shrugged. 'He won't get far without medical attention to that arm,' he whispered.

'Quiet! You've got three seconds to toss the weapons, Banks, and that's it for Miranda. Quite frankly, I don't care if it ends in a gunfight – at least I'll die knowing I've taken her with me. It's up to you.'

'Do it, Jed,' Chris said.

It went against everything he stood for, his own personal moral code and the ethos of the organisation in which he served, but Jed drew back his arm and flung his rifle into the Zambezi River. Chris did the same, watching where her weapon landed.

'OK, let her go,' Jed said to bin Zayid.

'What do you think my brother would have done in this situation, Jed Banks?'

'Let Miranda go.' Jed's voice was cool with menace as he took a pace towards his daughter.

'Keep still! Both of you,' Hassan barked. The mirth had vanished. 'Tell me first, or have a guess. What do you think my twin brother would do now? You should know, Banks, you met him.'

'Your brother was a soldier. I didn't agree with his cause or his methods, but I faced him down like a man, and he died like a man. I'd say that he would have abided by a deal he'd given his word on.'

Bin Zayid smiled. 'Iqbal, that was my brother's name, was a believer. He had the strength to do what needed to be done – not like me. I was soft, Jed Banks.' His voice started to crack and he sucked in a sob before it manifested itself in tears. 'I fell for your daughter, fell in love with her, because I was weak. I believed her lies and all along she was plotting against me and my family.'

'Let her go. It's over. You can leave.'

'My brother, Banks, would have done this.' Bin Zayid kicked Miranda behind one of her knees, forcing her to kneel. 'And this!' He put his boot in her back and drove her face-first to the dirt. He held the assault rifle, one-handed, and rested the barrel on Miranda's back, on the rear of her heart. 'Say goodbye to your little girl, Banks.'

'Dad!' Miranda cried.

Bin Zayid's finger curled around the AK-47's trigger. Chris and Jed started running towards him. 'No!' Jed yelled, knowing he could not make the distance before the Arab fired.

They all heard the gunshot, but none of them saw where it came from. Jed closed his eyes, slowing in midflight, unable to look at Miranda. Chris dropped to her knees.

Hassan bin Zayid felt the hammer blow of the bullet in his right shoulder and careened backwards, onto the ground, writhing in agony, screaming. The AK-47 fell from his hand, hit the ground barrel first and toppled over, out of his immediate reach.

Luke Scarborough yelled, 'Freeze!'

'Watch him! Give me the gun, Luke,' Jed called. 'Where the hell did you come from?'

Hassan rolled towards the fallen AK-47 and Luke, ignoring Jed's surprise, fired two wildly aimed shots that both missed their mark. Hassan tried to wrap his hand around the barrel of the rifle, but his left arm had been shattered by the earlier wound from Banks. Miranda was in front of him, starting to crawl away. The sharp tang of gasoline fumes filled the air.

'Keep him covered and get over here,' Jed said to Luke, who was still fifty metres away and advancing cautiously, the pistol held out in front of him. 'Good shot, by the way, kid.'

'I'd call us even now,' Luke said, smiling, the adrenaline leaving him wide-eyed and jubilant.

'He's not dead yet,' Jed cautioned.

'Look out, he's reaching for something!' Chris yelled.

'Miranda!' Jed screamed. 'Roll!'

Bin Zayid's right hand emerged from his trouser pocket and, in one fluid move, he flipped open the silver cap of a Zippo and rolled the flint along the front of his load-bearing vest. The wick ignited and he tossed the flaming cigarette lighter at Miranda.

Her gasoline-soaked cocktail dress ignited with a whoosh and bin Zayid scrambled to his knees. Miranda screamed and started to stand. Jed sprinted the remaining metres and hit his daughter hard, mid-section, in a crushing football tackle that sent her sprawling and the two of them rolling in the sand. Jed wrapped his arms around her in a bear hug and they tumbled. He ignored the pain of the flames on his bare torso and arms, dimly aware of the smell of his own hair being scorched. Over and over they rolled as he pushed her towards the river. There was a hiss of steam as he finally felt the warm river water on his back. He submerged her and held her underwater until he was sure the flames were extinguished.

Luke emptied the pistol's magazine at the fleeing figure of Hassan bin Zayid before Chris could stop him. None of the shots found their mark. 'You'll never hit him with that thing while he's moving,' she told him.

'God, I'm sorry,' he said, looking back at Jed and Miranda.

'Don't sweat it,' Chris answered. 'You probably saved our lives.'

27

'The burns on your daughter's left arm and neck are bad, but she will live, Mr Banks,' the Italian doctor assured Jed.

'That's the most important thing. Thanks, Doc.'

'We've got a plasma IV going, and I've given her something for the pain. I am sure that with some surgery in America there will be little sign of scarring. Your African friend was in surgery when I left the hospital. My colleague said his signs were good. He is strong, and he is in good hands.'

Jed nodded. 'Thanks, Doc. Can I see Miranda now, before she goes?'

'Of course. The helicopter is on its way, but I presumed you would be travelling with her, to the hospital in Lusaka.'

'No, I've got something else to do.'

'Your burns are not as serious as your daughter's but they need dressing.'

'Later,' Jed said.

Around them was a scene of escalating chaos. The Zimbabwean warden of Mana Pools National Park wanted to know what Willy Wylde and two of his employees were doing on the wrong side of the river in the middle of the night. A Zambian policeman argued with

410

a park ranger, and a siren wailed from another approaching police launch. From upriver came the clatter of a helicopter.

Luke was talking to Chris. 'I heard the gunshots from the river, and the boats. I grabbed the pistol I took off this guy who tried to mug me in Zanzibar, and ran down to the bank. That's when I saw you guys and bin Zayid pull in.'

Jed ignored them all for the moment and walked over to the stretcher on which Miranda lay. 'Can you hear me, baby?'

'I'm sorry, Daddy, so sorry,' Miranda said groggily through the fog of medication. 'Don't leave me . . .'

'I'll be with you soon, baby. Everything's going to be all right now. They're taking you to the hospital. Chris will be with you.' He swallowed hard, barely able to hold back tears as he thought about how close he'd been to losing her.

'Tell her . . . tell her, sorry . . .' Miranda closed her eyes, but Jed saw the rhythmic rise and fall of her chest as he took her hand in his. He bent over her and kissed her gently on the cheek.

Jed felt a blast of rotor wash-blown sand on his back and shielded his eyes as he turned. Another Huey helicopter, the same model as the one which had been shot out of the sky, touched down. Jed looked up and saw the grey-haired figure of General Donald Calvert jogging out, bent at the waist. Behind him was Harold Jones.

'Are you Banks?' the general called over the roar of the engine. His neck was wrapped in a blood-stained field dressing.

'Yes, sir, General,' Jed said.

'I ain't a general any more, Master Sergeant. You can call me Donald. However, my friends, and I hope I can count you and your lady friend in that company, call me Crusher.' The older man extended a hand and Jed shook it.

'I thought you'd be in hospital by now, General . . . Crusher.'

Calvert smiled and touched his neck. 'I was on my way – that is, until reports started coming in about your little pursuit here. I figured we might need to keep this helo on stand-by, in case there were any more wounded.'

'You were right about that.'

'How's your daughter? Ms Wallis filled me in on the whole thing via satellite phone.'

'She's going to be fine, according to the doctor.'

'Hell of a diplomatic mess, but at least those terrorist bastards didn't get what they came for.'

Jed thought that the deaths of the secret service and CIA agents, the Zambian helicopter crewman and the pilot of the general's aircraft was still a pretty high butcher's bill, but he held his tongue.

'What news of the man who got away?'

'He was carrying two gunshot wounds. Looked pretty unsteady, but he managed to get away on foot with his AK,' Jed explained.

Chris arrived next to Calvert. 'General, I've spoken to the US embassy in Lusaka. They'll have some people meet you at the hospital and will stay with you until we can arrange a flight home. I really think you should get out of here as soon as possible, sir.'

'Not without you, Master Sergeant Banks and his daughter, Ms Wallis,' Calvert said.

'Chris, look after Miranda for me, go with her,' Jed said.

'What do you mean?' she asked. 'No way, Jed, you're not going off on another crusade. Leave bin Zayid to the local police. It's out of our hands now.'

'She's right, Jed. Don't make me give you an order,' Calvert said.

Jed grinned back, though there was no humour in his eyes. 'You can't give me an order, *Crusher*. Jones,' he called to the CIA agent, 'give me your MP-5.'

'Can't do that,' Jones replied, shaking his head.

'Jones has to look after the general, Jed. For God's sake come with us!' Chris barked. 'You are *not* going to waltz off into the bush on a one-man suicide mission. Who do you think you are? This is real life, not the movies.'

'I know, Chris. This is very real. There's a wanted terrorist out there with a blood feud against me and my daughter. He won't rest until one or both of us are dead. He was hit bad. Look at those policemen. They're arguing jurisdictions while Hassan bin Zayid gets away.'

'Chopper pilot's signalling us, General,' Jones said. 'We really should get you and Ms Banks-Lewis to hospital now, sir.'

The Italian medical team had carried Miranda on her stretcher to the helicopter and the Zambian crew chief was strapping her in. The doctor climbed aboard. The pilot waved frantically towards the knot of people gathered around Jed.

'There speaks the voice of reason,' Chris said over the increasingly noisy whine of the helicopter's engine.

Luke had been hovering on the edge of the group, listening to and absorbing everything that was being said, a skill he'd perfected as a journalist. He still had the pistol he'd taken from the dead mugger in Zanzibar. He, too, was worried about bin Zayid's escape. The man had tried to kill him once – who could say he wouldn't be targeted again? He coughed and broke into the circle of people.

'Here you go, Jed.' He handed the American the pistol.

Jed looked at Scarborough. The boy had, to a large extent, been responsible for this whole mess. No, that was wrong – the reporter had simply done his job. Miranda had spied on Hassan, fallen for him, and Jed had killed the terrorist's brother. All the media had done was made sure everyone knew the truth – for better or worse. 'You probably saved Miranda's life, bursting in before like John Wayne, kid. Thanks,' he said as he accepted the pistol. 'You'll have a hell of a story to write tomorrow.'

'Hey, can I borrow someone's satellite phone?' Luke asked.

'Don't push it,' Chris said. 'General Calvert, Jones will escort you back to Lusaka.'

'So, you're going to let Banks go off on this wild-goose chase by himself?' Calvert asked.

'No, sir, I'm going with him,' Chris said. Jed shot her an angry glance. 'Oh, come *on*, Jed. I'm ex-Army, CIA-trained and probably a better marksman than you are. Drag yourself out of the goddamned Dark Ages, for Christ's sake.'

'Sir, let's go,' Jones said.

'All right, all right,' Calvert said. 'Jed, come with me. Don't worry, I'm not going to force you onto the chopper at gunpoint, but I've got something you might need.'

Luke stopped Jed with a tap on his shoulder. 'By the way, there's no ammo left in that pistol I gave you.'

Jed smiled. 'I know. I saw you empty the magazine at bin Zayid. But it did the trick. Thanks.'

'Don't mention it,' Luke replied.

'There's a seat on the helo for you, too, Luke,' Jed said as they walked.

'I know and, believe me, I'm taking it. I've had enough gunfights to last a lifetime.'

The aircraft's rotors were sending up a wall of dirt and twigs and leaves that stung Jed's face as he approached the waiting aircraft. He stuck his head inside the cargo compartment. Miranda was asleep or passed out, but the Italian doctor smiled and raised a thumb to tell him she was not in danger.

Jed leaned over, brushed a strand of blonde hair from his daughter's face and kissed her forehead. 'Goodbye, baby. I'll come back for you soon,' he said to her.

Crusher Calvert was inside the chopper, undoing a ratcheted nylon tie-down strap that held an assortment of bags. 'They retrieved this stuff from the airplane,' he yelled in Jed's ear as he slid out a long black nylon carry case. Calvert unzipped the case and pulled out a hunting rifle and a box of ammunition. He handed both to Jed. 'You might need this. It's a Weatherby Mark V Safari, .300 calibre. Those are Weatherby Magnum rounds with a hollow-point solid copper Barnes projectile. One of those'll gut and wrap him in one easy movement, ready for shipping, boy. Good luck. Only wish I was going with you.'

Jed took the weapon, checked it was clear by sliding back the bolt, and said, 'Thanks, Crusher. I'll bring it back in one piece.'

'Bring it back with a notch on it.'

Jed saw that Chris was standing on her toes near the front crew door of the helicopter, talking to the pilot through his half-open window. She had her hands cupped around her mouth and he was holding up one side of his flight helmet to hear her better. The pilot gave a thumbs-up and Chris ran to Jed's side.

'Get in,' she yelled in his ear.

He shook his head and made to leave the open cargo door of the chopper.

Chris punched him hard in the arm and screamed, 'Get in, you jack-ass. I'm getting the pilot to give us a lift across the river to bin Zayid's airfield. I've got an idea.'

Jed looked at her and saw she wasn't trying to fool him. He suddenly remembered the ultralight aircraft parked in the hangar on the Arab's property. 'You can fly?'

'There's a lot you don't know about me, Jed. I learned to fly in the Sudan.'

'I won't ask what you were doing there.'

'Good idea.'

They sat on the edge of the floor of the cargo compartment, their feet resting on the left skid. Jed opened the breech of the rifle, fed three rounds into the integral magazine, then chambered a fourth bullet. The helicopter crewman spoke into the microphone attached to the boom on his headset and the AB 205 lurched skywards.

The rush of air from the slipstream dried the sweat on Jed's body. Chris had her hands pressed against the aircraft floor. The wind snatched at her hair, tousling it. Even in these mad circumstances, with the threat of danger still very much present, he found he wanted her. It was more than sex; he wanted to be with her and to care for her. He held the rifle across his lap with one hand and placed his other on hers. She looked into his eyes and smiled. The river flashed beneath them, crossed in less time than it took to blink. They flew low and fast, to minimise the risk from ground fire in case there was anyone else lurking in the thick bush below. Bin Zayid's landing field was a scar of grey in the moonlight. The nose of the chopper flared up as the pilot brought her in. Jed and Chris stood on the skids, ready to hop off as soon as they touched down.

'Good hunting! Come back safe, the pair of you,' Calvert said to them.

They crouched on the short-cropped grass and shielded their faces as the helicopter departed. Once more there was silence.

'I'm betting the ultralight was part of some back-up plan,' Chris said as she strode to the hangar.

'Makes sense.' Jed instinctively kept the hunting rifle up, in his shoulder. He had the night-vision monocle on and he peered into the gloom of the hangar. 'Let me check for booby traps.'

Chris waited while Jed scanned under, inside and around the little aircraft. 'Looks clear.'

'Help me push it out,' she said.

They wheeled the ultralight out of the hangar and Chris began a pre-flight check. 'The helicopter pilot will refuel and return once he's dropped off Miranda and the general. He will bring some reinforce- ments – marines from the US embassy in Lusaka. If we can find bin Zayid all we need to do is keep him in sight until the helo returns. The marines can pick him up.'

'You're the boss,' Jed said as he checked the rifle and scope once more. Despite what Chris had said, he planned to kill bin Zayid as soon as he had a clear shot. 'Did I ever tell you I'm scared of flying?'

She stopped, hands on hips, and looked at him. 'You're kidding, right?'

Jed shook his head. 'It terrifies me more than facing hostile fire.'

'Well, you might get some of that, too, if bin Zayid's still capable. Harden the fuck up, soldier, and climb aboard.'

'Yes, ma'am,' he said.

28

'It's me,' Hassan said into the portable sat phone he had carried with him in his chest rig.

'This is not part of the plan. Why are you calling?' The voice on the other end was panicky, angry.

'The target is down, but not with me,' bin Zayid confessed.

'You have failed. You sound bad. Are you wounded?'

'Yes. I need you to pick me up, in your boat.'

'That was not part of the plan.'

Hassan choked back a sob. Whether it was from the pain and shock of his wounds, or the growing sense of helplessness he felt, he wasn't sure. 'Please,' he croaked.

'You have been compromised? They know your identity?'

Jed Banks would never forget him. Miranda was probably still alive. Everyone knew he was part of the plot to kidnap Calvert, but the man on the other end of the line would not risk a rescue mission if he knew the truth. 'No. No one saw me. They do not know my identity. However, if I am caught, it will not be good for any of us.'

'You should take the martyr's way,' the man replied.

Easy enough for you to say, thought Hassan. He knew he could never go back to his old life, but he was planning on staying alive long enough to construct a new one. Also, he was already looking forward to a time, maybe years in the future, when Jed and Miranda Banks had thought it safe to drop their guards. 'Pick me up or I will tell them how to find you.'

'Coward.'

'No. I'm a realist. I can help you, if you rescue me. I still have access to offshore bank accounts that no one else can touch. We can continue our fight. Without me, it is all gone.'

A pause at the other end. Hassan prayed that the one truly tangible deity of the modern world, the US dollar, would save him.

'All right. Be at the river. Call in two hours and give me a GPS reading. We will bring you out.'

'Thanks be to Allah,' Hassan said.

'Thanks be to your bank manager.' The line went dead.

Above him he heard the amplified mosquito buzz of an ultralight.

His night vision was good. He could see the target, leaning against a tree, looking skyward. In fact, they could both see him now. They worked well as a team and he found he was comforted by the fact that she was close to him.

The trick was to keep the target in sight and not lose him in the thick, dark bush. He needed to be able to see him to kill him. It helped if the target was moving. They circled a couple of times, searching in the bush for the slightest movement.

At last, the target moved again. The fool thought he was still invisible, but the movement made him stand out.

From his hiding place under an overhanging branch Hassan saw the ultralight pass over and head away from him. He wasn't sure whether he had been spotted or not. Either way, now was the time to make a run for it.

He held his shattered left arm close by his side. It was a little easier to carry the AK-47 in his right, although blood still oozed freely from the wound in his shoulder. He summoned his last reserves of strength.

His plan was to follow the edge of the river, so he turned back towards the Zambezi and ran as fast as he could. He needed to be under cover again if the ultralight turned back to make another pass.

The hunters bided their time. The target had been spooked and it was obvious he was heading for the river. Slowly, in no hurry, for they didn't want to let him know they were on his tail, they circled.

The bush thinned out as they came closer to the river. The target's tracks would be visible in the sand. They saw him again, in the distance, and she increased her speed.

In a matter of minutes they were close enough for the kill. The target had no way of outrunning them.

She was the boss – that was how it really was with most couples – but the killer instinct was guiding him. It didn't matter who was in charge. Now that the target was in sight, and in range, he was going to do the killing. It was a matter of honour, and a matter of life and death.

Without warning, without a reason other than pure survival, it was done.

In the ultralight, thirty metres above the valley, Jed Banks spoke into the microphone attached to his headset. 'See anything?' The frustration was plain in his voice.

'Nada,' Chris said as she scanned left and right. 'This is harder than I thought. We might never see him down there. Wait a minute. There's a boat coming up the river, a long way off.'

'Got it. Radio it in to the Zambian police. Maybe it's his pick-up. No one else would be out at this time of night.'

'The chopper pilot just called. They're on their way. If it is bad guys in the boat the marines can take care of them.'

'Roger that. Let's make another couple of circuits.'

'We can't keep searching all night, Jed. Fuel won't last. I think we should head back. Besides, we don't want to get caught in a firefight.'

Jed knew she was right, but the need to find and kill the man who had hurt his daughter burned his insides like a draft of acid. 'I want that bastard, Chris.'

'I know, Jed, and there are people ready to go get him. You've done all you can, and Miranda needs you now.'

He stared down again at the silvery Zambezi, the black tufts of the tops of the trees. They wouldn't find a man down there in a million years if he wanted to hide and knew what he was doing. He was torn between wanting to finish the fight and returning to his daughter. For once, he realised, he was making the right decision.

'OK,' he said. 'Let's go home.'

Epilogue

Sunday morning, around eleven. The newspapers by his side, a half-drunk cup of coffee in his hand. Virginia spring sunshine on his face, eyes closed, rocking in the swinging chair on the porch. For many Americans this was a normal scene, something they took for granted. But Jed had been here too few times in his life, and he was making the most of it.

A normal scene? Maybe. A normal life? Not really. They were a careful family. More careful than most. Part of that had to do with their occupation. However, if you discounted checking for bombs under the SUV and sleeping with a loaded Glock and a pump action shotgun under the bed, they were living a pretty quiet life.

'You look relaxed. Teaching's suiting you. If you get any more laid-back you'll pass out,' Chris said.

He opened his eyes. She was so beautiful he sometimes felt short of breath. Her face was fuller, as were her breasts, which he thought was sensational. Though she looked a little pale. 'Sick again, baby?'

'Baby? Don't say that word,' she said in mock anger. 'I haven't thrown up this many times since I was in college.' She eased herself into the swinging seat next to him. She smiled when he put his arm around her. She had never felt more fulfilled, happier or more in love in her life.

'Got something interesting to show you,' she said, holding up a sheet of paper.

'What? Your resignation from the Company?'

'Ha ha. You're just jealous because I'll be on maternity leave soon.'

'I'm picturing myself as a stay-at-home dad, who carries the kid in one of those chest rigs and does all the housework.'

'Yeah, right,' she laughed.

'And I'll be waiting at the front door, naked with a rose between my teeth and a roast in the oven for when you get home in your sexy spy-lady business suit.'

'On second thoughts, you've got the job. Now, be serious for a second. I just checked the emails . . .'

'And?'

'Luke and Miranda will both be able to make it here for the wedding. She says Canada is great and polar bears are a lot scarier than lions. He's only got a couple more months in Africa before he gets a posting to the International Press office in Washington. They're meeting in New York for a few days together before they come here.'

'Mmm, I'd better make sure the shotgun's loaded.'

'For the bears?'

'For the reporter. So, what's the good news?'

'Not sure if it's good or bad. It's from Africa. From the National Parks ecologist in Mana Pools, Zimbabwe. You didn't meet him.'

'No.' The hairs on the back of Jed's neck started to rise. 'He was away when everything happened.' Thoughts of his domestic idyll were expelled from his mind and replaced with the last sighting he'd had of Hassan bin Zayid as he'd tossed his lighter at Miranda. Miranda's burns had healed and, once her final operation was carried out next month, she would carry no more scars. But all of them had their own painful memories.

'I've kept in touch with him off and on. Here, read this.'

Jed took the email and read it.

You'll be interested to learn that it appears we have another man-eater in the park. Just last week two rangers came across some human remains – not much, just a skull pan and a femur. There was a rusted AK-47 and some military-looking web gear nearby. By the state of the kit they reckoned the kill was about three months old – possibly dating back to the time of your high adventures in the valley. They thought the remains were probably those of a poacher, though one of those terrorist chaps did get away, didn't he? I've been monitoring a small pride in the area – an extremely old, scarred male, and a mature lioness. She's just had a litter of three cubs. I'm fairly sure the male is the brother of the one you shot, although I only ever saw that pair a couple of times, so I can't be certain. It is highly unusual for a pride to start this way – a battle-scarred old male almost past his prime, and a lone female who may have lost her way. Just goes to show that there's hope for us all, I suppose.